THE LAST
LARNAERADEE

Book one in 'A Fairy's Tale' trilogy.

Shelley Cass

First Printed in Australia

First Printing: Dec 2020

Shawline Publishing Group Pty Ltd
www.shawlinepublishing.com.au

Paperback ISBN- 9781922444257

Ebook ISBN – 9781922444264

To those who have listened, advised, supported and loved me –
you have made me strong enough to build a new world.
You have helped to make the real world a place of magic.
Thank you.

THE LAST
LARNAERADEE

Locations and pronunciation guide located at the back of the book for reference.

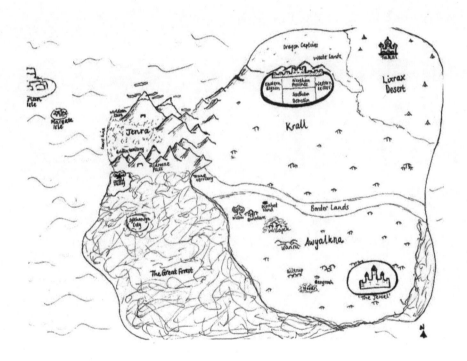

Shelley Cass

CHAPTER ONE

Beginnings

Gravity had been reversed in the Great Forest for moments that had felt like hours during the terrible standoff. Her green eyes had been wide, her auburn hair had been lifted to twist about her face, her lungs had tightened, and she had been unsure if even her magic–the magic of the Mother of all Nature–would be able to push his power back.

His energy had spread outwards towards them, like a ghoul sweeping up out of its host. Ready to consume the Lady and Forest dwellers.

It had been clear that they would only survive if they could banish the Sorcerer from their refuge within the trees, but the Elves had been such passive beings for so many years. The Nymphs were also frightfully helpless, having only just tumbled into their midst, weakened after fleeing the Sorcerer for so long. And as time had paused, she too had felt the Sorcerer Darziates' poison slowly overwhelming her defences.

With no other choice the Elves had been forced to truly awaken, the Nymphs had been made to use the last of their dwindling energy, and the Lady had desperately joined her power with theirs.

Their entirely pure magic had clashed with his unnatural force, shaking the Forest to its very heart. And it had been enough to hurt the Sorcerer.

Somehow, together, the Nymphs, Elves and Lady had driven Darziates out.

Yet it seemed that his shadow still haunted the outskirts of the Great Sylthanryn Forest, and his granite eyes scorched across her memory. His magic still bled from every blade of grass in the clearing. The air itself smelled of burning as ash rose and swirled on the hot breeze. And leaves were browning and shrivelling, recoiling from the decay that was left in his place.

She knew that despite their small victory the Forest dwellers had not really defeated him, and she was now only just managing to stand firm. She waited until the last of the Elves had tenderly carried away the few surviving Nymphs, taking them into the safety of the Forest, and then she raised a quivering hand to her heart–pressing at the white fabric over her aching chest as if she were staunching a wound.

She ached from his attack, and ached with the knowledge that a prophecy as old as time was coming true, as she had been warned would happen on her first day of life.

On that day she had woken to find that the Gods had given her two prophecies, each encased in a sphere of light.

The first prophecy had come to life almost as soon as she had. The globe had begun spinning in her hand, like a miniature world contained in a dazzling trinket box. Then it had opened, releasing the cautioning voices of the Gods.

We breathe life into you, so you in turn breathe our power into all things.
You will become stronger and healthier as the world does.
However, the world will weaken if its many races become separate.
A deadly threat will be born at the end of the ninth age, and will find a divided world easy to consume.
All races must be united once more to survive this threat.
If the world does not unite before the beginning of the tenth age, and the threat is able to succeed, all will be destroyed in a storm of ice and fire.
Spread the word.
You must try to live in joy and love. Create life and goodness.
Seek unity.
Guide the world to the steps to freedom.

When the first sphere had laid quiet on her palm and the second had not opened to reveal its secrets, she had turned to her task of nurturing Nature. And the threat had seemed impossible because everywhere she'd stepped throughout the empty world she had spread her energy and joy, raising life from the dust.

Each touch had coaxed new plants to burst forth from fresh soil. Empty lands had been blanketed in green grass and cuddled by rolling clouds. Animals had yawned to life out of burrows, and finally other beings had slowly joined them.

There had formed different races that were either of magical or mortal kinds, and she'd felt more hopeful still as each being was filled with the breath of divine life in new ways.

Gnomes and Dwarves had rolled out of the rocks. Others were born who could fly across the skies, such as the jovial Nymphs, and colossal, majestic creatures who scattered the clouds with plumes of fire.

There were Sprites who flitted from flower to flower, dressed in petals and leaves, and there had been the Larnaeradee Fairies, as well as Giants so tall they could cross the lands with mighty steps, and swim entire oceans for fun.

Centaurs had appeared, gazing at the stars, and Unicorns had galloped across vast fields while Elves wandered through the forests. Dryads had lounged in tree boughs while water deities had spread throughout the oceans to keep Nature's water safe.

The mortal races had also been born, and the Lady had watched human-kind sweeping the lands in wonder. The first people had green eyes, filled with Nature like hers, and though their lives were short lived, they flared like burning sparks. They were driven by passion, creativity and curiosity and they raised towering, bustling civilisations where there had before been nothing.

And together each race, magical and mortal, had prospered and flourished for a long time, growing closer still when the Unicorns and Larnaeradee created a common tongue known as Aolen, to unite all the races with speech.

Yet the Lady had at last grown worried as, while each of the races lived in friendship, they had started to develop separate lives.

The Giants, fire breathers, Dwarves and Gnomes had left the main land to dwell over the seas. The Elves had grown secluded in the Great Sylthanryn Forest and the mortals had formed divided nations of their own—the kingdoms of Awyalkna, Krall, Lixrax and Jenra.

She'd travelled far and wide to spread the words of the prophecy, however one human of the Krall kingdom—Deimos, had become so fearful that unity was unattainable that he had taken the world's salvation upon himself.

Seeking help, Deimos had gone so far as to use a piece of his soul as a way to anchor himself to another world. A place that had not been made by the grace of the Gods, but by Demons of the Other Realm.

In return for more pieces of his soul, the creatures of this Other Realm had granted him the supernatural power to force the world into unity, filling him with their powers and spirit, and birthing the first of the Sorcerers.

Then war had torn through the lands, and the Lady had grown so ill that she'd feared the threat had come true.

Refusing to be subdued, hope arose when the Larnaeradee and the Unicorns summoned all the magical and mortal races to unite, overthrowing Deimos with their Army for the World, and with the specific sacrifice of a Fairy named Sylranaeryn and her Unicorn Kinrilowyn.

Peace had returned, and the Lady had felt well again, until the world had neared the middle of the ninth age, and she had discovered Deimos' descendant and heir. Darziates—filled with dark magic that had amplified as it had been passed down through the ages, had strengthened quickly. He had bred himself a black-haired Witch for an assistant, and as the twisted pair had turned their life taking power on the races she'd brought into the world, the Lady had grown weak. For he, and his followers, would become the threat to the world.

The Larnaeradee and Unicorns were Darziates' first targets, and as they fell, their uniting gift of the Aolen language had also disappeared. Then the Centaurs and the water Nymphs had begun to vanish, and the Sprites had sickened–huddling and shaking in their flower beds. The Dryads had grown afraid, shutting themselves into their trees, and the Lady had found herself surrounded in failing purity and growing corruption.

Finally she had herself retreated to the confines of the Elves' Great Sylthanryn Forest so that she could protect the purity and magic there at least, and she had remained secluded with them until Darziates had just now chased the Nymphs into her bounds, where they had all battled beneath the treetops for their lives.

With a bruised and worried heart, she viewed the shrivelling grass, scorched leaves and poisoned trees about her. But the Lady was startled by a hurtling glimmer that caught her eye. Fearing some strange new magical attack, she quickly held a hand up, shielding her eyes as the sphere of light seemed to shoot towards her.

Yet instead of pain, she felt the light source–a globe–land in her palm gently, bringing with it a sense of something sublime.

As she realised what it was, the second prophecy at last opened, and the voices of her makers spoke once more.

As adversity is at its greatest, there are to be Three. Three to stand against the threat and unite the races against the Sorcerer and his war.

Of the Three, there will be a friend to bring the members together in their Quest, and to keep the partnership between them all strong.

There will be a leader to unite the lands of men, and to usher all mortals of the world through the Sorcerer's storm of thunder and lightning. He will be the Raiden.

And there will be the One, to summon the magical races together and to join them with the mortal races led by the Raiden. The One will end the darkness.

Thus, all races of the world will be joined against the threat.

You must guide the Three and bring the world to the steps to freedom.

The Lady now clutched at her heart for a very different reason as the voices of the Gods faded. As if heavy hands were being lifted from her shoulders, the Lady, Mother of Nature, felt hope again.

For, just as Deimos' line had survived in Darziates, at least one Fairy must have survived as well, living on to be the Summoner the world would again need. And there would be two others to join the Fairy to bring unity between all the races.

Her green eyes danced with life as she stepped free from the marred glade. Her auburn hair flashed like a challenge as she walked through pools of light beneath a rustling canopy.

THE LAST
LARNAERADEE

She would watch and wait. And she would help the Three to see their way on their Quest so that there could be a chance.

A chance for life.

CHAPTER TWO

Kiana

'Ohhh Frarshk.'

There was the agony of an unbearable weight across my legs, and the smell of freshly broken earth as dirt and rocks dug into my cheek.

The fingers of one hand were twisting in cool blades of grass, and my other hand was still tightly clasping my dagger hilt.

A groan gurgled in my throat as my mind stuttered back into action, registering each of these sensations, which were common sensations in a huntress' life.

The sweat of my adrenaline after that evening's desperate fight had become icy, and every breath made my clothes press coldly against my skin. But I was sure I hadn't been unconscious for too much of what little time remained of the ninth age.

A cough cleared some inhaled soil from my dried throat and I frowned, trying to move my legs from under the mass of the shaggy body pinning them down.

'Frarshk.'

It was too heavy.

Finally, I opened my eyes and lifted my face from the torn dirt, blinking the dots of light away from my settling vision. I saw that the sky glittered with burning stars, the moon was high, and the empty pasture had been ripped apart.

Across the field a large tree slanted on an angle, holding onto the earth with a few thick roots. Its trunk had been cracked open, and claw marks raked deeply along the wood.

Behind that a fence had been pulled free of its stumps, a boulder had been overturned–its damp underside now looking strangely exposed, and grass and dirt had been clawed and broken everywhere.

I sighed, brushing ingrained specks of broken rock and earth from my cheek.

One Awyalknian farmer would be very unhappy in the morning. His sheep had made a quick exit from the break in the fence, but he would be blissfully safe despite how close the threat had been to his family.

THE LAST
LARNAERADEE

I tried not to remember the times I had been too late to save other families, because Darziates sent more of his beasts from Krall than I could keep up with. His odd, terrible creatures were forever invading Awyalkna and anywhere in between, and I could never hunt them all in time.

I shut out the crimson images of what I often found in those broken houses and instead twisted my torso a little, trying to turn over onto my back. I grimaced as my legs strained underneath the massive carcass and something heavy seemed to weigh my shoulders down.

Puffing and labouring to glance over my shoulder, I saw that a matted, grizzly paw the size of my body was still imbedded in my quiver where the claws had become stuck in the leather as they had scraped for my spine until the very last.

Pushing to peer further behind myself, I was confronted by the nearby sight of wet amber coloured hair covering a fanged muzzle. Two of my own arrows were protruding from one of the beast's eyes. The other orange eye stared glassily at the sky, while a green tongue lolled out from a slack jaw.

My sword jutted from between its shoulder blades, and I winced as I remembered that the dagger still grasped in my hand had been my last defence against its attacks.

There had been hungry growls, hot breath and strings of spittle as I had tried with all of my might to keep those gnashing, foul teeth from my face. Those jaws had snapped together, inches from my nose, before I had buried my dagger into its bear-like throat, pulling at that blade until the shaggy fur and skin had torn loose.

Then I'd only had a moment to turn, to try to dive out of the way before the beast had slumped to land across my legs, and the collision had left me sprawling and senseless.

Now my blade, and all the way up to my forearm, looked as if they had been coated in rust and amber fur.

Grimacing, I struggled against the heaviness of my quiver and the massive deadweight of the huge paw. I squirmed and pulled until I had turned to lean back on my elbows while forcing my buried legs to rotate beneath the hairy belly of the beast.

I shrugged the quiver from my shoulders and felt the sudden relief of the monstrous arm slipping away. Then I carefully picked claws, each thicker than my fingers, from the strong leather and let the paw drop to the dirt, knowing that getting my legs free from the creature's bulk would be harder.

Gritting my teeth, I took hold of one numb leg and yanked on it, hearing dirt scraping and feeling sudden explosions of pins and needles as the movement sent blood fluttering back around my limb.

'Frarshk. Frarshk. Frarshk...' I moaned, and pulled until, with a sickly wrenching sound, one leg was free–completely whole, and with squashed boot intact.

I grimly manoeuvred the second useless leg free and cursed quietly as I used handfuls of the beast's fur to pull myself up.

I could hardly tolerate standing, and each limping step around the ruined paddock brought new explosions of painful life back into my numbed muscles.

But all the same I yanked leaves and dirt from my hair, staggered to collect various weapons and my bag, and then wearily climbed over the remains of the paddock fence to start the long trek home.

And with each stiff step back toward my new cottage on the outskirts of Gangroah village, I wished ardently that I had wings to fly me there.

I would open the bedroom window's shutters to a sky decorated with a frosting of glowing stars. Silvery beams of moonlight would illuminate the big old bed. And perhaps I would find restful sleep and healing dreams.

I rolled my eyes. Growing wings would be more likely.

Tonight's hunt had not exhausted me enough to avoid the usual night terrors.

Though I had spent two years crossing the lands to protect others from the Sorcerer's threats, I was never quite tired enough to escape dreams of the ghosts of my own past.

No point even trying for sleep and tempting nightmares of torn up pastures, crimson rooms in destroyed houses, or visions of the ones I had lost myself.

CHAPTER THREE

Agrona the Witch of Krall had spent her life being everybody else's nightmare. But tonight it was she who was sitting up in a cold sweat, shivering in the darkness of her chamber.

A chorus of sublime voices had woken her, but she was alone, and they seemed to whisper from inside her ear drums.

'Beware,' those voices warned her. The words hurt and reverberated within her skull, and, abruptly, her vision was also taken from her control. Her sight was somehow travelling, as if her gaze was being carried away from the dry wastelands of Krall and across a green landscape without her body ever moving.

'Beware what is coming.'

It was all rushing so much that the Witch's stomach roiled. But then, too quickly, it all stopped and Agrona's eyes could see a serene place. An enemy place.

She saw that the moon was high in the velvety blue of the sky, floating above Awyalkna's Capital City like an iridescent diamond.

A faint breeze rustled in the farming village outside the great Gwynrock Wall which surrounded the Capital City, and it nudged the yellowing leaves from their rest along the dark streets of the City within the Gates. She had only a moment to wish she could reach her magic out and make that breeze a hurricane–tearing all that peace away–before her vision carried her further in, past quiet dwellings. Oh, if only she could wake the sleepy inhabitants up. And drive them screaming from their beds.

But her gaze travelled to the Awyalknian Palace, which was a gleaming jewel of sparkling ivory marble in the night. Agrona couldn't wait for it to be theirs–Darziates' and hers. They would take it soon, before the tenth age began, and the pale blue flags of King Glaidin would be torn down from each so far un-accosted tower...

Again, before she could take in too much, her sight was pulled further along, and she was jolted once more by the sound of the voices.

'Beware what is coming!'

She cried out from where she was huddling back in Krall, raising her hands to her ears, but the voices continued to lash her mind. 'Beware the threat and what it will do to you.'

'I know of the threat! Darziates made me to join him against it!' she howled from her chamber, throwing her head forward to hide behind a veil of dark hair. But the vision played on in her mind.

'There will be Three to leave on a journey,' the voices whispered now. 'And if they live, they will be strong. They will seek allies for Awyalkna. They will seek to face your King. To end your menace.' Then–barely perceptible at the corner of her vision–there was a flicker of movement in a faraway hall of the Awyalknian Palace.

Two strange figures were creeping stealthily through the hall–only two, not three. Their soft feet crossed the smooth marble floor of the vast, lavish chamber, and they had sheathed swords and long coils of rope looped at their belts.

Agrona noticed them slip into the shadows of the decorative monuments that lined the walls, melting into the dark until the exact moment that the guards patrolling the area passed into the adjoining chamber. Then the figures crossed the expansive space to the giant Palace entrance.

The taller and leaner of the two figures placed his hands on the huge door, looking tiny in comparison. The other cast a quick, furtive glance across the hall again, then nodded for his comrade to ease the immense door open a slither.

Agrona forgot to be fearful of the strange phenomenon controlling her vision as she watched them dash across grounds that were abnormally quiet. Awyalkna's City was deliciously empty because most able-bodied citizens had left for the borders of Krall in a futile effort to march against her Sorcerer King.

The figures began climbing the inner Gwentorock walls now, and suddenly her vision changed, startlingly quickly, to carry her so close to the ears of the taller figure that she could sense his thoughts. Being so in tune with a mortal's basic mind made her cringe, and she heard the simultaneously cocky and jittery thoughts of a young man in the middle of growing up–sickened as his pure and ignorant intentions oozed from him openly.

His mind fluttered with grandeur: he was off on a noble Quest to save his beloved Awyalknian Kingdom. He was contemplating how he would seek the help of the Jenran mountain people. He pictured the glory he would find if he succeeded.

Then his thoughts became typically youthful and self absorbed. Would he really be good enough? Man enough?

If only he could hear the answers she would give. The Witch's sharp lips curled upward. Was this really the best Awyalkna had to offer? Why was she even being warned of these two, and a third who had not manifested?

Her vision panned out again while the figures next ran through green gardens, neat markets and down twisty City streets. They moved unfalteringly in a course toward the outer Gwynrock Wall's colossal Northern Gate.

The two figures stole closer to the closed Gate, treading silkily, and Agrona observed guards stationed as far as the eye could see along the top of the fortified wall. A set of guards also stood watching the foot of the stone ladder steps that led to the top, but as if the two sneaking figures knew every patrol routine, those guards began to patrol the surrounding area, checking the length of the base of the wall so that the figures could quickly move forward and scale their way upward.

Agrona's view was pulled along to climb with them, and her sight was positioned closer to the rounder figure this time. The Witch felt more amused than threatened once more as she again encountered a young male. This one was feeling queasy and... hungry with nerves. He was repeating: 'don't freeze up. Don't freeze up,' like a mantra.

She felt his relief when he saw that the soldiers on either side of the top of the ladder-like stairs were gazing out across the land for anybody trying to get into the City, not behind them for people trying to get out.

Blending into the dark in their cloaks, the two evasive figures pulled the extraordinarily long ropes from their belts. These ropes had fist sized knots running down their lengths, and the figures quickly joined their two lengths together before securely fastening one end to the rail at the top of the stairs.

They lowered the rope over the ledge of the walkway, and let it uncoil. It tumbled and unfurled down the length of the Gwynrock Wall to dangle and sway gently from side to side, its dully coloured line hardly noticeable against the stone.

When no cry of alarm came, one after the other, the two hooded figures climbed over the ledge, virtually invisible.

Agrona's view blurred and her vision was carried away from the escapees, to cross over boundless fields of neat squares like grassy patch work. She saw two packed bays tethered and waiting for the fleeing boys and tried to hiss at the mares to frighten them. Their black manes and tails twitched, and they stamped their dark legs. But then with a lurch she could see her chamber again, where she had been sitting all along.

She felt more certain of victory than ever.

Until the voices rose up again.

'Beware of what the threat will do to you!' they were repeating–howling with so much pressure now that she thought the pounding of her brain would burst her skull open.

And then they were gone.

She sagged backwards. Panting for a moment before she smirked delightedly. Darziates would praise her for a vision like this!

She was tearing out of bed and transforming into her other form–that of a raven, before her sheets had settled back down on the mattress.

CHAPTER FOUR

Dalin

'They underestimated us. Just like you thought,' Noal remarked wearily. 'They must have assumed we would aim for a village closer to the City.'

'Only hiding from one search group so far has been great. But I'm also incredibly insulted at how severely low everyone's expectations are,' I replied with a grimace.

I'd been grimacing all day as each rise and fall of my mare's gait made my muscles remember my rope descent from the night before.

'At least this part has been easier than escaping the City,' Noal commented, absently stroking his bay's dark neck with blistered fingers.

'We still can't let our guard down,' I warned him. 'Not until we get to the abandoned cottage.'

'Don't worry, I know,' he replied amiably, despite his fatigue. 'Your parents will search to the ends of the world to bring you back.'

I felt momentarily stung as I was reminded of my parents, and how acutely focused they had to be on affairs of the kingdom and the approaching war with Darziates. It felt like a betrayal to shift their attention to what would seem like a selfish flight on my behalf.

'Gods, we did well to get out though. Not even Wilmont, the world's most observant supervisor, realised we were capable of plotting anything of note,' Noal managed a smile. 'Let alone a Quest to seek aid for Awyalkna.'

My father especially would never have guessed my intentions to leave for Jenra. We had barely spoken in recent months, after he had refused to allow me to take any useful part in Awyalkna's preparations.

I had been trained from birth to face all circumstances, yet I'd had to stand resolutely with the remaining nobles, waving off the other young men who were leaving to face the impossible against Krall.

My father had argued that I was just a boy. And I had accused both himself and the King of being fools.

For, while Noal and I had been kept idle and safe, constant news had poured into the City of monstrous attacks within our kingdom. There had been news of invading Krall soldiers, but also news of other things invading too.

I had been especially devastated when the first invasion of Awyalkna had been reported. The entire population of Bwintam village, a place I had once visited on a festival day, had been massacred by Krall soldiers–along with a young, dark-haired singer I'd become enamoured with during my visit. She couldn't have survived.

'Do you think we'll reach small, out of the way, easy to overlook Gangroah soon?' Noal asked hopefully then. 'Otherwise we could keep our guard up, but stop for a bite.'

'The Quest has only just begun,' I chortled. 'We can't deviate from the plan already.'

'But I'm starving,' he sighed, mournfully hugging his paunch.

I turned in the saddle, rummaged through my pack and turned to him brightly.

'An apple?' Noal gasped as I tossed it to him. 'I'm used to finer things.'

'You can muster up enough energy to give me sparring bruises most days,' I told him. 'So I'm sure you're tough enough to handle the apples this Quest throws at you.'

He eyed the fruit balefully, but his reluctant, doleful crunches soon sounded around the rolling landscape while the sky gradually filled with inky darkness.

CHAPTER FIVE

Kiana

I had bypassed the big old bed, swapping weapons for a broom, and now the formerly abandoned cottage of little Gangroah village was beginning to appear less uninhabited.

In the lantern-lit rooms I was starting to see what my old neighbour, green-eyed Gloria, had meant when she'd insisted that this had once been the finest dwelling in the area. She had also regularly visited to comment on my lack of house pride since purchasing the place, so I was glad to be casting off the signs of the cottage's long neglect, and to be giving her one less observation to offer.

Sweeping my way across the bedroom and out into the hallway, I was also becoming increasingly glad that the cottage would now serve me for a base. A place where I could safely stow my healer ingredients, and where I could also heal myself between hunts.

A place that my parents would have approved of, after they had worked so hard to train me to become a village healer as my mother had been, or to run a smithy as my father had. Instead, I would be a secret village protector.

I only paused when I reached the so far unused kitchen, which was a nest of intricate cobwebs that stretched across the entire room. Dust flakes were hanging in line on each web like prisoners of war, and no matter how carefully I stepped my way in, I became caught in soft, clingy strings.

I paused again when I felt something heavy drop onto my arm. And the heavy, hairy mass moved quickly down my arm on many sharp legs, only stopping when it reached my hand.

'Frarshk,' I breathed slowly, raising my hand in dread.

My mother had once shown me a picture of a creature like this in one of her healer books, but she had explained that this creature's bite was something I would hardly have to learn to heal. Patients wouldn't live long enough for a healing.

'What is a Granx spider, the most rare and poisonous spider known to exist, doing in my cottage?' I asked it in an exaggeratedly calm, soft tone. 'What is a Granx doing on my hand?' I continued, stepping carefully toward the wooden table in the middle of the room. 'And by the grace of which Gods am I still alive?'

I lowered my arm to the table and, with a quick slice of my free hand, I tried to brush it off. Instead of running, I felt its blade-like, spiked claws cling into my skin, and my hand rubbed across a warm, round body and stiff bristles of black hair.

I inhaled while my heart stopped for a moment, but the bulbous creature just merrily dug into my flesh, barely troubled at all.

'Perhaps you are the friendliest Granx as well as the most poisonous,' I managed to utter.

The black Granx now happily waved its many claw tipped legs, as if to affirm that it was a terribly friendly fatal insect. It moved forward on my hand and I felt each tug on my skin as its little claws pulled out of my flesh and sank back in.

Its body was the size of my palm, so I could clearly see each beady eye, disturbingly fixed on my face, as it finally prickled its way off my hand of its own accord. Then it sat itself down on the table to continue watching me.

I crossed my arms, raising an eyebrow at it in evaluation—amazed that I was not convulsing on the floor. Yet instead of bringing me an early death, it simply seemed interested in my presence, and I couldn't help but crack a grin as it lifted a thin black leg and waved it imperiously, as if gesturing to the mess of the kitchen.

'You did that,' I told it. 'Perhaps you could clean it.'

The Granx raised another leg, bossing me about now.

So I bowed obediently, and began cleaning again—this time under the dictatorial, multiple eyes of a spider as I in turn kept it in the corner of my vision.

However, the Granx watched innocently enough until I had finished, even prancing up and down the table in encouragement. When it seemed as satisfied by the room as I was, it scurried down the wooden table leg and led me to the next room, where it found itself another commanding perch to sit on.

Confident and content now, I grew used to my new deadly friend as the Granx watched me fold and stack, tuck in and tame, dust, wipe and sweep until my face was flushed scarlet and my hands were pink and numb with effort.

Finally, when the little bathroom was sparkling too, I stooped over the basin to wash up and examined myself critically in the looking glass. A bruise that had coloured my whole eye socket the week before had nearly faded, and the flaming zig-zags of red veins in my eye had receded.

I wiped my face on the back of my sleeve and glanced down at the prickling sensation of many claws tugging at the skin of my bare foot.

'Yes, yes,' I smiled. 'Lead on.'

The Granx purposefully scurried across the adjoining bedroom and stopped next to a discarded satchel—the only thing still out of place in the whole cottage.

'Old Gloria will have to find another talking point now,' I told the Granx.

'Though she never struggles to do that.'

During one of her visits I had been caught listening to her for two hours about how Mother Nature must be ill, based on the weather and the state of the stall's vegetables.

I heard a faint tap, as a clawed foot was stamped indignantly on the floor, the spider demanding that the last bag be cleared. The Granx looked like it wanted to cross all of its arms at once as it waited impatiently.

I stooped to pick up my new friend instead. 'Thank you for the company,' I told it. 'But we both need to seek our proper beds once this final job is done.' I lifted it gently across to the unshuttered window and placed the velvety little ball on the sill.

'I promise,' I agreed as it waved at the bag again. 'Gods know I wouldn't argue with a deadly Granx anyway.'

It appeared contented then, and scuttled off as if its job was done while I turned to hastily scoop up the worn out, patched pack, stained from long and gruelling journeys.

But I frowned as something dropped out of the loose flap of the bag, thudding noisily against the floor in the warm silence.

It was a simple stone Unicorn figurine shining in the light. A token I had stowed away for two years–unable to bear the sight of it.

It had a faint fault line, like a healer's incision circling its entire body, but it was beautiful. Filled with reminders of things that had happened to the loved ones who had given it to me before I'd been a hunter. Before Krall's Warlord and Witch had crossed the borders into my childhood village to take everything from me.

At once, I flinched and reeled backward at the sight of it, tripping in my haste on the forgotten, dropped pack, knocking the lantern from its position on the stool. It toppled after me, both of us landing roughly while the lantern smashed into a thousand twinkling shards and the warmth and light of the merry candle died.

Darkness crept in, spreading slyly and cunningly like the phantom figure of an Other Realm ghoul. And with the darkness came the memories that normally haunted me in my sleep. But this time the ghosts seemed to trickle in around me even while I was wide awake.

CHAPTER SIX

Granx hurried straight down from the sill and scurried across the large, wild yard.

So fast.

Her legs; so powerful, and very, very dainty spiky feet, allowed her to grip her way over any obstacle.

She danced over the fence, graceful, lithe.

Then pattered over another sill, to where master Lady was waiting just next door.

Master Lady was old, old, old. Wise, wise, wise. But more beautiful than catching the freshest crickets with crunch. Even better than flies or sparrows with feather puffs. A Gloria-glorious master to belong to.

Master Lady, The Lady lady, had Nature running through her veins. Master Lady–Mother Nature Lady.

Magic.

Any dumb gnat would know that.

Except for tricks that hid the magic now–master Lady's old Gloria disguise. She put that on for Kiana girl. And because outside Forest, master Lady felt older and sicker anyway. Master Lady had been more ill of late.

Master Lady's hair was often now as silver as a gossamer web.

But could be as red as hurts with blood. She wore red hair at the moment, while nobody could see.

Master Lady had left the Forest, so big things were happening.

Hush things. Things to curl black leg hairs with fright.

'Well done my little friend,' master Lady smiled.

Granx hopped giddily in total agreement. So well done, so clever, yes.

'We needed to make Kiana remember, and to make her ready. But I will watch over Kiana now. I will check on her in the morning.'

Legs in the air: then what? Then what?

'We will lose her again.'

No good? Bad? Bad?

'She won't be alone,' master Lady's fingers were soft on the Granx's lovely, lovely velvet back. 'The Three of them are getting close to meeting, and soon everything will come together. But we must help her find the other two in time, and at precisely the right time.'

Dear, dear. Time business again.

'Yes little one. And I am afraid you have missed them. The two others made it to Gangroah and left already, with a little of my help in evading the search. They were outside while you worked with Kiana. I shall have to send you back.'

Back again. Make more friends?

'Not this time. This time it is best if you watch over them secretly,' master Lady said. She was beginning to change. Youthful skin now had delicate lines. Master Lady was putting on her Gloria face again. 'Don't draw attention to yourself. We don't want them to be terrified of you and not allow you to follow along.'

Other one loved me. Much to love.

'Indeed,' master Lady agreed, hair fading to silver. 'But just in case. We need to keep them safe, and you are the only one that can follow undetected.'

So fast. So clever. So true.

'So brave,' master Lady added. 'Now there's no telling where you will arrive when you jump back in time. Just try not to land anywhere that they'll notice you.'

Right, right. Secret. Clever... beautiful.

'Exactly,' master Lady's warm magic washed around Granx like webs.

Her lovely legs faded from sight, then her luscious body.

'Good luck,' master Lady whispered, as she sat back; an old lady settling into her chair to wait.

Granx was right. Big things were happening.

CHAPTER SEVEN

Kiana

Though I knew I was alone in my Gangroah cottage, I thought I heard the footsteps of a small child running through my hallway. As if my baby brother, Tommy, was here.

'Wait up!'

I thought I heard his tiny friend, Jin, give chase. His soft shoes sliding on my floor, just as they used to in our family home, before it was all destroyed.

Was that humming in my kitchen? My mother, Gwendis had always sung in our kitchen. She had passed her gift to me, and I'd become one of Bwintam's star singers. I had sung at the festival on the day of the invasion.

Could I hear whistling? It sounded as though it was coming from outside my cottage window. It was what I'd always heard as my father, Kires, had made his way home from the smithy.

It was all just echoes of my loved ones. 'It's not real,' I told myself.

'Oh Kiana,' the skin along my arms and back prickled as I swore I heard my best friend's voice, as if she stood behind me. 'I'm so happy.'

No—Joelle was gone.

'Get a hold of yourself,' I growled, squeezing my eyes shut. 'Send them to the back of your mind.'

But when I opened my eyes, I could see my past as if I were back living in it.

I was back in a warm time, when the sun had poured in over Joelle and I in her bedroom. The white of her bed covering had been almost blinding and we had traced our fingers over the delicate, raised lines of the lace.

Joelle had never owned anything so beautiful. Her mother had given it to her, just as a long line of once wealthy females in her family had prized it and passed it down. Most girls in any village could scarcely dream of such quality.

'One day I'll make this my wedding gown,' Joelle had breathed in wonder at her new adornment. 'It is too good for any bed.'

The pure, white lace enfolded in on itself in connecting patterns. The material had been magnificent.

'You will look like a Queen,' I'd told her reverently.

Her porcelain-like features had lit up as she'd risen to snatch a tendril of ivy growing about her window frame. Tiny white flowers made the plant seem strangely beautiful.

'And we will do your hair like this, some day when you are wed,' she had said then, placing the ivy about my head like a crown. 'You will be a Fairy.'

'Perhaps I won't marry,' I'd said frivolously. 'Perhaps I'll find a mythical Fairy Prince and just fly away with him.'

'You were quite taken by that green-eyed, gorgeous noble at the festival,' Joelle had teased then. 'The one who watched you sing. They always say green-eyed people have a lineage that can be traced right back to when the Lady first created humanity. And he did come with the royal party from the Palace. He may have been a Prince.'

I'd traced my fingers over the white bed cover coyly and tried to jest. 'Then I guess I'd end up being the Queen if I married him.'

'You know,' Joelle had faced me seriously then, 'I really can tell you won't be like the rest of us. My parents are hoping I'll marry next year, and that is all they hope for. Your parents have made sure you will have many accomplishments.' She had twirled a tendril of ivy between her fingers thoughtfully. 'Your father has taught you your letters and numbers, to ride and to hunt. He's taught you even to help him in the smithy—and nobody minds. Yet you fit into your mother's world as well as your father's dirty one.'

'No man will want me,' I'd laughed, feeling heat in my cheeks.

'Your mother will pass you the role of village healer,' Joelle had ignored me. 'You have the sweetest singing voice, are a festival day celebrity, and,' she'd smiled lightly then, 'the Gods wouldn't allow you to never have a wedding day with looks like yours either.'

Her light brown curls had spread across the white cover in loose twirling wisps as she'd laid back down next to me... But I felt myself frown then, as I glared through the brightness at her curls and the white cover.

The whiteness seemed to be tinged with pink.

Faint. Almost red. As if stained by wine that was spreading.

'Joelle...' I said falteringly as her curls lifted in a light breeze.

They were such soft wisps.

Then they seemed to whither and dry up.

I could smell burning.

I gasped. 'No,' I said, aghast. 'The attack was later. You didn't leave me yet!'

She couldn't seem to hear me as she played with the flowers and ivy she had picked.

'I never saw you die!' I begged.

I felt a moment of clarity. This was a distorted memory. I wasn't really with Joelle in Bwintam. But I was mortified as my mind played tricks and let the vision of Joelle start to burn up and turn to ashes before my very eyes. Her porcelain skin became cracked like clay, and her clothes began to break up and blow away.

I blinked in a haze of smoke as my mind shifted to a new memory of a time before the invasion, and I could hear the rhythmic clang of metal on metal as I passed my father, Kires' forge.

I could smell the embers, and peered in to find him, illuminated by sparks that were dancing with the heat. A hiss of steam burst outward while my father's strong arm lowered an axe head into the water.

I swung the hares I had caught over my shoulder and made to move toward him, into the heat of the smithy. Until I noticed the ringing sound ahead of me had stopped.

The heat was intensifying, the steam turning to smoke.

'But... it hadn't happened yet!' I whispered desperately, freezing in my dream-memory's tracks.

But I blinked up to find the vision of a burnt out ruin. A few collapsed beams. Smoke curling out of the remains.

'No, that never happened,' I was crying out, only to find that now there was the comfortable warmth of two small bodies snuggled against mine. This scene had taken place much closer to the time when Warlord Angra Mainyu and the Witch Agrona had come.

The memory seemed so real, I could feel it. The big armchair in the corner had enfolded the three of us, as Jin and Tommy had cuddled into my sides.

They had been tired, and messy, fluffy hair had tickled my nose as they'd leaned their cheeks on my shoulders. They had been my darlings. Jin with his wonder-filled eyes and Tommy, a miniature of father with the same sandy hair.

'I think I would like to fly one day,' Tommy had yawned.

'I'll fly if you do,' Jin had agreed comfortably.

'How will you do this?' I'd smiled, taking one of Tommy's sticky hands in mine, and Jin's in the other.

The lengths of their chubby hands had fitted comfortably within my palm, and their fingertips could not reach mine. Their knuckles were dimpled and their palms were like soft little cushions, warm and untouched by hardship.

'Look,' I had said. 'Such tiny wings you have.'

Then I noticed patches of crimson had stained their little palms.

The blood was spreading slowly, following the lines of their skin.

'No...' I said again. 'No, it wasn't like this.'

I tried to rub their hands clean with my fingers.

But I could no longer feel the warmth of their small forms as they nestled against me.

Smoke began to curl in through the windows with coiling tendrils.

I could barely see them. They would not move. And they gradually faded from view.

From where I huddled in reality, all alone in my spotless cottage, I felt winded–for when the smoke of my vision cleared next, everything of this final memory was ringing true.

Yes. This was when it had happened.

It had been a joyous day, and there had been the fragrance of flowers from outside, and the sound of faint, gaily played music had drifted from Bwintam's village square, in through the windows of our cottage.

I'd savoured the smell of baking bread as my mother had hummed and kneaded dough, and Tommy had run past, in the rush of a four-year-old, chirping, 'happy birthday!' before whizzing out the front door to wait at the gate for Jin.

I'd caught sight of my father coming home, his hand nearly covering Tommy's whole head to ruffle his hair in passing at the gate. Father was early, the festival being the year's most special rest day to celebrate a successful harvest.

Bwintam had been famous for its prosperity for the kingdom, and our merrymaking had even once drawn the King and Queen, and that handsome green-eyed noble who had watched me sing.

Father had bounced in the open door, still ruddy and rosy from the smithy, and I had followed him to the kitchen as he'd sat at the bread heaped table.

My father had been back for less than a week from a journey to find my gift and visit an old, auburn-haired aunt I'd never heard of. So excitement had made my heart flutter as mother had paused to lean against the bench keenly, and as father's big, rough hand had pressed a plainly wrapped gift into my own.

'It's beautiful,' I had gasped when the twine and brown paper had been torn away to reveal the white stone Unicorn with a faint line that circled the entire body.

My mother had looked as if seeing me with the little Unicorn was the proudest moment of her life, and I'd wondered at her expectant expression.

'You have reached sixteen years of age today!' father had beamed, putting browned hands on my shoulders. 'And your mother and I wish you to now learn some truths that may be hard to understand.'

I'd tried to keep from frowning.

'You know our families didn't originally come from here,' my mother had begun eagerly then. 'We were wanderers of the entire land. You can tell for yourself that we are a little different to others around us–'

'WHEEEEEEEEEEEEEEEEEEEEEE!!!'

Tommy had sped into the kitchen, flying the lopsided toy wooden bird I'd once carved him. He'd obviously tired of waiting for Jin outside.

'Thank the Gods,' I'd breathed. 'Festival day is not the time for long speeches.'

To my relief, my parents had been silenced, and I had smiled. I'd had all the time in the world to hear their stories.

'When you were younger,' my father said after a moment, stroking my hair and changing the topic. 'You used to wish every night to meet a Unicorn, and you would beg and plead until I tucked you into bed and told you the story of the Fairies and the Unicorns.'

'I remember,' I'd laughed, as I often had then.

But a rapping sound at the door drew my attention, and a moment later Jin's wide-eyed face had appeared at the kitchen window. 'Food's being brought out!' he'd squeaked elatedly.

And I'd quickly embraced my father's strong frame and kissed my mother's soft cheek, hurrying after the ecstatic Tommy to dance and sing with Joelle at the festival.

When I'd wandered contentedly away from the festival to rest beneath my favourite Willow tree, the largest on the border of the village, I had drifted to sleep with not a care in the world.

And had woken to find my village on fire, with Angra Mainyu's troops and a raven that could only have been Agrona the Witch of Krall leading an ambush against my people. This time when the smoke set in, it was exactly how it had really happened.

CHAPTER EIGHT

Dalin

We silently led our weary bays across the green plains. The moon climbed steadily higher in the darkening sky; the stars grew steadily brighter, and we both became steadily more morose.

I had almost lost hope and confessed that I'd probably led us astray before we finally saw the outline of a fence surrounding a field. If farmlands were close, then so was a village.

'Is it Gangroah, Dalin?' Noal was regarding the fence as though it was a revelation.

'Course it is,' I grunted. 'Did you think I'd got us lost?'

We both remounted, wincing as we settled back into the unforgiving leather of the saddles and began to pass small farms along a dirt road. The road ran between the fields and led us into the tiny village where the mares quickly sought the nearest water trough.

'It's smaller than the inky dot on the map back in Awyalkna Palace suggested it would be,' Noal observed of Gangroah.

The village almost blended into the fields, and the few brow beaten, sleepy farmers seated outside the tavern also seemed to fade into their surrounds. There were no stalls, but a few laden, sheltered wagons selling necessities that had been covered for the night. The tavern leaned over the road and some barns clustered across from it. The ten or so cottages were all small enough to be called huts, and they were lined up on the opposite side of the fields like aged comrades huddling in a group. Then the dirt road continued on to where the empty cottage we were headed for was meant to be.

The cottage was a distance away, and I remembered that the secluded blocks of land surrounding it were private and overgrown. The abandoned place would serve for a refuge if the search didn't come this far until our Quest could begin.

I'd been reminded of this place quite conveniently while I'd been planning our escape, as I had overheard the talk of one of the new young Palace maids. She'd had stunning green eyes like my mother's, auburn hair, and had been gossiping about the little old lady who lived in the other cottage at the end of Gangroah. I'd seen the cottages years before when I had passed through Gangroah to attend the festival in the now destroyed Bwintam village, where the dark-haired singer I'd given my heart to had lost her life.

'We'd best head straight to the cottage,' I commented as I turned to Noal, only to find that he was gazing with yearning at the tavern which was casting light out into the street as well as an aroma of cooking meat.

Noal opened his mouth to speak, still staring at the tavern.

'No,' I said firmly.

'But couldn't we at least buy a cooked meal–just quickly?' he pleaded.

I thought about the stale bread and cheese in our packs and he saw my expression weaken.

'The villagers won't be shocked if we just stop to eat and then pass through like most travellers would,' he seized his opportunity eagerly, grabbing both sets of reins to tether the horses by the side entrance before leading the way inside with a radiant expression.

He was resplendent with the idea of a meal when the leathery looking bar maid seated us by the unshuttered window.

I relaxed as we were served and began to feel sleepily contented under the merrily burning lanterns hanging from the rafters. It seemed like most of the farmers were gathered there, smoking pipes, lounging in the worn out chairs, talking over cups of ale, and not taking any notice of us.

I finished my meal and sat back, downing my own frothy cup of ale while Noal added a third plate to his pile and finished what was left of my second half eaten helping of stew.

He reached for some doughy bread next, and I gazed out the window lazily while many of the farmers now began to file out to get home.

The light spilling from the tavern lit the road outside, and everything was easy to see as I took a long mouthful and swilled it around my mouth, filling one cheek and then the other.

I only became more attentive again when an elderly woman passed close by, her striking green eyes meeting mine for a moment. I nodded out the window politely, but she gazed away pointedly and moved onto the road. I watched her progress with sudden unease as a group rode along that road from the same direction Noal and I had used, stopping in the village on their huge stallions.

I sucked in a breath while the group dismounted to question a passing farmer who had been stumbling drunkenly home. Each man in the dismounting group bore the Awyalknian coat of arms, gleaming on their armoured chests. But the old woman appeared to be creating a fuss to capture everyone's attention, and even in my rising panic I saw that many of the newcomers had at once become oddly drawn to her.

'Gloria at your service, sirs,' she cried. 'You must be tired!'

Oddly, almost everyone watching her really did appear to abruptly become highly exhausted. There were slumping shoulders and weary nods from all but one of the crowd.

A sharp eyed scout from the group, an archer carrying a bow, slipped gracefully from his mount and began to look about as the others watched Gloria in stupefaction.

I turned with exaggerated calm back to Noal, who was happily licking his fingers clean.

I swallowed the ale, casually scraped my chair back, and then pulled Noal up by his collar.

'Hey!' he protested, but then his eyes widened as he saw the search, many only now starting to try to escape the doting Gloria, or to question the intoxicated farmers.

I led us backward through the inn to the side door, stopping to watch until the one sharp-eyed archer scout had passed by, and then we slowly and naturally exited. We sauntered down to the wooden planks where our horses had been tethered, untied them and coolly mounted as a couple of guards finally entered the tavern by the front entrance. We continued down the road at an indifferent pace until we were at a safe distance. Then we kicked our heels into the water-filled bellies of the mares and rode away from the village like scared rabbits, all the way to the abandoned cottage and Gloria's neighbouring cottage on the town's outskirts.

I wondered how in the Gods' names we had made it without being spotted, but promptly decided it must have been those Gods and their grace that had sent the old woman and allowed it. Some kind of magic had happened there.

'Well, the search didn't overlook this village,' Noal surmised, panting and raising his eyebrows.

I couldn't bear the thought of it all ending like this. Being sent home to face my parents, and our supervisor Wilmont's ruffled, ringleted disdain.

'We can't stay. They're going to check this place over from end to end,' I said, thinking fast. I pushed to remember back again to when we'd passed this way, years before.

'There was a small woodland around here last time...' I turned this way and that in the saddle, getting my bearings while Noal waited nervously. 'It was somewhere in that direction,' I nodded past the two lonesome cottages.

But at that moment we heard the approaching sounds of galloping horses, and we both peered down the lane anxiously.

'Hide first, though,' I whispered. 'Then back on the road when we won't be spotted.'

He quickly followed my lead, and we both slid from our saddles, leading the bays into the miraculously overgrown grass at the end of the field. I wasn't sure, though I thought I saw a light in the abandoned cottage's windows in the distance before we pulled our horses down into the grass, quieting them with soft clucking noises and squatting down ourselves.

Moments after we were settled and safely hidden a good distance away, the search became visible as they rode in a tight band out of the darkness. They stopped only yards from where we had been, and four of them dismounted to walk quickly up and down the fences. The lithe archer sentry was one of them, and I held my breath. Awyalkna's archers were famed for their intuition and scouting.

But, as if the God of Concealment was watching over us, they walked right past, staring over us as we held our breaths before they rejoined the group.

I handed Noal my horse's reins so that I could creep as close to them as I dared. My vision was somewhat obstructed by towering grass, but I could discern the scene enough to note how disgruntled the soldiers were.

'It's too dark to spot much and these paddocks are pretty wild,' the archer scout reported to the leader at the front of the group.

'That green-eyed old lady out the front of the tavern already said no strangers had been here,' one of the soldiers crossed his arms. 'The other villagers around her agreed.'

'I don't know why we were sent out this far. Those two don't have the experience to make such a distance,' another soldier complained.

I tried not to bristle. I'd been relying on the fact that they'd miscalculate us, so that was a slight consolation.

'We're needed for more vital work than searching for runaways,' added another. 'Even valuable ones.'

'I've heard good things about them at court, but wasting soldiers at a time like this...' another man leaned tiredly against the fence.

I was feeling increasingly like a criminal, and the guilt of my necessary crime twisted in the pit of my gut.

'Enough,' the archer sentry said then, and stopped all the chatter. I raised my eyebrows at his slight figure.

'We can quickly look through the village again and question sober farmers in the morning. It's more than likely that when we get back to the City, the boys will have been found in a closer village. And,' he added, 'I have met those lads. They aren't just spoiled children.'

The archer had a strange air of self-assurance to him, and the group leader was nodding, almost in deference. This archer had to be one of the elite of Awyalkna.

'Of course you're right, Dren,' the leader demurred, and the men were all quieted as they followed his motion to remount.

I watched as they rode slowly back toward the main part of the village and the archer, Dren, turned once, seeming to scan the long grass just in front of me. Then they were gone.

As I found my way back to Noal I was feeling slightly reassured by Dren's kind words, and I wished that I could remember him as he remembered us.

'I can't believe our fortune,' I whispered on my way back to Noal's silhouette as it got clearer in the moonlight. Finally I straightened, stretching my legs and then dusting the damp from my pants. I tugged at the horses to get them to rise too before I reached for Noal, wondering why he hadn't stood for himself.

He was crouching pale faced and trembling in the grass, going cross-eyed as he stared at something sitting on his face, taking up the entirety of his forehead. I leaned in to see what it was, and found that it was peering back at me with rows of beady eyes, and with eight clawed legs that were either digging into Noal's brow, or waving about in the air in an almost friendly way.

'Granx spider?!' I hissed incredulously and fumbled immediately for my knife.

Noal wailed, and I worried that the search would hear, or even little old Gloria, who had probably finally got back to her home next door.

'Be calm,' I instructed with my own heart racing. 'I'm just going to scrape it away from your face.'

As quickly and precisely as possible, I slapped the spider off Noal's face with the blade. It tore away from his flesh, flew in a graceful arc through the air and landed with a thud on a tree a few yards away.

Its bulbous shape appeared almost indignant in the moonlight as it pattered away, but I didn't pause to stare, instead spinning back to Noal, who was still frozen. I grabbed the front of his tunic in my fist, pulled him up and pushed him to mount.

I mounted too, pressed his reins into his hands and slapped the flanks of his horse.

We took off at a light trot and I guided the mares in the rough direction of the woods until, with relief, I spotted a mass ahead that could only be the outline of the trees. I found a small clearing easily, and busied myself finding water and kindling for a fire before grooming the horses so that Noal could recover. He never handled fear well, and I'd seen him freeze up from it many times before.

It was understandable, and Noal had been like this since childhood after his family had been attacked by Trune raiders while passing through the rocky lands between Awyalkna and Krall. Trune raiders often came from Krall to find wealth and food by targeting those travelling on the roads, but this had been one of the first attacks where the Trunes had aimed specifically at the nobility of Awyalkna for a political purpose.

Noal had been bound and forced to watch his family die in brutish ways before the remains of his loved ones had been piled around him, and a letter to the

Awyalknian King had been left in Noal's pocket. That letter had promised open war on Awyalkna, or surrender and a peaceful takeover by Krall's King, Darziates.

Noal had been barely alive and never the same when they had carried him into the City. The nation had been outraged, the King grief stricken, I had gained an adopted brother, and both Awyalkna and Krall had started to prepare.

As I sat by the fire now, watching over Noal out of the corner of my eye, I saw him gradually come back to the present. He stumbled closer to the fire and huddled to stare into the flames.

'My forehead has never had such a close shave,' he joked hollowly with a thin smile, looking up at me from the fire at last.

I felt myself relax and crossed over to give him the water flask.

'Life doesn't get much better than this, hey?' I smiled back, squeezing his shoulder.

CHAPTER NINE

Kiana

The sun had burned gloriously above the debris, its rays as red as freshly spilled blood. Ashes had swirled slowly on a scalding breeze, dancing like snowflakes of death.

The still rising tendrils of smoke had coated my lungs. Choking with warm, cruel fingers. And the charred ground had crunched under heavy, steel covered war boots as they had come slowly closer.

I had been found, the sole survivor of Bwintam's massacre, and strong arms had forced me down on bloodied knees while Krall's Warlord had approached.

Angra Mainyu had brought his and Darziates' soldiers into Awyalkna's border lands. Into my village. And he had burnt away everything I had ever known.

He had towered threateningly over me, gripping a curved sabre that had glinted like a dangerous smile in the sun. I would be the last lamb to the slaughter, and I had truly hoped for death.

He had licked his lips, smudging the dirt around them, and then leaned in. There had been the reek of unwashed body and spilled alcohol, and his hulking shadow had blotted out the blood red rays of the burning morning, mourning sun.

His curved sabre had risen, ready to slide along my throat. But then a raven had landed near us. The Warlord had withdrawn, and it had become so much worse without him.

Worse without the sabre that could have ended the pain right then, sliding effortlessly across my throat, opening fine, soft skin so easily and allowing red blossoms of blood to bloom, blanketing me peacefully in nothingness.

Instead the raven, transforming before my eyes into the Witch Agrona, had wanted to keep me alive to suffer instead. And though I'd always thought magic was just in stories, she had placed her hand upon my shoulder to brand me with her magic so that the ghastly hole I was left with, both outwardly from her physical attack, and inwardly by my devastating losses, had rent me wide open much more effectively than a sabre could have.

THE LAST
LARNAERADEE

When the troop had gone, I had been left with nothing but ash settling on my eyelashes and falling down my cheeks. Everything had become dust, and when I had taken the hand of someone lying close to me, its charred fingers had disintegrated at my touch. More ashes had floated like funeral petals in the air about me. Settling in my hair.

That was how it had all happened. How I had lost them. How I had been left with only a little stone Unicorn in my pocket. And nothing else in the world.

Instead of scorched dirt I became aware of the cold, hard floor of my own cottage in Gangroah, and felt my shoulders slump forward as the last of the memories, flickering within my mind like wavering light cast across a wall, released me at last. Flashing, stinging and disappearing.

I blinked myself back to the present, wincing at how stiff my jaw felt after being clenched all night. Glass shards from the lantern surrounded me, the Unicorn figurine still looked up from where it had landed, and the pale sun of first morning filled the fresh room.

I frowned and rejected the heavy swelling feeling in my throat. Instead, I made myself blank and refocused on a new sensation. An instinct from the present. Something in this moment, in current time, wasn't right.

Snap.

I threw my head up. It was the sound of a twig breaking underfoot. There was somebody outside, the sound of their footsteps on the gravel outside the cottage carried in through the open window.

The steps were slow. Purposeful. Hushed.

A faint scratching noise came with each step, as though claws or talons were scraping the ground, and it seemed an enormous amount of time stretched between each step, as if the walker had irregularly long legs.

I noticed that the fresh air seemed to turn suddenly colder as the scraping footsteps drew nearer and watched as the breath began to issue from my mouth in icy clouds. A chill shot down my spine and goose bumps broke out all over me like a rash.

Then the scraping sound of the footsteps stopped, right next to my window, and I shivered involuntarily. My fingers were icy.

From where the steps had stopped came the sound of slow, deep breathing that hissed through the breather's teeth.

Gods, was I glad to have awoken to this. Almost as if they had been reminding me of my duty and motivation, the Gods had sent me my next unnatural beast. Hunting Darziates' creatures was the only way I could take a stand against the Sorcerer of Krall.

And this thing spreading cold paralysis into my cottage was not natural. This thing was not human. So this thing was mine.

I had fully awoken now, concentrating on it. Silently, I rose from the floor and pounced over the broken glass to land lightly next to the bed. I slid my hand under the pillow and withdrew my long dagger.

I began to slink toward the window, ready to drop down on the hissing breather and surprise the Frarshk out of it. But its senses were as acute as mine and I heard a quick hiss of surprise as the breather gasped, then I heard scraping and scratching on the gravel as the creature spun and began to run from the cottage.

As I reached the window, I caught a glimpse of an abnormally long, sharply pointed figure running across the paddock at an incredible speed. It loped so quickly across the land, stooping close to the ground as it blurred away.

A surge of blinding need sent me flying through the cottage, and I paused only to grab my sword as I passed it leaning on the wall.

I ached for a fight, for the healing thrill of a chase, and I raised my glinting sword as I sped through the kitchen towards the door.

CHAPTER TEN

Dalin

We had let the day pass, keeping to our hideout, and Noal and I were again by the fire, eating the stale bread and cheese we had avoided the night before.

I stared at the darkening sky through the treetops listlessly, lying on my back with my arms under my head.

Noal was scratching shapes in the dirt with a twig.

'Gods it's got cold,' I frowned, sitting up and rubbing my arms for warmth.

Noal sighed forlornly. 'As you said so optimistically last night, this sure is the life.' He pulled his cloak over his shoulders and shuffled closer to the fire.

'Wilmont would have expected us to be dead already, living this sort of life,' I reflected dryly, poking at the suddenly dwindling embers of the fire to stir them back to life.

'We were trained better than to die within a few nights,' Noal comforted me. 'Wilmont would give us a week at least.'

I cocked my head a little then, certain that I'd heard something beyond our camp. I peered through the dark trees. 'Did you hear that?' I asked Noal.

He paused in rubbing his arms for warmth to listen, just as another sound came from the darkness.

His posture stiffened and he sat up straight. 'There's something moving,' he whispered now.

I pulled my cloak tighter about me as Noal's expression changed to one of hope. 'Do you think it's a rabbit? I could do with a little meat!'

I rose to throw another few sticks and some dried leaves onto the struggling fire.

There was the snapping sound of another twig breaking, but it came from the opposite side of the clearing this time.

'Perhaps it's the search!' I whispered to Noal, suddenly concerned.

Noal got up too and began to creep toward where the original noise had come from. 'Let's have a look,' he whispered back over his shoulder.

He disappeared between the tree trunks in front of him and, certain that the fire was crackling strongly enough for us to be able to find it again, I cautiously approached where the second noise had come from.

Shivering, I shrugged away my sense of growing foreboding and stepped further away from the light of the fire until the darkness encased me. But then I grew painfully aware of how the trees stood close together in a suffocating way, and the air seemed to be getting colder. The night was endless, and I felt as though I were the only person left in the world.

An irrational panic began to bubble in my chest, but I pushed it aside and listened for any sound from the dead of the woods, realising how oddly quiet everything had become.

Why was it so cold? It didn't feel right.

The woods now seemed so ominous, so sinister that I was about to call out to Noal to prove to myself that I hadn't been struck deaf, when a strangled yell rose out of the woods from the opposite direction.

I gasped, and another strangled yell tore through the trees.

Noal!

I spun around at top speed and began to stumble back.

Gods, it was cold. I was running, swerving, and tripping over trees and roots. My mind felt like it was spinning in my skull and I craved warmth. I couldn't think straight. It felt as though I'd been running for hours.

I hunted for the clearing but couldn't find the light from the fire and started to panic and blunder again. But through sheer chance I stumbled over a bush and toppled out of the trees into our camp site.

'Noal?' I called loudly, no longer caring if the search was about.

The fire had gone out, and I ran to try to stir it to life as the horses showed the whites of their eyes and pawed the ground in restless fright from where they were tethered. Their manes were clinging to them with sweat, their lips curled back from their teeth in silent screams.

'Noal?' I yelled and then was stopped short when there was again the sound of a twig breaking.

The back of my neck prickled, and I had the feeling of eyes upon me.

'Noal?' I whispered into the clearing.

A long, low sound of hissing came from behind me, like the air rushing out from between jagged rocks. My breath billowed in an icy cloud as I whirled around with dread.

I saw the shadows of the trees begin to move, taking on the shapes of impossible beings.

They were advancing toward where I stood, taking sharp, jerking steps.

As the shadows advanced the fire weakened and died again, and two sets of piercing white eyes glared down at me from a great height. These things were not human.

The anxiety was swelling like a disease in my chest and felt as though it was choking me.

'What in the Gods' names...'

One of the moving figures was caught for a brief moment in a puddle of moonlight. It was easily three times my height.

'Oh Gods!' I moaned in fear. They didn't belong to this world, which had gone quiet around them, and it seemed certain that this was one of Darziates' unnatural beasts from Krall.

'Oh Gods!'

I tried to dart toward the trees, yelling with a hoarse voice, screaming for help even though I had led us too far from the village to be heard by anyone.

Sharp, torturous hissing followed my every step, and I ran wildly.

I glanced over my shoulder and saw a pursuing creature bend its wiry body and stoop. Time stood still as I watched it pounce. I saw it soar through the air like a spider, its long body twisting high over my head in the air.

Then it landed effortlessly in front of me and I practically ran into its arms.

CHAPTER ELEVEN

Kiana

Sword held ready and a snarl of determination etched onto my face, I peered around the door, opening it an inch.

The wild yard was empty. The morning light cast a fresh glow upon the field. Birds argued, the sky was cloudless, and even though autumn was still clinging to the fresh breeze, the sun was already beaming with a faint sign of warmth.

'Frarshk,' I cursed under my breath, slipping watchfully out and beginning to jog down the yard in the direction I guessed the strange figure had taken. The woods?

I was pushing vines, long grass, and scratching branches away with huge sweeps of my blade. I was focusing only on the ground as I ran, looking for some kind of evidence of what the thing had been. It had seemed nothing like any of the beasts I'd ever hunted through Awyalkna, Jenra, Lixrax, or Krall.

I saw a mark in the dirt for a fleeting instant as I ran past and started to push my legs harder, feeling my heart and my lungs working faster.

Slicing through anything in my way, I had nearly reached the end of my property and made it to the fence when I heard the sound of a twig breaking.

My legs and pulse worked even faster as I considered that perhaps this hunting trip was going to be a short one. I began to steady and raise my sword.

'YOOOOOOOHOOOOOOOO!'

My head jerked up in surprise and my eyes registered the dread inspiring, fearsome, waving figure of Gloria standing in my path.

I started to skid, but she was standing right in line with my careening descent and I was going too fast, with my sword still pointing forward.

I shouted in warning, but she didn't seem to hear as she smiled and waved. Perhaps her old green eyes couldn't see the sword.

I was sliding with momentum and she was just feet away.

Desperately, I angled my body backward and hugged my blade sideways across my chest. Then I stopped moving my legs, letting them slide forward while my body was dragged down to crash along behind them.

The air knocked out of me in a rush and my head smashed into the dirt so that my vision was filled with blurring earth as I was carried past Gloria. I kept my teeth gritted against the pain and my sword held tightly against my chest so that I wouldn't slip and slit my own arm or throat until I at last laid still.

It took a few moments of breathing heavily and blinking at the bright blue of the sky before the burning, stinging feeling of scrapes all over set in, and before I awkwardly flailed to sit up.

'Gods, Gloria!' I spluttered, struggling to stand and turn back to where she'd been.

And I found Gloria beaming away as if nothing had happened.

'Kiana! Are you well on this fine morning?' she enquired sunnily.

I stood dazedly, panting, with fire now running up my legs and back, and with an unnatural beast, ready for the hunting, instead getting further away.

'Gloria, what are you doing here?' I asked, trying not to sound agitated. 'I saw no one on my property a moment ago.'

'I noticed candle light from your cottage last night, and thought you may need something,' she replied reasonably. 'And it is clear that you do, dear, running about like that.' She gave me an appraising gaze. 'Let's get you inside and cleaned up.'

She was coming toward me as she spoke, and I glanced down at myself as she took my arm. I was amazed by how foolish I had nearly been, because if I had chased that thing with only a sword and night shirt to protect me from it and the elements, I would either have frozen or stood out in the woods so starkly that it could easily have spotted me.

As soon as I could be rid of Gloria, I would prepare and hunt this beast down properly.

But right then Gloria was guiding me gently by the arm toward the cottage. Like a mother would.

'The candlelight was glowing so late, you must be tired,' Gloria was saying, and I swiftly began to feel rather exhausted. My shoulders sagged wearily, and I nodded to her in surprise.

I let myself be led into the cottage where she bustled about exclaiming at how nicely I had fixed it up, and how there must be some hope for me after all, if I knew how to make myself a home.

She took the sword from my hand and leant it against the kitchen wall. She swept up the glass in the bedroom, then pulled me into the light spilling from the unshuttered window.

Fuzzily, I felt something about her... something warm and natural that boggled my thoughts and that my mind shied away from and couldn't quite grasp. Never had she actually touched me, and now that she had, I could feel a million puzzling things about her. But fatigue was weighing my mind and muscles down.

She tutted as she pulled glass from my hands and knees, and she regarded me with care. Such exquisite eyes that held me strangely fascinated. Something about her...

My own eyes were shutting, and I had to keep hauling them open, and when she pulled my arms over my head and yanked the dirty nightshirt off I only grumbled like a protesting child. I seemed to have lost my senses.

She shushed me immediately, just like a scolding parent, and her striking green eyes lingered on the mark on my shoulder for a moment, before she slid a clean shirt back over my head and guided me to settle into bed.

I had a dim awareness growing within me that, as dark and unnatural as the creature had felt, she seemed to be full of light.

The last thing I saw was Gloria bending to pick the Unicorn figurine up, putting it on a shelf and saying: 'My, my, what a pretty thing', before walking out.

When I awoke, it was with a dreamy smile on my face, feeling greater peace than I had in two years. I rubbed my eyes and stretched my arms out in front of myself happily, realising I hadn't been haunted by terrors and memories as I'd dreamed this time.

I glanced toward the open window where a dazzling sunset was filling the sky.

Then I sat bolt upright in bed.

I had slept through the whole day?

'Frarshk!' I hissed and threw off the blankets, crossing to the cupboard and pulling on a dark green tunic, trousers and my boots. I quickly combed my hair back with my fingers and wove it into a tight braid, then strapped on my quiver full of arrows, grabbed my daggers, slid my sword into its sheath, and threw a dark cloak about my shoulders.

This time as I made my way through the kitchen door I checked not only for lurking threats, but also for the enigmatic and fearsome old Gloria. I could not fathom how she had been able to surprise me in the yard earlier, how she had enticed me to let my guard down enough to allow her care for me, or how she had sent me to sleep.

Certain the yard was clear, I travelled quickly through my land, jumped the fence at the end and closely inspected the surface of the wood. Six scratches curled around the wood in the shape of a giant, narrow, clawed foot. The engraved mark looked as though it could have come from the foot of an incredibly unusual bird, but a bird that was bigger than most people or animals. I moved away from the fence and studied the dirt around the area.

Either the thing had vanished after latching onto the fence, or it had become more careful about leaving tracks, but I trusted my instincts that any creature in need of shelter would head for cover in the woods.

I ran across the grassy lands, scanning them keenly, and recalling how unreal the creature had seemed, even in comparison to those I'd hunted in the past.

But it was real, and the idea of how real it was, and how much damage it could do, spurred me on.

CHAPTER TWELVE

She tapped long, black painted fingernails on the arm of the steel chair she lounged in. Her eyes flickered impatiently around the candle-lit chamber. Tonight the Sorcerer's newest creatures were acting on her prophecy. They would seize the two Awyalknian runaways, and her vision would be proven invaluable. After years of toiling relentlessly, she would be proven worthy and invaluable to the Sorcerer King.

If all went well.

Agrona had met the Sorcerer Darziates when she had been twelve. He was a defender of ones like her and a protector of the world, he had said. He had strange abilities, just as she did. He had described how he had already hunted out many of their divided enemies, ending the separation by ending the magical races in these lands. Almost at once she had given her withered, young heart to him, and she'd spent her life fighting for his approval ever since.

He had been a young man at the time of finding her—a small, spiteful, vengeful wraith, and while she had grown he had never changed. He was the most beautiful thing she had ever seen after a childhood of being scorned, shunned for her wondrous abilities. She had been glad to follow him, and from the beginning Agrona had done as Darziates suggested, allowing him to help her use her abilities to poison her two greatest haters—her parents—until their faces turned black, their eyes rolled back and their throats gurgled for air. Agrona had then gone without question to serve him in his great cause and in his ascension to power in Krall so that now the mortal races could be dominated under one ruler too. She'd aided him in seizing his rightful throne, sweeping in with him to shrivel Krall's royal family of that time on the spot, and helping to terrify or magically manipulate and subdue the rest of the kingdom.

Together they had shared in the righteousness of Darziates' higher purpose, both craving to feel the sweet comfort of consistent, unified control. And if she were the right one, he'd said she would be his bride, working forever by his side to unify the entire world under his rule. Oh, how terribly she desired him, the most powerful being she had ever encountered.

She could feel when he was angry, she could sense when he was pleased, and she could taste the magic of him without even standing near. When she was near though, he sent thrilling sensations like shivers through her entire being. She delighted in it. It made her very blood spark and bubble with energy.

So she had done much in his name. She had scoured the lands in raven form, spying on what was to be his world, and finding the best places to attack. She had installed the Awyalknian spy, Wilmont. She had teamed up with Trune raiders, ordering them to ambush a noble Awyalknian family to get the war started. And she had overseen the destruction of Awyalkna's most industrious border villages to help break Awyalknians into fear.

Even though she hated the disgusting mortal soldiers she had also been given the job of dealing with, she still gladly performed her duties of keeping all Krall soldiers in check for Darziates too. The mortals repulsed her with their simplicity and scorn, the worst being Warlord of Krall, Angra Mainyu. But despite despising this tyrant militant human, who was allowed power in spite of being a mere mortal, Agrona tolerated him. Her master was amused by the animalistic Warlord and appreciated how loyal and effective he was with mortal soldiers. So she kept the vile human close. She would always whole heartedly obey her Sorcerer.

And the fact that men quailed at her beauty and her cruelty was nothing. Everything the Witch did was in an effort to please her King. She could control entire armies with a gesture or command. She could stare down any grizzled warrior. Angra Mainyu himself was transfixed by her. She could cut off a man's airways with a twitch. She breathed evil magic like air; it pulsed through her body instead of blood.

Yet still, Darziates was more powerful than she, and he remained indifferent to her as anything more than a second in command. Often even being seen as on par with the insane Warlord Angra Mainyu.

Agrona knew Darziates thought she wasn't the one, wasn't the bride he wanted, wasn't powerful enough. But who could be more powerful? More beautiful? Darker? More willing? Who could adore his work so entirely, other than his Witch?

She supported his genius with awe while he experimented and poured himself into creating new beasts to send into Awyalkna. She watched him bend the evil spirits he called to his will and appreciated the craft he used in contaminating the foully pure Dragons they had captured. Nobody else could truly grasp how terrible and deliciously warped his experiments were as he moved on from making brutish trifles that could frighten people, and began producing beasts of true darkness and subtlety. His talent was such that he was now able to call poisonous entities from the Other Realm to serve as the spirits of these newest beasts–the same ones that were now hunting down the Awyalknian runaway boys of her vision.

These beasts were the first attempts since Darziates' forefather Deimos had tried to bring spirits of the Other Realm into their own world, to meld even the different planes together in unity. And nobody had completely mastered the power of controlling the Other Realm spirits. Yet he had done it. The spirits responded to his compulsion, oozing into this world from their own to obey his summons, even though most died after undergoing his experiments.

She could see his brilliance and often despaired at how rare it was for the King to be moved to be impressed by Agrona in return. Until she had displayed the power to be a vessel of prophecy and vision only recently. She'd been ecstatic to go to him to describe her new skill, and how she had been warned that, by some twist of fate decreed by the Gods, the Awyalknian boys could be dangerous if they reached the Jenran mountain people. He had been pleased, and she knew that she, Darziates' Witch, had perhaps given her master something vital, something that could thwart the whims and threats of the Gods.

And when Agrona had kissed him, Darziates had allowed it, permitting a feeling of his magic to pass in wild thrills through her delighted body.

So she was sure that, after this night, if her warning did help them to avert the threat the boys posed, she would be recognised to be powerful enough. She would prove to him that he needed her. He would want her as his dread Queen.

Just as she hungered for him.

CHAPTER THIRTEEN

Kiana

For some time I stepped through the woods, checking dark groves and moving through the natural Palace of towering tree pillars. The chill was growing around me and I pulled my cloak tighter as I quietly stepped over fallen branches. I searched through a hollow in the ground that was shrouded in shadows and noticed that my breath was starting to spread from my lips in clouds.

When my heart increased in pace to raise an internal bell of alarm, I gripped my sword hilt firmly. I had to be getting closer to the menace of the beast.

I observed that nothing stirred. No sounds of animals or wind rustled the peculiar silence.

It felt as if something had sapped the liveliness out of the air, as if the atmosphere was being turned to ice—until suddenly the stillness was split by a desperate cry for help.

The sound tore at my instincts and galvanized my limbs into a jagged sprint over roots and bushes, and around shadowy trunks while I now un-slung my longbow.

In a blink the arrow was fitted and I rushed on, steadily gaining the sense that I was nearing the presence of whatever icy power filled the beast until at last I slowed, and on soft feet, with taut bow ready, I moved around the final trees on the border of a clearing.

Then I saw properly for the first time what had been outside my window.

It was the height of at least three grown men combined, with sharply pointed limbs. Spikes protruded from each joint, clawed out from each digit, and poked gruesomely out along the thing's spine. The legs were so long that they bent in a way that made the thing look constantly ready to pounce. It was insectile, with slit-shaped features and burning white eyes.

I steadied myself against the shelter of the nearest tree trunk, the rough bark feeling reassuringly real against my straining hand as it gripped the bow. I tried to evaluate the creature and the odd chill that spread about it like an incapacitating weapon, and saw that past the beast there were two horses bumping together with their teeth showing in panic. Then peering further across the clearing revealed that there was another beast blending into the shadows.

Worse, one human victim was dangling from the clawed hands of the first beast, which was intent on the victim's strangulation. The captive was gurgling weakly–still alive, which didn't always happen on a hunt. The second beast was holding another person by the leg–less urgent.

A name flashed unbidden across my mind for a moment–the name of Sylranaeryn, a mythical Larnaeradee Fairy warrior who had taken the path of self-sacrifice against dark creatures of Sorcery[1]. With that pure thought, I blocked out the swells of crippling, toxic emanations poisoning the area around the beasts to let myself be encased inside with the steel I always felt in place of fear.

I calmly loosed my arrow straight into the chest of the nearest beast, and then leapt lightly to a new position, drawing a new arrow. In an instant this was also hurtling into the second beast before I was again flitting to a better vantage point.

I paused, disconcerted to find that the creatures had not uttered any cry or shown any evidence of registering their grievous injuries. I slung my bow back over my shoulder grimly and unsheathed my sword again, sprinting forward from the trees to run a long slice across the nearest beast's spiked back before I disappeared again for cover in the trees and whipped around to observe.

There was no reaction on either of the inanimate mask-like faces of the beasts, they simply continued to focus on gripping their two captives and in particular on watching the dangling victim choke.

'Frarshk,' I panted. But without hesitation I threw myself out into the open and charged at the fiend strangling its prey.

I swung my sword with all the might I could muster into the outstretched beast's arm, forcing the blade to bite deeply into the flesh. And this time the towering fiend opened a mouth that had previously not been visible and began a hair-raising shriek that revealed black gums and pointed fangs lining its jaws.

Simultaneously, the other brute dropped its victim's leg and began toward me in a menacing slouch, but I determinedly sawed with my blade to the chorus of continued screams while the first beast somehow withstood the severing of its arm to keep a hold on the boy's throat.

I grunted with effort, driving the blade deeper until finally tendons, muscles and ligaments sprang apart under the force, and I pulled free and whirled away to its other side as the beast's hand lost function and the boy slipped down to the ground.

I raised my blade again and turned on the second being that had been circling with an arrow still embedded in its chest to try to get behind me. I darted closer, ducking under sharp, lashing talons, making a slice across its belly as I passed, and then slicing through the tendons and muscles behind its knees so that the beast toppled forward with a loud shriek.

I felt good until I glanced back at my original adversary, whose clawed hand dangled limply, disconnected from all nerves. But I gasped as I saw it reach with that flopping, nerveless, half-detached hand to pull my arrow from its chest, and as I saw the hole from the arrow re-seal with more shadowy darkness.

Then I saw the rent open gouge in its arm start to seal over as well, the muscles reconnecting and dragging the wrist and hand back up.

It flexed its long clawed fingers before its white eyes flickered onto me.

I quickly pounced to land on the second beast's back before it could recover too and began sawing at its spikey spine for a more permanent injury, but it roared and jerked around fast so that I was thrown off, and at once I felt myself being snatched up by its healed comrade's freezing grip as it seized my ankle and lifted me to hang upside down in a dizzying rush.

My mind was wiped clean for a moment as freezing ice seemed to shoot through my entire leg, but I began to wriggle desperately when its claws tightened, biting through my leather boot and into flesh so that it felt suddenly as though I was being sucked down into a frosty vortex of black water that could rip me from this world and into the Other Realm.

Frantically I kicked out with my free leg and my foot connected heavily with the thing's face. When it blinked at the blow, I took the opportunity to pull myself upright, bending upward with all of the tensed muscles in my stomach burning until I could reach with my blade and jab at the thing's neck.

The blade slid into its throat and it furiously raised its free hand to try to wrestle the sword buried in its gullet back out again. Then there was the throbbing agony of the second demon's clawed hand seizing my middle, nearly entirely enclosing my waist.

I cried out with the shocking barrage of bitter cold, fervently trying to twist free while also keeping a grip on the sword spitting the first beast.

Trying to still me, the second beast also now clamped its hold around my wrist before it took a step backward, pulling my middle and wrist along after it.

'Gods!' I shrieked in savage agony as I was pulled instantly in two different directions.

It took another step, and I screamed as my body was pulled taut between my two captors, ready to rip apart at the seams.

As if it enjoyed my screams, it gave a little teasing tug on my wrist and I heard my shoulder click while the creature's sharp teeth glinted in what could've been a smile. Then my knee made a popping sound as the first sword speared beast continued its agitated movements.

Agonised, I finally pulled my sword out of the first beast's throat and it released my ankle in its own pain.

The other beast hadn't been ready for this, and it was still pulling at me gleefully so that I, with my sword pointed forward, was miraculously tugged at great speed into its hard chest.

With a ghastly sound my blade penetrated deeply and those gloating, glowing eyes suddenly assumed surprise as I kicked off from its stomach to flip myself around its wrist, managing to twist free of the now howling beast's grip.

I dropped back to the ground, but those two hulking figures shuddered and were already stretching out their healing bodies, unfolding their limbs to their full, spike lined extent, appearing ready to chase me to the ends of the world.

Counting on it, I dashed away into the woods, only looking back to ensure they were pursuing me from the clearing as I sped through the trees and hastily dodged hurdles of the undergrowth.

I ducked under a branch that could have beheaded me, swatting its leaves from my face, but a few moments later I heard the same bough shatter as one beast ploughed straight through it.

As they came in closer, I sheathed my blade and drew out my bow again, refitting another arrow in a blur. Then with as much accuracy as I could manage without pausing, I fired my arrow straight into one slitted eye of the beast on my right and watched it career out of control to collide into a tree. The tree lifted with the impact, its roots ripping upward from the soil. Then I swerved to my left, refitting my bow and loosing at the other beast.

Immediately I skidded to a halt and dropped to the ground in front of a patch of bushes. I quickly tested the wind direction, making sure it was blowing away from Gangroah, the closest village, before I plucked two rocks from the ground and began to strike them desperately together over the bushes until they sparked and an ember began to eat into the leaves. Perhaps the legendary Fairy Sylranaeryn was magically assisting me to help a little flame to grow in the chilled air, because I was able to gently–if hurriedly nurse the embers to life.

I ran to a patch of fallen branches to create another spark, and looked about in a panicky rush, expecting to feel an icy hand around my neck at any moment. 'Come on … Please Gods, let it burn!' I whispered frantically, wishing again for Sylranaeryn's magic.

I gasped when I said the word 'burn', because as I said it, the pile of makeshift tinder seemed to magically listen and ignite. Flame abruptly caught hold of the sticks, bursting to life.

But I could only thank the Gods for another blessing and move on. The beasts were stirring, and I rushed to spout more arrows in their direction before fleeing to start another little fire.

I heard the beasts crashing loudly behind me as the next fire began to grow, but I calmly fired once more so they never fully regained their sight, and went through the same process.

I dashed to another clump of bushes and did the same thing, then to every bush that I passed. I yelled 'Burn!' at them and, as if by enchantment, they did.

I ripped a patch from my cloak and snatched up a branch as I ran. I wrapped the material around the branch and dipped it into a fire that was already crackling. The makeshift torch wouldn't last for long without the proper oils, but it was enough.

Like a wild woman possessed, I danced my way around the wood, lighting as many bushes as I could, crying out for them to burn. Finally, inexplicably, fires had begun springing up everywhere, as despite it being a fresh night, the flames were truly taking hold, not even diminishing when the beasts and their cold drew close.

Whenever I could, I scooped up leafy branches to dip them into the steadily growing fires, holding them out as I ran and lighting up all the trees I could get to.

I evaded my pursuers and spread fire until I was covered in sweat and ash, and my breaths were heaving. Only when smoke started to replace oxygen and the flinching, scorched beasts began to thaw and lag in speed during the chase, did I accept that soon the entire woods would be alight in a spectacular blaze.

Almost running out of arrows now, I fired once more at the beasts to slow them further, and to give myself the opportunity to run back to the clearing. I saw one beast jerk back with the impact, and it scorched itself on a burning bush. The flames started to crawl up its legs as if they were flammable.

I kept running, with the sounds of the creature desperately howling and beating at its legs echoing behind me.

The fires were joining together, and I crashed through the burning woods with my arm protecting my head and my sword now out again, cutting through anything in my path.

Branches were crashing from treetops to the ground like bodies raining from the sky, burning leaves dropped like snow and it was as bright as daylight around me when I finally burst into the clearing again, to find the skittishly prancing horses straining to get as far from the burning as their tethering allowed.

I also found one of the survivors awake and pulling at his comrade, who seemed limp and unable to move.

Breathless, I held my hands out in a sign of peace. 'I'm going to help you.'

The boy who was upright nodded, swallowing.

'We need to leave.' I said hastily as the flames gnawed at the edges of the clearing, their yellow light filling the area as they neared. 'Can your friend move?'

He shook his head, pale faced.

'Get him up, carefully. I'll ready the horses.'

The clearing was a furnace that would be alight soon, and if we didn't hurry the escape route I had planned on would be burning too, and we'd be trapped along with our enemies. But I steadily prepared the two nervous bays while the boy struggled to get the dead weight of his friend up.

I mounted one of the mares, still clutching the reins of the other, as the boy finally dragged his friend across and helped me to pull him up to lay over the saddle in front of me.

Then the blonde youth mounted hurriedly and obediently followed my lead towards the stream while the flames snarled at our heels.

The sight of the smooth dirt banks was a welcome one amidst a nightmare of suffocation and raining embers, and we gratefully steered our course into the stream just as, off into the blazing distance, two high-pitched shrieks ripped through the woods.

They were the shrieks of fury and agony from two dying beasts unable to escape the flames that were searing away their ice.

And with a grim smile, I leaned forward.

I could see the end of the woods.

CHAPTER FOURTEEN

Dalin

As my airways were constricted, I became detached. I was drifting away into a blackness so smooth and rolling I felt I was floating.

Then I saw, in the shadows of my vision, a person rush in to attack the beast, and I dropped in a heap–shivering uncontrollably, spasming and twitching, and unable to help the person who was surely a brave soldier from the search.

The poor soldier had used the last of his fortune when he'd found us, but I was just so cold that it hurt and any movement brought chilling agony that clawed through my anatomy. It felt as though shards of ice were tearing, ripping, slashing their way through my skin and muscles. Freezing knives had been let loose just beneath my flesh.

I'd not known real hurt until then, and I was paralysed by it. I couldn't even surface when I heard Noal urging me to wake.

He yanked on my arms, pulling me jerkily into a sitting position, and even in the roiling blackness of my mind my world lurched as I was pulled up and my head lolled to the side.

I did dimly hear a beautiful female voice and wonder if the voice was that of a guardian from the Gods.

I was relieved that an angelic guardian was here if I had to die.

At least I could be peaceful in the cold.

CHAPTER FIFTEEN

The night seemed darker in the lands of Krall. It was a vast, bleak country that looked as harsh and unwelcoming as the rumours accurately painted its King to be.

The castle slanted upwards, sprawling as it climbed the jagged desert landscape behind it. The castle was made of a dreary dark grey stone and, unlike Awyalkna's Palace, which stood like a jewel of incredible height and width, it was a massive six story high structure that spanned outward for miles rather than in height. It was known for its brutal occupants and for the foul activities it concealed rather than for aesthetics. It appeared more imposing than the looming rocks it perched on.

The whole capital was surrounded in a huge rock wall with massive gates at each divided city sector. Thousands of streets filled the areas inside the gates and around the castle, and the small houses lined within those streets displayed neat, but sombre. The streets were deserted, the houses dark and brooding. There hung a feeling of permanent suspense, of silent fear in the atmosphere. This was a natural state for a population that had to tiptoe fearfully around its easily displeased master.

The roads were of dirt and the rainy season had turned these to sandy coloured mud. That mud clung to every surface, and the splashes of it from carts along the roads had to be painstakingly removed from every house by every family. The gloomy tidiness had to be maintained.

On the stark walls around the castle there blew ragged flags, flapping about like wraiths. A crimson hand print was painted onto the darkness of each flag, like a warning sign.

Inside the castle were giant function rooms, bedrooms, ballrooms and throne rooms of brilliance, but they lacked warmth. It was long since those halls had held functions or gatherings. The servants who dusted the darkened, empty rooms barely noticed they were places of opulent richness and finery any more.

Even the sparsely scattered torches lit along the walls threw off little light or warmth. The dank atmosphere of the buildings seemed to consume them.

In a particularly foreboding, out of the way room that adjoined the King's own chamber, Darziates was sitting in a high-backed, intricately formed steel chair. His flawless face was framed by startlingly white-blonde hair, and had strong, striking features that would have made him unnaturally handsome. Except his eyes were too impartial, as hard as granite, and made his face disturbing to behold.

The Sorcerer King had the body of a soldier, and held himself regally, his hands on the throne's armrests as he regarded a short, terrified man in front of him.

This man's nose was pointed and his patchy goatee and tufty hair were the colour of carrots. His nose twitched, and he was kneading his hands. He wore a brown robe and hood.

'How did this failure happen, Agrudek?' the Sorcerer asked, his voice soft, but still echoing in the stony chamber.

The small man, the King's scientist, flinched. He smoothed his rough, brown cloak nervously. 'I–I'm not sure, Sire.'

There was a pause as cold, calculating eyes held Agrudek's for a moment, and unbidden, images of Agrudek's family were planted in the small man's mind. Agrudek quivered, certain that the King had forced him to see his family as a warning of what was at stake.

'Try to explain to me why those Awyalknian boys are still breathing.'

'Sire, I'm sorry, it won't happen again...'

Darziates stared down at the man cowering in front of him. The Sorcerer was impossibly still, and not a sound of life echoed beyond the stone-walled room.

Agrudek became paler, the blood draining from his face.

'It must be the spell we used to make the creatures. We–we don't have it right yet, Sire. But please, please Sire, we will.'

The darkness inside the Sorcerer on the throne made it almost impossible to breathe. Being so near such wrongness made a man's pulse race.

'The Evexus were to be designed with intelligence. I gave a plethora of energy to raise the shadows from the Other Realm to form them.'

'Yes, revered majesty... I'm terribly sorry, I just... just need to make some adjustments in their design... Sire...'

A montage of Agrudek's family ran through his mind again and he swallowed carefully.

'It's just that... my honoured Dread Lord... the Evexus followed the boys' scent. To a wood. And... attacked there.'

'Yes.'

'Somebody interfered, Lord... found a way to kill the Evexus experiments... really not my fault Sire... please... don't hurt my family, Majesty... '

'Who caused the interference, Agrudek?'

'I'm not sure Sire, but it has to be a man of great skill to be able to best two Evexus, Sorcer... Sire, Majesty, Darziates.'

'Four days. Modify the experiments. Make them smarter. End the 'attacker of great skill' and bring me the runaways. Otherwise, I must torture your family and mutilate you.'

'Yes... magnificent King... thank you so much my Lord...'

'Hush.'

'... Yes Sire...'

'Leave.'

Agrudek nearly ran from the room, scuttling and stumbling backwards at the same time as bowing. He walked quickly through the imposing halls; his footsteps echoing, and he exited with little relief. He looked over his shoulder at the dark castle that even at night cast a shadow across the streets. Shivering, sure the King still knew what he was doing, Agrudek started down the muddy road to his modest new house. He flew silently through the rooms and quietly sobbed with relief to see his wife and two daughters nearly perfectly intact.

Only a small token on the table made obvious how real the King's threat had been. One of his daughter's plaits had been left pinned to the kitchen table by a large knife. His family had slept through and not realised the danger.

He swallowed nervously and crept into every room of his home to double check that his daughter's piggy tail had been the only thing harmed. Then he took the knife from the table, put it out of sight, and exited the house. He walked down the deserted street, his eyes darting about and his head constantly twitching to glance over his shoulder. He stopped outside a workshop, and taking a deep breath, he pushed the way into the prison-like laboratory that the King had made especially for him.

He stepped over dark shapes and discarded gadgets, and brushed hanging tools and shiny articles aside.

The objects he was to create were not gadgets or creations of science or rationality. They were monstrosities. Life forms wakened by the strange power of the King and controlled by the logic of Agrudek's science.

Agrudek made the hateful empty shells for bodies, like giant dummies used in weapons practice for the soldiers. But these empty shells had levers and steel inside to create a framework and joints, to mimic the real insides of a body and to allow strength and movement. When Darziates got to them however, the evil that was poured in to fill these models took on a life of its own. The bodies warped, with the evil inside clinging to the framework and making the body its own. The steel and materials used to make a pretend skeleton were suddenly fused to life. Spikes and claws protruded grotesquely out of each body, with the evil unable to be cleanly contained in the shell, and a hideous light filled the eye sockets as a gruesome reflection of the new spirit existing within.

Agrudek pushed away thoughts of what these shadow Evexus creations could do to people. Instead, he fixed firmly in his mind the faces of his daughters, with noses like buttons, wispy curls of carrot-coloured hair and smiley, gapped grins. He pictured his wife, roly-poly and brimming with love.

Keep them safe, Agrudek told himself. They were all that mattered.

Then he rolled up the sleeves of his brown robe, ignoring the tears on his cheeks, and looked at the shadows all about him.

Agrudek shivered.

There was enough shadow in his heart to create an entire army of Evexus.

CHAPTER SIXTEEN

Kiana

In the distance behind us, the woods lit the whole night. Shadows were cast before us that danced and swirled and leapt like demons from the Other Realm, but the air was not tainted by smoke in a sign that the flames might have begun to follow us.

I set us a steady pace to leave the area I had earlier sprinted across, trailing beside the stream that would lead us all the way back to Gangroah. And I observed the overwhelmed boy on the bay next to me, seeing that he was entirely blanched of colour, even underneath the ash powdering his face.

'My name is Kiana,' I broached the silence. 'I have a cottage not too far from here where we can tend to your friend.'

It seemed like an effort for him to break from his stunned reverie. 'Well met. My name is Noal,' he managed. 'I greatly appreciate the aid,' he added resolutely. 'So does Dalin,' he said, and swallowed visibly as soon as he gestured toward his comrade.

I kept my reservations to myself as we neared my land, but the boy slung over the saddle in front of me hadn't shown any signs of life.

'This is... your cottage?' Noal asked in a startled voice, with a little vigour at last touching his tone.

'I purchased the property only recently,' I explained, lifting my eyebrow as I glanced back at him from where I'd been double checking Gloria's cottage was dark.

I steered us down to my gate and across the wild yard while Noal continued to regard me with surprise.

'You live by yourself?' he questioned in puzzlement, hinting at the oddity of a young lady living without others, and roaming the lands by night.

'Here we are,' I guided my bay to a stop outside the front door. 'Let's get your friend inside.'

He helped me to drag his comrade from the saddle and through the unlit cottage, into my newly cleaned bedroom.

'Could you light any candles you see around the place?' I handed him a box of matches. 'Try to get a fire started in the fireplaces too.'

Compliant and appearing glad to be useful, Noal lit the candles around my room and then left purposefully, giving me a moment to focus on the stricken boy–Dalin.

He had still not stirred with even a flicker of the eyelids so I put my hand close to his nose to feel for the light fluttering air that would brush my hand if he was breathing. It was either too weak for me to feel, or he wasn't breathing, and I quickly put my head to his chest to listen for a heartbeat.

The layers of clothing were too thick, so I unclasped the cloak at the boy's neck and felt my eyes widen as I noticed that a layer of frost had stiffened the collar of the boy's clothes. I untied the cords of his shirt and listened once more, waiting, scarcely breathing myself so I could hear clearly.

I frowned–and then there it was. A weak thumping that was so faint I could've missed it. The boy was barely clinging to life, and only with a weak grip.

'Gods,' I winced, rubbing at my throbbing ear from where it had been pressed to his chilled skin. He was unnaturally cold all over and I recalled with a grimace that those fiends had spread cold like poison through their touch. Perhaps the ice had spread through the boy's body, pumping through his veins.

In the flickering light I noticed an inky blue ring circling the boy's wrists and throat. Lifting his chin showed me the marks were unlike any kind of bruises I had ever seen. They spread around his neck with feathery patterns, as if a design had been painted onto the skin. I touched the mark curiously, but snatched my hand back hastily with my fingers pulsing as if I had been burnt.

I pulled my sleeve back to look at my own wrist, where the beasts had clamped me for a time. Then I lifted my tunic to look at my waist. I had blue marks from their touch too, but they were already fading because, though my struggles had seemed to stretch for an eternity in their hold, my entrapment had been only brief.

In comparison, Dalin was literally freezing inside and I had to find a way to purge the cold from his body, to prevent him from being frozen completely into a sleeping death. I couldn't set the poor boy on fire as I had the beasts, but I could attempt to concoct some kind of scorching fluid that could quench the ice inside, setting a kind of fire alight within him.

'I've lit everything I could find to light,' I heard Noal's tentative voice from the doorway, as if echoing what I'd been thinking. 'Do... do you think Dalin is going to live?'

'I believe your friend has been affected by the power of those two beasts,' I answered, and Noal gaped, aghast.

'He's trapped under some evil spell?' he wrung his hands anxiously.

I held up a placating hand. 'It appears that the chill from the attackers has made him too cold to function, so we need to warm him again.'

His face crinkled in consternation. 'Dalin is... very important to a lot of people.'

'For now to help you could try getting him into fresh, warm clothes,' I suggested, and he nodded, so I retrieved all the packs from the mournful looking horses outside, crooning to them and wishing I could tend to them immediately. But instead I delivered Noal his bags, and moved into the kitchen to open my own travelling pack, at once catching the rich scent of its contents.

It contained a precious stock of healing herbs, plants, powders, balms, and creams—all cures I had created or found on my journeys. A collection my mother would have been proud of, and that I was sure I could make a tonic out of for Dalin.

I hung my large cooking pot on its hook to boil water over the fire, then selected the herbs I knew to work well in heating the blood. After finely slicing them, I chose roots and plants commonly eaten to fend off colds and other sicknesses, and shredded them finely. Thoughts of my early healer training with my mother swirled about in my mind as I instinctively mixed some other assorted ingredients into the pot and then boiled everything together into a liquid. I tossed in a variety of spices and a dash of alcohol, and wished that I'd found a plant called the Rupta berry that grew in the Great Sylthanryn Forest. They were so potent when mixed properly, that magician performers could create explosions with them.

But I pushed aside all doubt. My mother had trained me exceptionally well, and on my travels I had helped to heal many injuries and sicknesses, including my own.

I felt my arms prickle then. And the back of my neck. As I imagined that I heard a content voice humming, just as my mother had always hummed in the kitchen of my childhood. There was the illusory sound of someone else's knife rapping on the chopping board behind me, but I didn't turn because I didn't want to see nothing, and lose what was for once a nice memory.

The sound of my mother humming became clearer and filled my heart with light. I could hear father whistling outside and yearned to be riding with him and our chestnut mare, Star. The smell of herbs tickled my nose.

'Everything you do is important. Every breath keeps you alive. Every sleep rests you for a new day. Every planted seed grows to feed a life.' I heard my mother's voice speaking now, as best as memory could reproduce it. 'The herbs you use could save a life. One pinch more or one pinch less could hold the balance. You can end the suffering of any living thing. You can feel it when everything is right. You'll know.' The voice became fainter. 'You could save lives, Kiana,' she said at the last. And I began my chopping again in real life, this time in tune with the rhythmic sound in the memory of my mother's knife as she left me.

I could still hear and smell everything from that memory, feeling for a few moments that I hadn't been alone. Even now, she was teaching me.

'That smells magnificent,' Noal said, looking famished as he sidled into the kitchen and I slid the last ingredients into the pot.

'I tried to warm Dalin, but I became cold too,' he continued then, disturbed as he inspected his blue tinged fingers.

'Stay by the fire for a while,' I instructed.

But the frown didn't leave his face as his eyes started to wander around the room.

'I'm going to see if this will help.' I motioned to the pot over the fire, filling a wooden cup from it. But there was no answer, and I registered a change dawning on Noal's face.

I saw his eyes alight on the foreign herbs, leaves, and pungent smelling roots scattered over the bench, alongside my medicine bag brimming with other healing ingredients.

He stared at the pot bubbling away. Then at the sword still at my waist, the knives I had laid on the bench and my bow and arrows dumped in the corner.

'What's in that exactly?' he asked pointedly, peering over the rim of the pot.

'Something that should put some warmth into the veins of your friend,' I replied, watching him carefully. 'I'm ready to try it.'

'No,' Noal shook his head then, becoming hard faced. 'Perhaps we should just see if he wakes up by himself.'

I stood straighter. 'Why the sudden change of heart?'

My brow lifted then as he backed up a little. 'I think we should go. Thank you for your help,' he answered evasively.

I tilted my head to the side, discerning what he was feeling. 'I don't mean to poison Dalin,' I stated flatly.

Noal crossed his arms in response, obviously summoning great courage to confront me, when I was beginning to understand that he was suddenly suspecting me to be somebody terribly dangerous.

'What kind of girl lives by herself on wild land, with a collection of potions? What lady roams the woods alone, starts fires, carries weapons and lures strange young men home with her?'

There was a tainted, sick feeling in my throat as Noal mistook me for the most vicious woman to have ever lived. And I could understand his mistake – Darziates had sent two magical beasts. Maybe the King of Krall had also sent his Witch. The Witch with long dark hair and pale skin like mine, who was a fabled mistress of dark magic and no doubt had her own bubbling pots and bags full of herbs and plants.

My face softened.

'I'm not a Witch Noal,' I told him. 'I'm not an evil Sorceress, I'm not even a seductress out to lure young boys back to my cottage. And I'm most definitely not about to murder your friend.'

'Why should I believe you?' he didn't relent. 'I'd never seen monsters outside of old book sketches until a few hours ago, but obviously they're very real and for some reason after us.'

I looked at him earnestly. 'Noal, if I was going to enchant you I would have done so, and I would have hardly saved you if I wanted you dead. This is not an elaborate plot to trap you.'

The air rushed out of him in relief, and his stiff posture relaxed to lean across the bench. 'Thank the Gods,' he gasped. 'It wouldn't make sense.'

'I breathe and bleed just like you,' I showed him the scrapes and cuts along my arm. 'I am flesh and bone just like you.'

He studied me for just a moment more, taking in the unthreatening expression on my face. Then he took a deep breath. 'I trust you. For some reason, I trusted you from the start.'

There was something within me that was also relieved. For a minute I had been worried that my solitary, violent life had done something irreparable to me.

He became sheepish. 'I'm not sure why I trust you,' he admitted. 'Or how I know you're not bad. I just know it. But,' he fidgeted a little. 'Why are you helping us?'

I relaxed now too. 'I hate Krall's King, Darziates,' I responded openly. 'Helping his enemies or victims is my way of standing against him.'

'But you're a lady,' Noal stated.

'I suppose it is fortunate I managed to rescue you, despite that shortcoming,' I was a little wry this time, and Noal was abashed.

'I meant no offence, it's just that... why? Why were you even there to help us?'

The underlying question was again why I was alone and living a life like this at all.

'Where do you come from, Noal?' I asked.

'The Awyalknian Capital City,' he fidgeted with a spoon on the bench.

'Have any hunting groups been sent out after the bizarre creatures roaming Awyalkna?' I questioned.

'Of course,' he glanced up again. 'They're threats from Krall. But, all the hunters sent out are male, and they don't often come back.'

'My goal is also to hunt down those beasts and make sure they can do no more harm. I have so far always managed to survive, but these beings are getting smarter.'

'King Glaidin is doing his best,' Noal said hesitantly.

'Yes, and I'm getting rid of as many unnatural threats as I can, to do my best and help in the only way I know as well.'

'Was that how you found us? Were you hunting those things?'

'Yes.'

'Why do you live alone?'

I shrugged. 'I just do.'

'But, don't you worry for your safety?'

I appealed to him to open his mind. 'You must understand that, if I can defeat those beasts, I can take care of myself against most threats.'

'Oh,' he weakened. 'Of course.' He peered back at the ingredients I had scattered everywhere. 'And why do you have them?'

I rested my hip against the bench. 'Those are plants that I've found on my travels. I often need to mix medicines to help patch people up. That's why I think I can help your friend.'

'You're a healer? At your age?' His face lit up. 'That's incredible!'

'Shall I help your friend now?' I asked him pointedly with a slight smile.

'Oh!' He straightened in alarm. 'Yes! Please.'

Taking the little wooden cup, I returned to my bedroom, where the flames of the candles were struggling to stay alight, and where the room temperature had dropped dramatically.

Unceremoniously, I leant over the boy to grip his jaw and tilt his head, and gradually poured the entire mixture between his parted purple lips. I massaged his throat and waited, but for now there was no reaction.

'Is that bad?' came a whisper from behind me. I started, thinking it was the unconscious boy who had spoken. But instead I turned to find Noal in the doorway again.

'Just different,' I answered, grimly remembering other healings I'd performed that had involved cauterising, packing or bandaging grizzly wounds. 'The tonic may take time and multiple doses to work its way throughout his freezing anatomy. I'll stay with him while he needs it, just in case.'

Noal nodded grimly. 'You are the kindest stranger I have ever met, and I will do anything to help.'

He seemed such a good-natured sort, and I wondered why Darziates seemed to have used his first intelligent beasts to target such a harmless pair.

Still thinking on it, I resolutely set up my station beside the bed, deciding that the Sorcerer would not snatch the life of the dying–no, healing, boy if I could help it.

CHAPTER SEVENTEEN

Kiana

The second night of my vigil was nearly over. The stars were just distant glittery specks in the sky, the moon a pale faraway globe hovering over the earth.

I had managed to keep strong the thread that the boy's life clung to, but he had still not stirred. He was continuing to make the very air inside the room frosty, and I sat with my cloak about my shoulders.

At one point during my watch I had been unable to endure the chill and had taken one sip of the potion I was regularly medicating him with. For two hours my eyes had watered and wept and my throat had burned horribly, reaffirming my belief that, sooner or later, my patient would respond to this treatment.

When the pale pink light of another morning began to kiss the sky and the sun crept up to peek over the land, I was still quietly confident despite his lack of response.

Cringing at the loss of my solitude, I had warned a crestfallen Noal to avoid the village in case he and his friend were still in danger. But I had found that he was a surprisingly good companion, and I'd regularly caught myself smiling when I'd heard him puffing and grunting under the weight of the water pails, before he proudly brought the water he'd fetched or scraps of food he'd found into the bedroom for me.

Noal and I were both relieved as another afternoon melted into twilight, and at last Dalin's breathing and heartbeat began to strengthen. His chest and fingers were thawing as they lost their blue tinge.

Heartened as the evening wore on, I left the room briefly to see how Noal was planning to scratch dinner together. I found him collapsed at the table, two rabbits waiting to be skinned in front of him.

'Good catch,' I congratulated his slumped form.

'I'm just so hungry,' he groaned into the tabletop.

'Oh, I see,' I teased with a half smile. 'You wealthy young lords must be used to things appearing on your plates fully cooked.'

He sat up. 'What makes you believe Dalin and I are wealthy?'

'Your travelling clothes are tailored to fit,' I started listing, raising an eyebrow. 'And they're more fashionable than travel worn. Your mounts are very well bred. And you balk at the idea of food preparation.' I leaned on the table. 'But no fear, status means little in my world,' I reassured him, and he smiled.

'You're right though.' He became glum again, eyeing the rabbits. 'I'm dying at the thought of food that can't be eaten instantaneously. It's got to be cooked.'

'Not to mention you still have to skin and wash each rabbit,' I agreed supportively. 'Big task.'

His expression managed to draw a laugh from me before I returned to Dalin, and my spirits remained higher than usual as Dalin began to breathe heavily, as if he were simply in a deep slumber.

I only became restless in the middle of the next night, my body brimming with energy despite not having slept since the strange incident with Gloria. It was as if she had settled me into an uncommonly restful sleep to prepare me for the challenges that had then been ahead. But now I felt listless and frustrated, as nights were for hunting, and I craved physically demanding action.

Dalin seemed peaceful enough, and finally, sick of idleness, I stretched my body in the early, dark hours of morning and pulled on a crisp set of hunting clothes and cloak, belting my sheathed sword at the hip.

I glanced at the sleeping boy and left the room quietly, walking across the hall to the kitchen to scoop up my quiver of arrows and bow, slinging them over my shoulders as I went back down the hall to the dark sitting room that had become Noal's domain.

I found Noal, a crumpled ball of blankets on the floor, and shook him gently.

'Noal,' I whispered. 'Noal, wake up for a moment.'

'I don't like the apple!' he groaned. 'I'm hungry.' His eyes were closed, and he rolled over grumbling onto his side, his back to me.

I smiled to myself and shook him harder. 'Wake up!' I whispered more loudly, and he opened his eyes to look at me in confusion.

'It's still dark,' he mumbled. 'What's wrong?' then he suddenly became startled and rolled back to face me, sitting up. 'Is it Dalin?'

'He's doing well. So well that I'm going out to hunt, and to get us food.'

He blinked blearily. 'Would it be better for me to go?'

I stood. 'Noal, I'm a hunter. I can catch us something more than pheasants and rabbits,' I said with emphasis.

'Yes. Right... Sorry.' He yawned himself back to sleep as I quietly left the cottage. And the fresh, early air invigorated me at once as I set off for a little freedom.

CHAPTER EIGHTEEN

Noal

I sighed, prodding the spoon around in the tonic filled pot dejectedly, knowing its contents would not be the solution for my rumbling stomach.

I was in Kiana's sunny kitchen, on the prowl for a snack.

I rummaged through some cupboards, in case I'd missed anything good, and when I got to the very last cupboard I sent an imploring look up to the Gods and knelt down to pull at the door slowly, looking hopefully inside.

Right in front of my nose there stood a round little jar with a lid, one of the kinds you'd find a biscuit in.

'Thank you!' I cried and swiped the jar, prying the lid off to peer inside, at something round, shiny and red.

I groaned at the apple, but sprawled out at the table to demolish it anyway, just in case Kiana didn't come home with food. But over my resentful crunching, I didn't hear footsteps on the gravel outside, or the front door opening, or steps coming down the hall. I only looked up when I saw her walk sideways through the kitchen door, just as I was nibbling the last chunk of apple off the core.

I was surprised that I hadn't heard her come in, because she was bent under the weight of a healthy sized doe slung across her shoulders.

'Wow!' I yelped at the sight. 'How far did you carry that thing?' I'd caught rabbits and found two injured birds when I'd decided to provide for us, and both those times I'd been out slinking around for half the day.

I sprang up and took it from her shoulders, and when I'd shuffled it across to mine, I immediately slumped under the weight.

She regarded me with a trace of humour. 'I'll let you do the gutting, skinning and cooking. You've grown so competent at that.'

'Sure,' I answered in a queasy puff, struggling to appear indifferent to the weight as I carried it outside and edged it down. But when I returned to fetch a knife and pail, I found Kiana asleep in a cushioned chair she'd brought into the kitchen to set by the fire.

THE LAST
LARNAERADEE

She looked to be already deeply dreaming, the sun falling across her in the chair like a blanket, and I quietly left her to rest.

CHAPTER NINETEEN

Kiana

His gaze pierced my own like a red-hot dagger. Angra Mainyu was drinking in my helplessness. His sabre rose to deliver the final, fatal blow and my heart was cracking inside my chest.

If only I could shake free and show him what I had become. That I could defeat all of them and not leave my family unavenged. I had become the saviour of villages in all the lands. I had grown strong.

But this dream was a nightmarish memory of the person I had been then. A girl who had powerlessly watched Bwintam village square and all the villagers' homes and fields being consumed whole by the appetite of flame. A girl who had stayed hidden in her Willow tree while others had their throats slit, and who had been too frozen to escape when the Krall invaders had seized her at last.

The girl I was in this memory had nothing left and now felt sure she would die too.

Will it hurt? I had wondered, as the sabre had begun to arc down.

I had pictured the cruel blade's tip entering my flesh, pushing and cutting through muscle, bone and life. I had pictured the galleons of hot blood gushing from my body. Draining from me to join the blood of my people absorbing into the scorched dirt at my knees. But at that time, I had not pictured a way to stop any of it.

I had expected that my life would end in terrible, blinding pain. My heart would be sure to pump all of my blood through the hole of the wound until I was empty.

He'd been standing over me, ready to kill me. As they had all been killed.

His sabre had been coming, coming, coming, and how I wished I could break free of the dream to beat him this time.

CHAPTER TWENTY

Dalin

I was tingling all over. Tingling with warmth. My scalp prickled, my fingertips smarted, the tips of my toes felt near to bursting with pins and needles.

My eyes drank in the sight of a sun-bathed ceiling, and I tried to remember what had happened.

Was Noal alright?

My tongue slid out of my mouth to lick dry lips, but I almost gagged with pain. It at once felt as though I had been swallowing boiling pitch, and my tongue throbbed and ached terribly as I tried to groan.

The rasping sound that scratched from my throat sent a fire raging down my oesophagus that spread itself to the outside and throbbed around my neck.

What was going on?

My eyes travelled down to search my surroundings. A small, neat room. A chair sat empty next to the bed.

I groggily tried to prop up on my elbows, but my arms trembled.

Slowly I pushed myself to sit up and to unsteadily use the bed to get into a standing position on limbs that felt like hollow cylinders. My knees were almost knocking together, struggling to lock into a standing position, and I searched for a way to protect myself in this vulnerable state.

My eyes settled on a dagger on a shelf and I silently thanked the Gods that it had been that easy.

Like a newborn lamb, wobbly and weak on new legs, I tripped and stumbled weakly across the room and clasped the hilt in shaking fingers. Then I made my way toward the closest door and quietly leaned out to see that it opened onto a hallway. I saw an entrance to this place at one end of the hall, and a room smelling of herbs and spices at the other. It would be so easy to wobble my way down to that front door and leave, but I had to find Noal.

Shuffling and sliding along the wall of the hallway for support, I managed to reach a kitchen. No sound came from inside, so I slowly levered myself into the room, clutching the blade out in front of myself with one hand.

That was when I saw her.

The sun poured in from the window and danced in golden rays about her sleeping form.

A guardian of the Gods? A resting angel?

I felt overwhelmingly drawn and wanted to be closer to her.

Dark hair spilled down slender shoulders, and her cheeks held a tinge of pink. Her features were sharp and defined, and her chest rose and fell as she breathed deeply and dreamed.

I didn't even notice that I was moving toward her, my weakness forgotten. I haltingly, stumblingly approached until I was standing over the angel obliviously.

Gods, she looked like the girl I had once seen sing in the fateful village of...

But in an instant my rapture became surprise as brilliant blue eyes flashed open, and her lips parted with a quick intake of air. I realised those eyes were staring at my hand with rage.

Oblivious, I glanced at my hands, one of which was clutching that cursed dagger.

In a blur that I would've missed if I'd blinked, she whisked a long blade, much like the one I held, from her boot, pounced from her chair and lunged herself into me so that I fell pinned to the floor, collapsing easily.

I was winded and my brain realised in shock that my wrists were pinned under her knees, the knife now useless in my hand as she held her own blade to my throat.

I squirmed and croaked in panic, seeing her hard eyes stare at me with incredible intensity, but without really seeming to take me in. Then she started to raise the dagger.

'Kiana!'

Her gaze blazed up toward a dumbfounded voice coming from a back doorway at the end of the kitchen.

'Kiana! Don't! It's Dalin!'

I could see Noal now as I squirmed manically to look at him.

My gaze darted back to the girl, with her dagger so dangerously poised at my throat, and her eyes met mine. Their intensity faded as they focused on my face properly, but the hardness in her stare didn't fade before she pulled both blades away, and stood.

In a few silent steps she reached the door and left without looking back while Noal ran quickly to my side.

'Gods Dalin, what in the Other Realm happened?'

My face had started to radiate with heat and I tried to sit up, but fell groaning back to the floor.

'Here,' he clasped my hand in his and pulled me up and into the same chair that the girl had slept so peacefully in.

'Are you alright Dalin?' he asked with worry.

'Fine,' I grimaced.

'What happened? What did you do?' he asked in a stunned voice, and I spluttered in disbelief.

'What did I do? I was the one with the dagger to my throat!' I declared incredulously. 'Who in the Gods' names was that, anyway? And why did you tell her our real names?'

He shuffled uncomfortably. 'Don't you remember what happened, Dalin?' he asked uncertainly.

'We were in the woods, but somehow now we're here, and it feels like somebody's been having a grand time strangling me—' I paused. 'Oh.'

'Somebody–something, *was* strangling you,' Noal answered quietly.

'Ambushed,' I sank back with wide eyes. The memories came seeping back of those awful eyes, that shadowy figure, and that crippling chill again. 'Surely that beast could not have been real?' I breathed, searching Noal's face.

He shifted and shrugged sickly.

'Real then,' I gasped. 'Darziates knows, and has taken our Quest seriously.'

Noal appeared just as flummoxed and horrified by the idea as I was.

'And we only escaped because of...' I remembered the brave stranger who had freed me from the beast.

'Kiana,' Noal supplied. 'The Gods had to have brought her to us,' he rushed on. 'She owns this place–the cottage we were going to hide in. And she happened to be a healer and hunter in the right place to save us at the right time.' He seemed somewhat awestruck. 'It can't have been all accident.'

I was frowning in disbelief, and also with regret for how I had just introduced myself to this saviour of ours. Kiana.

'Dalin,' he said meaningfully. 'She saved all of our lives. And I trust her.'

I nodded without speaking as he went on to describe the fight she had put up to save my life.

'I'm grateful to her then,' I admitted gruffly at last.

'But I don't know why she tried to kill you, after all of that,' Noal added curiously.

I sighed in agitation. 'I thought something had gone wrong. I didn't know where you were or what we were doing here. So I found a knife and searched the place. I found her asleep, and she woke up to find me in here with the knife,' I admitted.

'You must've been standing rather close,' he speculated with his eyebrows raised.

'It was still an overreaction,' I shrugged. 'Surely she could expect me to wake feeling threatened and disoriented.'

'It was odd,' Noal pondered, and I nodded tiredly.

Shelley Cass

'I'm sure I can fix things with her when she returns,' I told Noal confidently, but he gave me a knowing expression.

'I don't think she's quite like the girls who usually forgive you anything at the Palace,' he warned with a hint of amusement.

'We'll see.' I leaned my head back and closed my eyes, too exhausted to think about it all.

CHAPTER TWENTY ONE

Noal

The doe had been prepared, Dalin and I had eaten, and I'd stored the rest, coming to wait by the fire for Kiana a little worriedly while Dalin rested in the bedroom again.

Night had come, and I didn't know Kiana was even back until she made a coughing sound to signal her arrival. I twisted in the chair, surprised, and found her leaning against the frame of the door, arms folded, hair tumbling loose and tucked behind one ear. Her face was expressionless.

I bounded out of the chair, and a feeling of uneasiness I hadn't registered twisting in my gut unravelled. I realised I'd grown to rely on her.

'Kiana, you've been gone for an age!' I exclaimed. 'What was wrong? Are you well?' I sucked in some air. 'And, are you hungry?'

She smiled a small smile, but there was a grim steeliness in her eyes and I stopped talking at her.

'I don't wake well to armed figures standing over me. I went for a walk. Now I'll fix something for myself.'

'It's alright, I'll get your dinner, you can do your check up, healing work on Dalin,' I said, rushing to cut her some meat.

'He can rest for now,' Kiana answered bluntly. 'I'll see to him later.' She walked past me to the table, scraping a chair out and sitting down.

While I got her dinner ready, she cleaned one of her daggers, her face showing that her mind was turning over some absorbing thoughts. And as I watched her I knew with great certainty that I didn't want to leave her here when Dalin and I went on our journey again.

Dalin and I had to convince Kiana to join our Quest.

I just had to convince Dalin.

CHAPTER TWENTY TWO

Dalin

I was taking steps which were gaining in strength around the bedroom, but I was still feeling like I'd swallowed hot sand.

I paused to gaze at a Unicorn figurine sitting alone on a shelf, and reached to take it down, examining it on my palm with a little surprise. For in the abrupt and volatile meeting we'd shared the day before, I hadn't seen Kiana as the type to collect such trinkets.

I closed my fingers around it and resumed my careful pacing again—only to jump when Kiana stepped soundlessly through the door, crossing the room with a cup in her grasp.

'Sit,' she said as if nobody had dared argue with an order from her in her life, and I sat on the bed in an offhand sort of way, as if I'd been planning to be seated all along.

Now was the moment to make peace between us.

'I'd like to thank you for your help,' I told her winningly.

She gave a curt nod.

'You have such a wonderful, pastoral little cottage,' I went on with a big smile. 'Very cosy.'

'Please be quiet. I need to concentrate.' She put her palm against my chest and I froze. 'Stop that,' Kiana instructed. 'Breathe normally and stop being so rigid, I need to feel your heart beat.'

I tried to relax, watching her face as she concentrated on my heart.

Then she removed her hand from my chest, its warmth disappearing, and she bent forward to examine my neck, her face close to mine. She smelt like pine and flowers.

She lifted my chin to lightly touch the bruise around my neck, and I flinched at the sudden pain that shot through my skin. Her fingers stopped their gentle sweep when she saw me wince, and she drew back.

'The bruise around your neck is still concerning, but it's starting to fade. Your heart and the temperature of your skin is normal enough for me to stop checking. After some bed rest you should be well enough to leave.'

'Thank you again,' I sat up straighter and put my smile back on. 'By the way, this is a delightful piece.' I held up the white Unicorn figurine, still in my hand, for her to see. 'Did you make it?'

Kiana's eyes hardened from pretty blue to bitter frost, and the big smile planted on my face started to get hard to hold up. She held out her hand, and I quickly surrendered the Unicorn to her. She put it straight in her pocket and pushed the cup she'd carried with her into my hand in return.

'Drink that,' she instructed. 'You probably won't need any more after tonight.'

'Sure,' I answered weakly, though she'd already left the room again.

At a loss, staring after her, I gulped down the entire contents of the cup thoughtlessly.

'GODS!' I rasped, spluttering uncontrollably at the smouldering sensation spreading from my throat to the rest of me. It flooded from my core, around my chest, all the way out to my extremities. It felt as though even my fingernails and the tips of my ears would start glowing pink with heat.

'Frarshk,' I breathed huskily, rubbing at my throat as my tongue throbbed. 'Thank the Gods I won't need that anymore.'

There was a knock at the door, and I wiped at the streaming tears that saturated my cheeks, wheezing as Noal entered.

Noal stifled a laugh.

'You know, your nose is running,' he remarked. 'I thought our frilly, powdered Wilmont broke you of such flaws.'

Noal sat himself on the bed, wriggling his way into a nest like spot among the blankets and pillows without putting his shoes up to dirty anything on Kiana's bed. That was likely the eternally disappointed Wilmont's training too.

'Make yourself comfortable,' I croaked dryly, dabbing at my streaming nose while it still felt like smouldering pebbles had been tipped down my gullet and were burning grooves into the soft, pink lining of my innards.

'I did,' he reassured me with raised, wheat blonde eyebrows as he stretched out his long limbs. 'Because we need to discuss something.'

'Discuss what?' I asked cautiously.

'Now, Wilmont also entrenched the rules of diplomacy into you, so hear me out,' Noal began.

I groaned loudly.

'Just listen,' he told me, and I gestured with resignation for him to continue.

'I believe we must still continue on with the Quest,' he told me. 'But it has become clear that it's going to be fraught with more danger than expected. And,' he continued, 'I don't think we should leave Kiana here alone.'

'What?!'

He crossed his arms as I sputtered in shock. 'If you think about it, Dalin, she isn't a normal girl.'

'That's for sure,' I grunted.

'I mean,' he glared, 'she would be an asset. She's proven herself to be a better fighter than us. She's a hunter of the things we could be up against, a tracker, and a healer. It's a miracle we've found everyone we could ever need on a dangerous journey all in one.'

And I knew everything he'd said was true as he finished and clasped his hands over his rounded belly to sit back and wait for the inevitable.

'You're... right,' I muttered grudgingly at last.

'We're taking her?' he asked, his voice suddenly happy again.

'Fine,' I mumbled.

'Great!' he bounced up from the bed and punched me lightly on the shoulder. 'That's fantastic, Dalin!' he beamed. 'Now, you can help me to convince Kiana!'

CHAPTER TWENTY THREE

Time had nearly run out for Agrudek, and for the Awyalknian runaways. And though he had worked tirelessly to create only five of them, those boys didn't stand a chance against the Evexus now.

Soon Darziates would rouse the shadows that made up the Evexus. The Sorcerer would pour those shadows into the strange case-like dummies, fusing the shadows with the bodies and manipulating them to life. The darkness would corrupt the building materials within the case bodies, becoming one with them.

And though Agrudek felt sure he had done everything properly this time, that these modified Evexus would not fail, he knew the King would want more. He wanted an army. Yet worse, was the fact that so far Agrudek had been unable to find the boys or the brave one who had helped them. And it was clear that Darziates had known the task to be impossible for one such as the scientist—it was designed for him to fail. Agrudek was no spy and had never been asked to gather foreign intelligence before.

Nonetheless he had tried, desperately tried to do all the King asked, for the sake of his family. He had sought to get notes to the Awyalknian, Wilmont, for information, but no reply had arrived. Agrudek had even sent out some more minor beasts to try to track the missing targets down, but the fire that had killed the first Evexus beasts had erased all trails to follow.

Time was running out. He knew.

CHAPTER TWENTY FOUR

Great creatures writhed screaming in the wastelands outside of Krall. They stretched massive wings in agony, but were bound in the wastelands by a terrible magic that tormented and sickened them.

At every moment nightmares and hate were being pumped into their minds to warp and twist them into forgetting the wise, peaceful creatures they had once been. Their golden, gleaming scales had faded to lifeless grey, no longer an armour of light around them. They no longer spoke to each other, or even recognised each other. The evil ate their awareness away and broke them into beasts.

Dragons.

Outside of the wastelands, where the screams from below were faint and the size of each Dragon was reduced by distance, there stood a lone figure. Tall, straight, strong, immovable. His hair almost white in the desert sun, and his eyes harder than granite, Darziates watched the transformed, savage beasts writhing below impassively.

He strengthened the spell on the entrapments placed on the Dragons and lashed them with another vicious vision to scream over. He used the power of his mind, pushing and moulding reality, twisting and warping until what he wanted happened.

When he had discovered his true identity as heir to Deimos and as the world's last hope for a leader to unify it, he had returned to Krall as King and had begun using his gifts to take a piece of the world at a time. These Dragons were not really needed for him to win his wars, they were simply one of the pieces to take, and Krall had been another. Containing the other magical races had been a crucial step too.

Another series of howls echoed up to him from the writhing Dragons below, and he considered how he could still make use of them as he seized his next piece—Awyalkna. He already had more numbers than Awyalkna could stand against, and he knew he could win the war sheerly through his own dark power, with the remaining magical races too weak and isolated to stand against him. But unification rather than destruction was the goal.

Eventually even those weak magical ones left over would have to belong to him too, or he would not technically rule everything together.

He began to build his energy, readying to leave, but there was a squawk from the blue sky above him, and a circling black dot started to get larger, swooping down to meet the Sorcerer.

A raven with silky feathers, a harsh beak and cruel, sharp talons landed before him, screeching a greeting to its master. Then the raven's beak and feathers melted to become abnormally pale skin, a long nose and midnight hair. The outstretched wings twisted into themselves and split at the ends, becoming arms and fingers. Talons and legs stretched to become the legs and toes of a woman. Beady eyes became huge and beautiful, but just as dark as Agrona now stared at the Sorcerer in admiration and hunger.

'You have twisted these creatures so perfectly, my King. Now we have Dragons to serve the will of the world's saviour.' Crimson lips, standing out on the unnatural white of her skin, spread into a smile that would have been breathtakingly beautiful and terrible to behold for any other person.

'I have dealt with that little man, Agrudek's, family,' she purred when Darziates did not respond, and she moved closer to him with an expression of greedy fixation.

But the Sorcerer's emotionless gaze was fixed beyond her, having returned to the Dragons.

'It's that scientist's fault that the Evexus didn't stop those Awyalknian boys. But with the help of my visions, we will be rid of their threat before the end of the ninth age.' She moved even closer, relishing the proximity of the Sorcerer's power. 'I love you, my Dread Lord. And can help you in the future you are building.'

His magic stung her a little, as if she had flown too close to the sun.

'I will marry you, my Liege,' she went on lustfully. 'I'll breed with you the next generation of your world.'

He cast her a short glance.

'I must marry the most powerful woman to create the most powerful heir.'

Her laugh was low.

'I'm that woman.'

CHAPTER TWENTY FIVE

Kiana

I crossed through the bobbing, long grass of my field to the back of the cottage, lowering two heavy pails of water to the ground. Rubbing the red, handle shaped indents across my palms, I found both boys sitting at the kitchen table acting as though they were plotting something dangerous.

'What are you two up to?' I asked, and their heads shot up to look at me with startled eyes.

'Gods, Kiana! I never hear you come in!' Noal exclaimed as he clutched his chest.

I grabbed myself an apple from the jar at the end of the kitchen, automatically tossing one to Noal, who groaned, but already had his hand up to catch it.

I crunched into mine, letting the juice freshen my mouth, chewing slowly. I swallowed and said casually: 'The villagers say there were soldiers here some days gone by.'

I was satisfied to see the hurried glance of alarm they shared. I crunched slowly on my apple again, chewed, and swallowed.

'They were apparently asking for two nobles described to look much like you.'

Their eyes shifted to the floor guiltily.

Crunch, chew, swallow.

'I don't want an explanation, but I'll let you know that they left days ago, heading back toward Awyalkna Palace, and no others have been seen around here.'

Suddenly their faces brightened considerably.

Crunch, chew, swallow.

'Seeing as you're both recovered, the weather appears to be fine and now you aren't being searched for by soldiers or monsters in these parts, this would be a good time for escape.'

'Escape?' Noal puzzled.

'I'm not passing judgment. Lots of people don't want to die in a war.'

'No, no, no, you've got it all wrong,' Dalin cried.

Noal waved his hands, and the core of his apple, in dismay. 'We're not deserters!'

I shrugged and took another bite.

'Please, let us explain,' Dalin appeared personally wounded.

They both stood now, with the apprehension from earlier returning to their faces.

'What were you plotting about just now, then?' I asked with an eyebrow cocked.

'Approaching you,' admitted Noal.

I frowned in consternation.

'We need your help,' he explained.

I put my hands up. 'I've given you ample enough aid. I won't help you abandon duties in the war.'

'I beg you, Kiana, to listen,' Noal appealed earnestly. 'And then decide.'

I sighed and leant back against the cupboards, setting down the apple and crossing my arms to stare at them both, awaiting their explanation.

This time it was Dalin who drew a steadying breath and spoke. 'We seek your aid, because we're not trying to run from the war. We're trying to save it.'

They saw the cynicism cloud my face. Nobody could be that much of a terrible fighter, where not participating could save the whole war.

Dalin continued, undeterred. 'Everyone knows of the attack on Awyalkna's most prosperous border village, Bwintam, and that other smaller ones have already been sacked too.'

I tried not to stiffen at the mention of Bwintam.

'But those attacks, and the unnatural beasts you hunt, are just the beginning,' Dalin proclaimed. 'Spies have reported that the rumours are true. Darziates himself, and the woman he works with, are capable of impossible–magical things. Our enemy has in fact used his magic and terror to gather vast armies that are not entirely human.'

He looked at me imploringly now. But I wasn't ready to say anything.

'So Darziates has access to unnatural, even evil measures to destroy anything in his path. Which is Awyalkna. And we have no means to match such forces.'

'That's where we come in,' Noal asserted genuinely. 'We're on a Quest.'

Dalin was unwaveringly serious. 'Noal and I have been kept from helping in the war–held in the Palace securely because of our fortunate lineage. But while we stayed, we saw that there were ways we could help, options open to Awyalkna that our leaders have refused to consider possible. The threat became too serious for us not to leave to try whatever we can to give Awyalkna some chance of survival.'

'So, yes, we ran away,' Noal surmised then. 'But we plan to leave Awyalkna especially to enlist the help of our Jenran neighbours.'

'We would benefit greatly from your skills as a hunter, guide and healer,' Dalin finished solemnly.

I regarded them both dubiously for a moment, processing what they had said, but also remembering my experiences from when I had crept into that isolated, mountain ringed country.

I remembered freezing nights hiding from Griffins and clinging to cliff faces. I traced a finger across a particularly prominent scar across the inside of one hand, where the flesh had been split by a jagged rock hold during a particularly daring climb.

They could have no idea of what that terrain was like. Jenra had been cut off from the world for as long as anyone could remember.

'How do you intend to enter Jenra and inspire the people to enlist to fight in a faraway war?'

'I can try to put my years of diplomatic training in court to use,' Dalin answered naively. 'And we have some authority by noble birth to help us approach other leaders.'

The impossibility of this idea was so great that I understood why the Awyalknian leaders had hardly considered such a move. Still, I could see Dalin and Noal had golden intentions, and these were desperate enough times to try anything, no matter how futile.

'Do you know anything of Jenran customs, their mountains or their language? Will you be able to communicate?' I evaluated their expressions carefully.

Noal looked exactly like someone who had never thought of any of these things.

'I have studied antiquated texts about Jenra in the Palace,' Dalin admitted. 'But gleaned only a limited, outdated understanding. Jenra has been too closed off for Awyalkna to ever find much out about it.'

Their situation was beginning to look increasingly dire, and I couldn't help but feel that I had little choice in the matter. That I had been brought to this moment especially to add my skills towards this dismal, fool hardy, glimmering chance to even the odds against Darziates.

Perhaps my aid of these two would also be a personal opportunity for me to do more than just hunting down sporadic beasts, which wasn't near enough to really make an impact.

They were waiting for me to speak, and I folded my arms.

'I have seen much in my travels, and from what I know of the secluded Jenrans, I can hardly picture them, even as Awyalkna's nearest, non-hostile neighbour, listening to outsiders without royal authority. The chances of success for this Quest are less than slight. But Awyalkna does need some kind of assistance, and miracle.'

Noal was holding his breath.

'Will you help us?' Dalin asked.

I inclined my head. 'You're going to need it.'

CHAPTER TWENTY SIX

Dalin

Kiana realised at once that Noal and I didn't have much practical knowledge or experience with the lay of the land. The puzzlement we presented her with when she outlined the months it would take us to cross Awyalkna, the Great Forest and the mountains left her incredulous herself.

'How in the Other Realm had you figured on getting out of Awyalkna to find the Jenrans to beg for their help?' she demanded, the dagger she'd been using to point out our trail on a map now stabbing the parchment in her consternation.

'We're not against stopping for directions,' Noal answered truthfully. 'We would've managed.'

She stared at him disbelievingly. Then she gave a short bark of a laugh, sheathing her dagger and moving on from the map.

'I'm glad she's on our side,' Noal whispered as we left for the next room, heading to where we both now slept in bundles of blankets on the floor.

'She's on your side,' I grumbled, piling the bedding on top of myself.

'Ah!' he grinned gleefully then. 'You're not used to a girl who doesn't melt at the sight of your face!'

I hurled my pillow at him and went to sleep, grumbling into my nest of blankets on the hard floor.

But in my dreams I found no rest. My mind replayed the last day I'd seen my father, when I had quarrelled with him childishly. Wilmont had stoked my growing resentment when he had promised that I would never be sent to help in the war, and I had gone directly to my father to hurl all of my hurt and frustration at him.

In my parents' quarters, during the confrontation, there had been no trace of my mother, except for her favourite golden ring left on the bedside table. She had been busily preparing the City to withstand a siege, but I had found my father sitting wearily on the bed after hours in council. And I had pushed him relentlessly, arguing that it didn't matter if I died in the war and left no heir for our family. Because if the war was lost, there would be no Awyalkna at all.

When I had given up and stormed from his room, I'd stayed outside the door hoping he might come after me. Hoping that years of training would be put to honourable use. Instead, I had heard him answer a knock that came from the other door on the opposite side of the room.

'Is all well?' I had heard the deep sound of Warlord Chayten Conall's voice.

'Yes, of course,' my father had said. 'Just having some trouble with Dalin.'

'Lads his age are always out to prove themselves. He'll outgrow his pride to understand the difficult situation of his status,' Conall had answered.

'Yes. I hope so,' my father's voice had replied. Then after a moment: 'Now, what was it that you needed, Conall?' He'd already cleared me from his thoughts.

I woke to Noal shaking my shoulder. It was still dark with the early morning and I moaned into my hands, blinking in the dull candlelight.

'Good morning!' he beamed energetically, and I moved to throw my pillow at him again, but I realised I'd slept without it because he'd kept it from the last time.

'Come on you two,' Kiana's voice called. 'I'm going to close this place up.'

Noal ran out obediently, and when I joined him I found that Noal had already readied his mare. Her coat was gleaming, her gear was fastened, and Noal's packs were tied to the saddle.

'Hurry up,' he grinned at me. 'You don't want to upset a huntress.'

I pulled a face at him, but got to work all the same, so I was ready when Kiana joined us outside.

As soon as she appeared, our mounts crowded her eagerly, butting her with their noses for attention, their ears flicking backward and forward in excitement. She rubbed their foreheads affectionately.

'You seem to have a way with horses,' Noal commented.

'I had a horse named Star once. Roaming with her always brought me peace,' she replied, and then she straightened, back to being stern. 'We'd best get started.'

'Wait,' I protested as she swung herself up easily into the saddle of my bay. 'That's my horse.'

'Congratulations,' she shrugged.

'But, I was going to ride my horse!' I blabbered.

'Well, my thanks for the loan then. Until we find one for you to purchase for me.' She smiled a small smile, nudging my horse's sides gently, before cantering slowly down the field.

Noal was grinning as he pulled himself back into the saddle.

'Don't,' I pointed a warning finger and glowered at him.

'I didn't say a word.'

CHAPTER TWENTY SEVEN

Noal

'I'm expecting we'll reach Giltrup village by sundown,' Kiana informed us.

'Well thank the Gods,' I said with relief. 'So many days on a traveller's diet does not agree with me.'

'It's been three days,' Kiana stated dryly.

Dalin was smirking from where he walked beside my mare. 'And you've made such a great effort with all those apples we packed. You know what they say—an apple a day keeps the healer at bay.'

'I think not, my friend,' I grimaced with distaste. 'Apples could be the death of my tastebuds—of me—one day!'

'How tragic,' Dalin mused. 'And special. I've never heard of anybody else who has felt so threatened by a fruit.'

My nose scrunched in disdain. 'They're poison to me.'

'Whoever heard of a poison apple?' he snorted.

'You never know what a bad apple could do,' I warned. 'But if it's not death by apple, it could be death by tea,' I pondered. 'I hate tea too.'

Dalin shrugged. 'Well, I'll make sure to explain all of this at your funeral pyre, if you're certain.'

'As we get closer to the settlement, watch out for anyone approaching,' Kiana stayed focused across our banter. 'We'll tell them simply that we are travelling entertainers.'

'Because we actually amuse you?' I asked her light heartedly.

'It's a courtesy between travellers to swap stories. The real point is to swap information about the road ahead,' she answered decisively. 'It's beneficial to both parties, especially in these times.'

'That makes sense,' I reflected. 'But why tell them we're entertainers of all things?'

She turned to glance at my attire. 'You are being sought by Darziates' creatures and by Glaidin's men, who may have described you in their search. Looking as richly dressed as you do, and carrying as much as we are, can be explained away by being wanderers like entertainers. They have no base, need to carry a great deal, and wear their costumes for a living.'

'That's a clever plan then,' Dalin commented politely.

Kiana turned back to gaze ahead and nudged her horse into a canter. As had happened every time Kiana had roamed away freely, my mare snorted back at me, glaring with one jealous eye.

'Kiana has already connected better with our transport than she has with us,' Dalin commented, still clearly stumped that Kiana hadn't warmed to him as others usually did.

'Oh, she connects with me just fine,' I needled him. 'But the horses do seem incredibly attached to her,' I grimaced as my mount eyed me judgmentally again.

Kiana had been offended to learn that we hadn't checked the names of our horses when we'd hurriedly chosen two to send out beyond the Gwynrock walls. She had promptly named them Ila and Amala—and amazingly the horses seemed immediately adoring of and responsive to her names for them.

Kiana sped up and galloped the distance back towards us then, and we watched her easily lean to turn Amala and keep riding beside us.

'There are three travellers approaching. Don't say anything, try to look a tad less noble and don't react when they mention you,' she instructed calmly.

'Why would they mention us?' I asked.

'With nothing better to take their minds off the war, talking about the scandals of nobility will be common, I think.'

'Really? That's nice, I feel important.' I raised my eyebrows with a flattered expression.

'Being egotistical could give your status away,' she jibed dryly.

'Got it,' I affirmed, smoothing my brow.

Sure enough, we soon saw three specks ahead that gradually drew nearer and took the shapes of worn, stooped elderly men. Two shaggy workhorses pulled their full cart, which was brimming so much that none of the weary travellers were able to sit on the cart's seats.

'Frarshk,' Dalin swore under his breath. 'Those men are not fit to be travelling with supplies. They'll be going all the way to the Palace.'

'They're the only ones left to deliver their village's share of the crops to stock the City for war,' Kiana replied gravely as the men neared.

'Well met,' one of the old farmers gave his raspy greetings as our two groups came together. 'How fares your journey?'

'Well met, friends,' Kiana inclined her head. 'We mean to stop at Giltrup village, so we don't have a great distance left to cover.'

'We're bound for the Palace,' a second, toothless man said. 'We hail from Giltrup ourselves.'

The third farmer's balding head and face were sunburned, and he mopped at his brow wearily.

'Giltrup is quite a suspicious and closed place in these times,' the first, raspy farmer warned.

'We understand. But, we're entertainers, and must brave the lands to make a living,' Kiana explained flawlessly.

The three old men nodded sagely, seeming to accept and be sympathetic to that, as Kiana had thought they would be.

'We've not heard much news, apart from those two Palace lads going missing,' the sunburnt one stated then. 'We all hope it's not some kind of kidnap from blasted Krall.'

I saw Dalin slump slightly, as we both felt relief that the search had not elaborated on exactly which nobles we were. I wondered if these old men would have regarded us suspiciously if Kiana hadn't been with us.

'Apart from that, there's been a few strange beasts spotted in these parts, so be careful and light fires at night,' Kiana told them in exchange.

'Thank you, friend. The way to Giltrup from here should be easy, and the best place to stay would be the Firetree Inn. I'm not sure you'll find fortune or even welcome there though,' the first farmer informed her apologetically.

'Of course,' Kiana answered reasonably. 'Thank you, friends,' she added warmly in return. 'Be well, and I hope we shall meet again.'

They waved as they slowly moved off with their rickety cart once more, but we kept their words in mind as we at last made our way into Giltrup and saw the truth of their warning.

Similar to the worn travelling farmers, the other villagers were either aged men, or unsmiling women and children. Most people we passed did not look up from their chores. They continued sweeping the landings outside of homes, brushing down sagging work horses, calling each other to dinner, pulling in worn-out washing from lines and returning home from the fields.

Only some of them glanced at us and away again, and a few watched us with a mixture of suspicion and fear.

'What is your business here?' a man with greyed hair and tanned, lined skin asked. He was approaching from a house to the side of us, guided by the arm of a young girl, and I saw that he was blind.

The people around the village square hushed a little as the grey haired leader approached and Kiana dismounted to stand undaunted under his towering height.

'Friend, I am Kiana. My companions, Dikin and Nop, and I are entertainers.'

He cocked his head as he listened. He was judging our intent with every word.

'We have no need for frivolity or entertainers in this time,' he at last answered gruffly.

Kiana remained composed. 'As we can understand. We simply seek shelter and will move on tomorrow to Wanru Valley. We will pay for a night's stay, buy supplies in the morning and be on our way.'

'Where have you come from?'

'Through Gangroah. We passed three gentlemen headed that way with a cart of food bound for the City. They recommended the Firetree Inn.'

His frown lessened a little. 'Yes,' he nodded at the mention of the old men we had met. 'Stay then. But you must not push for an audience.'

'I appreciate your position,' Kiana told him respectfully. 'But forgive me for believing you to be wrong about entertainment. Sometimes a little light to ease the darkness is all anyone needs to keep persevering.'

His cantankerous disposition didn't worsen at her words, but the villagers all appeared to be observing us with curiosity.

'Perhaps in better times we will come back and give you that light,' Kiana finished.

'Perhaps,' he answered grudgingly, his forehead crinkled more with thought now. Then, as if waking, he turned and allowed himself to be guided back to his dwelling.

Kiana jerked her head in the direction of the Inn, leading her bay, Amala, as we quickly followed with Ila.

'Dikin and Nop?' I asked her as we left the horses in the care of the stable boy and headed to the Inn.

She gave a half smile, only one corner of her mouth curving upward.

'Pretty names, I thought.'

CHAPTER TWENTY EIGHT

Noal

After a meal and homemade brew, I had been in high spirits when Dalin had hefted me up the stairs to the room the two of us were sharing. I was chuckling merrily when he pulled off my boots and gave up the bed for me.

But when I woke in the dead of night to a strange sound outside our room, it was with a racing heart.

Dalin had been asleep on the floor, and he had heard it too. He was propped up on his elbows, listening.

'What was zat?' I asked groggily.

He frowned. 'I thought I heard a cry from Kiana's room.'

Then we heard her scream.

Dalin sprang to his feet and darted to the door, opening it and running across the hall to Kiana's room. He tried the handle, but it was locked and he banged on it loudly with his fist.

'Kiana? Kiana, open the door!'

There was no response, despite how the noise he made echoed through the otherwise empty inn.

I started banging on the door and yelling too but, cursing under his breath, he pulled me back.

Angling his shoulder toward the door, he braced himself. Then he rammed the old wood with such force that it gave way. He caught himself with his hands in the doorway.

Both of us fell silent, and I looked over his shoulder uncertainly.

The room was now completely quiet and dark. The only movement came from an open window. The moon floated like a ghostly face in the sky, casting its wraith-like light into the room, and the window's thin white curtain danced on a slight breeze.

'Kiana?' Dalin could see no danger and walked in without fear towards a door that had to lead to the bedroom. I followed, despite the dizzying, shaken feeling that usually had the ability to swallow my senses when I became afraid.

The door was ajar, and beyond it there was no sound. Cautiously, Dalin angled the bedroom door open and then paused to stare at the bed.

Kiana lay in the middle of a mass of chaotic blankets and sheets, asleep. But not just dreaming.

Her face was contorted with anguish and her hands grasped her head as if she was trying to escape whatever she was dreaming about.

Dalin took a moment to absorb what he was seeing, but then quickly crossed to lean over the bed, putting a hand on her shoulder as I stepped nearer too.

Kiana's blazing blue eyes flashed open at once, and Dalin and I both took a hasty step back, nearly bowled over by the force of her gaze.

Her hand shot under the pillow at her head, withdrawing a dagger. Quick as lightning she had sprung up and lunged toward Dalin, dagger and hate-filled eyes trained on him.

His reflexes took over, and he caught her wrist, stopping the dagger's journey toward his heart. But the force of her lunge sent them both to the floor. She continued trying to push against his hold on her wrist to drive the blade toward his chest.

Her fierce blue eyes raged at him, but she was not truly awake.

'I was weak when last we met!' she hissed at him. 'Now I am strong.' The dagger moved closer to Dalin as she drove it with all of her might.

'Noal, get the knife away from her!' Dalin cried, and I suddenly unfroze from my shock.

I sprang forward, leaning over her shoulders and clasping onto her wrist, though she barely took her searing glare from Dalin.

I strained to pry open her immovable fingers, but even with both Dalin and I putting our strength into staying her hand, the blade was gradually moving closer to Dalin's skin. He was gritting his teeth with effort, and I desperately tried to wrangle the hilt from her grasp again.

'Kick her!' he grunted.

'What?' I gasped. 'I can't kick a lady!'

'She'll not stop unless you stun her!'

The dagger was inching closer.

'Ooooh, sorry, sorry...' I babbled to Kiana, who wasn't listening, as I lined myself up.

'HURRY!'

I winced at how improper it was and kicked at her stomach.

She barely blinked.

'DO IT!' Dalin shouted now.

'Oooh!' I groaned, aiming a proper, hard kick into her stomach. I felt my boot connect with her body and this time she doubled over, robbed of breath so that I could hurriedly snatch the dagger out of her suddenly limp hand.

'I'm sorry, I'm sorry!' I again apologised guiltily, but she ignored what was happening in the real world.

'Frarshk,' Dalin swore, startled as she began a new assault, raining down with her fists while she still pinned him. He blocked her from his face with raised arms, but she drove her fast, jabbing punches into Dalin's chest as she got her own breath back, almost as if she could collapse his rib cage.

Desperate, Dalin rolled, clasping Kiana's upper arms, dragging her with him to try to gain the upper hand and immobilise her. She kicked him hard in the shins as he threw her to the floor and she tried to push him off by rolling too, until they were both caught in rotation. Kiana attacked with gusto while Dalin defended and tried to stop her.

Finally, her head connected hard with the floor and she was startled long enough for him to in turn pin her down with his weight. He used his arms to hold himself up enough to avoid crushing her.

'Kiana!' he panted. 'Kiana, wake up!'

She shuddered and grimaced, shaking her head. But her eyes started to change, to focus.

Gaining awareness now, she stared up at Dalin in shock, seeing him truly at last. The shock quickly turned to withdrawal–her expression immediately becoming closed and guarded. In wakefulness she now found it easy to slip out of his grasp with a firm, deft movement, and she at once put distance between us.

'I would like some privacy now, please,' she said stiffly, crossing her arms tightly.

Dalin pulled himself up too, pale after having had to fight her for his life just a moment before.

'Kiana,' he said in exasperation. 'That wasn't a normal nightmare. I think you'd best tell us what that was about so we can help.'

'I am well again now, thank you,' Kiana replied in a low voice, her posture only becoming more closed. Her eyes were guarded and directed at the floor.

I noticed Dalin follow her gaze, and I did too, to find that there was a beautiful figurine of a mythical Unicorn lying on its side on the floor.

'Just go.'

Dalin clenched his jaw and then walked out, baffled frustration written across his face. What horrors kept possessing her?

I placed the dagger on the bed and followed Dalin out before he closed the door that he had only recently charged through.

CHAPTER TWENTY NINE

Dalin

I heard Kiana walk out at first light, her footsteps almost too quiet to hear, but I'd been listening for them all night. I heard her pass our door, headed toward the staircase, and I felt drawn to observe her. I waited until I was sure she would have descended the stairs, then crept after her, squatting out of sight on the faded mat spread over the top step of the staircase.

Kiana was in her deep green hunter's garb once more. She was pulling one fitted glove used by archers onto her slender fingers, the other was held between her teeth. Yet she didn't carry her bow and arrows, and I became aware of an innate sense of relief that this meant she wasn't sneaking away to leave us.

She pulled on the second glove and threw her dark cloak about her shoulders. For a moment she glanced up at the staircase, as if sensing me watching, and I pressed myself against the wall that blocked her view of me. Then, drawing her hood up, Kiana stepped outside and gently closed the door.

I released my breath and stood, padding back to the quarters I'd shared with Noal and finding that his head was bowed, his chin resting on his chest. He'd been taken by dreams while he'd on sat the bed, leaning against the wall as he'd listened for Kiana too.

'Noal, wake up,' I instructed, shaking his shoulder.

'Mmmm?' His brow creased sleepily as he opened one glassy eye.

'Kiana's gone.'

He opened both eyes. 'As in, she's left us?' he asked, sitting up.

'I don't think so, not completely. But perhaps we should take some time to watch and see what's going on with her.'

He nodded uncomfortably. 'Not like spying, just seeing she's alright?' he asked for confirmation.

'Yes, of course,' I reassured him, already dressing in readiness.

Noal continued to look glum as he searched for his tunic. 'I still feel it's already bad enough I kicked a lady, now I'm snooping on one too.'

I grimaced. 'I don't feel like Kiana is truly a risk, but we are not experts, and need to be more careful. So far we have both felt able to trust Kiana to come on this Quest, but what if the secrets she conceals are dangerous to us? Or alternatively, what if we can help her?'

Noal sighed. 'You're right,' he said uneasily. 'It may be an idea to go into her room to see if there are any clues with her belongings then.'

As we made to check her room, we both felt as low and sly as Wilmont had always been when he'd revelled in trying to catch us out for any slight misdeed.

We found that Kiana's bed was now neatly made, with no sign of the struggle from the night before. Her packs were full and ready at the foot of the bed, and on the pillow of the bed stood the figurine of the Unicorn.

'Pretty, that,' Noal observed.

'Yes. It is. We'd better see where she's got to, then,' I turned to go, but as I passed the little table in the next room, I stopped and stared.

'She left a note?' Noal asked with a sick expression.

I picked it up and read it aloud.

'I've gone for a ride with Amala. I'll return soon. Do not follow. Be useful and get supplies for the journey to Wanru. It will take three days with only the two horses. Stock up enough for Noal's appetite and ours. Kiana.'

'Well, that's embarrassing,' Noal huffed.

'What is?' I asked, staring at the beautifully shaped script on the scrap of parchment.

'Kiana knew we would come prying,' he fretted. 'What must she think of us?'

I hardly listened. 'She has been educated,' I stated in surprise.

'Dalin,' Noal scoffed in wonder, 'not all commoners are illiterate. And it turns out not all nobles have the good manners we were meant to be ingrained with.'

'Of course, you're right,' I replied more humbly, and folded the paper carefully to put it in my pocket.

But once we had done as she had instructed, I found myself watching for Kiana and wishing to gather more information about her. I was craning to see the road into town from my window when I at last saw her ride back into the square, only to be heralded down by two villagers. She listened as they spoke, then dismounted to follow them.

'She's back.'

Noal followed me hurriedly to find Kiana, now in the square consulting with the grey-haired, blind leader.

'Friend, I am glad you have not left,' we heard him address Kiana, and I wondered at the change of heart.

'My companions and I do plan to leave as promised,' she replied calmly.

'Yet before you leave,' he said sincerely, 'I must request something of you.'

She remained silent and unsurprised, allowing him to continue.

'I have been thinking on your words and have also had requests from my people. And,' he continued with lifted eyebrows. 'We believe you were right. We haven't been given any joy here for a while. No light to ease our minds.' He moved his head to the side. 'We all believe that it may be time for some of that light now.'

'I see,' Kiana answered.

'Will you perform for us?' he asked earnestly.

Noal and I stared at each other, gulping. We had no talent whatsoever in the field of entertainment.

'Should we flee?' Noal whispered in horror.

I held my breath as Kiana spoke.

'Unfortunately, my companions had a little much of your village's home brew last night, and are feeling too delicate to perform.' Then she shocked us. 'But I shall sing for you, if you wish it.'

A smile broke across the lined face of the old leader. 'I thank you, Lady, for being willing to offer us a few moments of reprieve from our toil and fear.'

So within the hour that we had been planning to leave by, instead of mounting up to leave, we were watching the growing gathering of people in the square who had come at the word of entertainment.

A table had been brought out to be Kiana's stage, and she stood on it now.

'What are you going to do?' Noal whispered up at her wildly. 'They all think we're real performers and that you can truly sing!'

'I'll think of something,' she told him steadily without looking down.

Noal and I both stood back nervously as she straightened and the crowd quieted. I wondered what she was going to do to get out of this fix.

Expectant, worn, dirty faces gazed up at her with hope.

'These are terrible times,' Kiana called for them to hear. 'Many of us are already hurting from what the war has cost, before it has properly begun.'

Each villager was listening and watching attentively. I myself felt caught by the charismatic power that seemed to resonate from this reserved, strong woman. 'And yet,' she called, 'we have more hope than Krall. We have more power than Darziates.'

There were not even slight frowns of disbelief, and everyone watched on as if enamoured by her composed presence.

'You have proven this,' she said. 'You, and your loved ones rallying on the borders stand against the crippling fears of what may come, and refuse to be broken. Every time you push aside thoughts of hopelessness, and will your hands to keep working... you prove this.'

There was a hush, and many of the villagers were standing taller, beholding her serenely as if enchanted. I felt my own flesh prickling, as if her words were laced with some kind of bewitching magic that stirred the blood and inspired the heart.

Then she started to sing. A slow, haunting song that rang with a warning to our enemies and with galvanising energy to our people.

Where darkness breeds,
And light flees.
Where terror entraps,
And hatred leaps.
Where pain is glory,
And suffering seethes.
Where loss stabs deeply,
And doubts creep.
Look and see.
That's where we'll be.
Duelling fear,
And ensnaring greed.
Fending off ghouls of hurt and grief.

Her words were at once captivating. Kiana's voice rang around the square like a low bell of sweetest clarity, as though it could spread heat and feeling. And each of us in her audience were lifted with determination; carried higher to live and breathe what her words gave us.

Our oath, our pledge, we swear to thee:
We'll never sleep,
Our courage will stay...

In that moment she seemed so like the young, dark-haired village singer that I had once heard sing. When I had stood, youthful and wide eyed, at the foot of a stage at the yearly festival in the now destroyed Bwintam—and had lost my heart. Kiana was different to the smiling singer of Bwintam—so grave and dark. But like those of the young singer, Kiana's words washed over me and were spell binding.

Our fight won't end,
We'll light the way.
Until the night dawns into day.
Until the threat has been chased away.
We will not break,
Or stop and fade.
We will be strong,

We will be brave.

We were all surging closer to the magnetism of her voice. With every rise and fall of her song, I felt all uncertainty drop away.

We will cast off chains,
Of dread and hate.
We will face each trial,
And test our fate.
Our strength is great,
The risks have been weighed.
We'll march unshaken,
In unbreakable waves.
It is a path to freedom that we shall pave.
It is freedom
Freedom—that we crave.

Her eyes were closed, but she lifted our hearts and carried them to the heavens with her. When she outstretched her arms to us, we all were warmed by her embrace without touching anything but her voice. And I felt at a loss when it ended.

People were leaning against one another, but not in the worn out way they had earlier. They were hugging.

Kiana stepped down from the table, as people embraced and began to talk; laugh, even. She discreetly moved away, unnoticed, to where Noal and I were gaping.

She gestured for us to follow her to the stables so we could leave inconspicuously, and she remained thoughtfully silent long after we had left Giltrup behind and set up a new camp for the night.

However, despite how easily she had moved on from her performance, I hadn't been able to shake my wonder at the sound of her voice for the whole day. I'd found myself watching her in fascination—hoping for just a word or two more. At last, when she'd left Amala and Ila's coats gleaming, she had come to the camp fire to sit with us. But it still seemed she was out of our reach, gazing into the flames.

Noal seemed a little bashful and intrigued too, staying hushed around her.

Finally, looking for an excuse to hear her voice once more, I cleared my throat.

'You gave hope to those villagers with your song, you know Kiana.' I watched her face keenly, waiting for a response. 'You're quite the hero if you think about it,' I prompted.

Kiana's eyes rose from where they had been lost in the flames. They focused now on me completely.

'You're wrong,' she said simply. 'I am not the stuff of heroes.'

I was taken aback momentarily, unsure of where to go from there.

'Well, you *have* nearly killed me in your sleep twice now,' I said then, trying to be jovial.

I saw dark brows lower over hard blue eyes. 'You have intruded on me twice.'

I frowned too, suddenly feeling defensive, but not quite sure of why. 'I had thought I was saving you on the most recent occasion.'

Kiana rose without answering, crossing back to Amala. Her hand rested on Amala's neck and the mare nickered while Kiana ignored me.

'I can't understand you,' I exclaimed then, in mystified exasperation. 'You don't communicate with us. And there's obviously something very wrong–' I barely stopped myself from finishing the sentence with 'with you'. But the unspoken words seemed to float around in the space between us.

She turned back to me. Her eyes were cool enough to dim the feel of the camp fire flames heating my face.

I had never come across someone so reclusive and confusing, and my inexplicable frustration built into an outburst. 'Earlier you were singing liberation and hope to those villagers with incredible kindness. Last night you tried to murder me. Then you went back to being quiet and now you're rebuking me when I was trying to be friendly! You never explain yourself. For all we know, you could be a crazed threat to our safety!'

Kiana regarded me impassively. 'I do not feel obliged to share myself completely with you just because you demand it. I shall share what helps the Quest. But I wonder at what life you have had, if you have come to expect everything of the people around you with little in return. And I wonder if you've ever truly spent the time to solve the puzzle of a person, to know them deeply, if it vexes you so that you don't have what you desire from me after a matter of days.'

I was taken aback for a moment, glowering with a hanging jaw. 'Look,' I told her, regaining gusto. 'Just tell us what's going on, and we can help. It can't be that bad.'

'You prove to me that you are the one person who cannot understand someone as crazed as I,' she answered calmly, and I winced.

She turned to Noal. 'I crave peace tonight,' she told him simply. 'I shall be back by morning, and I will make sure nothing is about tonight to harm you.' Then she swung herself easily onto Amala's bare back.

'Where are you going now?' I demanded.

She whispered something into Amala's ear. My bay at once broke into a canter at her command, and they disappeared into the night.

I slumped in dismay, dumbfounded by the exchange. I hadn't meant to be so cruel.

Noal, who had not spoken at all during the exchange, turned to me. 'You need to apologise.'

'She had a part in it too!' I defended.

'You need to apologise.' Then he laid down, back to me, and closed his eyes to sleep.

I knew he was right.

And sleeplessly I watched the stars, burning like silver jewels of fire, and I wondered what it would be like to fly away from the guilt of leaving my parents, escape fear for Awyalkna, and fly away from the confusion of Kiana, to those beautiful buds of light.

CHAPTER THIRTY

Dalin

I woke to someone shaking my shoulder.

I opened my eyes to find the sky was now pale with an early sun. Kiana was kneeling beside me, having come back as she'd promised, but as soon as she saw I was awake she moved to rouse Noal.

Both horses were saddled and had the packs tied neatly onto them. Traces of the fire had been covered with dirt and leaves.

Noal yawned and rubbed his face. 'Time for breakfast?' he asked blearily.

'We'll have breakfast in the saddle,' Kiana told him authoritatively. 'I want us to get started and travel until we reach Wanru Valley tomorrow morning.'

'Will we stop for lunch?' Noal asked, alert with surprise now. 'Or dinner?'

'We'll stop riding only to rest Ila and Amala. But then we'll go on foot ourselves instead.'

Noal put his hand to his forehead, looking queasy.

I cleared my throat. 'Can I ask why you feel we must hurry to the next township?'

Kiana considered me for a cool moment. 'It's a hunter's instinct. That's all. There have been no signs that we are being followed, but it is a wise caution to perturb a search and lose ourselves in crowded areas quickly while we can. Mix up our scent with that of others for a couple of days to throw any unnatural followers off our timing and trail. Wanru is also isolated enough by distance and a bordering ring of hills that they may not have heard news of two nobles being on the loose.'

'I agree with you,' I told humbly, and she appeared faintly surprised. 'For whatever reason, Darziates may still be interested in our progress. The thing is, if we want speed, I need a horse, and we only have two.'

'It'd be too heavy with both Dalin and I on poor Ila, along with our packs,' Noal surmised the obvious fact.

'I know,' Kiana stated simply as she stood for action. 'Dalin will be riding with me.'

I gaped in astonishment, astounded at how easily she'd accepted me to ride with her.

But Kiana just shouldered her pack and dusted her trousers down; business like.

She held out her hand to Noal and he let her drag him to his feet before she moved off to Amala.

As I helped my own self to my feet and Kiana swung herself up into the saddle, I saw why she had so easily accepted me to ride with her.

'Kiana … Won't I be the one holding the reins?' I asked tentatively.

'No. You can take your leisure at the back.' She braided her long hair quickly, perhaps out of pity for me and the lashing it would have given me otherwise.

I gritted my teeth instead of arguing, and huddled in the saddle behind her, quickly losing all heroic visions of being the gallant knight and assertive lead.

Instead I, the great and noble Dalin, held onto Kiana's waist, like a good emasculated damsel in distress.

However, my bitterness quickly faded as we moved quickly over the land, saving my legs–and occupying my arms with an embrace around Kiana's waist. She still smelt somehow as fresh as newly picked flowers and pine. And surprisingly, I had to begrudge the moments when we alternately dismounted to walk when I could behave like an empowered marching soldier once more.

I'd completely given up being disgruntled by the end and was snuggling against her back quite contentedly when at first light we saw the large hills Kiana had said would be surrounding the basin-like valley of Wanru.

I forced myself to sit up with at least a scrap of dignity as we rode down through the hills, following a steep, rocky path into the village at the bottom of the deep basin.

I was musing that Wanru was a larger village than Gangroah and Giltrup, expanding in the protection of the huge hills, when I felt a sudden flash of dismay as Kiana slid lightly from the saddle in front of me. There was the abrupt loss of her warmth against my chest, and I sagged a little.

'All seems well,' Kiana observed with a slight hint of relief. No leader came rushing out to ask us what our business was, and children roamed without a care– chasing each other gaily, tussling and laughing as they played. Womenfolk bustled about, and while there were no young men left, people didn't seem worn or miserable here. Nobody appraised us with suspicion or gave unwelcoming stares, some of the children even waved as we passed.

'I don't understand how well it does seem,' Noal remarked. 'This village is one of the closest to the borders of both Krall and where the massacre of Bwintam was. I would expect them to be more wary of strangers.'

Kiana shrugged as we considered the peaceful town scene. 'It's hard to feel threatened by outside forces, no matter how close, when you've lived in a private bubble like this for all your life. The worry of war fades when you feel the protection of those hills and hear barely anything of what goes on abroad. Wanru has always been lulled into a feeling of security.'

I spotted a pretty young woman scrubbing at some clothes in a wooden wash tub outside one dwelling, and saw her watching us with interest rather than fear as we moved towards her, following Kiana to the Inn.

'We're likely not to need our travelling entertainer story here, in the absence of distrust or rumours of two nobles being missing,' Kiana continued, ready to pass the girl and continue along the road.

'Well met,' the girl greeted us warmly as we approached, pausing in her scrubbing.

'Well met,' Kiana replied politely, but I noticed the maiden's eyes were on me.

'If you're looking for the Inn,' the young woman commented hospitably, 'it's at the end of the market square on the left.' She pointed further down the road, to the exact place Kiana had already been heading.

'Yes. Thank you,' Kiana nodded to her, but the girl wasn't listening.

'Staying long?' she asked me with big eyes and dimples flashing in her cheeks.

I leaned forward in the saddle to oblige her with an answer. 'Only a couple of nights, unfortunately, before we must move on. I can assure you it won't be nearly long enough.'

She laughed and blinked long eyelashes.

Noal snorted into his hand and I noticed Kiana roll her eyes.

'Well, we best move on and get our rooms at the Inn,' I told the girl, who nodded and daintily smoothed her skirts. 'Be well,' I said courteously.

'Be well, and I hope we shall meet again,' she replied with a gratuitous smile, watching me with her big eyes.

I looked to see if Kiana was going to jump back into the saddle in front of me.

She lifted her eyebrows at me. 'Your head seems swollen. There's no room for me up there,' she commented. Then she turned to Noal, held out her hand for him to obediently clasp and swung herself lightly onto Ila behind him.

She let him take the reins.

CHAPTER THIRTY ONE

The raven screeched harshly. Relishing the grey skies and frigid air as she swooped away from the castle. In her raven form she was still sharp minded, sharp sighted, but also free of the burden of her earth-bound body, and her own inexplicably growing dread.

Ever since the Evexus had failed to capture the Awyalknian boys of her vision, something about the supposed threat from those runaways had been nagging at Agrona, making her feel almost personally endangered.

Darziates was as unconcerned as ever, but Agrona was glad that he had decided she would be sent with Agrudek's perfected Evexus this time. When the inventor was done, she would make sure things went well. Prove her loyalty. Her love. In fact, she was now on her way to organise a soothing surprise for the Sorcerer to make her approaching journey even more of a success.

The Witch swept easily over the grounds, squawking over the muddy streets, high above the reek of humanity. She enjoyed the sight of those ducking and running under her raven shadow below, only slowing when she reached the military training grounds for mortal soldiers, where they hit at each other and ran in formations and stank like cattle.

As she circled down to where the Warlord Angra Mainyu stood and barked orders, the men closest to his hulking, solid figure quickly moved away before she had even melted into her own form, resplendent in a crimson gown with fabric lined by glittering rubies.

'Agrona,' Angra's harsh voice rumbled through a forest of grizzled, sweaty stubble, his eyes on her body as it changed. 'I've missed your visits.'

'Yes. We haven't made our mark on the world as much of late. But I've had an idea,' she purred. 'Soon I will be leaving to complete the Dread Lord's tasks, and I think you should go out with me at the start, and have some games once more.'

His eyes lit up. 'Where are we attacking? I will follow you.'

Her painted lips twisted in a false smile at how easily the Warlord succumbed.

'Then to Wrilapek village north of the Awyalknian hilly lands you must follow. They are a horse rearing village with beasts Krall could use.'

He grinned at her in a repulsive snarl half obscured by his lumpy, swollen nose–

and all the while Agrona considered how delightful it would be to rip that gross face off and be rid of the Sorcerer's only other trusted underling.

'When do we leave, Sorceress?' Angra glowered with desire, his eyes burning as they often did with an uncanny light, which many people believed was the light of an Other Realm spirit who had possessed him.

Agrona was certain Darziates had experimented in some such way on the Warlord and suspected that that was the only real worth Darziates found in the demented human. But the light was also likely a mix of Angra's own blood lust and madness after having been too close to Darziates for so long.

Angra was eagerly watching her lips as she started to reply, but then she felt a sharp calling from her King.

'Agrona.' Darziates' voice seared across her mind, plucking at her spirit.

A thrill rippled through her body and at once, every other priority faded. She immediately brushed thoughts of Angra aside, while he continued to froth with excitement.

'It will be soon. The King is calling,' she answered abruptly, eyes back on the castle.

'Agrona, I can't stand waiting. Let us ready to go!' Angra's coal-black eyes glinted red, and his voice changed, becoming harsh and commanding.

'I am to be instructed first by our King. I'm needed now.'

She'd lost focus on him, but Angra Mainyu's arm shot out and a grime covered, meaty hand seized her wrist.

That demanding, clammy hand swallowed nearly up to her elbow, and the Warlord brought his face close to the Witch's, his breath hot on her deathly white cheek. She could see the red light in his eyes more clearly now; the brokenness and insanity others feared.

Agrona glared at him icily, and with a wave of her free hand, made her captured wrist suddenly become red-hot while not feeling any pain herself.

He held on as his hand quickly began to blister and smoke, leaving a smell of burned flesh in the air. Then as the pain in his hand throbbed, the red light in his burning eyes faded, and he looked up at her with a smirk, dropping her wrist.

'You forgot your place, Angra,' she snarled. 'And you are lucky to still have a hand. You'll wait for my summons and be ready.'

'Thank you for not taking my hand.' He lowered his eyes, and she was grimly satisfied to have reminded him of who was ranked just a little more highly out of the two of them.

She melted back into raven form before him, squawking, and then swooped back across the sullied streets to the castle to sweep in through the open window of the King's council room.

She found that the King was already seated, straight-backed in his steel throne.

Darziates' face was emotionless, but for the power of his icy eyes. White-blonde hair was pulled away from beautiful pale features, revealing a noble brow.

As she flew across the room to perch on the high back of his throne, she saw they weren't alone.

Apart from the twenty armoured guards that lined the hall, standing at intervals at the walls of the room, there was a snivelling heap on the floor. The ratty man with the carrot-coloured hair. Agrudek.

Agrudek was kneading his hands in sick terror. 'Please... Sire, Dread Lord... I've made five of the Evexus this time, and, and I am sure they are perfected for you to replicate them.'

The King furrowed his brow almost imperceptibly.

The little scientist leaned forward on his knees, his face white. 'Please, my King... where are my family? I went home, and... it looked like there had been a struggle... Majesty, don't harm them... please. Sire?'

Darziates still didn't respond, only moving slightly in his chair. 'Agrona,' he acknowledged the raven.

She screeched back her greeting, revelling in his attention. All twenty guards flinched and averted their eyes. Agrudek quailed, whimpering.

'Please, Sire, there's no need to disturb the Witch...'

Darziates let the cold of his glare burn Agrudek for a moment, and the quivering little man quieted.

'Agrona, this thing has only made five Evexus. He does not have the information I require,' he paused, looking up at her. 'He was also the one who spoiled our first opportunity to act on your vision. Does he deserve his family?'

She observed Agrudek beadily. Then flew from her perch to the floor between the terrified Agrudek and her master's throne. As she grew, merging into her other form, every eye was upon her. Every breath but the King's was held in apprehension. From where he cowered at her feet, Agrudek watched helplessly, his eyes following her upward as she transformed. At last, she stood before them all, looking down at the wretched man. The hem of her draping skirts swept inches from his flinching face and she saw him regard her as all mortals did—with awe for her beauty, with fear and with loathing.

'King Darziates, this man is worthless. He has betrayed you in his continuing failure, and deserves punishment, not reward,' she said slyly, thinking back to Angra and how great an impact taking a hand could have.

'Yes.' Darziates affirmed indifferently. Agrudek had already been condemned, and the moment was over in the King's mind.

'Though this fool deserves death,' the Witch of Krall paused as Agrudek gasped. 'You are kind and wise, Majesty, and will spare his life.'

'For what purpose?' the King asked, cold eyes passive as she played her games.

Agrona's voice was of velvet and poison. 'Agrudek must be punished and must redeem himself,' she mused. 'For redemption, he must journey into Awyalkna and find those boys himself,' she resolved in playful glee. Agrona knew, everyone in the hall knew, that he would never get through Awyalkna alive, or find the boys to save himself or his family.

Agrudek cried out. 'But, Lord, you need me... the Awyalknians will kill me as an enemy from Krall...'

The scientist was silenced again by the ice of the King's eyes. 'And for punishment?'

An inspired smile stretched Agrona's angular face. 'I will remove something that he needs in compensation for the trouble he has caused you, and to pay for his family's lodgings in our prison.'

She felt Agrudek's heart spasm wildly. She could even feel the disgust of some of the guards. Others were more corrupted by the Sorcerer and were enjoying the show.

She moved closer and Agrudek's eyes were near to bulging out of his head as she motioned for him to outstretch his arm.

Forced by her magic, his arm haltingly extended even as he strained to pull it back. And she took his small hand in her hard, bony grip and let heat engulf his fist. She'd been unable to go as far as she'd wanted to with the Warlord, and so she relished the chance to test how far she could go with the inventor as he screamed. His knuckles blistered, and the skin cracked and she was delighted as his hand slowly burned.

She let it burn down to nothing.

And all the while she smiled, filling the air with the aroma of cooking meat and showing her Sorcerer how ruthless she could be for him.

CHAPTER THIRTY TWO

Kiana

I found myself a rock pool cuddled protectively amongst the hills where I could wash all cares away as the boys ate and slept away all of theirs.

It was afternoon, and the sun was hot and high when I dressed again and wandered back, catching sight of the boys lounging on the veranda of the tavern with some old men. They were talking and drinking mead. And, being nobles, they seemed very excited to be experiencing this side of life.

Noal waved, but as I was heading across the market towards them I felt a tugging on my belt.

My hand automatically flew to the hilt of my sword, concealed by my long cloak, and I turned quickly. But I found two little faces looking up at me and relaxed. Just two little boys.

'Well met!' smiled one.

'Well met!' smiled the other.

'We're bored!' stated the first.

'Know any stories?' asked the second.

'We've heard all of Wanru's stories, and they're boring now,' said the first.

'You could tell us a new story?' appealed the other.

'We asked your companions, but they said you'd be the better entertainer,' shrugged the first.

'We're bored,' they repeated, as I glared toward Noal and Dalin.

'Can't you play with your friends?' I smiled, turning back to their youthful faces.

I pushed down a flash of memory, of Jin and Tommy sitting against me, their small hands in mine.

'They're all bored too. Could you tell us a story?' asked the first one again.

'Pleeeease?' added the other.

I noticed ten or so children, probably not even five years old, standing in a band, watching us and waiting.

'Are those your friends?' I asked the two little ones in front of me. They really did look just like Tommy and Jin.

'Ahuh,' they both nodded in harmony, motioning with little, soft hands for their friends to come rushing forward.

'Well,' I said, forcing good cheer to cover any melancholy, 'I guess I could tell you one story.'

They cheered and instantly pressed in, taking handfuls of my shirt or grabbing onto my arms to pull me toward a grassy patch in the shade of a tree. They sat me down on a rock and were gathered around before I could blink.

'What kind of story would you like?' I asked, getting my breath back helplessly. I noticed Dalin and Noal sauntering across to join the entertainment.

'A magical one!' they cried.

'With Fairies and magic!' called some little girls.

'With blood and gore!' shouted the little boys.

Dalin and Noal sat themselves on the grass too grinning at me.

'A story about magic,' I mused. I didn't let knowledge of what I'd seen magic do cloud my mind or darken my face. Because when I had been young, my mother and father had told me good stories about magic.

These children surely had heard the basic myths surrounding the tale of the Larnaeradee and the Unicorns before, as every child grew up hearing them, but my audience was as captivated as I had always been by my parents' detailed version.

'In ancient times. The times of heroes, kingdoms and magic...'

Father had always whispered the last word. Leaning forward so that the stone held at his throat by a fine chain had glittered, and a thrill danced down my spine as my voice took on a similar tone to his now.

'...Times where mortals and magical creatures lived in harmony, roaming freely, and animal and human treated each other as kin, there lived the two fair races of legend. The Fairies and the Unicorns. The Fairies, or in their tongue the Larnaeradee, were a magical kind. They were fair and elegant, with eyes of brilliance. The Larnaeradee cared for the land, were strong and agile trackers and hunters. But their greatest wonder was that, at the time of their sixteenth year, their elders presented them with an earth stone necklace, and the ability to fly.'

I tried not to remember my own sixteenth birthday, and how I'd thought my parents had forever to tell me what they'd wanted to, to explain their own gift of the Unicorn figurine.

'The Fairies were particularly devoted to the Unicorns, a race they saw as kin after, by chance, a young Fairy drew them out of their seclusion in their mountain refuge, Karanoyar. They had hidden years before out of fear of enslavement, as their non-magical horse cousins had faced. To draw them out, the Fairy Farne had to make a big mistake in order to create a bigger miracle...'

I described how the legendary Fairy Farne had been rescued by Treyun, and convinced the Unicorns to come back from their isolation, beginning the age of the Larnaeradee and Unicorns. A peaceful and prosperous time when a language called Aolen had been created to unite all races.

My voice stopped at the end, as father's had stopped, and I glanced about at the little faces staring up at me, and at Dalin and Noal's faces watching me too.

'Is that it?' asked the first boy who had come to me with his mate earlier.

'That was lovely!' chirped a little girl at my feet, her eyes dreamy.

'It was good,' agreed the other original little boy. 'But there wasn't any blood or gore. You've got to tell a second story.'

I could swear I was looking at Jin. Craving attention, just as he had every time I had minded him with Tommy.

'Don't you have chores to do to help your mothers?' I questioned.

'Done them,' said the first boy a little too innocently.

'Done them,' agreed the second boy, his tone just as questionable.

I raised one eyebrow in doubt, looking at Noal and Dalin for help.

'We've done our chores too,' grinned Noal and Dalin at me.

I sighed resignedly. 'Right...' I gave in, without any real annoyance. 'As we know, the Unicorns and Larnaeradee shared a unique bond never before shared between any other race. They grew in skill together, sharing powers, connecting as pairs with a link between the Unicorn's golden horn and the Larnaeradee's precious earth stone. With their magic so completely melded together they were more powerful than all others. For hundreds of years, after Farne and Treyun's adventures, the Larnaeradee and Unicorns lived in harmony. They devoted themselves to keeping the world at peace, and during this time all living things flourished.

'Every magical race, whether in the seas, on faraway islands, or within Sylthanryn, was bonded–and the four kingdoms of men were also allied peacefully. From the rocky bounds of Krall, the green planes of Awyalkna, the vast desert lands of Lixrax, and the cliffy, mountainous country of Jenra beyond the Great Forest.

'During this time of amity, with the Larnaeradee and Unicorns acting as the keepers of the peace, there was no such thing as war, and death came only to the old. Fear and hunger didn't exist, and it was hard to believe in them. With the guidance of the Larnaeradee and Unicorns, the world shared the common language Aolen, and connected easily.

'Yet, the age of peace and goodness was ended as the first Sorcerer of Krall, Deimos, introduced corruption and greed. The natural world began to die and, to protect goodness, an Army for the World rose to face the darkness. And great sacrifices had to be made.'[1]

---

[1]The 'Tales of The Army for the World' and 'Sylranaeryn and her Unicorn' are included at the end of this text.

THE LAST
LARNAERADEE

I poured myself into the story of 'Sylranaeryn and her Unicorn', letting the legend I knew so well roll from my tongue until I reached the conclusion.

'It has been told that the Kingdom of Krall fell into waste, and that, out of the ruins of the royal family, a babe was smuggled away into hiding. But nobody is sure if the heir of Deimos lived. Many believe that Darziates is part of that bloodline and has reclaimed the throne. It is believed, though, that if evil were to ever rise once more, the Larnaeradee and the Unicorns shall live again to unite another Army for the World. The ancient pledge may still hold true for the earth's pure protectors...'

My voice ran off, and I stared into memories of my father as he had told me those stories. I only stirred when I heard an awed voice say, 'I wish I could see a Unicorn.' Just as I had always said.

I smiled down at the young faces around me.

'Me too,' I answered truthfully.

CHAPTER THIRTY THREE

Kiana

I'd felt a terrible sadness closing in on me as I had finished the tale my father had always told, knowing that father's stories now only lived for me through my own voice. As the children had left in a happy garble of sound, I'd felt myself stiffening in response to the rising misery in my chest.

'What a captivating storyteller you are,' Dalin complimented me as he and Noal crossed to where I was still sitting. 'I've heard shorter versions of those stories many times, but your telling was remarkable. It felt like I was there and that it was all true. It's like there's magic in your voice,' he grinned in a friendly manner. 'We don't have such good storytellers even at the Palace. It'd be nice to meet the one who taught you so well.'

I felt my face hardening against the emotions, just as I'd trained it to, as I thought of how Dalin would never meet the storyteller I'd learned from, or anyone in my family.

I could feel that lump of hurt, an angry tumour in my throat that should have signalled the coming of a vulnerable outburst—instead prompting rising internal shields.

It was helpful to always be able to seal my internal sense of loss—or horror, at things I had witnessed on the hunt—behind a flawless mask. Being detached kept me from crying now, and at other times reduced hunting memories to just fleeting slashes across my mind.

Yet the mask also kept me separate, and Dalin was smiling obliviously as everything inside me flared up and was then locked away, and I knew he couldn't understand.

'I thank you for your praise,' I replied, and heard the armour that was constricting my voice box turn my words to stone. My face was immovable, and I saw the inevitable flicker of hurt in his own expression.

Knowing conversation was hopeless from me for the moment, I rose and moved past Dalin, leaving for the solace of my private room.

'I guess she's not forgiven me,' I heard Dalin murmur, and I pictured his puzzled face with a twinge of guilt.

But it was impossible. I had to reclaim my sense of calm without the aid of a wild hunt as I usually would. So I closed the door to my apartment with resolve, separating myself from them effectively. And the sun was in the late motions of setting before I next heard from anybody – with a tap at the door breaking my solitude.

Feeling sufficiently personable once more, I opened the door in anticipation of finding Noal or Dalin.

Instead, three dimpled, ample chested, beaming young women stood on the doorstep.

'Yes?' I asked, disconcerted.

'May we come in?' questioned the more robust girl of the three, glancing about herself furtively. Then before I'd had a chance to answer, they all toppled in, squeezing past me to perch themselves on the bed in a preening flock.

'Can I help you?' I asked them with an eyebrow raised, pushing the door closed.

'Yes, we want to question you,' nodded a curly haired, blue-eyed girl.

My eyes narrowed warily.

'You're not in trouble! Far from it! We just want to learn of one of your companions,' giggled another.

I immediately put my guard up, suspicious that these girls may have recognised Dalin or Noal as the noble runaways after all.

I fixed a smile on my face. 'What do you wish to know?' I asked with the best girlish tones I could muster, sitting on the bed amongst them to make myself part of the flock.

'Well, this matter is delicate,' confessed the robust one, drawing the words out annoyingly slowly.

'Don't fear!' I encouraged.

'The tall one, with the dark hair – is he yours?' burst out the giggly one, giggling again.

'Mine?' I almost laughed myself.

'Are you together, or promised to each other?' asked the blue-eyed blonde.

'No,' I answered bluntly. 'Not at all.'

'Isadora saw you together, sharing the same horse when you arrived,' robust girl said.

'Isadora?'

'You met Isadora when you first got here. The wretch has been boasting of how much he liked talking to her,' the giggly one became less giggly.

'Oh,' I sat back, crossing my arms.

'I couldn't stand it if she had her way with him first!' sighed the blue-eyed one dramatically.

'And Isadora's whole group is going after him tomorrow!' the giggly one complained, surprisingly with no giggling at all now.

'Her group?' I exclaimed in disbelief. 'How many girls are chasing him? And why?'

It sounded as if he were going to be attacked.

'There's Isadora, Betsya, Doreen, Lorai, Dertors and Perimay,' listed the blue-eyed blonde.

'So, there are six of them, and the three of you wanting that boy?' I exclaimed. 'How in the Gods' names was he fortunate enough to manage that?'

'Oh, he hasn't done anything. Hasn't spoken to any of us except you and that wench Isadora. It's terribly vexing!' gushed the robust one, rocking back.

'He's exquisite!' wailed the blue-eyed one. 'Quiet men are mysterious men!'

'He's gorgeous, he is!' giggly one. 'Those striking green eyes! They say green eyes make you a descendent of the first men in the whole world.'

'And the way he dresses, he must be rich,' asserted the robust one.

'He's tall, and muscular, and he's witty, and handsome...' the blue-eyed one was now also starry eyed.

'How did you manage to find out so much about him, if he hasn't talked to you?'

'Isadora has talked about him non-stop,' pouted starry blue eyes. 'But this morning we spied on him when he was dining with that round boy, and we just happened to overhear him talking. He's so clever, and, and...'

'Male,' I finished with an effort not to sound condescending.

Sighs filled the room.

'You were spying?' I asked dryly.

'Perhaps,' giggled the giggly one, predictably.

'But at least we came to you to see if he was promised,' defended the starry-eyed one. 'Isadora and her rotten mob didn't care.'

'Yes, that is so,' I nodded.

'But the game's afoot tomorrow,' declared robust seriously.

'We are leaving after tomorrow night,' I warned. 'There is no future in pursuing him.'

'It's of no matter. If we can save him from Isadora, that'll be enough.'

'And a quick taste of those lips each would be nice,' giggled giggly.

'I think your fathers would worry if they were here,' I told them.

'Of course,' agreed robust. 'But they're not here, so we can jump at every rare handsome opportunity that presents itself.'

I tried not to grimace as the robust one stood, ushering the others up too so they could prepare for a competitive day. But I put them from my mind until the next day when I was interrupted from pouring over a map I already knew by heart.

And again, the interruption came with a tapping on the door.

I did grimace this time, suspecting the girls again, until Noal's mournful voice sounded, smothered through the door.

'Kiana, Dalin's off with the billions of girls throwing themselves at him. Can you come and play runes with me?'

'Oh, you're such a nuisance!' I told his glum face as I opened the door and he stepped in.

'I need guidance,' he said piously. 'There are some old men that we were drinking with yesterday who said I should join in their runes game today. But, I need your wisdom and help to make sure I don't gamble and drink away the coin that serves to fill my stomach.'

'I might be the one you lose to,' I warned.

'I'm quite talented at losing, so there's a fair chance it could be one of the others as well,' he answered humbly.

I laughed. 'Very well, but you're buying my drinks.'

He beamed with enthusiasm at once. 'My, my, I thought ladies didn't partake in liquor.'

'I'm no lady,' I informed him as he led the way to the tavern next door, where some smoking, laughing old men were already lounging about a round wooden table on the veranda, each with a mug in their hands.

When we got to the table and they saw Noal had brought me, they stopped.

'You can't bring a lass to a runes table,' rumbled one with rosy cheeks, as he picked some meat out of his teeth.

'A lady would just get confused,' another burped into his salt and pepper flecked beard.

'Aye, a lady might,' I smiled evilly. 'But decrepit old men hardly stand a chance against a woman.'

Of course they took the challenge, and it was evening and the terrace was lit with burning torches when Dalin finally came over to find us. He leaned against the wooden railing that bordered the veranda, close to our table.

My fellow gamblers were all in an uproar, the old men and Noal singing drinking songs or griping about their losses, while I sat lazily beside my huge pile of winnings. My feet were up on the railing beside Dalin, my legs crossed comfortably. I rested my elbows on the arms of the chair, lounging in triumph.

'Noal can't hold his liquor well, can he?' I smirked, flicking a coin up in the air and catching it.

'Heyy! I caaan tooooo!' he protested happily, sloshing some ale onto the wooden floor.

Dalin shook his head, 'I'm surprised he got through that many pints,' he laughed, nodding at the six empty beer mugs on the table in front of me.

'Nah, I didn'. Those one'sa Kiana's!' Noal hiccupped. 'Thosea mine,' he pointed to his three empty mugs.

Dalin snorted.

'Wanna joinus for the nex game?' Noal asked him.

There came a drawn out, female call from behind us. 'Dalin! Where are you?'

'We just want to talk to you!' called another girl's voice. 'We'll be good this time!'

I rolled my eyes at him.

'I'm in demand,' he shrugged airily before magnanimously walking back to where the voices had come from.

After another game I had won all that my purse could hold, and I decided it was time for Noal to go his chuckling way to bed. I slung his arm over my shoulder and helped him stumble, still singing cheerfully, to his room. I dropped him on his bed and left him to do the rest, but wasn't tired myself and went to get some fresh water. Grabbing a pail, I headed down the path to the stream, listening to the night sounds of crickets chirping in the grass and a horse whinnying in the stables. But I frowned when I heard something different ahead.

I was close to the stream now, pail still in hand, and when I reached a small thicket of bushes I heard a giggle come out of the darkness.

Standing by the clear stream, illuminated by the silver light of the stars and the smiling moon, stood two figures.

It was the girl we had met when we had first arrived.

Isadora.

And she was kissing Dalin.

When their lips parted she giggled again, batting those weapon-like eyelashes at him like before, and he smiled impishly back. His tunic had been pulled off. It was crumpled at their feet on the grass. She was holding his hands to her waist as she smiled, and I found that my teeth were clenching.

She took her hands from his, and her fingers started untying the cord lacing the front of his shirt. She stopped when his shirt was open to the navel, and started circling her fingers across his chest, tickling his skin lightly. Tracing the muscles there.

There was obviously no care for honour from either of them and I felt judgment cloud my face, for the noble gentleman in particular, and was just about to turn to leave when the dim-witted, selfish sot of a boy spoke, looking down into Isadora's adoring eyes.

'This is nice,' he smiled.

I nearly felt my eyes roll out of my head.

'But I really only wanted your help,' he finished.

I paused. How could Isadora help Dalin in a way that Noal or I couldn't?

'Isn't this helping?' she asked playfully, and she started to caress his bare chest with her lips.

'Mmmmmm,' he agreed slowly, as she kissed his skin. 'But honestly, if you were angry with me, what could I do to apologise? I don't have access to the nice gifts I could give to someone from my home, and I doubt that buying gifts would help in this instance.'

She tore herself away from kissing his chest to stroke his cheek. 'But I'm not angry with you. In fact, I'm very, very happy.' She kissed him again.

He pulled away after a few moments, thinking. 'But what could I do?'

She sighed, considering. 'I would love the bought gifts you mentioned. But if you had to, you could give me a flower.'

'I'm not sure cliché tricks will work in this instance either,' Dalin replied doubtfully.

'Find a special flower,' Isadora shrugged. 'Doesn't matter, the effort will say everything.'

He nuzzled at her cheek, kissing her softly all the way down to her collarbone. 'You're an angel!' he said at last, grinning down at her.

'Is this for that girl you came with?' she asked without any hint of concern as she went back to tracing her dainty fingers along his chest.

'Yes,' he nodded. 'Thank you for your help.'

My jaw dropped in surprise.

'You shouldn't worry about her. I'll make you forget your troubles.' She said it slyly, and her fingers started to move south, travelling down his chest and past his navel.

My mouth dropped open a little further in amazement.

But Dalin gently clasped her fingers, stopping them as they roamed and stroked their way down to his trousers and began fiddling with his belt. He kissed her hand, holding it, then kissed her lips and pulled away, beaming.

'You taste nice,' he smiled. 'But, now I have an important errand. I'll have to find the perfect flower, in the dark.' He kissed her again, a long slow kiss, then a quick one, and then stooped to pick up his tunic.

'Well, come to say goodbye before you leave on the morrow,' she looked at him suggestively.

'I am indebted to you for your help, fair maiden!' He bowed comically, so that she laughed, before he turned and set off on his hunt in the trees opposite the stream.

She looked after him for a moment, then left too, walking past the other side of the bushes I sheltered behind, back toward the village.

'What happened Isadora?' I heard excited whispers from further back as she withdrew.

'We have a true connection,' she gushed. 'He said he loves me.'
I nearly snorted as I heard them squeal as they departed.
Not long after, I filled my pail and headed back too.
But, for some reason, I wasn't angry anymore.
The girls who had visited me had been right–spying could be beneficial.

CHAPTER THIRTY FOUR

Dalin

It was already late when I found the best flower in the hilly tree lands around Wanru.

I'd been traipsing all around the area, thanking the Gods for the moon's light, when I'd almost tramped on it.

A wild gardenia.

To be more exact, it was a fragrant patch of wild gardenias, but just one, raised above and more delicate than the others, caught my eye. It was beautiful, looking silvery white in the moonlight, with petals opening to become a star shape.

I gently stroked the soft, velvety petals with a fingertip before carefully picking it, and cradled it like a baby on the way back to the village while rehearsing what I would say as I walked up to the room Kiana was staying in.

It was very late, but the light of a candle could be seen behind the curtains of the window, and for some reason drunken butterflies began crashing around in my stomach.

I stood on the doorstep for a moment, breathing deeply, then knocked lightly on the door. When it opened, Kiana stood in the doorway as if she were a framed and mesmerising portrait.

She gave me an appraising look as I stood speechless on her doorstep with a flower and a bashful expression. 'You're out late,' she commented. 'Did one of those girls try to kidnap you?'

'Yes,' I said seriously. 'It was awful. But, with the bravery and strength of a lion, I courageously fought my way to freedom.'

She gave one of her half smiles. That was a good sign, when she normally didn't smile at anything I said.

'Kiana...' I cleared my throat nervously. 'I braved my way through all of those nasty girls because I had something to say to you.'

'Yes?' she encouraged. My face was colouring, and I was sure I looked like an absolute fool.

'I think...' I cleared my throat again. 'I think we've got off to a bad start.'

Kiana raised an eyebrow.

'I know how much you've helped us, and I've not shown you as much respect as you deserve. I do truly think that we need you to get safely to Jenra, and I'm sure we can work together and cooperate. But even more so, I hope that we can also be friends. I really want you to know that I can do better.'

I stopped there, smiling at her hopefully, and held my perfect gardenia out to her.

She regarded the flower, and me, carefully. Then slowly she held out her hand and took the flower gently from my fingers. She inclined her head.

'Thank you.' Her eyes were soft instead of impartial as they looked at me. 'We must try to get along, my friend. I am also sorry for treating you harshly.'

I was more elated and relieved than I'd guessed I could be as she stood twirling the flower in her fingertips.

'Thank you Dalin,' she said again with her smile, and then quietly closed the door.

As I hopped down from the step and made my way to the small apartment that Noal and I shared, my heart sang with a happier beat than it had since before Noal and I had planned our Quest. And the next morning as Noal and I made our way over to Kiana's room, I still felt buoyed with optimism with the thought that there was no longer any frostiness between Kiana and I.

Her door was open when we got there and we found her leaning a wooden chair back lazily from the rickety dinner table, flipping her knife up and catching it playfully as she waited. A map was laid out on the table.

'Please stop that, it makes me nervous,' Noal pleaded, watching the blade spin in the air as he sat by me on the edge of the bed.

She let all four of the chair's legs fall forward to the floor and slipped the dagger back into her boot. 'Right,' she swivelled to look at us. 'Here's the plan.'

Kiana proceeded to inform us that the horse breeding village of Wrilapek was our next and likely our last populated place to visit and try our fortune at buying another mare. She also explained that we needed to move much faster to cross Awyalkna, Sylthanryn and the Jenran mountains within a limited number of months.

But I was looking at her contentedly as she talked. Because, sitting at her ear, soft and white against the coal black of her hair, nestled the flower I had picked for her the night before.

CHAPTER THIRTY FIVE

Noal

Kiana and I had been farewelled from Wanru by our baleful runes opponents, who had eyed Kiana's bulging coin purse regretfully as we rode out. In contrast, Dalin's farewell party had been much larger, more feminine and more tearful as they'd watched us riding out of the hilly basin.

But as we rode from then on, there was no longer any tension between Dalin and Kiana, and Kiana even spoke to us as a friend rather than a distant guide.

Her light heartedness lasted for a few days, though I noticed something change about her as we roamed into more isolated lands. She became quiet, and I could see that her eyes regularly scanned the land, and even the sky. Her face became increasingly worried the further we journeyed, but more disturbingly, as she became withdrawn, the horses also became increasingly skittish as we travelled too.

Dalin finally asked: 'What is it, Kiana? You're watching ahead as if for danger and behind as though you believe we're being followed. Are you worried we've been found?'

She waited for a moment, as if deciding what to admit. 'Can you feel anything out of the ordinary?' she replied with her own question.

'Feel what?' I asked with deepening apprehension.

She hesitated.

'Be honest,' Dalin encouraged her. 'We know your hunter's instincts must be keener than ours.'

She straightened her shoulders resolutely and peered around the open lands once more. 'I have a... sense of foreboding. Something feels wrong to me, as though someone vile was thinking of me or looking for me, lurking close.'

Her solemn face was pale, though I knew there were few things that could shake her.

Dalin leant around her back to look at her. 'Perhaps you're catching cold, or perhaps you're tired.'

'No. I am aware of some wrongness that's not part of me, but is around me. I am dreading something, I can feel something rotten.'

'We should definitely be careful then,' Dalin answered, sounding concerned. 'But perhaps we should stop for you to rest.'

I saw Kiana assemble a reassuring smile across her features and consciously relax the tension in her posture, which only added to my own growing anxiety.

'I'm sure all is well,' she replied. 'In fact, I'm probably just restless, and in need of exertion.'

At that, she slipped herself out of the saddle, even as Amala was moving, and tossed Dalin the reins as she took up the pace to run easily beside us.

Dalin and I swapped expressions of unease, and I noticed that we both started furtively glancing over our shoulders and scanning our surrounds.

By the end of the week I felt a strange disquieting feeling gnawing at me too. Similarly, Dalin seemed pensive, and we all sat quietly and agitatedly close to the light of the fire, huddling away from the darkness each night.

CHAPTER THIRTY SIX

Kiana

A white hand, so skinny as to show the bones of the fingers like claws, slapped my face.

A woman, tall and pale as a ghost, more beautiful and terrible than any mortal, had stopped Angra Mainyu's sabre from its path to my body. But it was no relief.

I quailed as she smiled at me, and I prayed for death.

I could feel her evil in the air, churning through the atmosphere. I was choking on it as it spread from her like poisonous vapour that stung my throat and scorched my lungs as I was forced to breathe it.

I wished for the sabre's cool touch. A quick rip.

Or for the burning. For the fire that had raged before to have taken me, biting up my fingers and hair so that I crumbled and blew away like everyone else had in Bwintam.

The Witch smiled as if she had seen my thoughts.

She told me I would go on alone. Lost.

I would weep, she told me. I would grieve forever, in the darkness, alone.

Then her claw-like hand gripped my shoulder so that she could leave a branding as a reminder upon my skin to carry always.

There was blinding pain as her evil seared my flesh. The skin she touched smoked and hissed and steamed so that I screamed.

When she was done, there was a tear drop shaped burn on my shoulder, and her form twisted and Agrona suddenly melted before me, oozing into the form of a raven.

She, the raven, screeched at me. And I knew, as she screeched and flew away to leave me with the torture of life, that I would weep and face the darkness of life alone. I sat up, sweating, panting and weeping quietly in the darkness.

Alone?

Alone and a coward, weeping into the darkness?

No. Not alone. I could see the sleeping forms of Dalin and Noal next to me.

The nightmare was gone, but the feeling of wrongness remained. It had been growing steadily with each day, with each hour, with each moment as we drew closer to Wrilapek.

It was close. It was real. It was something I'd felt before, and that inspired nightmares from the past like the one I'd just had.

I had felt the wrongness in the beasts I always hunted.

And I had felt it in her. In the nails she had dug into my skin when she'd left her mark on my shoulder, the day the Witch and Warlord of Krall had come to Bwintam to destroy it all.

As if the dream had been forewarning, a small ache was growing again now in my shoulder where her hand had burned me two years before.

And I was afraid.

But if the wrong I felt, the wrong even the boys now felt, was what I dreaded it to be, then our Quest was more important than ever.

CHAPTER THIRTY SEVEN

Darziates would love her for this, Agrona had thought as she'd drifted lazily over her marching soldier pawns.

She would burn Wrilapek and steal its crucial stores of horses for Krall. And she would find for her Sorcerer the elusive Awyalknian boys and their helper.

Though she couldn't manipulate time through the Other Realm as Darziates could, she had moved Angra and his army across Krall's wastelands and into Awyalkna within days instead of months. She had flattened their dust, stifled the sound they made, hidden them from sight and bolstered their energy.

The Witch had even been getting ahead on her next task, bending her will during the entire journey towards the Awyalknian boys and their guide, sending her malice towards the blurred snatches of images she could catch of them when she tried–to hinder and worry them wherever they were.

Now as her soldiers closed in on Wrilapek she sent out one last spiteful thought, not caring at the pain it caused her to hurt the three figures across the distance again. She was happy to dimly see one of the blurred forms even fall from their horse this time. Agrona hadn't realised she had sent such a potent spell.

But then the sound of Angra breathing heavily brought her back to her current task.

Night had begun to creep over them and her pawns were all in place, spread amongst the thick growth of bordering trees around oblivious Wrilapek so that none of the villagers could escape.

The men were in an intoxicated state, euphoric with anticipation, and she enhanced this with a gesture until they were almost howling with a want to kill. Angra Mainyu was frothing at the mouth and the red glow of insanity was again showing through his bulging eyes.

'Darziates will love me for this,' Angra rumbled so hungrily that his words sounded slurred.

Agrona scowled at how he echoed her thoughts.

'He will love *me* for this,' she glowered.

'You only offer to kill his enemies and to share his throne,' Angra chortled. 'You're just a body to him. Something he can use to make an heir.'

'What could possibly be more valuable than all of that?' Agrona hissed.

Angra fixed his glowing gaze on her. 'He wants my soul. He said I can give him pieces of it, and help him create his new army.'

Agrona fixed him with a withering stare in return. 'You're basically an animal already. What will you be like with less of your humanity?'

'Invaluable,' he husked darkly.

She rolled her eyes. He would be the only mortal in the whole world who was already so corrupted that Darziates could dissect him. She refused to be jealous.

'Just focus on the treat ahead,' she scowled, turning her gaze back to Wrilapek.

Angra stared fixedly between the trees. 'Yessssss...'

Beyond the trees, deaf to the army amassed and watching, people chattered in the streets or settled in at home with soft candle light showing through their windows.

As she listened, laughter rang from the tavern. A horse whinnied from the stables in the distance.

All was perfect.

'Pleeease,' Angra begged. 'Lift the spell.'

She waited just one more moment to spite him.

Then she released her men, removing their invisibility and unleashing their sound to let them sweep away the peacefulness.

CHAPTER THIRTY EIGHT

Dalin

We were crossing bleak, rocky planes. Noal and I led Ila while Kiana roamed ahead on Amala.

My focus had been on guiding Ila between rocks that could make her stumble, until suddenly I heard Amala whinny ahead of us, and my head jerked up.

Kiana unexpectedly cried out too and stooped forward in the saddle. Her cry was one of instant and terrible pain, and as she slumped, she clutched her shoulder.

Before I'd processed what was happening, she was sliding sideways out of the saddle towards the ground in front of the panicked Amala, who backed up anxiously.

I sprinted toward Kiana as her body collided with the rocky ground, and Noal rushed after me, still pulling Ila along.

I skidded to a halt and knelt at her side hurriedly, lifting her to lie in my arms.

'Is she awake?' Noal asked with the sound of rising panic in his voice.

'Take Amala's reins before she bolts,' I told him, and he was distracted by the task. The mare had reacted to whatever had hurt Kiana before even she had. I didn't understand what that could mean, but I didn't have the time then to contemplate it.

Noal approached the skittish Amala, dancing on the spot a short distance away, while I turned my attention back to Kiana.

She was still and pale, her eyes not flickering. I supported her in one arm, and stroked her hair from her face, only to find that her skin was as cold as ice.

'Kiana, you have to wake up,' I said urgently. 'Kiana, you're the healer, I don't know what to do, please wake up.'

Relief flooded me when her eyes blinked open, but then I saw that there was a distress in them that I'd never expected to see in Kiana.

She immediately tried to sit up, but then clutched at her shoulder, groaning in agony as she collapsed back and curled in my arms.

'What is it?' I asked fretfully. 'Has something happened to your shoulder?'

'Don't know,' she managed. Her eyes were still closed, and I was scared she was going to lose consciousness again.

'Let me have a look–' I started.

'No,' she cut me off, speaking through gritted teeth and gasping.

'Kiana, let me help,' I was aghast.

She gripped my shirt with the hand on her uninjured side, her gaze asking me to understand. 'No,' she repeated. 'The pain will pass,' she said with certainty, and released me from her gaze. 'I've endured worse.'

'What can I do?' I asked and felt her relax a little in my arms as I accepted her wishes.

'We need to keep going to Wrilapek. It's now the most important thing. To keep moving for the Quest.'

'Alright,' I agreed, and her eyes closed again. She looked disturbingly fragile and vulnerable.

I glanced over at Noal. His face was white, except for two little red circles in his cheeks. As if they had been pinched. But he had not given into his fear.

'I need your help,' I said as he watched me with wide eyes. 'We'll have to trust that the horses won't bolt if you drop their reins for now.'

I had a feeling that these bays wouldn't leave Kiana easily anyway.

'I'll mount up and you'll have to lift Kiana up to me.'

Noal nodded his head. Holding my breath, I put an arm around Kiana's back and an arm under her legs, lifted her, and stood. She made no sound, but her face contorted as she was jostled.

Ila and Amala stayed their ground as Noal let go of their reins and reached for Kiana.

'Carefully now,' I said as I let her body rest in his arms. She was biting her lip, and it was clear that whatever ailed her was not a normal injury.

I quickly pulled myself onto the waiting Amala, and reached over for Noal to carefully lift Kiana up to me. I pulled her over to sit sideways across the saddle in front of me, and my heart skipped as I saw that she fought to hold back tears that were wetting tightly closed lashes. I slid one arm around her back to support her as she sat against me, and the other in front of her to grasp the reins.

'You're finally letting me take the reins,' I whispered jokingly as Noal mounted too, and a weak smile played faintly across her pale face.

'Don't go easy,' she whispered back. 'Gallop when you can.'

'It'll hurt,' I warned her with concern.

'I can manage.' Her eyes were still closed, and she leaned with her side against my chest, her head against my shoulder, her face close to mine.

'Alright,' I said again.

I saw her wince as I kicked Amala into a smooth canter and motioned for Noal to follow. But, as she said, we kept up our pace until first dark when I decided to call a halt.

Kiana had fallen asleep and had barely stirred from her position in my arms for the entire journey. Noal helped me to lift her down, and we set up a bed for her near our camp fire. I spent the night fighting all of my better judgements to search her shoulder for a wound as she slept unmoving before me.

But by morning, when Noal and I woke, we found Kiana sitting up as ready as usual.

'You're well!' Noal exclaimed with undisguised relief. 'We were so worried.'

'No need to be worried.' She smiled a smile that didn't reach her eyes. 'I have an old injury that was playing up.' She was still smiling unconvincingly, and sat with her arm held lightly, gingerly.

'In half a day we'll get to Wrilapek where we can have a freshly cooked lunch,' Kiana said then, and effectively stopped Noal from questioning her.

He scuttled up, making ready to leave at once, and I moved to help him break camp, kicking away any traces of our fire and sweeping up telltale signs of our stay.

We mounted and I didn't say a word when Kiana positioned herself on Amala behind me. She put her arms around my waist and laid her head against my back as we rode on again.

CHAPTER THIRTY NINE

Dalin

I felt the cold against my back as Kiana straightened to sit up alertly for the first time in hours.

'I can smell smoke on the wind. There's been a fire ahead,' she said.

'I can't smell anything,' I replied nervously.

'Something's not right.' She sounded troubled. 'Watch for signs of anything strange ahead.'

As we rode onward that uneasy feeling I'd had for the last week seemed to intensify. With each of Amala's strides, I felt I was being drawn closer to something rotten and inexplicable.

Eventually Noal and I could smell the smoke Kiana had warned of, and now we could see steady tendrils of it rising up into the clouds in the distance, close to the woods that Kiana had said bordered Wrilapek. My stomach began churning with nerves as, the closer we got to the expanse of trees and village beyond, the thicker the smoke became.

I moved to steer Amala around the trees, but Kiana stopped me. 'Go through them,' she said grimly. 'We may want cover.'

'Cover from what?' Noal asked a little shrilly. 'What do you think has happened, Kiana?'

'I can only guess.' She didn't elaborate, but with thudding hearts we moved into the cover of the trees, our eyes darting toward every stirring leaf and shifting blade of grass.

Finally, stepping around another row of towering trees, we saw the brighter light ahead that signalled their end. My eyes were watering with the smoky air and my lungs laboured to make use of the unclean oxygen swirling visibly around us.

'Halt here,' Kiana ordered quietly, and she slid out of the saddle while Noal and I followed compliantly, tethering our reins to a low branch and trailing Kiana silently to the break in the trees.

Though Wrilapek should have been just beyond the opening of the trees, there were no sounds of life, no indications that any people lived near.

'Keep quiet, no matter what you see. Do not move beyond the shelter of the trees unless I say so,' Kiana whispered back to us as we reached the edge of the woods. Her dagger was already in one hand, and the other hovered over her sword.

Following Kiana's lead, we moved forward to each take shelter behind a tree, and, after a nod from Kiana, we peered slowly around their trunks.

Kiana cursed softly.

Noal gasped and fell heavily against his tree.

My stomach felt as though it had dropped to my feet, and I saw nothing but the ruins of Wrilapek.

The sun was setting over charred and smoking remains. A still graveyard.

It could not have been from natural causes. There was no way that a fire that had engulfed an entire village wouldn't have spread to the trees or become a beacon to Awyalknians far and wide. But worse, there was a feeling in the air, as though the atmosphere was sizzling with some hair-raising, corrupted power. It felt thick and lingering, with invisible filth that coated our skin, foul and gritty.

Noal had sunk down to the ground, nauseated.

'How could a village, a whole village, be lost without warning?' he gasped, and covered his mouth, ready to gag. I sank down beside him, also feeling as though I would be sick if I breathed too hard.

'Magic,' Kiana was stony faced. 'It is exactly like Bwintam. It is exactly like the other border villages.' She drew her sword, still holding her dagger in the other hand and ignoring the pain in her shoulder.

'What are you doing?' I whispered, reeling with shock.

'I'm going to see if anyone's left,' Kiana replied flatly.

'You could find anyone. Good or bad!' I tried to keep my voice low.

'That is my plan.'

'We need to tell someone what's happened,' Noal babbled.

'We won't need to,' she told him in a quiet, reasoning tone. 'Some traveller will pass and see what's happened and this place will be crawling with people. Though it will do no good for the dead.' She peered beyond the trees grimly. 'But I can look for survivors right now and tend them, or look for enemies and avenge the dead.'

I stood up too. 'I'll go with you,' I told her shakily.

'I will be fast and thorough alone. Remember, I am a hunter. Stealth is my way.'

I made to reply, but she shook her head to quiet me. 'Enough,' she ordered me softly. But the confidence behind her natural tone of command left no room for argument.

'I will return. Do not move from the shelter of the trees. Soon enough, we will all face danger.'

Then she simply turned and left the protection of the trees, stepping lightly and melting into the cover of the shells of buildings.

Noal and I were left to huddle together, shuddering and staring away from the chaos as the darkness of growing night and magic swirled in the air around us.

I barely knew Kiana had returned until she squatted down in front of us. Noal flinched.

There was blood all over her tunic and dust covering her hands.

I sat forward in concern. 'Where are you hurt?' I croaked.

'The blood is not mine,' she answered, and my stomach twisted.

'Was there anyone... anyone at all?' Noal asked sickly.

Kiana shook her head. 'Nobody.'

The blood and ash covering her was testimony to the fact that she must have searched each body for life.

'I walked through every burned out room and street. I only found day old tracks returning to Krall.' She straightened then. 'But now we must move on. We cannot stay at the gateway to a graveyard. Especially when our feelings of foreboding are not gone.'

I realised she was right, and shivered at the thought that, while the mortal murderers may be gone, the evil thing, the magical one that had been here, could still be about.

Kiana did not have to say that it could be the same magical one that Darziates might send specifically after us.

Noal was staring at the ground numbly, but she rose and leaned toward him. 'Come,' she said, sheathing her sword and holding her dusty hand out.

I was about to tell her that he could not talk when he felt this way. But he stared up at her hand. After a moment he clasped it and stood, allowing her to lead him back to the horses.

We turned as Kiana quickly poured flask water over her face, hands and arms, and discarded her bloody clothes to put on a new shirt and tunic from her packs.

Then we rode out the night and into the next day, with blank faces and with Kiana pushing us to put as much distance as possible between ourselves and the village of dead.

CHAPTER FORTY

Noal

We had been largely silent in the days following Wrilapek, until Kiana had given us an invigorating tonic. It was of her own mixture from her healing bag, and we were relieved enough by it as we settled into our most recent camp site, that we tried hollowly to create some kind of functioning communication again.

'You do remember that apples will be the death of me one day,' I grimaced as I always did at the sight of them when Kiana handed them out for our frugal dinner.

'Or tea,' Kiana added quietly for me. 'You've pointed out a hatred for tea as well.'

Dalin tried half-heartedly to involve himself. 'And I've just as often pointed out that I always thought Wilmont's scorn would one day be the death of me,' he shrugged. 'You never know.'

'He could kill with a glance,' I agreed, but then I noticed Kiana had frozen. Her body had become rigid and she peered out through the darkness beyond our camp.

'What is it?' I asked in alarm at her sudden change, also trying to look about myself.

It was then, chilling and sudden in the dark of the night, that we heard two sounds in the distance, very far off.

An inhuman shrieking call from one direction that was answered by another call in the distance.

The wild echoes were so faint, and sounded so ghoulish and unnatural, that one could almost question whether or not they had been real.

But Kiana stood quickly, her head sharply turned to listen. And we could not hide from the truth. We had heard unnatural calls like that before, when two beasts of cold darkness had first attacked us.

'What do we do?' I whispered in horror, wondering where in the world we could hide.

'We can do nothing,' Kiana was composed. 'We are far from where they are and we have tired our horses and must rest them. We do nothing, safely, but ride hard tomorrow.'

My heart raced, and it felt suddenly as if white glowing eyes were peering out of the darkness at us from everywhere, as if the shadows beyond the light of our fire were moving and breathing, pressing in.

I imagined them getting closer with every passing moment... loping and clawing their way across darkened fields to find us and freeze us with their cold grips. The usual clammy feeling of fear spread across my palms and sent tingles along my back. My breath began to quicken.

'We knew we would be pursued,' Kiana said simply, her voice cutting across my clouding panic. 'Take this as a compliment that Darziates still regards this Quest as important enough to worry about.'

Dalin's face was grave, but we said nothing as she calmly spread out her cloak to nestle in for the first watch of the night.

Following her lead, we laid in shivering bundles on the grassy floor. But I peered around myself and squirmed with every crackle of the fire or rustling sound of some little animal scurrying harmlessly about in the night.

CHAPTER FORTY ONE

Agrona had been enraptured as she'd swept across the chaos of Wrilapek, blasting dwellings to oblivion. Fire had raged through happy homes, screams had echoed down every lane, children had cried, thick blood had spattered the ground and her men had been laughing.

Agrona had sent out thoughts to keep the villages' horses penned safely in their stalls and carefully prevented any fire from spreading out of the borders of the village into the trees. Not because she hadn't wanted to set Awyalkna alight and roasting, but because it would draw more attention than was necessary so early. Angra's soldiers would be safely back over the borders before Glaidin could retaliate.

She'd paused to squawk encouragement as an elderly man had been stomped on and had taken delight in the finality of the crunching of his bones into the dirt. She had stopped to admire Angra Mainyu's undeniably effective methods as he'd slit the throat of a shrieking old lady. And Agrona herself had set a wailing child on fire.

When the men had had their fun, when there'd been no more blood to spill, she'd let them rummage around for whatever trinkets they could find. Then she'd rounded them up, made sure each man had a horse, before they'd set off for Krall with laughs of merriment and pockets full of bounty, blanketed once more with her power. She only saw them out of the remains of the village and across the borders, before she turned back to start her second task and to meet the five modified Evexus back at the ruins.

She felt exhilarated as she swooped in again to the remains of Wrilapek–but nearly toppled out of her tree when a second vision, like the one that had visited upon her months ago, swamped her mind.

She saw a girl. A woman. Beautiful. Powerful. She saw the two boys again. They were with the woman. She was their guide! They had been here, at the remains of Wrilapek. They had stayed a while but then had fled. No, not fled, but set off on their Quest again.

If the woman were to live, the boys could succeed. Krall would be made equal to Awyalkna despite numbers and despite the magic of the Sorcerer, of herself and of

131

the Evexus and the Dragons.

But worse, if the woman were to live... Darziates would desire her. More than he desired his Witch. She was a threat to Agrona and to Darziates' Quest.

Agrona lurched back to reality with a harsh cry of fury tearing from her raven's beak. She was sure she had seen the woman of the vision somewhere before. Where? How had she never known that the woman was so powerful? That the King would want her?

She must kill the woman. To save Krall, and to save Darziates for herself.

Her feathers stood on end in livid indignation, and her beak snapped open and closed as she angrily flapped up from her perch. She refused to believe it. None before in hundreds of years had been as powerful as herself or the Sorcerer. Not even the foul Lady of Sylthanryn, in the Great Forest of old.

But then Agrona's sharp raven eyes alighted on an ash and blood covered shirt and tunic discarded on the leafy floor. And when she gripped them with her talons and sent her thoughts out to find the owner of the garments, a chill ruffled her feathers again as she felt suddenly ill at the touch of them, and she found that her mind was indeed drawn back to the same three shadowy figures she had sensed those other times.

But now there was something else she could sense. Something threatening. Something that felt a lot like the owner of the shirt had magic of a sort, or was being protected by magic somehow.

Agrona's sleek, dark middle roiled inside as she raged at the idea that this was possible. And as she puzzled over how it had happened, when all good magic, except that of those in the protection of the Lady of the Forest, had been wiped out in the mortal lands by her own cherished master.

She hissed with resentment, clawing and shredding the shirt material and only calming when she felt the presence of comforting magic instead. She looked to find the five Evexus slinking their way through the trees to meet her, and she obscured for a moment into her other form.

'We have work to do,' she hissed.

And as Agrona left with her beloved's Evexus close behind, the Witch bent all of her ill will towards that obscured, hidden woman. Stabbing out at this surprise foe in hatred.

CHAPTER FORTY TWO

Kiana

My shoulder was aching, and all of my hunter instincts felt betrayed as I led the boys away from the sounds of the beasts.

We rode endlessly, pushing Ila and Amala as hard as they could go. Then we ran alongside them when we had to.

I had worried that Noal would be unable to keep up with Dalin and I, but he maintained a stubborn, unwavering speed. They both rasped for breath and cramped often at the start, but I increased each challenge steadily to build their endurance.

As they strengthened, I hid the fact that every footfall sent a jarring impact through my shoulder. I made sure my face never contorted.

By each nightfall the boys had to stop, and I would scout ahead to find a sheltered area, just as I now directed them under some trees that ringed a very small clearing. The boys collapsed into moaning heaps, while I left them to meticulously check over and water Ila and Amala.

The boys finally roused when I had filled our flasks and hunted and cooked us three plump birds.

'Is it safe to have a fire? It could serve as a beacon,' croaked Dalin, sitting up from a near comatose state.

'Who bloody well cares!' moaned Noal, flopping onto his side from a starfish position to look at the meal. 'After all these days... it's meat.'

'I've decided that a fire shouldn't make much difference,' I answered Dalin soberly, not mentioning that I felt they needed the meal. 'The beasts seem to operate well by each of their senses so they could use our own scents to track us. And the only success I had last time was with fire.'

My shoulder felt as though a knife was twisting through it, but I showed no pain on my face.

'I don't know how they could follow my scent,' rasped Noal, always first to recover a sense of humour. 'It must be you two. I smell like a dewdrop.'

I smiled as my shoulder pounded. As if the socket had been crushed and shards of bone were tearing through the muscle.

I was feeling dizzy with the pain. It was biting across my chest now.

The boys, however, were utterly exhausted. So after they ate dinner and drank a hydrating concoction from my healer bag, I offered to take first watch.

'I won't put up a fight to that suggestion,' Noal agreed gratefully. 'My muscles, it feels, have turned to liquid.' He flopped like a sack of flour back onto the grass, resuming his starfish position.

'You've probably just wet your pants,' Dalin yawned, not even putting effort into his jibe.

'Probably,' Noal had already shut his eyes.

After first watch, I sat with Dalin at the start of his turn until he lost the glassy-eyed look. And apart from a slight stinging, prickling feeling covering my skin feverishly, I was actually feeling more settled as we shared a companionable silence.

It was a comfortable hush that spread between us, only broken by little snores coming from the lump that was Noal in the dark. Until the peacefulness was broken by a shrill, screeching cry that tore across the night.

It was faint, like last time. But it washed dread over all of us, even making Noal cry out in his sleep.

It was close enough to mean that all feelings of comfort were again gone, and we would need to ride hard tomorrow.

'You should get some sleep,' Dalin told me gravely, sitting straight-backed and cross-legged at the fire.

Nodding, I spread out my cloak, feeling increasingly unwell with every gesture. My shoulder felt as though a cold inferno was seeping through the flesh, eating through muscle and sawing into bone.

I couldn't lie on my side. At times my shoulder felt stiff and heavy, almost dead. At other times it felt hotter than fire or colder than ice. But at all times it hurt, and I took it as a sign.

A sign that I was afraid of.

CHAPTER FORTY THREE

They had found the trail of the travellers easily enough, but every night when they were right upon the three they hunted, it was impossible to find them.

Sick dread gnawed at Agrona as their elusiveness confirmed that some power or cloak really must be over the group, keeping them out of Agrona's reach.

Late every morning, after searching out finally where the group had been hiding, the spot was always empty, and the three were ahead again to repeat the process.

Agrona was almost exploding with desperation after a fortnight of this strange search, and every day she was galvanised to send out her will to try to hinder and hurt the group. But it was getting harder to even see their shadowy forms.

She should have been terrified when one night she felt a strong pulling on her very essence and recognised Darziates' call—along with his obvious disdain at her lack of success. Instead, she groaned with pleasure as his magic erupted around her, pulling her from where she stood to then make her reappear in the training room of the King.

Only he had the unnatural power to manipulate travel like this, through the Other Realm, to trick time in their own world. And he waited in front of her, barely an arm's length away. Boundless black magic pulsing around him, through him.

She breathed it, drinking him in. White blonde hair. Bare chest and stomach hard and powerful. Only the light of a fireplace showed him to her, but it was enough. She etched every detail into her mind.

'Agrona,' he uttered in his low voice.

'My King,' she purred. 'Much has happened,' she began to report delightedly, her dark eyes reverent. 'After the successful attack on Wrilapek and escorting Angra's troop back to the border, I returned to await the promised Evexus.'

He was void of expression.

'While I sat alone amongst the trees, another vision came upon me, in like to the one that was sent to me some months ago. First, I saw the two that I had been warned against, and then I saw their companion.'

'What man was it?' he asked quietly, crisply.

'It was no man,' Agrona glowered bitterly, but she had resolved to completely block all images from her mind for once, as he always saw everything there. She

135

would reveal nothing of her fears that this woman had enough power to interest the Sorcerer.

'My vision told me that if this woman were to remain alive and help those boys, they would be successful in their Quest, and Krall would be made even with Awyalkna.' Better for him to want her dead.

Uncharacteristic amusement touched the hard eyes of Darziates. 'A woman?' he asked softly. 'An Awyalknian peasant woman managed to save two young noblemen and kill two fledgling Evexus,' he mused. 'And now the fate of my own divine calling is resting upon her shoulders.' He raised his eyebrows imperceptibly. 'How can this be?'

'I do not know,' Agrona retorted, still frantically trying not to reveal everything that her vision had warned. But in the process of holding some things back, Agrona all at once remembered she'd recognised the strange woman somehow.

Darziates' eyebrows rose again slightly, and her heart skipped a beat as she knew she'd let him catch that thought.

He studied her as she hastily closed her mind again.

'How would you come to know the face of an Awyalknian peasant? None has lived to tell the tale of meeting you.'

'I have no idea,' she scowled. 'I have never been one to become acquainted with many mortals.'

A bead of sweat rolled down her brow as she strained to keep everything from slipping out.

'Perhaps you came across this woman during a visit to the Awyalknian Palace spy,' he said.

'She wasn't from the Palace,' Agrona frowned. And then an idea struck her. 'Perhaps it was during one of the attacks on Awyalkna when I first saw the wench.' She paced away, thinking.

'I wouldn't have guessed you would let anyone survive any of those village invasions.' With a glance, he stopped her in her tracks and whirled her around.

She revelled in his rough magic's touch.

'I remember that I may have found the kindness in my heart not to kill everyone in Bwintam.' The delight was plain in her voice, and he showed no surprise at her games. 'How many survived?' he asked.

'One,' his Witch replied slowly, a smile spreading across her lips. 'A girl.'

He dragged her forward, her shoes scraping the floor and her hair whipping back. 'Why didn't you kill her?'

'She wanted me to,' Agrona laughed, feeling better that this girl couldn't really be such a threat after all.

'Your mistake has put my cause in jeopardy.' The Sorcerer's voice was still low, but she scowled at the rebuke. 'You do not want to fail Agrona.'

The Sorcerer didn't move and his voice never changed in tone, but the implications were clear. And for it she feared him and loved him and lusted for him with all of her being.

'Now that I know the wench involved, I can track them more easily,' Agrona boasted confidently. 'I scarred the girl with my fire brand the day that I spared her life. I can search for the echo of my power and follow the feel of my own work. I can also give her more pain than she has ever felt in her life.' Agrona glared past the King, seeing the beautiful face of the mortal wench from the vision.

Even if this girl wasn't an all-powerful threat, she would be tortured for the trouble she'd caused, and then obliterated... just in case.

The Witch moved forward to kiss the Sorcerer, but his magic pushed her away and she felt herself being buffeted and rushing back through time and space across the Other Realm to where she had left the Evexus. Not a moment had passed.

CHAPTER FORTY FOUR

Kiana

Screeching, cruel laugh-like squawks shredded my mind. There was the sound of swooping wings and the click of a sharp beak snapping.

The raven watched me being dragged down into blood and ashes before Angra Mainyu.

But then the raven swooped in, becoming the Witch of Krall.

What had been a glossy wing then became a bone-white hand taking hold of my shoulder. Her touch sent a jet of boiling heat into my melting, blistering flesh.

But the smell of my skin burning and the perversive, defiling feel of some dark sickness being sent in to invade my body was hardly as painful as the tearing in my heart.

Her eyes were alight with gleaming, greedy joy as she felt that my heart was broken, and told me that I would weep into the darkness. Alone.

'Kiana!' a new voice seemed to call from very far away.

My shoulder was burning. I was burning, Bwintam had burned. Everywhere ashes.

'Kiana!' the new voice called again, and it sounded concerned. It wasn't laughing, and it wasn't hurtful.

I turned toward the voice. My eyes wouldn't open, they rolled with the dizzying agony. The memories were clinging, smothering me.

I felt hands upon me, and because my skin felt feverish, it throbbed at the touch. But these hands weren't cruel in their grasp.

Then my eyes dragged open finally, and I jolted from sleep into reality.

Dalin was leaning over me on one side, and Noal was at my other side.

I sat up quickly, my vision lurching with the throbbing agony of my shoulder. I felt bile burn the back of my throat, but I somehow managed to launch myself up to stagger a step away, swallowing the sickness and the embarrassment.

I also swallowed the slashes of memory that the dream had reignited, teetering a little as I forced down the images of Bwintam, and then of Wrilapek. Churned up, mangled bodies with staring eyes and gaping mouths. The sickly smell, like off meat. The dark magic causing premature rot.

I stopped myself from remembering the sabre, the hand on my shoulder, the raven.

Tommy's little blue hands, little blue lips.

'Don't push us away this time,' Dalin said, breaking my reverie as I firmly pushed away everything else. 'You were calling out in your sleep again. Something is troubling you and we want to help. We are a team now.'

I smoothed my face and steadied myself inwardly and outwardly. 'It is my own problem. It's not of your concern,' I spoke in an almost inaudibly low voice at last.

'I do have some business in it,' he stated, though not unkindly.

My mask was firm as I turned away, trying not to swoon with the nausea and agony. It roiled in my stomach and bunched in my shoulder.

'You cry out in your sleep, and though I know you don't mean to do it, the sound could compromise our hiding,' Dalin explained in a reasoning way to my back. 'If we understand, we may be able to help you. We could watch over you as well during our watch for the enemy–if we know how to calm you in your sleep.'

I remembered remorsefully the violence I'd confronted Dalin with when he'd disturbed my delirium in the past.

Holding my shoulder and closing my eyes tightly, I sank to the ground gingerly. 'You are right,' I admitted with a sinking feeling.

For this Quest to work, we all had to trust each other, and we had to be able to perform as a team. But keeping myself separate was an armour I had built so effectively, that I hardly knew how to remove it.

I opened my stinging eyes and stared into the fire. The flames consumed all else from my vision and seemed to dance and shift. 'Please, come and sit with me.'

My voice sounded hollow and my heart raced as I imagined my invisible armour breaking away to expose the withdrawn person I truly was, huddling and struggling to cover too many fracture lines and unhealed wounds.

Dalin knelt down beside me. 'You can trust us. We want to support you.'

Noal put a hand on my shoulder and I didn't even feel the pain. They sat on either side of me, as if providing a new kind of protection. A shelter at my sides to keep me safe as I stripped that armour away.

The taste of sickness fouled my tongue again, but I looked only into the dancing flames. Like twisting demons.

A faint screech came again from the distance, and we shivered. The pain in my shoulder exploded into a feeling of a thousand pins being wedged into sensitive flesh. But I began to speak to them, and to explain.

'I was not raised to be a hunter,' I began. 'Though my family taught me many great skills that helped me to become as I now am.'

I sighed deeply. Readying myself.

'I only chose to hunt after suffering the loss of my family. Before I lost them, my life was one of great happiness and normality.'

I sank back into my nightmare, with this time a waking heart.

CHAPTER FORTY FIVE

Kiana

My voice got stronger as I spoke, and I didn't pause when Dalin and Noal gasped as they began to truly understand.

'I'd slept the end of my birthday and Bwintam's festival away peacefully beneath a Willow tree. But when I woke, it was in fright at the thundering sound of pounding hooves, screams, and the smell of burning.

'The sucking wind of an inferno whipped my hair, lashed my skin, and plucked at my dress. Flames lit the night as they tore through the stage, stalls and pretty cottages, when before there had only been the cheerful glow of the village torches. Worse, in the blindingly ignited streets there were the silhouettes of dark figures on horses, charging and slashing through villagers who were running in all directions.

'I sprang from my distant resting place in terror and hooked my arms around one of the Willow's lower boughs, swinging my legs up and pulling myself into the safety of the branches to cling to the trunk like a child.

'Over the thundering raiders there swept a black bird, a raven, and it seemed to stir the Krall warriors into an even greater frenzy. They swung axes and curved sabres, hacking at anyone in their path. And it was from the Willow that I saw my own father in their path, standing protectively in front of my mother and brother, Tommy. Two warriors on horses bore down with their curved, ugly blades raised.'

I felt Dalin's hand grip my leg in support, but I hardly registered it.

'My father raised a hand,' I continued bleakly. 'As if he thought his gesture could magically stop the attackers. Something did make the first rider topple, but the second rider continued to swoop and I saw the sabre slicing and father falling.

'I heard Tommy's squeals as mother cradled him. But then she was down too, and there was no one to protect him. I remember it too clearly. Tommy's hands, smaller than my palm, were held up in terror. His tiny lips, which still gave awkward, wet kisses, were shaped in an 'o'. His uncoordinated little legs were stepping this way and that. Then he was caught in a frenzy of stabbing.

'All the while I clung to the Willow as night lightened into the blood red sky of morning. Everyone I knew had been turned to ash and even the raging flames in the dwellings were dying back to leave only smoking shells.

Meanwhile, the rough voices of the warriors laughed out from the smoke as they used their butcher's tools to cut and plunder, and I hardly thought of my own self until the black bird–the raven, circled out of the sky, down to the Willow, and let out a harsh cry.'

Neither Dalin or Noal said a word.

'There was no time to try to camouflage myself,' I said resignedly. 'I sat frozen as the warriors found me clinging pathetically to the trunk. The whole horde massed around the Willow's roots like a hungry pack of dogs, shouting and jostling in a sweaty crowd as one warrior pulled himself up into the tree and his grimy hand snaked up to grip my leg and tug. The warriors below bayed greedily in an excited uproar as I flailed downwards and screamed, only to be caught by snatching hands that ripped at my dress. I was tossed from one man to the next, caught and pulled and clawed at in a tug of war as I was jerked to and fro. It only ended when an order was barked and then I was pulled through the crowd and through Bwintam to be set down on my knees, my arms pulled roughly behind my back.

'I didn't dare to look at any of the nearby charred remains for fear of finding a familiar face among the piles, but fear engulfed me as instead a pair of heavy, steel covered war boots walked into my line of vision. Then my eyes rose to behold the Warlord of Krall. Angra Mainyu's returning gaze was as bloodshot red as the burning morning sun, and every inch of me was shaking when he lifted his sabre. But I closed my eyes and was comforted that it would all end. I could not face the idea of living with what had been done.

'Then, almost as if in response to that very thought, I heard the swooping rustle of the raven's wings, and I opened my eyes to find the Warlord's blade poised inches from my chest. He and everybody else were now looking to where smoke rose, spewing from the burnt earth to swirl around the place where the black-feathered raven had landed.'

Noal stifled a moan as I swallowed and remembered the next part. Dalin just continued to hold my leg as if he could keep me grounded.

'Uttering a single, horrible cry and spreading wide wings, the raven began to grow into a completely new shape until finally the Witch of Krall stood in the shroud of smoke. A regal black dress hugged her overly thin frame and black hair framed a beautiful, terrible face in darkness. And instantly a feeling spread from her that dispelled any final beliefs I could have that magic was only in stories.

'She asked me my name, and her eyes and voice held a foul power that silenced the entire army. They were transformed from a shouting, jeering pack into a subdued crowd of quieted sheep shifting nervously in the background. Many warriors bowed their heads or averted their eyes, and even Angra Mainyu lowered his blade and stepped away–leaving me to be her prey.

'I couldn't even think of defying her power myself, and told her my name as she stepped close–sending the smoke and ashes that had been drifting about the hem of her dress into a writhing, swirling frenzy of dancing spirits.

'Leaning in like a poised snake readying to strike, her face was almost touching mine as she whispered: 'Do you fear me Kiana?' so close to my ear so that my scalp prickled and my tongue moved of its own accord. Betraying me with a quavering 'yes'.

'Then abruptly she straightened as her hand, so wiry as to show the bones of every claw-like finger and knuckle, slapped my face. It made me gasp as her blow seemed to imprint on my stinging cheek with reverberating shockwaves of poison.

'I remember I began to pray for Angra's sabre to return. I would have preferred him to wet his blade with my blood than to face her and this new awful world alone.

'Oh no,' she told me. 'You made your choice to live when you hid for your own safety and watched your family die.' Her eyes had glittered. 'I did notice you never lifted a finger,' she remarked, and traced her own long painted nail in a line of fire down my cheek.

'I prayed to any God who would listen to let me die. But her lips curled in delight, and I knew I would live.

'I am kind,' she said. 'I will brand you so you remember the choices you made, and I will allow you to live in grief. Weeping,' she told me, nodding with a smile. 'And facing the coming darkness alone. It is your punishment, and your reward.'

'Then without warning her claw-like hand gripped my shoulder, pressing what felt like the end of a flaming torch into my skin so that it seared, smoked, hissed and steamed as I convulsed until her hand withdrew and I hung limply in shock.

'Under my grace, your branding will remind you of what you've lost and must live with. It will remind you of all you never did, and never shall do.'

My burnt skin was left bleeding and melted, but only in one spot, where there was a scarred mark in the shape of a tear drop.'

The boys were beginning to understand now, what the pain in my shoulder could mean. I saw their faces blanching with realisation.

'Then her form twisted,' I said, 'back into the raven. She screeched and rose into the smoke hazed air, and the army broke apart like storm clouds scattering.

'I was dropped and my face rested in the dirt, which became mud as it mixed with my tears. And with whoops and roars, the soldiers ran around and past and over me. Some of them spitting on me, or kicking and slapping at me as they passed while I yelped in a scrunched ball in the dust.

'In moments they had swarmed back to remount, wheel about, and thunder on nightmarish steeds out of the village. Then with one last screech from the raven, the entire army disappeared as if they had never been, leaving me alone in a village of corpses.

'It took time before I at last staggered up from the dirt, finding and clutching my Unicorn figurine, my final gift from my parents, as I dragged myself down all the village lanes in a daze.

I found that the lovingly tended fields were now squares of black char. My own home and Star's stables were destroyed. And when I got too close to the burnt bodies that remained, they broke and disintegrated.

'I picked my way through the scattered parts of people I'd always known, realising it would be impossible to ever reassemble all the limbs for each of the dead to have an afterlife without suffering. I saw things like a baby tooth laying in the dirt. Not even as big as my smallest fingernail. It had been kicked out of a small mouth, and I thought of Tommy and of his little friend, Jin.

'I was still retching from that alone, when I found the three forms that I'd dreaded seeing most, but that I had been searching for unconsciously.

'My mother's body was charred and father's chest was open. Tommy, a fallen little soldier, could have been alive the way his face looked, except for how blue it was. A slit had been made in his tiny neck, and there were holes all over him. A baby pincushion.

'I was shaking wildly, but I quickly leant over my parents. Glittering under ash, the jewels at their throats that they had always worn were somehow still there, and now I took the stones from their necklaces.

'When I came to Tommy, I closed his eyes and took his hand in mine. But his small fingers were cold and stiffening, and little patchworks of blood spattered across the chubby cushion of his palm. So, moaning, I put his hand down and felt in my darling little one's pocket for the wooden bird I knew would be there.

'I cradled and kissed those treasures, not looking back at the bodies, and found a patch of clear earth to bury them in.

'Alriynn, ingruda una dess boundesslyn,' I'd whispered; something I had heard my mother say over those whose healing beds she had always stayed by until the last. 'May your spirits always run free.'

'Then, as if I were being chased by a demon of the Other Realm, I ran. I ran and ran for what seemed like all of eternity, stumbling and falling when it became dark, and sobbing and choking when it became light again so I could claw my way numbly forward.

'When it stormed I took shelter in caves like a scared animal burrowing down. Wet hair clung in strings across my face, and the chattering of my teeth echoed off the walls, as, racked by shivers, I stared at the grey light seeping gradually in through the mouth of my cave, spreading to almost touch where I sat, before gradually fading to night.

'For a time I remained unmoved, and surely would have died if some strange hallucinatory voice had not started in my mind and pushed me to run on.

'I followed the delirious compulsion witlessly, even when I sometimes had to drag myself across the grass on hands and knees. Then at last I pulled myself along on my belly, grasping my way right up a small hill, to come to a stop–blinking at the sight of lights and sounds of a village ahead.

'Seek the blacksmith'–my hallucinatory voice was urging, and I limped my way through that unknown village, hardly aware of who I was myself. Falling, rising, and swaying my way to the smithy, I knocked on the door with a dirty, tattered hand.

'The Gods must have helped me to get to that place, because though I was a stranger, a grim companion and a wisp with no appetite, Marlin, the smithy, cared for me and even adopted me as his own daughter when I was physically well once more.

'In return I hunted our food, honed my abilities to perfection and brought great prosperity to Marlin's forge with the skills my father had given me. I made my weapons and strengthened each day. Though I dreaded sleep each night, suffering plagues of nightmares, and could never really settle.

'Foul rumours often disturbed me further, with tales of Darziates' movements towards war, of more villages being sacked, and of dread creatures spilling into Awyalkna.

Finally, while I was hunting one day, I came across a creature feasting on the remains of a traveller. Some innate reaction took over. I felled the beast, and then I knew I had to do more.

'When I left the warmth of Marlin's home, I surrendered to a wanderer's life. But I found incredible, driving purpose that pushed me to make new discoveries in healing, that spurred me to triumph over fiends I could hardly believe in, and that led me to track monsters amongst new cultures and nations.

Alone, but compelled, I have kept to that purpose ever since.'

I sighed again, swallowed thickly, but didn't look up as I finished.

I registered that Dalin's hand was still on my knee, but it was some moments before at last he spoke.

'You're not alone anymore,' he said. 'You have purpose–with us, and we're all in this together now. The three of us.'

I felt gratitude warm every part of me. Spreading outward from my core.

But before I could reply, a loud, unnatural wail sounded in the distance. Then another sounded, returning the call, closer than the last.

Noal and Dalin's expressions became anxious as they looked to me, and I felt desperately glad to still be regarded in the same way by them.

'Together, then,' I affirmed, and pulled myself up with resolve.

CHAPTER FORTY SIX

Noal

We had been in a race of blurring days. They blended together with riding, running, hasty stops, and following Kiana into invisible hiding places each night in exhaustion. Yet tonight I laid fretfully awake, staring up at the dark, cavernous roof of the burrow-like cave we were stowed in. I swore I could hear talons scraping the dirt over our heads.

'All will be well,' Kiana soothed me, sensing my distress even in the darkness while Dalin slept. She was on sentry duty and never seemed to tire after running circles around us all day. I had confided my own story of loss and crippling anxiety to her, and she now seemed to recognise my growing, silent panic. But in contrast, she was used to this life, and seemed as unmoved as ever at the scuffling sounds above.

'Every night the calls sound closer,' I whispered back nervously.

'We have tethered Ila and Amala far from here, and if our four-legged decoys are sniffed out, they will break free and flee, leading danger away,' Kiana's quiet voice was assured. 'Besides, we have not yet let our pursuers get close enough to see us during the day,' she added calmly. 'And when the time comes for us to meet, we'll face the challenge.'

I shivered, certain that I could feel their spreading cold and dread, and certain I could hear wailing screeches all around our hiding place as they searched for us. I prayed to the Gods that they would not sniff us out or find the opening above us that looked no bigger than a rabbit hole once we'd covered the small entrance.

'Noal,' she said softly, firmly. 'When the time comes, you will have courage. For you will be protecting not just yourself, but Dalin, who you love.'

'And you,' I sighed, feeling a little comforted.

She slung a reassuring arm over me and began to whisper tales of other lands to help carry me to sleep. And Kiana must have taken the watch all of that night, because when we awoke she wasn't there.

I could see traces of early light filtering through the little gaps in the leafy branches that covered the small entrance, and we were becoming alarmed before she slid expertly through the hole at high speed.

'Kiana!' I exclaimed, clasping my chest. 'Gods!'

'Shush,' she scolded, but she grinned quickly. I noticed that she'd remained sitting where she had landed and was clutching her shoulder.

'Where have you been?' Dalin asked, concerned. 'Is your shoulder giving you pain?'

I covered the hole back up as she talked.

'While you slept last night, the calls of the beasts got closer. There sounded to be at least four of them, but at first light their noises grew fainter.' She winced, clasping her shoulder. 'I thought I'd check out how things are with the enemy on our tail.'

Dalin grunted. 'You should have woken us.'

But Kiana took no notice. 'I scoured the lands all about here after checking that the horses were untouched and found that there were tracks five hundred yards from here.'

I spluttered as Dalin cursed.

'But I was wrong in my guess of how many there were,' she added consolingly.

'Less than four of them?' Dalin asked hopefully.

'No. There were tracks enough for five. I was one off,' Kiana replied. 'But my guess is they'll have lost our scent until we surface and move again.' She leant over to grip my hand for a moment. 'I don't think we will be so lucky as to trick them by simply hiding for too much longer. A confrontation may be approaching, just as we predicted.'

I nodded dumbly as she squeezed and released my fingers, but I mostly felt my shuddering pulse and fluttering courage instead.

'I think I can lead us in ways that will confuse them for a little while longer. But once we meet, we will have to defend, escape as unscathed as possible, and then evade them again. And we'll possibly have to repeat this process for our entire Quest, unless we can somehow lose them in the Great Forest before we reach the Jenran mountains.'

Dalin was looking grim. 'What do you think the ache in your shoulder means?' he asked. Now that we had a greater understanding of what it could represent, it only filled me with further foreboding.

She paused. 'Likely it means that the Witch is close by, searching for us too.'

'I guess we best get moving as far from here as possible then,' I said miserably. 'Might as well put our scent out there.'

I wondered if we would hide so successfully again at nightfall, or if today would be our last day.

I also wondered if I truly would have the courage, if we did have to face our last day.

I wondered the same thing every day for two weeks as I got fitter outwardly but more unsettled inwardly, listening each night to the bestial wails in the distance.

'That's amazing,' Kiana remarked one night as I sat tensely waiting for the wails to begin. She lounged on a fallen tree trunk that was creating a bridge above Dalin and I, eating an apple.

'What is?' Dalin took her bait with curiosity.

Kiana dropped her apple down to Dalin, who caught it automatically, and she slid off the tree trunk fluidly to land beside me. She drew her dagger.

I didn't have time to process her movement as she swiped her blade over my shoulder in a rush of air.

I felt something brush off my tunic, and saw a dark, hand sized shape land on the grass a yard away. It had long, sharp legs with dagger-like tips and rows of beady little eyes.

'A poisonous Granx,' she replied speculatively, eyeing the deadly insect as it waved at us and pattered away into the bushes.

I choked and felt as if the skin around my skull had tightened while the skin at the back of my neck was rippling.

Dalin's jaw was hanging.

'They're very rare, and yet I've seen two recently,' Kiana explained, as if that was why we had been struck dumb. 'Or the same one twice.' She sheathed her dagger with a business-like swish.

Fear began to take hold of my breathing even though the danger had passed. I began to feel exactly the same kind of sick anxiety as I had when I'd been a boy and my family's cart had been taken over by Trune raiders.

'Noal?' Kiana asked then.

I heard Dalin try to explain and excuse me.

Then Kiana's face was thrust into my vision and apparitions of my screaming family faded. Her hands gripped the sides of my face. 'Noal,' she said calmly, firmly. 'Snap out of it.'

I thought I heard Dalin plead with her to let me come out of my freeze in my own time. 'He can't help it,' Dalin was saying sadly. 'He can't help freezing up.'

It's true, I thought to myself. I'm afraid. I can't help freezing up.

'Noal,' Kiana said authoritatively. 'Stop it. You can, if you decide to. Overcome the anxiety.' Her voice refused to be ignored. 'You just have to force your mind back into this moment.'

It's too much. I thought to myself. I can't fight it.

'Your greatest personal battle is now,' she told me decisively. 'You can fight your fears instead of succumbing. Snap yourself out of your reverie and focus on right now. Or you will have never truly escaped those raiders.'

My eyes honed in to concentrate on her face.

'Don't be crippled, don't let the raiders take your life or your mind,' Kiana was saying.

I took a careful breath and felt myself surfacing.

'You need to end it. End the fear, or the attack on your family and yourself has never been finished.'

I took another sharp breath.

I could hear each of her blunt words distinctly now, not as if I were underwater.

Then I cleared my throat. 'I'm alright,' I said shakily, and I heard Dalin gasp.

Kiana gave a curt nod of approval. 'That is the greatest battle you'll ever face. You have shown your courage, and will not freeze when the time comes.' She went to reclaim her apple from Dalin.

CHAPTER FORTY SEVEN

Dalin

'Next week it's my birthday, and exactly two years since the loss of Bwintam,' Kiana remarked as she looked into the fire, which was the most comforting aspect of our whole campsite, and had drawn all of us close.

We hadn't had any particularly sheltered area to hide in that night, and the trees were the only thing that provided us with any cover.

'Oh Kiana...' Noal didn't know what to say to her.

I was reminded again of the beautiful village singer I had fallen in love with as a boy at a festival day in Bwintam and felt a pang of remorse. I had mourned when I'd thought she had been murdered, but even though I was now quite certain that I had found her again, in many ways she really had been lost.

Kiana rubbed her arms with the growing night's chill, and I rose to fetch her cloak and drape it over her.

'You'll have us,' I reminded her.

'A true gift,' Noal agreed.

I felt her brief, grateful touch warm my hand on her good shoulder as she wrapped herself in the cloak. But then I had to rub my fingers together for heat as I crossed to calm Amala and Ila, who were stamping nervously and shifting their weight, their ears flicking backward and forward.

I noticed that their velvety flesh was cool to touch, not radiating like usual. I rubbed Amala's cold forehead, and Ila snorted nervously at me when I scratched at her twitching ears.

'Your lips have turned purple,' I observed when I turned to Noal, who had started poking at the dwindling campfire to keep it going. It did suddenly feel as if winter had begun without bothering to wait its turn in the cycle of seasons.

Kiana shifted, rubbing at her shoulder with a grimace.

'It has got cold,' Noal complained, his breath producing misty clouds. 'The fire won't stay alive.'

'The horses are sure skittish, too,' I commented, trying to keep my teeth from chattering.

Kiana's posture stiffened. 'It's near the end of spring,' she said alertly. 'There's rarely anything more than frost during this time.'

'Sure there is,' Noal frowned, and he was shivering.

'Not that feel this unnatural, when only moments ago the night was just a touch fresh.' Her words finally sank in.

The campfire completely died now as Noal paused in stirring it. The shadows seemed to press in and the trees loomed darkly over us. Ila whinnied in fear.

'Oh dear,' Noal uttered in a shaken voice.

Kiana sprang to action at once. 'Saddle the horses, gather your things, have your weapons at the ready.'

'What are we going to do?' asked Noal, hastily stuffing things into his pack as Kiana started to saddle Amala. 'What can we do?'

'We are going to get out into the open.'

'Is that such a good idea?' he gasped. 'We won't have any protection. They'll be able to see us!'

All of my equipment was packed, and I began to saddle Ila for Noal.

'It would be no use hiding from beasts that can smell us out just as easy as spot us.' Kiana pulled herself into the saddle and loosened her sword in its sheath. Her bow, quiver and arrows were slung over her shoulder within reach. 'It will also do no good to have five beasts hiding behind trees, unseen by us.'

'When you put it like that,' Noal looked ill as he swung himself up onto Ila.

'We must confront them. They are too close for us to flee unless we do something to slow them down so we can escape.' She reached for a large, thick branch, hacking with her dagger, and then strapped the bough onto Amala as I mounted behind her.

'There's a place not far from here where a beast I once hunted unexpectedly exploded and scorched the earth into a perfect arena for us. And I have some tricks in my healer bag that could be helpful,' she explained.

She was not in the slightest unnerved, though I could see Noal's pinched face, and I felt my own heart racing.

'I have a plan,' she promised, and then led us at a gallop away from the trees and across the green seas of grass.

CHAPTER FORTY EIGHT

Yes, yes, yes, Agrona gloated to herself with each beat of her raven wings.

The Evexus loped like panthers beneath her, crossing ground that was covered with the Awyalknians' fresh scent.

Before tonight, it had become too clear to deny that some unfathomable power had been deflecting her efforts as the hunt for the three Awyalknians had dragged out. Agrona's doubt had flared up and festered into true loathing for the woman from her vision in that prolonged time of hunting. The infuriated Witch had been able to sense Kiana the whole time–in fact, Agrona had been almost able to taste the poisonous dart of her own dark magic branding the dark-haired beauty–but every night the Evexus had failed to flush the three out of hiding, and Agrona's hunger to end the threat had swelled.

This was unheard of. She had never encountered a block like this.

Ahhhh, but tonight the three hadn't shielded themselves well enough. Tonight they would be hers.

There was a growing light of fire in the distance now and the Evexus gained in speed, drawing towards an incredible, ballroom sized arena of charred earth, which was ringed by a border of flames.

The three were standing in the middle of the strange pitch, back to back near their horses, with weapons drawn. Kiana herself was carrying a blazing torch as the Evexus fanned out around the intensely burning barrier, and Agrona could smell that the flames had somehow been created by chemicals. Possibly unquenchable chemicals. And the perfect circle of burned earth prevented the risk of the arsonists being burned alive themselves.

Nevertheless, the Witch was not wholly impressed, because the fiery ring, even with those unquenchable chemicals, was not hot enough to deter the new Evexus models for long.

Agrona smugly blotted out the diamond glow of the stars and circled high above the arena while Darziates' five beautiful beasts awaited her call. They looked like nothing more than tricks of the flickering light, and the night seemed to hold its breath. Until Agrona released a commanding screech that made the three duck, and that sent the Evexus charging right through the blaze.

The Evexus screamed in agony for but a moment as they passed through the inferno wall, but then they continued on, already healing.

The female–Kiana, loosed a fierce cry before charging to meet the three Evexus closest to her, crashing fearlessly into battle with them. The raven hissed as Kiana skilfully spun and ducked and wove and sliced and parried and lunged and dodged their whirlwind attacks of frenzied, spiked limbs and biting cold.

The two boys followed Kiana's lead, hurling themselves into battle with the remaining beasts.

It was obvious that the boys too had been well trained. As she watched, the dark-haired, tall male was ducking instinctively beneath a spiked arm. The lad quickly pulled his sword out from between the Evexus' ribs and dodged behind his winded foe, hacking at a new place on the Evexus' body in a strategic effort to keep it off balance.

Oh yes, Agrona could see evidence of fortitude and talent from each of the three, with none of them showing the self doubt she'd relished in each of them previously. But it would do them no good. Every strategy they could concoct would of course be unsustainable–the Evexus healed from any wound.

She watched one of her Evexus snatch up the blonde haired lad, who struggled gallantly to reclaim the right to his life.

Pointless, but fun to watch.

CHAPTER FORTY NINE

Dalin

Dark, treacherous limbs reeled around me, claws whipping past just inches from my nose as my heart thumped a maddened beat in my chest.

With a grunt of effort, I put my entire body into wielding my shining blade in an arc that whistled about my ears.

The snarling fiend swung around as my blade sawed into its back, and I was suddenly confronted by snapping fangs and soulless eyes. I jumped away, but it whipped an arm after me that sent me hurtling backwards.

The breath rushed from my core as my back connected with the scorched earth and my head followed, smashing heavily so that I felt a throbbing ache erupt behind my eyes. Before my vision had cleared, the feeling of a crushing iceberg slammed into my chest, and more air wheezed out from my slackened jaw.

The coloured lights bursting before my eyes slowly evaporated so that I could see a gruesome foot pinning me down, pressing with enormous weight to prevent the oxygen that I craved from being sucked back into my desperate lungs.

Claws were digging into my tunic and the massive weight on my chest increased as the beast leered down, bending so that it could look at me closely, as if I were a fascinating insect it had stood on.

As it bent its long, knobbly leg to arch its body closer, pushing its ghastly, pointed face down towards mine, its spiked kneecap drew inches from my eye. However, at the same time it had brought itself close enough to be helpful to me.

Wheezing, I swung my sword as hard as I could into those cruel features, cringing as the blade squelched and crunched through one grisly white eye. Then I pulled it free again and cut deeply at the foot.

Its flailing arms flew up and its leg stamped away from my constricted chest, so that I could suck in gulps of air, roll away and unsteadily pick myself up.

The beast was clutching at its eye and screeching at an abominably high pitch as I lunged, stabbing at its legs to make it fall heavily.

Behind its recoiling and kicking in the dirt, I saw Kiana moving like one possessed, jabbing and burning one beast with her torch while stabbing ferociously at another two in an unwavering attack that meant they could never get close enough to assail her. Instead, they charged and stumbled away from her, one after the other.

Then my eyes sought Noal, and found him struggling in the grip of his beast, high in the air while it held him by his sword arm, his sword being forced uselessly upward.

Noal was gallantly throwing his free fist into the beast's face as I recklessly charged away from my own beast, across to where he was dangling.

Growling, I drew my sword up and swung a mighty blow into the exposed, leathery belly of the monster. The beast doubled over with a grunt and Noal slipped from its grasp to land safely on his feet.

'Thank the Gods I have you,' Noal panted at me. Then he jumped back into the fray, slicing and cutting different parts of the monster's body like a crazed butcher dicing meat.

Before I could even think to turn back to my own beast, it came for me. I was torn from my feet, lifted into the air and tossed far across the circle.

The world disappeared in a wave of vertigo until I pounded into hard ground. I blinked stupidly, feeling as if I'd swallowed a slab of granite while the flavour of blood made my teeth taste salty. But before I could even peel my face out of the dirt, I felt the ground shudder as the beast landed next to me.

The back of my tunic was suddenly pulled tight in the beast's grasp, and I heard the quick tearing sound of claws ripping into the material. I groaned as the skin of my back was also pierced and pulled into a scrunched handful, and cold spread from the claws to seep beneath my broken skin.

'Frarshk,' I wheezed as I was dragged backward across the dirt, then lifted over the beast's shoulder at a great height. Then suddenly I was heaved away again, tearing out of its grasp as my skin ripped free, shredded out of its talons.

I soared at top speed out of the centre of the circle, turning in the air and yelling while I hurtled down to land and drag along on my back until I was only an arm's span from the border of Kiana's chemical flames.

I hadn't landed in the flames or broken every bone in my body, but with a surge of panic I realised my hand was unbearably empty of any weapon.

I stared across the distance to see my beast bending close to the ground, getting ready to push off and soar through the air.

So I did the only thing I could think of.

CHAPTER FIFTY

'Kiana!' the dark-haired male yelled.

Agrona saw Kiana look over her shoulder at her comrade even as she stabbed an Evexus through its chest. While the Evexus she had impaled tried not to topple, two more were charging at her from different directions.

Yet in a matter of moments she had pulled her sword free and climbed up the leg, back and neck of the buckling, wounded Evexus so that the other two Evexus raced uncontrollably into the first, sandwiching it while Kiana perched safely on its shoulders.

As they all fell in a heap of knotted limbs, Kiana dived and rolled away, then pounced up to throw her sword, sending it arcing through the air much as the brunette boy had flown only recently.

He clutched her hilt gratefully as Kiana in turn ran to seize his sword from where it had landed nearby, turning easily to face the Evexus once more—as if the great beasts were nothing.

Agrona seethed. The fun was quickly winding up, and she began to consider killing the boys as well as Kiana, instead of just apprehending them for her master. This feeling heightened while she watched the galvanised brunette boy begin attacking his Evexus even as it landed from its great leap.

He was struck to the side of the head, clipped by a claw that opened a red line across his ear and jaw, and he hardly seemed to falter.

The blonde lad was even sitting on the shoulders of his Evexus now, chopping with all of his might at the neck in front of him, while the Evexus could only slap in a frenzy at his hacking blade.

Looking back, Kiana had begun pinning her opponents to the ground, her daggers keeping one Evexus' arms staked into the dirt as she aimed a blow in between its eyes that made it go limp. Agrona felt rage like a bubbling oil slick in her stomach as she saw that the Evexus was both trapped and unable to heal while the daggers remained in the wounds.

The boys began to mimic Kiana's strategy, and before long, another beast was impaled with a crunching sound as a blade was forced through its skull and driven into the ground by the brunette boy.

'Dalin!' Kiana shouted at the brunette boy, as she ran with two Evexus on her tail. 'Catch!' she called.

She threw his sword and her burning torch to him before she drew her bow and loaded it quickly with an arrow. She fired her arrow directly into the chest of the beast gaining on her fastest, and it careened wildly away from her with a yowl.

Not hesitating, she again loaded her bow in readiness and ducked under the legs of the next charging beast, squatting down calmly as its massive legs passed over her head. She then fired her arrow straight into the back of its head so that it collapsed into a thrashing heap, sending scorched dirt everywhere.

Kiana began conferring a plan of some sort to Dalin, and before Agrona's eyes, her master was insulted as his creations laid disabled in the dirt.

No, no, no, she thought to herself with each wing beat.

Oh, the battle would begin for real now.

CHAPTER FIFTY ONE

Dalin

Kiana sprinted in my direction, free for the moment of pursuers.

'It's time for you and Noal to get the horses.'

'And you?' I wheezed.

'I have a plan. But make sure you retrieve my sword from that thing's head before you go.'

I waved my hand at her in exasperation. 'If we're getting ready to ride, what will you be doing?'

'I'll draw all of the beasts to me in the centre here, so I'll need you two and the mares safe and ready for us to flee. I may need help at that point. Use the liquid in the red bottle in my healer pack to quench a small span of the flames,' she instructed inflexibly, glaring in a way that suggested I had no choice but to do as she said.

'You can trust in me,' I responded reassuringly.

'I know,' I heard her pant before she turned and began running back toward the beasts that had plucked the arrows from their bodies and had started to thrash upright again.

She dodged them easily, darting and running around them, and they were forced to follow her in chase like confused puppies.

She ran toward where Noal was being tossed around by his beast, and she sliced across its back with an arrow in her hand.

Its attention immediately turned to Kiana as it registered how the other beasts all seemed especially intent on her too. It dropped Noal with a squeak to the ground and joined in the chase of Kiana, who truly was the most dangerous of our group.

I sheathed my own sword and then yanked Kiana's blade out of the skull of the flailing beast in front of me, and didn't wait for it to start to heal itself. Kiana would gain its attention somehow.

I discarded the torch and ran back to where Amala and Ila were huddled in complete terror. But they didn't bolt or buck as Noal joined me, and I tied Kiana's

158

sword safely down before mounting.

'Kiana says she has a red bottle that can clear a way out of the flames,' I puffed to Noal, watching as the screeching pack of beasts tried to catch a dodging, spinning, arrow firing Kiana.

'How is a red bottle going to save us?' Noal panted back incredulously. 'Gods give me strength.'

I rummaged in her healer bag and pulled out a bottle with red glass.

'That looks explosive,' Noal groaned, but we kicked the horses into action and galloped across to the opposite side of the circle from where Kiana was madly shooting her arrows.

From Amala's back I quickly uncorked the bottle and poured the gluggy liquid straight over a length of the flame, breaking the perfect ring of fire with a doorway.

We rode out into the darkness and safety beyond the circle, but still felt the terrible intensity of the arena as we watched Kiana wrench her daggers free of the final pinned beast so that she now had all five of them chasing her.

We watched, dumfounded, as the raven above shrieked in fury. Vicious wings swooped with rage, and cries of spite echoed piercingly above the scene.

Then suddenly I felt an odd surging density in the air—as if I were being pulled at or the atmosphere was building in pressure. It was a foul kind of thick sizzling that I could almost taste, and that left a toxic residue.

'Can you feel that?' Noal whispered anxiously, gazing at the sky and the raven with dread.

'Gods,' I moaned. 'Of course the Witch wouldn't let us just best her pets and then leave.'

And Kiana had certainly known that and had sent Noal and I away.

The intensifying heaviness in the air made it feel as if the Gods were compressing the entire world.

Then an abrupt explosion burst from the raven, and a wave of sound and light tore the night.

Wind gusted against us and Amala reared in fright as a great bolt of red lightning split the sky, forking downward with an audible crackling and sizzling sound. It struck the ground hard, ripping the dirt and sending ash flying from the impact. A smoking crater was left in its place, and though it had missed Kiana, one of Agrona's own beasts had been thrown backward by about ten yards. It shrieked horribly in pain and the raven screeched in fury.

A second red bolt rent the night and the raven's rage was almost tangible as Kiana dived out of the way at the last moment again, leaving only the beasts who had been on her tail in the line of fire. Now another two beasts had lost their balance and were scratching at their startled ears and eyes.

'Gods!' Noal echoed as we both tried to control Ila and Amala, and as we felt another building surge of power.

The gravity of the world seemed to pull upward for a moment, up to the raven. Then there was the release.

Another red bolt ploughed down from the sky like deadly rainfall, exploding into the ring of fire. Another, and another in quick succession.

Red forks were appearing from nowhere, tearing at everything in their path and hitting beasts instead of Kiana. Vortex, twister-like winds were bursting outward from each boom of magical lightning, whipping at us so strongly that I strained to keep Amala steady even from where we were.

Yet soon Agrona's relentless, blind attacks had left all of the beasts sizzling on the ground, trying to rise or writhing with the unnatural electricity that licked at their skins.

While in the very centre of the circle of chaos, Kiana stopped – the last one standing.

'Is she mad?' Noal yelled over the noise. 'She's going to get hit!'

I held an arm up to shield myself from the ash and dirt whipping through the air. We watched as red bolt after red bolt hit the ground all around Kiana, sending earth and fire exploding into the air. But she paid no heed, simply loading her bow with an arrow.

My heart stopped when I saw her lift her bow to aim at the sky. When she had secured her shot, she fired.

I heard the furious, agonised squawk of the raven as the arrow pierced the breast of the midnight bird. I saw the winged demon plummet from the sky. And then, in an instant, I saw the Witch disappear before hitting the ground.

I saw Kiana suddenly double over with pain, clutching her shoulder as a couple of the Evexus began scrambling their way up.

'Stay here!' I shouted at Noal and kicked Amala into action.

Faster than I had ever felt any horse race before, Amala nearly flew in her effort to reach Kiana. We passed through the opening in the ring of flames, the mare's hooves hardly touching the ground. We skirted around craters in the earth at breakneck speed.

'Kiana!' I yelled and saw her fight to straighten and raise her arm.

I held my own arm out to her as we raced forward, and, not even contemplating missing her hand, I stretched out, leaned forward in the saddle, and finally grasped her forearm, swinging her so that she could seat herself in the saddle behind me.

I felt her arms encircle my waist before I turned Amala back to race us away from our scorched battle field.

CHAPTER FIFTY TWO

The Witch was dragged backward through suffocating layers of the atmosphere as her master's harsh magical grip reached out to grasp her. But all Agrona's mind could fixate on was how that mortal wench had had the nerve to lead the beautiful Evexus around like dumb animals.

And how that mortal wench had shot the Witch of Krall.

Perhaps Kiana truly did have power to take a Sorcerer's dead heart and make it beat too.

Agrona's feathers sparked and smoked as she was mercilessly tossed through the embers of the Other Realm, and yet her innards burned more fiercely than all else as she focused irately on the one who had managed to hurt her. Her gut writhed with boiling knots when she skidded into reality along the cold stone floor of her master's chambers.

She opened her eyes to see the Sorcerer's booted feet, only inches from her face. So close that she could feel the cool of his power radiating from his body and over hers. As if she was lying next to a pillar of ice.

There was no scowl upon his beautiful face. There was no anger, or in fact any feeling in his granite eyes. He actually stooped and bent close to her so that she could see his face.

'You are failing me again,' he said softly, his breath cold on her prickling neck. 'I am displeased.'

He was so flawless, like a perfectly sculpted statue of marble.

'No!' she rasped, made both ecstatic and terrified by him. 'I will still catch them for you.'

'Try, Agrona,' he almost whispered. 'Try.'

Then he wrapped his powerful hand around the arrow buried deep inside his Witch's left lung, and without emotion, he wrenched the arrow out.

Agrona didn't stop the shriek of pain it caused her, as he made no effort to stop the arrowhead from grinding against her bones and tearing through flesh.

She licked her lips and smiled at him hungrily. But before she could touch his cheek, he pushed her back against the stone floor and she was sent hurtling even further—back through space and time to where the Evexus awaited her in confusion, still scorched and smoking.

CHAPTER FIFTY THREE

Dalin

We rode ceaselessly until first light, when Kiana, shuddering in pain against my back, called us to a halt near a stream.

The horses were exhausted, their mouths frothing with foamed saliva and their sides heaving beneath a sheen of sweat.

'Kiana,' Noal said, dismounting and coming over.

I felt her head lift from my shoulder. He held his arms up to catch her and helped her walk across to sit by the stream as I dismounted and led our two sagging mares to the water.

The early sun was bright and warm when Noal and I finished tending Ila and Amala, and sat cross-legged beside our fatigued companion.

'Well,' Kiana visibly composed herself as she held her shoulder. 'We make a fine team. And none of us lost our reason or our lives in the fray.'

Noal grinned back and winced when a split in his lip opened again.

Kiana raised a sliced eyebrow. 'So the Quest is, for now, still alive and thriving. But we can only afford to take a short time to patch ourselves up.'

She gestured for Noal to show her his hand, which was blue and stiff from being squashed by the beast he'd faced.

She was flexing his fingers as I moved to refill our flasks, and after an intense examination Kiana decreed that none of the little bones in his hand seemed fractured. 'Though by the colouring of the bruises it was a close thing,' she observed. 'Your hand was too small for the beast to clasp tightly enough.'

Noal gazed skyward piously. 'Thank the Gods for my petite features.'

She was not worried by a surface wound staining his blonde hair red, or by his swelling eye, but pulled out a flask from her healer bag that could help to ease the cold from the beasts' touch.

'Whiskey!' he husked with delight and went to take another gulp before she retrieved it from him and corked it again.

'That's enough, young man,' she said sternly. 'Your session is now over.' Then she turned to me.

'I didn't get whiskey when I needed heating up last time,' I complained as I came back to them and sat in front of my healer.

'You got a cup of molten lava instead.' Kiana's blue and gold-flecked eyes scanned me for all of my hurts, but I could see her own bent, pained posture and felt a twinge of annoyance that I couldn't do anything to ease her as she was able to ease us.

Her cheek was swollen and scratches and bruises ran along the lengths of her arms and across her collarbone–but her shoulder seemed to be the only true bother for her.

'This will scar,' she commented, clasping my chin lightly with warm, slender fingers and turning my head to the side to inspect a stinging cut.

Noal grimaced guiltily. 'Did that happen when you were helping me? I saw your beast catch you.'

'No, not that one,' I reassured him.

Kiana dabbed with an ointment at the slice across my ear, following down my jaw line. 'This will get rid of anything nasty in the wound. I'll have to put the same on your back.'

Obediently, I untied the front of my shirt and winced as I tried to tug my tunic up over my head. Raw bruises had spread across my chest from when the beast had trapped me under the pressure of its foot at the start of our scuffle.

Noal tutted at the sight of my chest. 'Did I cause those?'

'No, these were my own doing,' I shook my head.

'Still not feeling remorseful then,' Noal smiled and crossed his arms.

Levering my arms to lift the shirt and tunic right off, I felt the cuts on my back stretch further open, and felt the trickling warmth of blood.

Noal whistled and rocked back.

'You did that,' I informed him.

'Great, still no need for guilt then,' he said, his eyes crinkled and mouth scrunched in distaste.

'Turn,' Kiana told me curtly, and I did as I was told.

'What a mess,' she muttered, and I tried not to flinch away as she thoroughly cleaned each slice. 'I've seen whip lashes that have cut as deeply as this once. I can help them heal without infection.' She mercilessly scrubbed out all of the dust and dirt that had become trapped in the wounds while I'd fought. 'This paste hardens a little and should help to seal the wounds quickly and keep them clean.'

She tapped my side, and I carefully turned myself around to face her again, watching her features as she looked at my chest with concentration–her fingers lightly brushing over ribs and tickling over my collarbone.

'No breaks or fractures beneath the bruising, so fortune was on your side too,' she reported.

Then she began cleaning roughly at her own cuts and wounds as Noal scrunched me into a new shirt.

'You look a bit rumpled. But it'll do,' he scrutinized me critically.

'Thanks,' I replied dryly.

After barely a moment's attention to herself, Kiana was satisfied. 'Now we're all in order, we'd best set off once more,' she said, observing the sky.

My attention was drawn to an odd building of dark, surly clouds roiling thickly on the otherwise clear horizon in the distance.

'Looks like a storm has been building over where we came from,' Noal frowned.

'I think that storm could be designed to follow our trail and spread out to reach us,' Kiana grimaced.

'Like it could be purposefully seeking us out?' Noal paled.

'We have been uncommonly blessed so far, and can't count on that to continue,' Kiana told him honestly. 'The Witch underestimated our stealth and then our endurance in a hopeless battle. But we are pitted against magical foes.'

'We have our own strengths,' I mused. 'You made Agrona herself into an irrational liability and a target,' I remarked, and Kiana inclined her head.

'Though from now on I think we must aim to flee across to the southern brink of the Great Forest, which is closest to us if we curve our path. The Forest is less dense and is quicker to travel through at that point, so Ila and Amala will not struggle.'

'It'll also mean we skirt away from Bwintam,' I realised quietly, and she nodded, gazing at the glistening surface of the stream. Dark, scattered rags of cloud were beginning to scud closer to where we were, distorting the otherwise serene reflection on the water.

'Another worthy reason,' Noal agreed. 'I wonder if we can flee both the beasts and the weather.'

However, as the afternoon dwindled the weather continued to take an unnatural turn. The sky became a brooding ceiling of grey that twisted and throbbed above threateningly until the looming storm finally broke and released overwhelming torrents that pelted down over the world like falling arrows.

CHAPTER FIFTY FOUR

Kiana

The wind had groaned, and the rain had been driving down in an unremitting, blurring sheet for all of the night and day. This was no natural miserable rain that obscured and distorted the green plains. It fell onto our skin, saturated us through our cloaks, and seemed to hammer right down to the bone with an icy intensity.

I ran ahead in an effort to lead us safely over uneven ground, though I could hardly see or even breathe through the sheen of water that had replaced our air. Noal huddled close to Ila, his golden hair dripping in torrents while Dalin slouched on Amala, his cloak hood pulled up and his face a bitter grimace as the wet slanted sharply inwards.

I would usually have handled brutal weather and lack of rest easily, but the unnatural power of the tempest beating its gusty fists against us, and the pain growing in my shoulder, seemed to make every step into a murderous sacrifice.

A hazy outline of Great Forest border trees gradually grew in the distance, but as I began to feel some hope, a shattering wave of throbbing agony washed over me, clawing out from the tear drop scar hidden by my wet clothes. And at the same moment, the wailing shrieks of our enemies sliced distinctly over the booming thunder and blustering wind.

The sounds broke out of the gloom impossibly close to us and as my stomach curled and dropped like a stone weight in my middle, I immediately turned to jog backwards and let Dalin wetly clasp my outstretched hand to swing me into the saddle behind him.

I held on with my knees and readied my bow and arrow just as, like shadows separating themselves from the darkness, five monstrous figures appeared at our flanks and at our sides. They surrounded us as though we were sheep to be herded.

Goosebumps exploded all over my skin, with the unrelenting rain gathering force to add to the cold those beasts issued forth. I shuddered, firing an angry arrow out into the night to hear one of the beasts slide along the ground before retaining balance and rejoining the chase.

Ila and Amala hurtled over the wet ground even faster, but the beasts did nothing to attack. They simply pressed closer, their shadowed bodies growing larger as the distance between us lessened.

They weren't close enough that I could reach out with my fingers and touch them. But my teeth chattered, and I shook so uncontrollably that I had to sling my bow back over my shoulder and grip onto Dalin for fear of being swept off Amala by the raging wind as we pounded through the curtains of rain.

I knew that they were forcing us in a specific direction, and away from where I had planned. But we had no choice and were lucky to simply face herding rather than attack.

I scrunched my eyes closed to feel the water rolling down my face and over my eyelids in steady streams. I was aware that, like demon hell hounds herding us through a dangerous frenzy to the Other Realm, the beasts would lead me back to Bwintam in time for my birthday.

We would have no choice but to take shelter there and await Agrona's next move.

My stomach continued to feel like a lead weight was dragging my insides down as we got closer to my destroyed home, and—satisfied—the beasts slowly let the space grow between us. They slowed their pace, no longer chasing, but fading into dark obscurity behind the veils of rain.

Soon when I turned I could only see five indistinct figures standing still in the distance behind us, and as I watched, they seemed to melt away. It was clear, that if we tried to change directions, their figures would reappear to herd us back on the track they had chosen.

I unclenched my teeth and tugged at Dalin's sopping shirt so he would strain to hear me.

'They're gone! We can stop a moment!' I shouted over the howling cries of the wind, and the words seemed to be whipped away from my lips.

Dalin's head rose at the sound of my voice, and he looked about in disbelief before he waved his arm at Noal to gain his attention. They pulled the stumbling, heaving Ila and Amala to a grateful stop, and we slid stiffly from our saddles to fight our way into a tight group.

'What happened?' I heard Noal shout over the wind, though I couldn't clearly make out either of their faces.

'They pulled back! We are now on the course they wanted us to take!' I shouted over the thundering booms of the storm. I peeled the clinging strands of my hair back into a knot that started to loosen and whip about crazily as soon as I let it go.

A huge gust of wind sent me almost stumbling backward, and both Noal and Dalin caught hold of my arms to hold me upright.

'This isn't natural!' Dalin yelled.

'What are we going to do?' roared Noal. 'They've taken us off course, and we need shelter!'

I felt nauseous. 'We have to take shelter in Bwintam's ruins!' I called back, just as Agrona must have wanted. 'Or we won't last.'

And they wouldn't be far away; our devilish guardians.

Dalin and Noal said nothing, but as another huge fist of wind nearly bowled me over, their hands were firm in holding my arms and I stayed upright.

'Come!' I yelled at the top of my lungs. 'Stick together!'

The mares were tossing their heads, and the rain rolled off their backs in cascading waterfalls, but they followed us as Dalin gripped Amala's reins in one hand, and clasped mine in the other. Noal clasped Ila's reins in one hand and mine in his other too.

We moved like that, as a linked chain, constantly fighting and almost leaning and pushing against the rain and wind, while our link never broke.

CHAPTER FIFTY FIVE

Dalin

Kiana squeezed my hand and gestured to the right of us. I managed to make out a half-collapsed fence, nearly overridden by unfarmed wheat grass and weeds. I guessed that this was where Bwintam's first field had started, and I remembered a road should be where we stood, but there was no trace of it now.

My mind then shied away from thinking of the death and horror that had marred this once peaceful place, as a huge gust of wind threw Kiana into my side and Noal and I helped her to get her usually unerring balance back, dragging ourselves onward against the onslaught and through the ensnaring prickles of the wild fields.

Our progress was laboured and slow, but when we began to pass through the remains of Nature engulfed homes, there was no comfort.

Signs of the fire that had destroyed this place still scarred the twisted tree trunks, but otherwise the area was covered in tall weeds, creeping vines, gigantic barbs and contorted, bare bushes that clawed upward with deformed branches.

I could see the Great Forest lurking as a show of vitality and life far away in the distance, and on the border of these village remnants I was sure I could see Kiana's Willow, where she had taken shelter from the Krall attack. But the savage torrents of wind had stripped the nearest trees, and their leaves tore around us in a cruel whirlwind like coloured daggers.

Kiana turned toward the vague forms of dwelling ruins that rose above the weeds, so we staggered toward the empty structures, ploughing our way to one cottage that had an intact roof and that looked stable enough to house the horses and ourselves for the night.

I caught the door which was hanging off its hinges awkwardly, hammering against the wall with loud crashes in the gales of wind. The shutters had fallen away from the windows, blasted inward, into the cottage.

I pushed Kiana in ahead of us and Noal steadied the mares enough to help them squeeze one by one through the door, before I backed my own way in after them.

I dragged the door closed, trying to wedge it shut so that it couldn't beat on its shattered hinges anymore while Kiana forcefully tied the rattling shutters down over the two gaping windows. At once the storm was shut out, and we were left shivering and creating puddles in the dark.

'Look for firewood,' Kiana chattered, and we fumbled our way out of the main space and found that there were only two other rooms in the darkness.

The room we first entered had a bed in it, and Noal broke up the frame so that before long we had a weak fire burning in the stone hearth at the centre of the main room. It cast a wavering light on damp, sullied walls, which looked to have once been whitewashed.

'I've never been so cold in my life,' Noal croaked through blue lips. 'Or wet.' He sank down onto the dirt floor.

'Take off your wet layers and try to dry them by the fire,' Kiana instructed quietly, and she laid her own outer layers of clothing on the dirt before taking wet saddles and packs off Ila and Amala.

We spread out our cloaks and laid in frozen heaps near the fire while Kiana rifled through our weatherproofed bags and found all of our belongings were just as saturated as ourselves.

I shut my eyes as Kiana wrung out her cloak and upturned the bags to pour pools of water out of them, but when I woke, she was no longer in the room.

I groggily pushed myself up and looked about, wincing at the pain from the welts across my back as I dressed once more in damp clothes.

There were rotted tapestries and half broken household items like plates and cups visible in the dirt. The grime caked walls were now decorated with clinging plants that had climbed upward with leafy hands, and the windows were choked with green plant tendrils that were wedged under the shutters Kiana had forced back into place.

I moved quietly past Noal's sleeping form and past where Ila and Amala were clustered together, following a hallway lined with steadily climbing ivy. I glanced around the leaf covered door of the first room, but Kiana wasn't in there, so I turned to the next door, which was slightly ajar at the end of the hallway.

This door was almost completely covered by ivy that leaked down from the top of it and swept all the way to the floor. Through the tendrils, the faint, wavering light of a candle cast a small glow out into the corridor, and I parted the leafy curtain with a swish to step through the opening.

Kiana was sitting on a bed in the middle of what had become an ivy palace. A window and the walls were so overgrown it was as if a giant green net had been cast over them and water drops twinkled and drizzled down from a hole in the roof.

On the dirt floor a grimy lantern with cracked glass created a glow that hardly reached beyond the bed, and the mildewy bed itself was a mound of roots and ivy, as tendrils of creeping leaves entwined around the bed legs, tiptoed up the frame and poured down the wooden head. Little white flowers had budded and opened upon the vines like tiny stars knitted into a green sky. Underneath this green blanket were traces of what had been a white, lacy quilt, which was now so mouldy and damaged that the ivy was growing through it, weaving itself into the material and becoming a part of it.

Kiana was cross-legged and her head was bowed while one of her hands rested on the damaged white cover and the other cradled her shoulder. There was an odd hush in the room, though the storm raged outside, and I wordlessly crossed to sit on the end of the damp bed of lace and ivy with her.

This felt like such a sorrowful place, and I shivered as the water splashed from the hole in the roof and the candlelight flickered weakly around the garden bedroom. And when she finally lifted her chin so that her hair fell away from her face, I saw that her pale cheeks were wet with tears. She seemed unwell and looked right through me.

'Are you ill, Kiana?' I whispered, glancing at her shoulder. Another shiver ran down my spine at the same moment that a chilled breath of air rustled along the green leafy fingers covering the walls.

Her voice was dull when she responded. 'I hurt everywhere all at once. I hurt all over. I hurt on the inside. Being here is just one part of it, but really there's no rest from the hurt.'

Kiana blinked drowsily, half in a dream state.

She held her shoulder as if somebody had broken it, and I saw cuts and welts along her arms, as well as old scars and bruises. But I knew she wasn't talking about any of those pains.

'Try to find rest now,' I told her gently. 'You won't be alone, I'll keep watch.'

She leaned further back into the bed of leaves, silently surveying the green curtains of ivy, and the glistening drops of water pattering down from the roof.

When the candle had burned lower, I heard the faint swish of Noal coming through the ivy at the door. He, too, took in the eerie room and our silence, and crossed to sit beside me quietly.

The candle light was fading quickly in the stillness when Kiana spoke softly once more, her eyes not leaving the droplets of water as they twinkled their way into the dirt.

'What is your age?' she asked.

Her lips were purple.

'We have both reached our eighteenth year,' Noal answered carefully for both of us. I saw a brief flash of colour with the memory of the party Noal and I had shared for our coming of age back in the Palace, surrounded by smiling faces.

'I reach my eighteenth year at midnight tonight.' She ran her fingers over a small patch of clear, lacy bed covering. 'And Joelle would have reached her seventeenth year within a month.'

Kiana paused, gazing at the tendrils of ivy that were swallowing the rest of the bed covering.

'This was her cottage. This was her bedroom. And this was her bed.' She dragged herself backward, wincing, and leant into the stream of ivy behind her, looking like a Queen leaning upon a throne of green. 'We used to pretend this was her wedding gown.' Kiana drowsily stroked the lace cover with her fingertips again, closing her eyes and shivering.

After a while she became still and her breathing became even with sleep as she rested upon the pillow of leaves.

The ivy in the room rustled as another icy breath of air issued through the hole in the roof. It stirred the leaves on the bed, along the walls and at the door, making each green finger wave and whisper.

The light of the candle died as if a ghost had stirred in the room, and Kiana looked faintly blue now. The ivy she laid upon twisted a green crown of leaves through her midnight hair and over her arms and legs, as if it was trying to take hold of her just as it was creeping over the whole cottage to make it disappear.

I shuddered suddenly and pushed myself off the bed. I quickly stooped over Kiana, swept my arms under her legs and around her shoulders and lifted her. She didn't stir but felt chilled to the touch.

'I don't like this room,' Noal shivered in agreement and quickly pulled the creeping ivy that was veiling the door aside for me to pass through. Once I was through with Kiana he came out behind and shut the leafy door on the cold, still room forcefully. The ivy's fingers were jammed in it tightly, and he hurried to follow me out of the hallway.

CHAPTER FIFTY SIX

Noal

We remained helpless and in need of shelter as the storm continued to rage, and there had so far been no signs of our enemies. So we wrapped Kiana up beside the fire and left her in peace. She did not stir in her slumber for the rest of our first night in Bwintam and the following day.

I was sharpening my sword and Dalin was brushing down Amala when we finally heard a sigh from Kiana.

'Good morning,' she greeted us lethargically.

'Good afternoon,' Dalin corrected and answered her at the same time.

She frowned.

'We decided not to wake you and enter the wrath of the storm again,' he explained calmly.

She sat herself up, still wrapped in our cloaks. 'I've held us back,' she said blankly.

'No,' I smiled at her. 'It's still too wet for me out there.'

'And the horses were too fragile to be back on the trail just yet,' Dalin added, flopping a cajoling arm over Amala's shoulders. Amala flicked an ear with disinterest.

'You're going to blame the horses?' Kiana asked.

'Entirely.' Dalin asserted. 'They're slowing the team.'

Amala peered back over her shoulder at him and he smiled winsomely at her. She snorted in his face and went back to chewing at the bent grass that was jammed in one of the windows.

'They're very touchy about it,' Dalin explained laconically, wiping his wet face and smoothing his hair.

Kiana moved to sit in the warmth created by Ila as the bay laid stretched out in a corner. Amala at once left Dalin's brushing so that in the end, Kiana nestled between the two mares and they nickered comfortingly at her.

Kiana seemed soothed, and it was a while before Dalin glanced back across to her. She was still tucked amongst the horses, but she was staring intensely at something held in her hands. She looked shaken.

'What is it?' Dalin asked, his previously light voice suddenly concerned.

She didn't break her gaze from whatever she was holding.

'Kiana?' I asked.

'It's alright,' she finally lifted her eyes away from what was in her hand. 'Perhaps I'm not adjusted to inaction. I'm imagining things and getting as eccentric as Gangroah's old Gloria,' she held up her hand to show us her Unicorn figurine. 'As I held this, I thought I felt a spark of heat emit from it,' she explained.

I remembered she had been given that figurine as a gift for her birthday, and that it was her birthday now once again.

Dalin rose and crossed to her. 'Come, sit by the fire,' he encouraged, and held out his hand to pull her up from the protective circle of the sleeping mares. But when she held out her hand to him, he looked at it closely with surprise. 'There is a red mark on your palm!' he exclaimed.

'I probably held the figurine too tightly,' Kiana answered, her voice uncertain.

Dalin drew her to the fire, but instead of sitting, she tucked the Unicorn back into one of her dried packs, and lifted one of her daggers from where it had been set aside.

Kiana traced the flat edge of the blade. 'I'm restless. Perhaps I could go out to scout the area, or to find us some fresh meat.'

'We have biscuits and dried food in our packs,' Dalin told her, not sitting down either.

'It can no longer be classified as dried after the downpour we went through,' she raised an eyebrow.

'Don't worry,' I implored. 'I ate some before and I'm fine.'

Kiana smiled her half smile, but looked towards her cloak. 'Even if I don't find us game, it would be good to see if the storm has abated enough, or if trouble is about. I don't like waiting to be sprung upon.'

'Kiana, it's not wise to leave our shelter now,' Dalin reasoned with her earnestly. 'We know the storm is still dangerous, and we would have no advantage stumbling through it blindly. You would also fare no better if you did find the Witch, or went through the ruins to see things that you don't really want to see. Try to think only of what is best for the survival of our Quest.'

Kiana's shoulders slumped slightly. 'You're right,' she agreed finally. 'We're helpless and at the mercy of the storm and what the beasts desire.'

'What do you usually do when you have too much energy?' I asked to change the topic. 'Apart from going for a hunt and killing something nasty,' I added hastily.

Kiana frowned—but allowed herself to be diverted and balanced the hilt of her dagger on a fingertip before bouncing it up and catching it in the air. 'I train.'

Kiana proved herself to be a patient teacher as we both eagerly took part in distracting her. She demonstrated and guided us through drills that seemed to match an expert dancer's moves, albeit a dancer who was also skilled in wielding deadly weaponry. Her movements were captivating and fluid, and Dalin and I became genuinely absorbed in trying to mirror her talent.

The repetitive drills all noble boys completed each morning back at the Palace could hardly be called elegant. But then, we'd never had to train alone, and this independent weaponry dance incorporated fighting stances, as well as being focused on careful movement and exertion.

A mist of sweat covered my brow, and I had forgotten the horrible wailing of the storm as she guided me to lean at an angle that made my core burn as I held the weight of my sword.

'You must begin slowly to wake your muscles and teach them to be controlled in their pace and movement. It takes discipline to keep the movement steady despite the weight of your weapons,' Kiana explained as she tilted Dalin's shoulders for him. 'You must continue breathing evenly and soundlessly to practice stealth.'

She moved now to extend my arm unbearably slowly, so that I understood the challenge, and I saw Dalin shaking with the effort to maintain balance and the slowed pace as he completed the movement at the angle she'd set for him.

'Your speed only increases as your heart beat does. It becomes your personal rhythm,' she advised.

'My heart is already rebelling,' I puffed.

'Control your breathing, or you'll give yourself away to your invisible enemy,' she told me with her half smile, and I tried to stop inhaling gulps of air so noisily.

'Your breathing must always be regular. And when you do quicken your speed, you must continue to be infinitely precise in each movement and in fluidity, while maintaining silence.'

Dalin's expression was intense as he grimaced and raised his sword. The sword tip was shaking more than he liked.

But when Kiana stood on the other side of the fire, the flames looking as though they danced about her legs, and started the weaponry dance properly for herself, we both stopped to watch; entranced.

I saw her breaths, and her careful rhythm as she followed the steady, musical drumming that guided her in her chest. And the precision of each movement was so clear as to be almost audible.

It seemed suddenly that I had never seen such a beautiful and accurate demonstration of the distinctive and powerful movements that I'd previously only considered to be mindless drills.

Like ripples across a lake, Kiana swept the shining sword directly, slowly away from herself while she drew her dagger upward to point to the roof. Her arms were straight and unwavering. But before fully locking into that position, they were already sweeping out in front of her body, the blades glinting in the firelight.

When she gradually built into a flurry of action, I became breathless myself, as lost in the noiseless fight as she was and Dalin was. I could almost picture the invisible enemy she fought, defensively blocking and attacking in a blur of action until her dance was ended with a ferocious lunge–leaving us gaping and with our own weapons now trailing in the dirt as we stared.

'You were both doing quite well, until you stopped,' Kiana broke our reverie, and straightened from her stance to stow her weapons away once more. 'And it feels much more beneficial to end in a more empowered position when you do decide to finish.'

We both immediately shook ourselves and puffed up our chests with vigour as we sheathed our own blades.

'One day I would like to learn to do that properly,' Dalin told her enthusiastically as we returned to being seated at the hearth.

'We'll try to find time to work on it,' Kiana granted, massaging her shoulder and looking more awake than ever.

'Ready to go to sleep now?' I asked hopefully, flopping down on my cloak. 'We'll have a nice big day of fleeing the enemy tomorrow.'

She grimaced.

Dalin leaned across to where Kiana was still rubbing her shoulder. 'Let me try,' he said, and she didn't give him her usual wary glare.

He pushed her hair away from her shoulder and started to gently massage the muscles there. At once her frown of discomfort cleared with relief. 'Harder,' she murmured, closing her eyes.

'You know, Noal,' Dalin said as he kneaded her shoulders. 'I'm starting to think that it's not actually you who smells like a rosebud in this team.'

'Well it sure in the Gods' names was never going to be you,' I huffed.

'But how can Kiana smell like flowers all the time?' he asked, ignoring me.

'Perhaps she eats them,' I supplied, rolling onto my stomach lazily.

Kiana didn't reply, but seemed much more at ease as she relaxed with the massage, so I no longer felt concerned at her restlessness.

I sank into sleep for the night, and Dalin must have soon done the same, because neither of us heard Kiana leave.

We didn't feel the blast of wind or the spray of rain that flashed upon us for a moment as she opened and slipped through the door; quietly closing herself out into the loneliness of what had been Bwintam.

CHAPTER FIFTY SEVEN

Kiana

I couldn't sleep through the storm howling around me and inside of me at the same time. And I couldn't sleep... because I had a growing sensation that something was calling to me.

My leg muscles bunched in restless frustration, wanting to carry me away. My heart seemed to be lifted in my chest, as if invisible fingers were pulling it upwards to make me rise. My teeth gritted on edge and I bunched my hands in agitation until I could stand the odd feeling no longer. I felt compelled to move.

I wrapped my hair into a tight bun, laced my boots and fastened the tie of my cloak about my neck. Each of my weapons felt as if they had returned home; part of me, as I secured them all in place.

I hushed Amala when she lifted her head to eye me mournfully, and I subdued a strange feeling that I wouldn't see her for a while as I swept past the sleeping forms of Noal and Dalin. They wouldn't understand this. I couldn't wake them.

I felt as if a spirit was tugging at my collar, beckoning for me to go out into the storm. Beseeching me.

I quietly opened the door, and the fire whipped about as the moaning wind gushed inwards. Then I closed the warmth in behind me and I was alone again in the graveyard that had been my home, already saturated to the bone once more.

The rain seemed almost spiteful and the stars were veiled by rags of black rain clouds that dragged moodily across the sky. But, following the deep urge to move onward, I started to fight my way against the wind through what had been the village square. I struggled across the dark grounds, tangling and untangling myself in grass and weeds, moving ever forward in a sure, straight line. And as soon as I saw the Willow I knew that it was to there that I was being drawn.

I forgot the raging storm and the effort it took to claw through the wild growth, continuing intently until I stopped at the Willow's familiar roots and gazed up at those protective boughs. I felt removed from myself, as though I were watching from afar and had been wiped blank.

THE LAST
LARNAERADEE

Numb, empty, calm – I ran cold fingers over the wet, knotted trunk, feeling the rough, gnarled surface. And I remained completely unmoved, even when the surface before me began to shift, to take on the tough features of a wisened wooden face.

I had somehow known all along that the Willow was more than she had seemed, and I was not afraid.

Kiana. Heavy wooden lips formed creaking, whispering words, and a smile of relief grew upon my lips.

'What are you?' I breathed the words, not registering the chill or the fury of the storm at all anymore.

I am a Dryad, and friend ever of your kind. Each word seemed to rustle and to come from far away. But each word was filled entirely with kindness and warmth.

'Why have you not revealed yourself before?' I asked wonderingly. 'I grew up playing in your branches and beneath your shade.'

Your time for knowing such things had not yet come. Your own mind and magic were not ready. Now, your time and need has come. You must heed my advice.

'What advice would you give me?'

Flee at once from this place, for it is marked by evil. Make haste to Sylthanryn and find yourself truly. Then you can be the One to end the darkness.

'We are to leave for the Great Forest tomorrow,' I told her. My voice, my mind, was so steady.

You must leave this night. Already the Witch recovers. Even now she approaches. You cannot yet face her in earnest. You are not ready to match her darkness.

'I must go back to get us ready to leave,' I replied, and at once I felt a warm rush of energy burst around and through me. Suddenly our packs had materialised at my feet.

'What about my companions and the mares?' I asked.

Call, and they will hear and come forth.

'I am not magical as you are, Willow. I cannot send out my power.'

You are the One oft told of. In Sylthanryn, you will learn this.

'I'll bring our group back here for our belongings,' I promised. 'Then we'll risk our journey to the Great Forest once more.'

But as I turned to leave, a shudder ran from every root to branch tip of the Willow. Her leaves fluttered and a groaning creak ran through her trunk as if she were suddenly in pain.

Abruptly the serenity that had blanketed me suddenly broke, and I felt with sick realisation that darkness was approaching, just as the Willow had warned.

You must leave now, the Willow's voice groaned.

'It's too late,' I murmured, and grimly drew my sword.

Agrona was coming, I could feel it.

An odd prickling feeling rippled over my dripping body, becoming sparks of agony in my shoulder.

Then I blinked, and found her standing quite still, just feet away.

'Well met once more. My friend.' The words curled from poisonous lips, radiating malice and foul intent.

I realised that somehow the storm wasn't touching Agrona, and she stood poised in the darkness, watching with glittering, evaluating eyes like a snake coiled to strike.

'Did you enjoy the arrow, friend?' I asked, my world spinning as I faced her squarely.

'You did not play nicely, Kiana,' she almost purred, and advanced with a slight step forward.

I had to force myself not to step backward in response. 'I did not follow fair rules,' I agreed stoutly. 'But you, yourself, follow none.'

Agrona tilted her lovely chin to look down at me. 'No. I make the rules. And you have followed my rules so well until now. Lost and alone. For so long.' She stepped closer again. 'But now that you've found solace with others, I'll have to take them from you too, because my rules are sweet and absolute.' Closer.

I lifted my sword.

'That won't do much good,' she smiled, and at once my shoulder seemed to explode. As if she had plunged her own hand into my flesh to pull the grisly bone and socket out in that white fist.

The sword dropped from my grip and I collapsed to the ground.

'Hold still,' the Witch crooned, advancing until she could press her hand to my forehead. 'This may hurt.'

Agrona's touch sent me into a writhing fit and the red magic flowed cruelly into me like water rushing in to suffocate a drowning victim. It surged through her fingers, through my flesh, through my skull, and in, in to darken my mind. Madness, vapours in my head, in my brain, like disease.

And she toyed with my memory until my eyes filled with the vision of a small boy screaming.

Tommy was so beautiful. But he was screaming.

He looked at me as he screamed. Then he wasn't screaming anymore.

He was laying in the dirt. His eyes were still open. But he wasn't moving.

Blood was gushing from a slit made in his tiny neck and his face was turning blue.

Suddenly he sat up, blood still pouring from his throat, down his ragdoll body. He gazed at me with his beautiful, innocent face. And his eyes were so sad.

'Why didn't you help me?' he asked, in his high tearful voice. I groaned out loud as my patched heart began re-breaking.

The Witch's fingers dug more deeply into my temples and my little Tommy reached his arms out to me. He had a hole in his belly, and punctures littering his small chest.

'Why?'

Something inside me broke with a physical snapping sensation as I began to convulse. And a scream of anguish louder than the storm rose high and terrible from the pit of my stomach to flood out of my mouth.

It was a scream of grief that rang right from my soul.

CHAPTER FIFTY EIGHT

Dalin

Noal and I both woke with a start to the scream, looking wildly about the cottage.

Kiana wasn't sleeping across from us anymore.

'The packs are gone!' hissed Noal.

Only our swords and the travel stained clothes we had worn that day remained in a heap next to the nervous looking mares.

The scream had stopped, and I had an awful feeling, as though I were about to lose something important. I jumped up and dressed frantically.

'What do you think has happened?' Noal gasped as he did the same.

'I don't know,' I grunted. 'There's no time to saddle the horses, they'll have to stay.'

He belted his sword around his waist and rushed with me to the door, which nearly tore out of my hands when I pushed it free, before we both stumbled out of the safe light of the cottage and into the storm.

'Kiana!' Noal and I shouted over the gale, but we could barely hear our own voices or see through the sleeting rain.

Our progress around the ruins was agonising until we paused at the heart of what had been the village square. Then I nearly fell forward as, in an unexpected and abrupt instant, the storm abated.

I stopped in my tracks to hold my head, wondering if I had been struck deaf.

Noal slapped wetly at his own ears and shivered with wide eyes. 'That can't be natural, and can't be good,' he whispered through what was now just a soft mist of rain.

I peered through the darkness desperately. 'Let's try this way,' I croaked, and began to move off before I was tugged back by Noal's vice-like grip tightening around my wrist.

'What?' I hissed.

'Over there,' he groaned back.

I followed his horrified stare with a sickening sinking feeling that took over the little gap in my abdomen where my stomach should be.

At the end of the grassy lane, surrounded in the collapsed forms of what had once been the homes of those now dead, was a little girl.

Her hand rested upon a broken fence and her feet stood perfectly sure inches above the weeds and grass. An ethereal light illuminated outward from her glowing hair, skin and dress. Despite the light giving shape to her features, I could see right through her translucent body, and I could see that there was a hole in her back.

Dread swamped me as her colourless eyes regarded us without emotion.

'What do we do?' Noal whispered desperately as the little girl stared.

'Ignore it. We have to find Kiana,' my voice wavered. I started to back away, dragging Noal after me.

'I think I'm lost,' the little ghost suddenly sighed through colourless lips.

'Why did this happen to us?' groaned another voice, echoing, but close at the same time.

Noal and I whirled around and drew our swords simultaneously.

A beautiful woman pulled herself up out of the grass but a yard away from us. She glowed as hauntingly as the little girl did behind us. A split tore her flesh from navel to chin and her limbs were at odd angles. 'Won't you save me?' she asked, broken arms bending awkwardly out to us.

We both dodged away, but our escape was cut off as another form gripped his way up from the earth to float in our path. A broad, strong young man. Dead.

'Am I going to die?' he asked, looking down at his gruesome injuries. 'I don't want to die.'

'Where is my son?' begged an elderly woman who was missing half of her head.

'Where is my mama?' sobbed a toddler, an arrow sticking out of his throat.

'Help us!' a large man groaned.

'Will I be alright?' cried a woman as she clutched at a split in her side.

The night was suddenly filled with slain, glowing figures as more and more deformed shapes floated up from the ground. The air was torn by cries, shrieks, sobs and pleas for aid as the beings surrounded us, pressing in. The dead of Bwintam.

I grabbed Noal's wrist in one hand and swung my sword into a man without any legs floating closer to me. He shrieked and burst into a thousand pieces of cracked light before dissipating.

I dragged Noal behind me, swinging my sword crazily in front to keep the freakish ghouls back, and we burst away from the forms in a sprint. We pounded together toward the dark mass of trees near the border of the village, and I looked back only once.

I didn't stop as I saw more ghostly forms floating up to join the sea of others massed and following us. Their cries of torment and fear rose, with their voices joining so that we were followed by a heart wrenching orchestra of gibbering yowls.

I pushed Noal in front of me and we sprinted across the open plains in terror until I saw the majestic Willow from Kiana's story. Barely thinking, I swerved us toward it as the pale, ghostly light grew and the dead kept following.

But as we drew desperately closer, and the emanating light of the spirits illuminated the Willow, I was suddenly struck by the sight of a female figure beneath that tree. And it wasn't Kiana.

'Oh Gods!' Noal gasped in shock as he made out the dark figure watching us now too.

Noal and I tried to skid to a stop with wheeling arms, no longer caring that there were ghosts behind us. Because, though we had never seen the woman under the tree in human form, we knew immediately who she was. And, even more confusing, we could see the face in the tree behind her.

We yelped helplessly as, before we could change our course, the Witch raised her hand and gestured as if asking for us to join her. At once an incredible force seemed to sweep around us, invisible fists of the Witch's magic that threw us up into the sky and pulled us forward through the air.

I roared in horror as we flew rapidly in an arc, kicking and struggling uselessly across the distance toward the Witch. We rushed in a blur right up to her, yelling and fighting–only to be brought to an abrupt stop, caught rigidly like insects in a web.

We had touched down, jerking to a standstill, but it felt as though my legs had been encased in stone, and the air around my arms was so heavy that they couldn't budge. I cursed and struggled madly, hearing Noal gasp and curse too.

You will not harm the Three! a strange whispery voice demanded, and I registered that it was the great Willow that spoke.

'Your companions have joined us, Kiana,' Darziates' creature smiled wickedly, and I saw Kiana's slumped, unmoving figure behind the Witch's feet. 'It won't be long now.'

Agrona gestured to us then. 'Don't struggle. I've got you.'

Then the Witch held up her hand towards the glow of the advancing dead, so that the yowling crowd stopped approaching immediately to wait. But in their light I saw Agrona stoop to stroke Kiana's face.

'It looks like this could turn out to be quite the reunion for you,' the Witch trilled, and at her slight touch, Kiana's back arched unnaturally, as if her body was controlled by a marionette master.

I gritted my teeth in fury and started to struggle against the invisible power holding me back once more.

'I'll let you join your people, just as you once wanted,' Agrona promised Kiana soothingly, and she reached out a skeletal hand–pressing it into Kiana's shoulder.

Kiana's body jerked and she let out a horrible, pain filled cry. Her back arched again, and she thrashed desperately in agonised convulsions.

'Leave her!' I shouted in outrage, straining so hard to reach Kiana that I managed to move forward a step.

'Why?' the Witch asked. 'She wanted this.'

Agrona stood and Kiana immediately fell back into the grass.

'She doesn't anymore,' Noal growled beside me.

'Hmmmmm,' Agrona smiled slowly, the sharp edges of her painted lips curling dreadfully upward as she left Kiana to stalk toward him.

'Kiana's got us now,' I quickly added, trying to draw her away from Noal.

'She had you,' Agrona asserted, reaching for me instead.

I swallowed nervously, feeling invisible, churning waves seeming to ripple through the air about her, stealing my breath and dazzling my mind. Her fingers rose to hold my face for a moment and I flinched under even that quick touch, dazed by an overwhelming vision of decay.

I could hear Noal thrashing beside me, and I could also dimly hear the inexplicable creaking voice of the Willow, but all I could do was try to blink my vision clear and focus on more than just the icy burn searing across my cheek from where her fingers had briefly rested. I could taste the rottenness of her power on the back of my tongue, like sick bubbling on my tastebuds.

I felt her face draw close to mine, and my skin bristled and stung as her breath brushed against my lips, as if next she wanted to kiss and end me. I shuddered with revulsion, unable to recoil.

Then there was the distinct song of a blade being drawn.

The Witch hissed and I felt the relief of her face drawing back from mine as her eyes widened in shock and she whirled to face the threat.

Somehow Kiana was standing, sword in hand. And she lunged suddenly for the Witch with her blade.

Agrona was caught off guard, but spun hastily out of the way and threw a flash of burning red light in Kiana's direction. Kiana easily lifted her sword and sliced through the magic, letting it explode in sparks over her blade.

Agrona laughed with self-assurance. 'You will die.'

Kiana inclined her head. 'It just proves that you were mistaken not to kill me two years ago,' she reasoned, circling around so that the Witch moved unconsciously too—away from us.

'It proves only that I kill!' Agrona shrieked, her mask of calm breaking with fury. 'Your entire village is evidence of that! Your world is full of the ones I've killed!'

Agrona waved her hand in a whirlwind gesture, and at once the glow of the ghosts started to grow again, and their voices grew louder.

Kiana turned, horrified as she became aware of her people, her dead, sweeping in like the tides. They flooded about us in moments, reaching out pleadingly and pressing in—one little ghost boy's translucent, glowing hand now nearly touching

Kiana's cheek.

Kiana was transfixed as Agrona started to sweep toward her again with wolfish delight, but I vaguely noticed the wavering voice of the Willow trying to break through the noise of the surging figures.

Look closely, Kiana! The voice was crying. *See clearly the truth!*

Agrona's bony fingers were curling, readying with magic, but Kiana tore her eyes away from the ghouls and squinted at the Willow, listening to the creaky words with a frown. Her eyes flickered back to the little ghost boy, then focused more closely on all the illuminated ghosts as they swarmed in chaotically.

Suddenly relief fluttered across Kiana's face. She fearlessly waved away the white form of the little boy, as if he was nothing more than smoke.

'That's impossible,' Agrona gasped incredulously, her steps faltering. 'Their touch is poison!'

'Perhaps they'd have been potent if I'd believed in them. But you made a mistake,' Kiana told the confounded Witch simply. 'I recognise none of these figures.'

I gasped in understanding, but Agrona drew back from Kiana, suddenly unsure.

'No mortal can see through my tricks...'

But as the Witch whirled around, the glowing figures began to fall apart, melting into white shapes in the air. Their voices started to fade as they bobbed in uncertainty, bumping each other in confusion.

Agrona roared and threw her arms upward violently. Two things instantly followed her motion: the storm burst back to life as the sea of spirits dissipated into nothingness. And Kiana was thrown up into the air.

With a fiercely clenched fist, Agrona punched the air and Kiana flipped wildly higher. Then the Witch brought her fist roughly downward and Kiana plummeted at incredible speed, falling and twisting, only to be jolted to a halt–suspended an arm span away from the ground.

With a motion, Agrona lifted Kiana and turned her to hang upright in the air. Then the Witch threw back her arm as though reaching over her shoulder for a weapon. As she drew her arm downward a sword seemed to appear in her hand out of thin air and she moved toward Kiana.

Kiana's heated gaze never faltered. But the Witch did, when an incredible, booming voice nearly threw her from her feet.

YOU SHALL NOT HARM THE ONE!

The ground shook and the gale force created by the shout knocked Noal and I out of the air. We suddenly found ourselves freed, but now soaring backwards, seeing blurring rotations of the grass below and dark clouds above as we were blown like toppling leaves in the wind.

At last I bounced and skidded to a stop beside Noal, where we both dizzily sat up, gasping and holding our heads.

'How are our necks not broken?' Noal puffed in wonder, looking at grass stains rather than mortal wounds covering his body. 'How did the Witch not kill us?'

'What in the Gods' names...' I gaped across the distance at the sight of the Willow. A powerful silver light was emanating from its trunk now, and unlike the false glow that the ghosts had created, this illumination was pure and overwhelming. It spread in increasing strength to brighten the night, and everything the light touched seemed to become clean and fresh.

In complete awe, we watched the Willow's roots break from the ground. Its creaking trunk swayed and stretched out, and its arm-like branches reached for the Witch.

Agrona shrieked in terror, sending blasts of red magic into the face of the Willow while roots as thick as normal-sized tree trunks wrapped themselves like snakes about her waist and legs. Quickly the Witch was enveloped by branch fingers and gnarled, leafy arms.

'Let's go,' a voice from behind us said calmly.

We whipped around to find Kiana with sword in hand.

'Kiana!' I groaned in relief.

'Tree! It's talking! Battling the Witch... magic!' Noal stuttered in disbelief.

'We have to leave for Sylthanryn now,' Kiana told him steadily. 'The Willow can't fight the darkness forever. She can only slow Agrona down. And the Witch is too strong for any of us to face.'

'Ila and Amala?' Noal blurted, still in a state of loss.

'We'll have to leave them. I have our packs,' she said with a grim face. 'Let's go.'

The bellowing screeches and blasts of power colliding against each other were loud enough to shake the foundations of the earth. Explosions of silver and red dazzled my eyes, but Kiana slung her packs over her shoulder and we followed her lead speechlessly while the ground lurched under our feet.

We ran, hand in hand, against the wind and rain and through the lightning and thunder until the flashing battle and the explosions of power were far behind us.

CHAPTER FIFTY NINE

Agrona's eyes were wide as she turned to see the glaring eyes of the Willow. The tree entity had truly, finally awoken now—after years of inaction. And too late, the Witch realised that the first place that she should have sunken her sword into was that wooden face.

Her three prisoners had been freed and lost, and Agrona was wide mouthed as she saw Kiana stand and dust herself off not far away. The girl looked from the Willow to Agrona and made a graceful bow to the Willow before walking away.

Agrona could do nothing, though, as the earth beneath her began to surge. A silver light, brighter and more horrible than anything Agrona had ever seen, was growing from the Willow's roots to its top-most leaves. She had not felt the pure magic of an ancient creature of goodness since Darziates had cleansed the other magical races from this part of the world. And as the night seemed to flee before the Dryad's light, Agrona knew that now she would be the one fighting for her life.

Eyes wide, rotten heart thumping, Agrona lifted her sword, and it burst into red flames. But her conjuring paled in comparison to the brightness of the Willow.

With black hair whirling about her skull-like face, the Witch poised herself, holding her ground as the Willow's roots broke free, the earth simply crumpling away in a rumbling movement.

Agrona didn't wait, but lunged with her glowing, crimson sword, scratching up and down the trunk so that the voice screamed.

The Willow whipped her with a branch, and then tripped her with a root, at once trying to wrap more roots around her body before she could get up.

Agrona blasted the roots away from her torso, turning them into blazing, withering ropes that shrivelled before her eyes. Then she screeched, running forward again to try to hack at the aged face on the trunk once more. She thrust her burning blade deep into one kindly eye, laughing as the Willow tried to pull her away with a branch.

The potent magic burst out of Agrona now like a glowing red dust storm, whipping around the two of them, lighting up the snarl on Agrona's face. The red light swelled gloriously, rushing like a triumphant tornado. The red magic even began to overflow—the darkness oozing out like wisps of smoke from the Witch's nostrils, and it rolled down her face like smoky tears. But Agrona didn't relent, hoping she could at least claim this victory to please her master.

The Willow managed to push Agrona away, and she took the blade with her, wrenching it free savagely so that the entire Willow shuddered.

Agrona was lifted off her feet and swung high into the air by a branch, but freed herself and threw a red lightning bolt so that the Willow nearly lost its strangling grip and toppled like a felled tree for firewood.

The Witch spun and sliced and jabbed and burned, trying with all her might to set the tree alight. But, no matter how hard she tried, the Willow continued to smother her attacks.

The ground rumbled as the two powers clashed in battle. The sky was lit with flashes of red and blasts of silver that could be seen from all across Awyalkna, and that made even the stars themselves cringe and hold tighter to the velvety night.

At last Agrona managed to throw flames into the tops of the charred branches so that the Willow's whole sea of leaves caught fire, but one of the Willow's undamaged roots took a firm grip around the Witch's ankle, and as soon as she had fallen, she knew she had lost.

The Willow pinned her to the ground with massive roots that were intent on strangling her, and she couldn't get away.

One root stabbed its way through Agrona's thigh, and another quickly sliced into her wrist, pinning two of her limbs to the ground. The pure magic was vicious as it flowed into her rotten veins.

More roots as thick as normal-sized tree trunks wrapped themselves like snakes about her waist and legs, pinning her hands too so she couldn't get loose. Agrona felt herself being enveloped by branch fingers and gnarled arms covered in burning leaves. She screamed as she was swallowed whole...

Until, she felt an unexpected blast of comforting malevolence.

One bolt. Stronger than anything Agrona had been able to achieve while fighting the Willow herself.

Then the Willow shivered. And the Dryad began to sag.

Agrona was shrieking as the Willow began to fold in over her. The Witch was still writhing as she felt the familiar rushing sensation and found herself falling backward into the Other Realm.

She was sent soaring across space and time, her limbs ripped free from impalement, before she was slammed hard onto a cold stone floor–and found her King sitting in his steel throne, staring at her coolly.

'You return to me shamed.'

So simple. So scathing.

She felt her world collapsing in. The game had gone wrong. She had failed.

'They are going to make it to the Lady's Forest, where neither you nor I can enter.'

Darziates' voice was even, controlled, composed. His face was blank. But she could hardly breathe with the frothing malice and darkness storming around the large room.

'The five are still there!' Agrona pleaded, 'I will send them on a chase!'

'I will have to send men into the Forest to capture them now.' His eyes pierced her as if she were a pig being spit through the stomach. 'Because you have failed me.'

She scrambled to her knees, grovelling with her head cowed as he watched her impassively. His power swept her easily from the floor and into the stone wall, hard enough for her skull to crack and hard enough for her arm to snap.

Physical injuries could be healed, but the scorn of his punishment, and her disgrace, would take years of recovery.

'Leave.' His voice was low. 'You have proven your magic and your wits to be inadequate.'

She peeled herself from the floor and stood, turning toward the door.

His final words were like lashes across her back. 'This is why you will never be my Queen.'

CHAPTER SIXTY

Kiana

My feet pounded the earth, and though the slippery ground was no longer quaking, every footfall was jarring beyond words.

The night broke into a stormy grey dawn and I tried to forget the impossibilities we'd left behind, and to focus only on the fact that I couldn't stop running, or let go of Noal and Dalin's hands as they gripped mine on either side.

The pain in my shoulder sometimes made me lose clarity and stumble for a moment, but the two strong hands holding mine never let me fall, and the billions of tree trunks spanning before us like a wall of brown and green were now so close.

We were panting and crying out in exhaustion, just a league away from the ancient shelter of Sylthanryn when we heard the chilling calls of the beasts.

Close. And coming fast.

I squeezed Dalin and Noal's hands. 'Run as hard as you can and for as long as you can to the trees,' I called between my gasps. 'Perhaps we can lose them. This is just another chase!'

I heard Noal groan to the Gods over the thunder, but we all let go of each other and somehow managed to increase our pace.

I squinted behind as I ran. The beasts were still just inky specks in the distance. But they were sprinting and leaping closer, gaining incredible lengths of ground with every stride, or loping on all fours like hounds of the Other Realm.

It seemed they were not playing Agrona's odd game of cat and mouse anymore, and would no longer be merely herding us. We were being hunted.

Even as I watched, two of them crouched to the ground and lunged in a spidery jump into the air, arcing across the sky toward us. They would land on our tails.

'Frarshk,' I panted. 'Keep running!' I called to Dalin and Noal, and pushed them forward before I skidded around in time to see the two shadow beasts landing before me.

Long spiked legs straightened from their heavy landings and I unsheathed my sword as my eyes followed their extending height. Then the creatures lashed out.

Instinctively, I dived below them and then swung my sword as they lunged again.

One beast caught my blade in its clawed hand mid swing and wrenched it from my grasp, sending it hurtling all the way to the trees behind us. Then the three others caught up.

It was clear that I couldn't fight the five of these things now. I had only lived previously because I hadn't been taken seriously. Nevertheless, I quickly drew my dagger.

Almost at once I felt the freezing grip of one of the first two beasts close around my waist, and I was hefted from one beast to instantly be caught by another. Another lurched over and seized my feet while a third clasped one of my wrists.

I desperately flung my little dagger about and knew that while it was making slices in the skins of my attackers, there was barely any damage being done. Their icy coldness sent sharp shards of pins and needles throughout my body so that through sheer touch they were delivering more painful blows to me than I could deliver them.

I was wheezing with each useless stabbing motion until finally the other two beasts joined in. One wrapped its clawed hand around my chest while the other clenched my free wrist, and I felt my dagger slip uselessly to the grass below.

Then, purposefully, they began to pull my body taut so I could not even wriggle. Just as their predecessors had done when I'd first saved Dalin and Noal in the woods, these beasts sought to wrench me apart. But this time the injuries would be final.

My mind went blank with the excruciation of being torn in five different directions, but I screamed in agony as I felt my spine, joints and sockets all crackling.

One stray talon would have done it—would have punctured my soft, unprotected body. But the beasts didn't seem to want to take any chances.

This entire scene had only spanned across moments, but I felt aware of each torturous move from the beasts. And I also became aware of a terrible thought—that once they were done tearing me apart, these fiends would move onto Noal and Dalin, and then the Quest would be ended.

Something within me was bolstered and galvanised into mental resistance. I had never let physical pain, or allowed any unnatural beast created by the Sorcerer, to get the best of me.

I felt my jaw clench as I fought unconsciousness. I heard the squelching, snapping sound of my shoulder getting ready to dislocate, then with a pop, my good shoulder was loose. Next, my second shoulder wrenched out of the socket.

Bit by bit, I would break, and so would the Quest...

'No!' my own voice cried out above the pain, and the clouds in my mind cleared with lucidity and need.

Fight! I told myself.

Yes.

Fight.

Live.

Live to fight.

I imagined my burning desire to survive and resist the darkness was being joined with my mother's strength, my father's, and that of everyone I had ever known and loved. Rising as a single goal. That one driving purpose of mine, joined by that of hundreds of others, was so clear. So strong. It tripled my own energy, seeming to gush outward and spread through my body, heating up every muscle fibre, every bone and hair follicle.

It swelled within me so much that I suddenly felt I was on fire with the need. New life burst through my stretched, breaking body, sent out from my mind, and my eyes opened with blazing motivation.

Every ounce of me was concentrated wholly on how I had to be free.

I needed to be free.

I wanted to be free.

Suddenly it was as if white hot sparks were dancing over my skin. I felt my loose shoulders reconnect with the sockets. The arms had somehow been drawn back in.

Each of the beasts lurched forward as if I had yanked them back in close.

A burst of silvery light engulfed us. Lightning from the storm?

I felt clawing hands drop away as if they had been burnt.

Then unexpectedly I was lying upon the lush grass, cushioned safely.

I blinked rain from my eyes and sprang up to find five sprawling bodies scattered over the ground, covered in burns that were already starting to heal. One spiked arm reached to swipe at me weakly.

I didn't pause to wonder. I grabbed my dagger from where it had fallen and shot away from the strange scene to race towards the trees of the Great Forest. I heard a scrambling chase and confused screeches from beasts in pursuit behind me.

I could see Noal and Dalin shouting and reaching out to me from between the trees as I ran for them.

I was spurred on by the sense that one beast was breaking ahead of the others and was reaching out a clawed hand.

I felt the beast grab hold of the end of my cloak which billowed behind as I sprinted desperately, but I felt the material shredding and tearing free.

And then I dived head first into the outstretched arms of my comrades, crashing into them, between the trees and into the Forest.

But as soon as we fell in a heap, there was immediate silence.

CHAPTER SIXTY ONE

Kiana

'What in the Gods' names?' I panted incredulously, looking over my shoulder at the beasts—all snorting and beating manically against the trees.

Dalin and Noal scrambled to untangle themselves, turning to gape at the towering monsters that were gibbering in frustration, ramming at the trunks as if barred by them.

'They aren't following?' asked Dalin in confusion.

'They aren't following!' rejoiced Noal, and they both took hold of my arms to pull me up.

'Why aren't they?' I asked, gasping and wincing as they dragged me back hastily to be cautious.

The beasts howled in outrage and flung themselves towards us again, shaking the trunks ferociously so that leaves dropped and bark splintered from the trees. But somehow they were unable to cross into the Forest.

Together we backed up further, and turned to hurry into the Forest before, in astonishment, we all froze.

The sounds of the raging beasts had been cut off the moment we turned.

Dalin's jaw hung wide. 'Sunshine?' he gasped in shock, looking up to where golden rays streamed through the treetops as if the storm we'd been hounded by outside had never existed.

Noal stared down at himself with boggling eyes. 'I'm not drenched anymore,' he gulped. 'Are we dead?'

'No,' I commented, completely baffled. I turned us back to face the brutish beasts, and we at once could hear the tumultuousness of the outside world.

'They can't enter. The dark magic that made them, and the unnatural storm, don't seem to touch here.'

'Bizarre,' Dalin breathed. 'There have always been myths about a Lady of the Forest protecting Nature here. But let's not test it.'

We hurried from the scene, at once enfolded again in the serene peace of the

Forest, as if everything terrible beyond it had never existed.

'Thank the Gods,' Dalin panted as we moved quickly away. 'Our lives are bombarded with one uncanny occurrence after another, but finally we have a completely positive one.'

'I thought I would never want to walk again during our final dash,' Noal winced and clutched a stitch at his side. 'But I am content to put as much distance between those things and myself as possible.'

'Are we anywhere close to the course you wanted us to take?' Dalin asked, helping me limp over a large, fallen bough.

'We're not at the thinnest part of the Forest, where I'd hoped we'd get to, but I've often wandered through Sylthanryn, and once went right through to Jenra,' I answered. 'So I'm sure we'll find our way.'

'Well, I can see why you would visit this place often,' Noal commented, brushing his fingers over the giant pollen face of a flower that was as large as his head. 'Magic really must be at work here.'

'Perhaps it's as magical as the Willow tree,' Dalin mentioned, shivering a little at the memory.

'It is something to take comfort in,' I soothed, clasping his hand in recognition of just how overwhelming our journey had become, and how impossible it seemed that we had suddenly found a reprieve. 'After all of the signs of evil magic I've come across in my journeys, it's encouraging to know that good magic does exist as well.'

And as we stepped further into the haven of trees, our hurts seemed to ebb away. The sunlight turned golden with the onset of an early summer afternoon, and I finally judged it acceptable to call a halt.

Noal immediately dropped his packs and flopped straight down onto the grass in a patch of sunlight.

'It really does feel safe here,' Dalin agreed speculatively. 'Not like when we could feel the cold of the beasts or the rottenness of Agrona.'

'And I simply must rest a moment, even if we can't trust this tranquillity,' I conceded, my muscles bunching and protesting as I sank down onto a log.

Dalin smiled then. 'This will cheer you up.'

I felt my eyes widen as I noticed that he had tied something at his hip, over his own sheathed sword, and in a moment, he held my sword hilt out to me.

I reached for it gratefully, feeling its familiar, comforting weight fill my hand. 'I had given it up for lost when the beast hurled it away,' I remarked in true delight. 'I'm glad to see it again. It took an age to craft it, and it's like a partner after all the hunts we've had together.'

'Apart from it nearly spitting me when it was tossed my way, it's one of the best swords I've held,' he agreed. 'Especially seeing as you made it,' he shook his head in wonder.

'Flattery doesn't mean you'll get a cheaper price if I forge you one,' I gave him a small smile, sheathing it as he grinned and stretched out on the grass beside my log. 'But when I've patched up our ailments, I'll go catch us something fresh.'

'Thank the Gods,' Noal chirped dreamily. 'A hot meal. I'm salivating.'

'I only have three arrows left though, so we have to be careful. I'll need to reuse any that we shoot for catching food.'

'You should be more careful of yourself. Your patching up might take some time,' Dalin regarded me with his serious green eyes.

'Worse than bandages, I've wrecked another good white shirt,' I yawned. 'I hate mending.'

'Well, perhaps you should take better care,' he suggested, rubbing at the scar that had formed along his ear and narrow jaw line. 'And not let us think you're behind us, when you're actually off fighting five beasts so that we get away safely while you get torn up.'

'That's right!' Noal piped up, dragging himself upright. 'We turned around to see you getting pulled apart and there was nothing we could do about it.' He crossed his arms.

'I apologise,' I responded calmly. 'I wanted to give you both a chance. But I was fortunate to get away with only a few cuts and bruises.' I cringed inwardly at the memory of that one sided fight and looked down at the slices that gaped in my tunic and cut all the way through the shirt into my skin. I knew without looking that my elbows, shoulders, knees, ankles, wrists and waist would be swollen and bruised, but miraculously no serious damage had been done.

Dalin pushed a lock of dark, sweeping hair out of his eyes and rolled onto his back. 'You did give us the chance we needed. But we're meant to be a team,' he said at last.

'I am glad to have a team,' I admitted, and went through my healer pack for a poultice to use on the chilled slits in my skin, feeling comforted by my comrades, and by the beauty of Sylthanryn itself.

CHAPTER SIXTY TWO

He stood with his hands behind his back, under the full glare of the burning sun. The sand at his feet shifted in the hot breeze, every grain like a burning ember. But his focus was on the Dragons, and his eyes pierced through the wavering air as it danced and melted in the heat.

They had grown while he had kept them locked in the wastelands. They had swollen in size, pumped full of his magic, and he considered how ready they were as he watched their gleaming, greyed bodies twist magnificently in the sun.

Darziates judged that the Dragons were prepared enough to be his next move in the war against Awyalkna while he awaited Glaidin and the Awyalknians.

The Awyalknian forces were right now readying to march into his reach for themselves, and all he would have to do would be to seize their Palace, the other mortal lands, and then the magical ones beyond the seas.

Domination rather than death was key. A ruler needed populations alive in order to conquer and unite.

Even as he watched and considered, the Dragons slashed and scorched each other in a thunderous row. The creatures were definitely equipped to be his tool to demoralise the Awyalknians so that mentally they would have already lost the war before their forces finished their long march to his doorstep.

He sent out a mental key to unlock the invisible bonds on two particularly vicious Dragons. They stopped their gnawing and crashing instantly to look about blankly, as Darziates had ensured that they couldn't quite function independently any longer. He forced an image of the location that the Dragons were to seek, and instructions of what the two were to do into their minds. And the brutes pawed at their eyes and heads in a frenzy of pain.

Then the creatures obediently hopped away from their companions, flapping to stretch their wings at last.

There was a cacophony of noise from the others as the two lifted their bloated bodies into the air. Then the wasteland was swept into a sandstorm and covered in soaring shadows as the Dragons finally pushed themselves across the sky like heavy, sluggish swimmers.

'Sire?' a shaking voice called over the dying ripples of air, interrupting his thoughts.

He didn't turn to face the speaker.

'What is it?'

'Sire... the Witch has sent me...'

So Agrona had further damaging news that she did not wish to convey to him herself.

'Speak.'

'She said to inform you that... the five failed, and the Awyalknians are in the Forest...' there was a frightened pause. 'Apologies Sire.'

Darziates had expected this. They weren't the most updated Evexus after all. They were weaker. But no matter, he had recently used Angra Mainyu's help to perfect Agrudek's creatures—beyond any of his and even Deimos' previous models and their short comings. Darziates had only to awaken the new five that he had made, and this time they would not just be beastly imitations. They would be properly possessed by intelligent spirits of the Other Realm; poisonous demons that he had promised freedom to, once they had helped him to become ultimate King.

Angra had certainly become more bestial while the Evexus had become more cunning, but that just made the Warlord endearing. And he would be useful for further experiments quite soon.

'She, ah...' the man coughed. 'The Witch said she would prove herself to you by breaking the barriers and going into the Forest herself.'

Darziates would have shuddered at Agrona's stupidity, if he were ever moved to such extremes. But he had already sent mortal troops into the Forest to capture the three. Mortals, though basic, were the only ones under his command who could enter the Forest. They were the only corrupted ones not barred by the Lady's power, which guarded against all malevolent magical beings.

He had known that it would be difficult to catch the three elusive children on their Quest, as this was why he had been warned to heed them at all. And they did seem to have forces in the world helping to cloak and defend them. A tree entity would not reveal herself or awaken for just a normal group of people.

'Sire...' the servant added from behind him. 'The Sorceress said that, uh,' he was nervous, 'the five got a hold of the girl, but something blasted them away from her somehow...'

He would look into who this girl was.

'Sire?'

'You may go.'

'Thank you Sire!' obvious relief. He heard the servant running away, happy to be escaping with every feature intact.

Darziates squinted up at the sun blazed sky. The foreboding shapes of the Dragons were already small in the distance, hurrying to complete their task in Awyalkna.

CHAPTER SIXTY THREE

Dalin

After our first full day of marching through the Forest, Kiana was sitting by the campfire, humming as she stitched her tattered scraps of material back into a tunic, and I let her light voice wash over me.

She was wrapped in my cloak because hers needed fixing too. The claws of the beasts had torn through the strong fabric easily.

'There,' Kiana stated triumphantly. 'Finished.' She held up the open tunic, looking it over.

'Not quite. You missed the slice across the back of it,' Noal observed.

She turned it around. 'Frarshk. I don't remember that happening,' she muttered in annoyance.

'Language!' Noal yawned at her from where he laid, waving an admonishing finger like old Wilmont used to do when I had been 'impertinent'.

'Perhaps you should check to see if all of your back is still attached too,' he added sleepily.

'I hate mending clothes,' she sighed, her face crinkling with distaste, and she slapped the tunic into her lap and threaded her needle again.

I grinned to myself.

Despite the crescendo of events that had led to this moment, I had never been quite so content in all of my life. Away from servants, courtly scrutiny, and the weight of being measured up against my father by Wilmont.

Soon Kiana gave a soft laugh from where she had finished her mending. I turned to see her sneaking towards Noal, who was now snoring gently.

'What is it?' I asked, unable to see what her sharp eyes had spotted as I sat up.

She didn't respond, but bent over Noal silently to scoop up something that must have been creeping on the grass close to his face.

She came to sit quietly beside me, and as she opened her cupped hands slightly, we peeked down at what she had captured.

Long, black, hairy legs with sharply spiked tips waved up out of the crack between her hands in an almost friendly fashion. Beady eyes stared up at me from a little hairy face. Two fangs glistening with poison smiled charmingly out of the darkness.

'Granx!' I exclaimed, jerking my face away from the bulbous shape in Kiana's hands.

'Hush,' she told me laughingly. 'Don't wake Noal.' She didn't look up from inspecting the deadly insect.

'How in the Gods' names do these Granx spiders keep finding us?' I hissed. 'I thought they were meant to be rare!'

Kiana didn't say anything for a few moments. 'It could be that this is the same Granx we keep coming across.'

'Surely not,' I snorted. 'Out of all the things that have been following us, how did we attract a deadly spider?'

'Perhaps she's in love with Noal,' Kiana jested.

Even as I watched, the Granx was trying to wriggle her way back over to Noal. Kiana gently lifted it back into her palm, getting flailing arms that were reaching to Noal in response.

My mouth hung agape.

'Why not? Stranger things have occurred recently,' Kiana shrugged.

'Put it down,' I grimaced. 'Aren't you bothered that it could kill you?'

Kiana sighed. 'I'm more disturbed by the thought of what may have happened to the Willow for sacrificing herself in defending us, and if Ila and Amala are safe.'

'I bet they're following your trail as we speak,' I told her, eyeing the spider in her hands warily.

Kiana laughed and stood once more. 'Don't look so worried!'

Still cradling the black Granx she disappeared for a moment into the trees.

I stared after her, considering the spot where her graceful, soundless form had melted into the darkness–and I didn't hear her footsteps as she exited from a different clump of trees behind me. I started when I turned and found her sitting beside me, which made her laugh again and brought a smile to my lips.

I didn't mind that she laughed at me.

It wasn't often that she gave one of her real laughs and I liked them.

It reminded me of my great certainty that Kiana was the cheerful young singer I'd fallen in love with when I had visited bountiful Bwintam's festival, long before Krall's attack.

The festival music had been nothing like that of the stuffy balls I'd always attended under Wilmont's displeased eye, and the dark-haired singer– Kiana, had shone from the stage. At that time Kiana had beamed and laughed along with the crowd easily, and when she had sung her voice had held her rowdy crowd in enraptured ecstasy as if enchanting everyone with a spell.

THE LAST
LARNAERADEE

'I still have your cloak,' Kiana said now, and she laid it out for me, close to hers. Taking my place beside her, I slept easily, with a happy feeling growing inside of me, and when I woke that feeling didn't go away.

CHAPTER SIXTY FOUR

Finally in her nightgown, Queen Aglaia of Awyalkna rubbed her eyes and leaned against the railing of her high up chamber balcony. She was exhausted by her task of managing the Palace, as the City within the gates was now full of refugees who had come from defenceless villages all over Awyalkna.

But despite her fatigue, she knew she would suffer another sleepless night. Her thoughts forever fixed on her husband, who had marched away with Awyalkna's soldiers to face certain defeat. Or she was unable to stop focusing on the spontaneous Krall attacks that had left no survivors in Awyalknian villages, along with a shortage of horses and a strain on food supplies. Though despite how heavily those things weighed on her mind, she was especially consumed by thoughts of her missing sons.

Her Prince Dalin, and her darling Noal.

Aglaia sighed, twisting a gold band ring around her finger worriedly and looking out at the sprawling City–before the night was pierced by a shout.

'ENEMY ATTACK!' the sentries from the Wall called in alarm.

Almost immediately a great roaring sounded that was so unbelievably loud it was as if the world was collapsing in on itself.

Aglaia gasped as her eyes discerned two massive figures blotting out the stars as they flew across the sky toward the City.

Within moments a soldier was bursting into her room and she whirled from where she had been staring, transfixed.

'Majesty, people are going to be evacuating to the Palace underground! You must go too!' he had to yell to be heard over the rushing sound of the monsters' wings.

'No. Hand me a robe!' she ordered, clinging to the balcony railing as the whole Palace shuddered.

He was obediently helping her into her robe when the enormous body of what looked like a giant lizard with wings soared past. If she had reached an arm out, her fingertips could have brushed glittering, spiked scales.

'Majesty!' the young soldier yelled in warning as a spiked tail longer and thicker than a watchtower lashed past, whipping across the balcony. She felt the young soldier's arms around her as he lunged and dragged her down to the marble floor, covering her body with his own.

The giant, horned cudgel-like tail tore right across the railing where she had stood moments before, so that all of the intricate metal was ripped away and both the soldier and the Queen of Awyalkna were nearly sucked off the balcony by the sheer air pressure.

Only once the roaring monster had careened away, smashing into a tower far below, were they able to drag each other to safety.

'You need to get below!' the soldier shouted anxiously, pale as a ghost.

Aglaia saw the second monster open its cruel jaws at the other side of the City and shoot flames down upon the market place beneath as if the Gods had loosed a waterfall of fire.

'You need to get me to the Gwynrock Gates!' she shouted back.

His eyes were startled and wide. But he nodded. 'Come on!' he held out a hand. She took it and they tore across the room and down the grand hallway, skirting around fallen tapestries, antique statues and golden ornaments.

The young soldier and the Queen skidded as the floors lurched, and she heard windows smashing on the other side of the Palace. Then moments later all the windows on their level of the Palace exploded simultaneously as a great twisting reptilian body tore past; the rush sending the glass in every window into explosions of hurtling shards.

They held their arms over their heads and ran through the raining glass amidst crowds of servants and nobles, all speeding down the halls.

One young maid was thrust into a wall as she tried to squeeze through the crowd, and at once began to scream. Aglaia yanked on the soldier's hand and steered him toward the maid, battling through a sea of people.

She gasped when she saw the screaming maid, whose shaking hands were covered in blistering burns, and then looked to the wall that the young girl had been slammed into. The wall was emanating with an orange light, and even from where Aglaia stood she could feel heat radiating from the marble where fire blasts had absorbed into it. The halls were slowly being filled with many such patches of the growing orange light.

Aglaia caught the arms of two fleeing women who were rushing to the underground shelter.

'Take this girl with you,' she ordered, and the two women hurriedly curtsied, scooping the crying maid up between them and half carrying her off along with the rest of the crowd.

'Stay away from the walls!' Aglaia yelled in warning, and even through the panic, she heard her order being echoed. She nodded and her soldier pulled her back into the stream of running people.

Finally the Queen and the soldier burst into the throne room with a swarm of others, and were carried forward to erupt from the great entrance doors, spilling out into the chaos of the City.

Soldiers were already hurling weapons and arrows into the sky, aiming everything they had at the passing winged monsters, which were snaking their way overhead and throwing explosive fire balls back at the crowd. But there were also hundreds of ordinary citizens rushing to join the armoured men, or trying to quench enormous fires and pulling friends from smouldering wreckages.

'The Queen!' came an echoing cheer as she rushed past the crowds, despite the fact that she was dressed in her nightgown, robe and slippers.

'Majesty! Take my horse!' one elderly man called as she hurtled past. He slipped out of the saddle and the soldier vaulted into it, pulling the Queen up behind him.

'Thank you, friend!' Aglaia cried over her shoulder as the soldier kicked the old plough horse into a gallop that carried them down the paved City road to the Wall.

She saw the great Gwynrock Walls covered by masses of her citizens, all swarming shoulder to shoulder with the soldiers, and torches along the wall lit up the scene like some kind of epic standoff to be portrayed in a tapestry.

'Did anyone go to the caves?' she called to the soldier as they galloped onward.

People cheered when they saw her coming to a halt within their midst, and the crowds parted so that the soldier could get her to the ladder. Hands reached out and thumped her on the back, and a wave of voices hailed her as she rushed past.

She practically flew up the ladder and was pulled by dozens of strong arms up onto the walkway, with her soldier coming up behind her. Her soldier pulled her to a cleared spot where one of the four Generals who had remained with the City in case of attacks such as this, stood shouting orders.

General Sumantra, with his massive voice, massive chest, massive arms, massive strength and massive sword was an Awyalknian champion, and even at the age of fifty, he retained a fearsome reputation. He was a good friend to the King and Queen and she was glad to see him in charge of the defence of the Northern Gate.

As the great body of the winged fiend swooped horribly over the Wall, the General raised his sword and boomed: 'LOOSE!'

A cloud of arrows flew whistling through the air, soaring towards the scaled belly as it writhed above the crowds along the Wall. There were shouts of warning and everyone ducked and gripped the rock Wall ledge to stop themselves from being plucked over by the suction of air created by the huge thing careening past.

It flicked its tail violently as it passed, and one soldier's armour was pierced by a thick tail horn. He was dragged over the wall to suffer a terrible drop, while at least twenty others were also sucked forward to crumple heavily against the stone Wall.

'STEADY!' General Sumantra bellowed as the fiend turned, roaring gleefully and opening massive jaws to release a stream of fire into the Wall that sent many people, including Aglaia, tumbling backward.

The beast passed high over them and people stood and shot arrows determinedly after it.

'HOLD YOUR FIRE!' General Sumantra ordered to avoid the wastage of good arrows.

It was then that he spotted the Queen standing barely three paces from him in her gown and slippers; dirty, scratched, climbing out of a pile of rubble and with an expression of grim determination on her face.

For the first time in his life, the unflappable General did a double take.

'WHAT IN THE GODS' NAMES ARE YOU DOING HERE AGLAIA?!'

'There's no need for you to shout at the moment, Sumantra.' She brushed some shards of glass out of her hair.

'My Queen, it is not safe, you need to get to the underground shelter...' he was spluttering.

'I'm here with my people Sumantra. Where I should be,' she answered flatly. 'I'm as safe as anyone else. And this good soldier has helped me to stay alive.' She gestured toward the young man at her side, who looked sheepish.

'Sorry General, she wanted to come,' he said forlornly.

Sumantra rubbed his face with a big dirty hand. 'I've witnessed dozens of people burned to dust tonight. You better guard her with your life.'

With a pained grimace at having to accept the situation, Sumantra turned back to concentrating on the beast.

The winged devil had taken up blasting the South Gate now, and the shouts and booms could be heard from across the City while the explosions lit the night spectacularly.

The second beast was still swooping around the Palace itself, pelting fireballs and bowling into its marble towers as if trying to knock the whole lot down.

'Dren! Report!' Sumantra bellowed.

A young man who had been standing amongst the archers nimbly jumped from the walkway onto the thick Wall ledge itself, quickly and skilfully running along it to land before the General. He bowed to Aglaia and then saluted the General with his bow still in his free hand.

'What can you tell me?' Sumantra demanded.

'I've seen a few weak spots,' Dren replied. 'And they're our only chance. Arrows aimed at heavily scaled areas are just rebounding.'

'That doesn't leave much to aim at,' the General remarked sourly.

'It leaves unprotected eyes and wing joints,' surmised Dren. 'I'll need a few of the sharper-eyed archers with the best aim.'

'That'll mean suicide,' the young soldier who had helped the Queen gasped, then blushed furiously again as the General and Queen turned to him.

'It's an undesirable possibility,' Dren clapped the soldier un-reassuringly on the back before turning to gesture at the ledge. 'The archers will need to be standing up here, so that we have a clear shot. But it can only be the few of us, so our fire doesn't get lost in a cloud of arrows, and so that the thing is happy to get close. Then I can guess we have a chance of harming the brute.'

Sumantra nodded grimly. 'You don't have much time. Get to it.'

Dren bowed again pleasantly, and leapt easily back along the ledge.

'Don't get yourself killed,' Sumantra growled after the confident archer.

'We gotta 'elp 'em General!' came a few cries from the crowd as Dren pulled four other young men to stand on the ledge with him and they readied their bows.

'I certainly won't let five of my best die because of a winged reptile,' he told the crowd gruffly. 'Spread the word that when the beast comes next NOBODY looses. Everybody keep low. Secondly, you lot,' he pointed at ten or so men standing at the ledge where the ankles of the five archers were within reach. 'You MUST grab our archers as soon as they've fired. Understood?'

There were shouts of agreement and cheers from the crowd as news of what was happening spread along the Northern Wall.

'IT'S COMING BACK!' came the warning.

'DREN!' Sumantra bellowed.

'We're set,' Dren replied, at ease and rocking to and fro on his heels expectantly.

'DOWN!' Sumantra roared, and as if an amazing wave had been created, hundreds of people simultaneously sank down to crouch out of the way; with Sumantra and Aglaia included, the young soldier shielding her as best he could.

A great shadow approached, and the Queen saw the massive body hurtling towards the Wall, turning elatedly in the air and loosing mighty roars that made the Queen put her hands over her ears.

Dren and his four young friends were unwavering, and every eye turned to these heroes, as the dreadful winged monster spotted them. At once, instead of writhing aimlessly, it roared in delight and charged with cruel jaws open.

'Ready!' Dren yelled to his archers and to the crowd waiting to pull them back.

Their longbows were cocked, with the bowstrings drawn and latched. The five arrows were held precisely at nocking point on each string.

Then as the spectators along the wall watched, riveted, Dren's lips formed the word: 'loose'. And the archers each smoothly mirrored one another in elegant release, sending five rotating arrows across the starry sky.

Two arrows plunged towards fierce reptilian eyes, and one hit true.

Another arrow glanced off the beast's quickly closing mouth while the last two arrows aimed to skewer the meaty joints that connected the great wings to the beast's body. One deflected harmlessly against scales, but the other buried itself into the small wing joint, penetrating the soft, unprotected cartilage and muscle there.

The results were instantaneous.

The beast that had been plummeting toward the archers threw its head suddenly backward in blind agony, and its whole body sagged to one side. It jerked away from the Wall and somersaulted, scratching at its face and shoulder wildly.

Those behind the ledge had already leapt forward to yank the archers down to safety, and the entire crowd along the Wall remained crouching and clinging to whatever crevice or boulder they could find as the torrents of wind sucked them forward in the beast's wake.

A deafening call sounded from within the City before the second monster joined its crazed kin. At once they turned away from the City altogether to quickly disappear into the night as the entire City came alive with ecstatic relief.

Even afterwards, when the general talk had all arrived at the same conclusion—the beasts had to be like the Dragons told of in childhood fables, Aglaia knew there was a new level of morale in the City. The population of defenders and refugees had now realised that they were strong.

Aglaia was in fact heartened, somehow feeling better than she had before the attacks, after she had gathered the reports in her throne room. Despite the shock, the population was already busily at work to right everything and to reinforce the City.

She had even managed to sit back almost restfully in her throne for a moment, until an oily voice sounded at her shoulder.

'Awyalkna has proven her strength again,' the voice said quietly, and Aglaia jumped, springing out of her thoughts and back to the present.

'Wilmont,' she said in surprise. 'I didn't hear you come in.'

A fleeting instinctual sense that he was a threat reminded Aglaia that Dalin had never trusted Wilmont, and she certainly noted now how he could catch one unaware.

'May I help you in some way?' she frowned.

He didn't look like he needed help. He looked as prim as ever. His ringlets had been oiled into place again and his rich costume was cleaned and pressed. He had been one of the few to have gone into the underground shelter during the attack, claiming to have led the elderly to safety.

'Nay, I but came to ask you the same question,' he simpered, arching his sculpted eyebrows.

'I am well enough, Wilmont,' she rose from her throne.

'Yes.' He continued to stand close, regarding her as if he had a report that he had to write about the state of her health.

'Good night,' she said curtly, thinking again of how she had always presumed Dalin had simply chafed at being chaperoned when he'd complained of this man. Wondering if there had been more to her son's distaste than first thought, she walked away from Wilmont with a shiver.

Her young soldier, who hadn't left her side since Sumantra had ordered him to protect her with his life, stepped forward when she passed through the throne room doors. He looked over his shoulder with narrowed eyes as Wilmont stared after her.

She laughed, less unnerved with distance. 'Don't be silly, dear,' Aglaia scolded the young soldier, Elan–or 'Friendly' as every other soldier seemed to call him–'It's only Wilmont.'

But Friendly continued to return Wilmont's stare with a decidedly unfriendly look.

CHAPTER SIXTY FIVE

Kiana

I had sent Dalin and Noal off to wash in the stream while I made a campfire for another settled night in the Forest's protection. But now, in some amusement, I listened to the two of them trying to sneak back, straining to catch me unawares.

I caught Noal by the wrist as he reached for me, and he emitted a yelp of surprise as I tugged him into a tumble to land beside the fire.

'You breathe too loudly,' I told him as he puffed up at me from the grass, and as I whirled an arm back and around Dalin's legs to bring him to his knees. 'And you,' I told Dalin, 'need to watch how heavily you're stepping.'

Dalin's green eyes crinkled with humour. 'I was always told I had a light, elegant step by the dance masters.'

'I was always told I didn't,' huffed Noal. Then he realised his huff was the kind of heavy breathing I'd remarked on and quickly deflated himself with a grin.

'The way you two move about, Jenra won't be the least bit surprised by our arrival,' I teased, laying my cloak out contentedly in our glade.

'Couldn't you at least have pretended not to have heard us?' Noal complained.

I fixed him with a glare. 'You wouldn't learn.'

'We must be nearly in Jenra by now,' Dalin half kidded, rubbing his calves after another full marching day. 'It's been weeks!'

'Have you spotted a mountain?' I enquired with a half smile.

'And have you thought about how good it is staying in here?' Noal added. 'No trouble around every corner... Nothing to disturb the peace...' he stroked an oversized flower and sent a butterfly flitting away, irritated.

'Nothing but you,' Dalin corrected him.

'We have made it quite far into Sylthanryn,' I informed them. 'The stream is becoming deeper and wider each day.'

'And I do wish to save Awyalkna, and Quest ever onwards,' Noal sighed, fluffing up some velvety ferns dreamily. 'But this place has healed me right down to my soul.'

I silently agreed with him, considering how gentle my dreams had become, how relieved my shoulder had felt, and how happy my days had been since arriving in this tremendous garden of bursting colours–this time with companions.

The abundant Forest, in its timeless splendour, was luring me into a sense of security that I found hard to shake.

And really, I didn't want to.

CHAPTER SIXTY SIX

Dalin

Kiana had been unsuccessfully trying to teach us one of her songs to pass the time as we travelled onward.

'It sounds like someone's killing you both!' she laughed, collapsing upon the grassy floor and clutching at her ears.

'I'm close to a breakthrough,' Noal assured her, and he opened his mouth to try again before his voice did break unbearably, at a particularly high and dramatic point in the song.

Noal closed his mouth abruptly as Kiana roared with laughter.

I elbowed Noal in the ribs and nodded at him.

'We may not sing like a choir to the Gods, but we do have other skills,' I warned her.

She wiped an imaginary tear of mirth from her eye.

'Right!' I told Noal, and we both lunged.

'Gotcha!' Noal roared as we made to tackle her.

She cackled and rolled easily out from underneath us, turning the play fight around to end with Noal and I, face down, in a heap, with her sitting on top of us as if we were a conquered mountain.

'Your other skills?' she queried gleefully.

'I surrender!' came Noal's muffled reply.

Kiana chuckled once more and released us graciously, picking a leaf from my hair.

'You caught me on a bad day,' I told her demurely, brushing my tunic down with dignity.

'Well, I tell you what,' Kiana said coaxingly. 'If you collect some firewood, I'll hunt us a meal.'

'I forgive all transgressions,' Noal waved a hand at once from where he still laid as she grinned and left with her bow and three arrows in hand.

I nudged Noal to get up so we could complete our own task. 'We'd best have a fire started before she gets back.'

'You're right,' he acknowledged. 'Even facing Kiana's wrath in jest could be dangerous. Perhaps worse even than Wilmont's rage that time you set his ringlets on fire.'

I smiled with the warm glow of satisfaction that I still always felt at the memory of our past supervisor's smoking curls while we wandered at a leisurely pace, picking up random sticks and twigs.

Noal started to sing the song again, lumbering about fearlessly, and we were unprepared when we stepped around a clump of trees to find a troop of Krall soldiers all calmly aiming their weapons at us.

CHAPTER SIXTY SEVEN

Kiana

I had been completely focused on a shot at a small wild pig when a shout of alarm echoed through the Forest.

I froze as my prey trotted away, snuffling and snorting while I forgot about it and felt my heart bounce crazily in my chest.

'Frarshk!' I swore under my breath, and slung my bow quickly back over my shoulder, moving rapidly and quietly back to where I had left Dalin and Noal, only to find that the glade was empty of everything.

Even packs were gone, which gave me hope that my companions would be alive and kept as prisoners, if indeed that single shout had been because of an attack.

I followed the imprinted trail Noal and Dalin had left in the grass, tracing their meandering steps as they had wandered in search of firewood, until their tracks stopped abruptly.

My eyes spotted evidence of many more heavy footprints encircling where my boys had last stood, and I could see the squashed indents in the grass where a number of men seemed to have been hidden behind trees in wait. I could also see where Noal and Dalin's footprints were replaced with marks that suggested they'd been dragged from the site.

I hurried on after the skid lines and stomping marks that had surely been made by stout Krall warriors, maintaining caution but wondering how long I had before the attackers left the Forest, and for my companions to be lost to Darziates.

A glance at the sky through the treetops told me I had three hours of light before the sun would set. Three hours to find Dalin and Noal, and to have a plan ready to get them away safely.

Even when their trail became lost in wildly growing roots, I rushed onward until at last I heard the muffled, distant sound of people and movement ahead.

I began moving from tree to tree, observing the area around me and steadily getting closer to the increasingly loud noise, which was in fact made up of many rough voices, of outbursts of laughter, of barked orders, and of a camp being set.

I noted as I approached that the trees sloped downward, and the great din of their camp site echoed up to me from what had to be the bottom of a steep drop in the land.

Creeping carefully towards the growing rabble of an army deep below, I found myself on the edge of a jutting cliff, where the ground suddenly dropped away as I'd suspected. I pressed my body against a tree on the brink of the drop, feeling its wooden roughness against my cheek and palms, and edged my face around the thick trunk.

It was the largest clearing I had seen so far in the Forest, sprawling outwards at the base of the cliff I peered over. And within that clearing a formidable camp for what had to have been over a hundred Krall soldiers had been constructed, with their harsh voices rising even more clearly now to greet me.

Numerous camp fires were already lit both around the border and within the camp itself, with each border fire accompanied by some armed, raucous soldiers loosely doing their duty of watching their surrounds. There were further fires within the camp for food, and one monstrous bonfire in the centre of the clearing had also been lit.

Such magnificent light would dazzle me if I approached, and make it impossible to get close to the camp without being seen, but I wondered at their extravagant measures when Sylthanryn was normally void of people—and when they surely knew there were only three of us to contend with. I considered again why Darziates may have needed to send a force of mortals who were being so watchful now, and why his magical beings had been unable to come after us in the Great Forest themselves. Perhaps the Sorcerer did believe in a need to be wary of the mythical Lady of the Forest.

Beyond the abundance of campfires, I counted three tents that had been pitched in a circle around the enormous bonfire at the centre of everything, obviously for the use of higher ranking members of the troop. The larger tent of the three was set up regally and topped with the black Krall flag, marked ominously by a crimson hand insignia which waved on the material like a warning. I guessed it to be the General of the troop's abode, but squinted past it to see that a separate canvas structure had been erected a short distance back—almost blocked from view by the size of the General's tent.

It did not have its canvas windows open, and two guards in demonic, spiked armour stood at its closed door, armed with their sabres.

I felt my fingers grip into the flaking bark of my tree. That segregated, darkened shelter, huddled out of the fire light and away from prying eyes, had to contain my stolen friends.

'All or nothing to get them back,' I told myself resolutely.

CHAPTER SIXTY EIGHT

Kiana

My mind raced with the need to beat all odds and use the setup of their camp against them. I considered many unlikely possibilities of how I could try to breach my way in and somehow get back out again with Noal and Dalin. But as I discounted one useless idea after another, I scoured every inch of the top of the cliff, following its bite shape around in a curve and scrutinising the camp below from different angles.

During my surveillance of the impenetrable complex, another layer of challenge was added as I discovered ten skilfully camouflaged sentries positioned at intervals along the cliff top's edge–watching for anything out of the ordinary, or anyone like me who might try to creep up on the camp.

I was cursing internally as I at last moved away from the cliff edge and silent sentries. For, including the sentries, there were roughly one hundred and ten men– and my usual methods of stealth didn't seem to offer any hope in the face of such a brightly lit camp. In fact, I needed to grow wings, or to adopt the exact opposite kind of approach to my usual ways.

'Need to attract attention,' I muttered almost inaudibly, scrambling up a log.

'Need to create the illusion that I have numbers.' I slid down the other side, searching for inspiration.

'No healer bag of tricks to help me,' I grimaced. But when I peered over another sloping ravine, I grinned at what the Gods seemed to have sent me.

'But those will do.'

Growing out of the jagged rocks was an evil looking weed covered in potent red fruits that I knew to be called Rupta berries. The most explosive ingredient anybody could ever ask for.

I eagerly scraped, clawed and skidded my way down the ravine to where the prickle covered in flaming coloured berries grew, and I wedged my boots into some cracks in the sloping wall before I dug out the entire plant with my dagger.

As I climbed my way back up, a tiny prickle punctured the soft pad of one finger tip–and my entire hand suddenly felt as though it had slipped into a vat of burning oil. Sweat broke out across my brow, and red blotches spread along my hand and arm, though fortunately that was the worst of it.

'Thank you!' I whispered up to the Gods, a somewhat plausible idea beginning to formulate in my mind.

Rupta berries were incredibly rare, and usually highly sought after by the worst types of people. They did not grow for long, as the sun's touch or even the slightest nudge of a warm breeze could cause them to combust. A crater would be left wherever they exploded, and most of the time the roots would burn away. A messier scenario occurred if people tried eating them.

I clasped the prickle's stem lightly in my teeth then, while I sweated the rest of the way back up the rocks. And even as I pulled myself back up onto level ground, I fought not to let the heat of my breath touch the shiny, round sides of the berries, though my mouth still stung as if I'd consumed something horribly spicy as I set the plant gingerly down in the shade.

I fervently searched further into the Forest; climbing trees, scaling rocks and tunnelling through roots before I was satisfied that I had found the most volatile plants on offer. Then I selected twelve palm-sized rocks and brought my collection together cautiously, maintaining a safe distance from the cliff edge and camp.

My developing idea revolved around things I had learned in my travels to Lixrax and around isolated desert clans, where I had witnessed how to cause little explosions by making pastes out of certain ingredients. I had witnessed temple priests using these flares for effects to scare superstitious followers, but I had developed the little detonations into big ones in my time, and now I focused intently on combining my ingredients into a paste without melting my own hand off.

I used water from my flask to cool the sparking tingles running along my fingers as my skin singed and reacted, and smoke wafted from the mix as it began to thicken and glow. With smarting eyes I at last finalised the paste I'd made and cautiously dipped the rocks into it. The resulting covering quickly dried and hardened like shells on the rock surfaces—making the best explosives for dramatic effect that I had probably ever designed.

I hoped that these lethal rocks might make the many fires in the enemy camp an advantage for me. If I could find a way to get those rocks into the fires, the paste on the rocks would melt, the heat would grow so intense that the Rupta berry ingredient would activate to explode, and shards of rock and acidic juices would be thrown out at the soldiers.

However, I had not yet sprouted wings or figured out a way to actually get the explosives into the fires.

I left the real weapons safely stowed away in the shade, but made my way covertly back to the camp to experiment with dropping normal rocks from above into the fires.

A couple of soldiers down below rubbed their heads and cursed loose pebbles that seemed to be dropping from the cliff top where I hid, but the distance was too great for me to be able to reliably hit anything other than one unsuspecting head at a time down there.

There was a slope entrance down to the base of the camp, but it was too obvious, so, sighing at the prospect of using my throbbing hands, I took cover in a wall of swaying branches and vines that covered the cliff face, and made my way down the rocky wall so that I touched down a small distance away from the camp.

I crouched in the cover of the trees, taking aim at the outer-most border fire with an ordinary rock as another trial from ground level this time.

Unfortunately the rock made a distinct 'poing' sound as it ricocheted off a helmet that had been set down next to the fire.

At once the confused, dirty warrior who had removed his helmet stood up.

My idea once again seemed quite impossible as I noted how hard it was going to be to toss rocks into heavily guarded flames – without drawing a crowd to where I'd thrown it from.

I rolled my shoulders and drew my dagger as the soldier peered in my direction.

'Whawasat?' he growled in a thick Krall accent, grasping a heavy bludgeon.

'Unno,' the soldier closest shrugged. 'Falling branch.'

The first warrior spat and growled like a rabid bear, stomping away from his disinterested comrades, and into the trees where I waited.

He peered into the dense shadows to my side, and I quietly ghosted back a few trees, running my sensitive fingers over leaves to create a swishing sound.

He grunted, and stepped further into the trees, squinting his small eyes.

I skipped lightly backward once more, and then found some fallen leaves to crunch on so that he turned completely in my direction as I hid in the shadows and he followed the sound.

I took hold of a lower hanging tree branch while he stomped straight past, and I was afforded the opportunity to lightly swing my body up to land on his back.

Before he could let out an alert, or bellow like a dumb animal, I rammed his windpipe with the hilt of my dagger. Kicking off from his stocky back, I slid around his wide body; clinging to his neck, and propelled my feet into his stomach.

Instead of battle cries, there was only a sucking vortex of air as he sank to his knees.

I rammed my dagger hilt into his skull to knock him out then, but was momentarily surprised to find this human being had one of the thickest, most protective skulls I'd ever come across.

As I stepped back his eyes did roll, and he continued to wheeze, but instead of losing consciousness, he suddenly launched at me, bludgeon and all.

I ducked and reflexively slid my dagger under his raised arm, and because of the blade's purposeful length, I knew its coldness would have touched his heart.

A little gurgling bubble sounded from my opponent, before he was gone after a very quiet fight.

I withdrew my dagger and wiped it clean on the grass with a flicker of regret that I suppressed.

I rationalised to myself that, though I was used to battling animalistic beasts, many mortal lives were going to be impacted if I could find a way to make my plan work. So I calmly dragged his heavy body over to rest against a trunk and hacked down a heavy branch so that it looked like it had fallen on him.

My dagger mark had been clean and had left a barely noticeable piercing and stain under his jerkin, so I hoped nobody would suspect an intruder just yet. I needed time to find some other way to get my rocks to the camp fires, because I could not just quietly kill another one hundred and nine thickly skulled soldiers.

Once back at the top of the cliff and a safe distance away from the camp again, I wasted time trying to shoot one of my arrows in practice with another harmless rock attached to it. But it was too heavy, as common sense had warned. And three arrows would never help anyway.

I wandered on again for a while, searching for some new form of inspiration, and feeling time slipping away until at last I sank down to lean against a tree, thudding my back into it with a grunt.

'Well!' a small bird squeaked in alarm and flapped out of the branches above me; shocked by my abrasive entrance.

I blinked stupidly. 'What in the Gods' names...' I leaned forward to look around and the small bird landed at my feet.

'You're in a bad mood,' it said. 'Can I help?'

And my eyes widened with shock.

CHAPTER SIXTY NINE

Kiana

'By my beak, you creatures are so simple. Shame, shame.'

The little bird puffed up and enunciated its trill sounds this time. 'CAAAN I HEEELP?'

I clutched my chest.

'Ahhh,' I floundered in uncertainty. ' ...Yes? Please?'

It hopped up and down in excitement. 'Oh good, good!' It flapped. 'I knew this dialect was not a dead one! Everyone else said not to bother, but no, I persisted, and now look, I've found one!'

'One what?' I asked weakly, feeling faintly ill.

'The One! One like you!' it said matter-of-factly. 'The others will understand you. But they'll sound like thugs if they try to respond.'

'You do seem surprisingly eloquent...' I pressed the back of my hand to my forehead, at a complete loss, and fearing for my health. Perhaps the Rupta berries had done something to me.

'I'm fluent! Living in the Forest helps,' it peeped happily. 'Now what can I do?'

My pulse was pounding so strongly, I felt it vibrating in my temples, in my throat and even in my digits.

'Krall soldiers have invaded the Forest,' my voice shook as I told it.

'Yes, we've been complaining of their smell all day,' the bird tittered with distaste. 'Filthy magic is in them, but they're not magical themselves–so they get to drag their filth around the Forest without anything to hold them back.'

'Yes,' I said nervously, wiping my palms on my trousers. 'They have taken my friends prisoner, and I could use any help possible to get them back.'

'Sure, sure,' it moved its head up and down in a wise nod. 'I can see why you were so flustered before. Like a worm was still wriggling in your throat. You wait here and I'll see if any of the others can spare you a moment.'

'Thank you, friend,' my voice was a wisp as the little feathered ball fluttered away to leave me waiting and trying to compose myself.

I hadn't quite felt myself take a secure grip on my sanity once more before my tiny helper returned gaily with a loud, chirping crowd of assorted birds that alighted all around me.

I stared at my winged audience and the original little bird flitted closer and nodded encouragingly.

Feeling my face heat at this madness, I cleared my throat.

'Well met...' I started falteringly. 'I appreciate your time.'

Immediately the gathering stopped chattering and cocked their little heads to look at me.

'Don't worry, they're comprehending you. They just speak Fairy tongue like oafs,' the first little bird who was helping me explained. 'I announced that you need help to get your friends back from those corrupted men,' it prompted me as I gaped around myself, at a loss once more. 'Just tell them what you need.'

I felt pins and needles all down my back and across my palms as though I had been drinking liquor. But my mind did somehow feel completely lucid, and within me there was the sense that something was falling into place, like when a dislocated joint clicks back into the right spot inside, and everything seems to fit more smoothly in your body.

'I am Kiana,' I began again more calmly, my mind shying away from the surreal situation. 'And I have a great favour to ask each of you, which none of you are bound to accept.'

They watched me with intelligent eyes, listening patiently and not uttering a peep.

'I am only one against that great troop of Krall. I need sentries, and I need helpers that can carry heavy, eruptive rocks to drop into the campfires below.' I swallowed the disbelief that still pounded through my sense of logic. 'If you understand and are willing to help me, please remain. But to do so will be dangerous.'

Not one bird moved.

I regarded this strange gathering awkwardly and gratefully. 'We have work to do then.'

I collected my cooled off rocks and returned to the cliff edge, where the Forest suddenly plateaued and where the Krall camp was set up below. I directed smaller members of my feathered army to spread themselves out around the tops of the cliff. From above the campsite they could watch the Krall sentries positioned on the same level of the Forest as myself and serve as alarms.

When I at last found myself a sheltered ledge, I dispersed the average-sized birds of the flock to keep watch around it, and I kept the larger birds with myself to serve as rock bearers.

I gritted my teeth and lowered myself over the lip of the cliff, climbing down a yard or two to reach the ledge, which jutted out from near the top of the rocky wall, but which was out of view because of hanging vines and leaves that spilled down from the top.

'Easy does it,' I whispered as the twelve largest birds swooped their way down to join me, each gingerly carrying their dangerous rock burdens.

I crouched amongst them and peered at the sky above the canopy. It was awash in coral pink and orange colours, and every time the sea of leaves moved in a breeze, a billion slivers of colour from the sunset above made the Forest a mass of glittering lights.

'It won't be long,' I told them softly. 'Before we ruin this serene evening.'

I reached behind myself to take hold of some of the rope-like vines that spilled over my ledge like a curtain, and all except one of the twelve birds nestled themselves into the foliage behind me too.

'You're sure you want to do this?' I asked the only bird not taking shelter. It was a broad-winged Forest hawk, and it seemed to dip its head in acknowledgment. Then it took a careful grip on its rock.

'Aim for a border fire. Fly away as soon as the rock leaves your talons,' I whispered as the leaves around the ledge stirred at the beating of the hawk's strong wings.

The noise of the massed men below echoed uninhibited up the cliff as we watched our tawny comrade swoop down towards them. They did not suspect anything as the hawk lightly flew overhead and dropped its burden directly into the chosen flames.

It took a few moments for the rock and its encasing mixture to heat.

But then my breath was taken away, and I felt my lips blister as an explosion of air and light shook the Forest.

The shock waves rolled over us endlessly, the heat and roaring voice of the fire breaking loose like a storm. I squinted at the blinding, blazing light that swelled before fading, leaving a hellish imprint of anguish filled images and contorting bodies across my vision as I blinked.

The Forest continued to creak and moan as the force of the detonation swept outward from the clearing, but it took a few moments for the soldiers below to begin their screaming.

I hoped to the Gods I hadn't harmed them all and frantically scanned the camp to make sure I had been right—that the one prisoner tent was being kept too far from the fires to have been accidentally impacted. Relief flooded me when I saw that, while the tents looked a little saggy on their frames, they all stood firm. And the prisoner tent was definitely out of range enough to remain relatively untouched from now on.

The vines covering the ledge rustled as my unlikely renegades surfaced from beside me with ruffled feathers and glinting, exhilarated little eyes.

The tiny figure of my original bird—a scurrytail no bigger than my palm—flitted down to skip about where I crouched. It cocked its brown head to the side and fluffed its feathers in anticipation for the next blast soon to come.

'This is exciting,' it chirruped.

'And perilous,' I whispered back to all of them, trying once more to subdue the flutter of sensation in my stomach as they comprehended me. 'It's going to be a big night. And it has already been quite the surprising day.'

'It's true. Whoever thought there would still be a biggun who could speak Fairy?'

CHAPTER SEVENTY

Those two Awyalknian boys had been caught by bad men. Worse than bugs in a web.

Granx had seen their beautiful heads get cracked by nasty, nasty sabres.

And not in the delicious way that a good egg can be sneaked from a nest and cracked for breakfast.

She was running for help as fast as pretty spider legs could carry her. So fast.

She had lost the Three of them so many times across their journey, but this time she had kept all of her eyes on them, and had seen the trap, had seen them carried off like juicy flies for crunching.

Thick black hairs stood up along her back. Her beautiful blonde Awyalknian boy—in trouble! Along with his friends.

But ... strange. As she got further from the Three, she knew it would be harder to find them again. Strange, lulling, lovely magic seemed to hide them.

Tricky, tricky, tricky.

Lady—not Gloria—must hear of this.

Awful Sorcerer-blinded people were making the Forest reek. And had taken her blonde boy.

Trouble was growing, like a poison filled bite.

Not acceptable.

Run, run, run!

CHAPTER SEVENTY ONE

Kiana

The first explosion had been very successful.

I gazed down at the groaning mass below, rolling unsteadily to their feet and staggering around with hands groping at heads and eyes. Most of them would have a little headache, and those who had been looking directly at the blast would be seeing only white.

The sentry nearest to the explosion was out cold, while others appeared to have been hit with surface wounds from the stone shrapnel.

The canvas doors to the tents for superior officers had burst aggressively open and I had been relieved to at last glimpse the leader of this force, and to see that it was not Angra Mainyu. He immediately began barking orders, and the least effected soldiers stumbled to their feet and fell into a tactical formation.

The General was built much the same as every man of Krall, with compact, thick legs, muscular arms, massive chest and broad shoulders – and as soon as he had entered the arena, the frenzy had dulled.

'Report!' he bellowed.

Straight away the soldiers began calling out from one to one hundred and ten, giving a number rather than a name, and most who didn't answer were accounted for. Even the hidden sentries on the same lofty level of the Forest as myself called out their numbers from where they hid in the dense trees at the edge of the cliff top.

The General accepted when all but one person had been accounted for. Probably my friend with the bumped head and punctured chest in the trees. But one man missing obviously didn't seem like enough of a problem.

'Change positions!' the General bellowed, referring to the cliff top sentries who had just given their stations away.

Then he immediately called for every man able to stand to join the few still able to see on the border to watch. Incapacitated soldiers were carried away, and throughout this process, a select few soldiers were taken off watch to search the immediate area around the clearing, and another group of ten were sent to climb to my level of the Forest to scour the top of the cliff as well.

The slanting slope I'd avoided earlier served the ten soldiers as a rough trail to climb from the camp, up to the cliff top. But I didn't feel worried by them, even though I was now sharing the cliff with twenty enemies intent on spotting me, as my winged watchers would alert me if an opponent got too close.

The next bird set to fly, a black crow, was already perched calmly near the explosive rocks so that it could perform its duty too.

I silently thanked the Gods for what could only be their divine blessing upon me and the Forest animals, and when enough time had elapsed for the camp to have settled into wariness rather than uproar, I nodded grimly to the crow which at once seized one of the eleven remaining rocks and flew for the border fires of the camp— this time on the opposite side to the last attack.

The other birds took shelter once more, but I tightened my grip around the vines and watched the rock drop unnoticed into the flames.

First, a whirring sound began to invade the oblivious camp as the air around that fire was sucked inward, as if a breath was being taken. The sound grew faintly at first, and was accompanied by the swelling of the light.

Soldiers everywhere were turning their heads nervously, trying to discern the source of the sound, then backing away from it when the whirring and hissing of the rushing air grew louder.

Then the heated rock and its encasing had reached their peak, and at the last moment I tightly squeezed my eyes closed, as heat radiated outward and the whirring sound reached an ear-splitting shriek. The rock got to bursting point and the shrill sound was abruptly replaced by a booming explosion and a surging wave of wind.

I could see the incredible light from beneath my eyelids, and it was only slightly less intense when I opened them to blink against the rippling force of the rushing air still assaulting the cliff and the trees at our backs.

The trees on the higher level of ground behind me shuddered, and the earth rumbled, my own ledge creaking and groaning while the cluster of birds around me toppled backward until the pressure swept past us and faded.

My ears rang, and I heard the camp echo with howls and moans of pain. But I felt my face set grimly while the Krall men again scrambled to find their attacker and reorder themselves.

Once again the uproar settled into confusion before I lightly rubbed the next bird's silken feathers with my fingertips. Then, without a rustle, it had launched away and was soaring easily below the dark canopy, swirling purposefully and watching for its target. This one was to land its rock inside the borders, as if the camp had been breached.

I held my breath when I saw the crow stop circling to drop the third rock.

The Forest around us and the birds at my feet tensed.

'Close your eyes,' I whispered a reminder to the birds around me, but didn't close my own yet, until another spectacular blast gripped the night.

After that one, I laid on my stomach to peer over the ledge as the General stormed about his shaken camp, agitated as less of his men responded to their number call.

Anyone who was able now moved about below in a gratifying frenzy, holding their weapons nervously, and I was only distracted from sending the fourth explosion when an angry cheeping sounded from the undergrowth above my jutting ledge.

It was a warning that one of the ten soldiers sent up to search the cliff top now approached.

'Wait only a little while between each blast, and move further into the camp as you go,' I whispered to the rest of my winged soldiers. 'I need them to feel like they must have me in their camp, alive, to explain all of this,' I said, before rising to climb the short distance back up from my ledge to the cliff top.

The angry cheeping had stopped, so the soldier had likely passed by thinking he had stepped too close to a nest. I thanked the cluster of birds in the foliage quietly and then turned to hunt the nearby soldier out.

He was much more obedient than the first soldier I had thumped on the head, falling silently unconscious at once when I came from behind to crack the hilt of my dagger into the back of his skull.

'Good boy,' I muttered as he toppled, his spiked armour only making a faint clinking when he landed upon the grass.

I heard noises of foreboding from below as the General made his roll call and found that my recent victim was unaccounted for –not even being one of those collapsed from the stunning explosions.

And I proceeded to ghost my way around the cliff top as time passed and explosions erupted from below at random intervals.

By the end of the eighth explosion I had picked off the ten soldiers sweeping the cliff top in search of me, and as fewer and fewer of the search responded to the General from above, those below became more spooked.

I began picking off the sentries that had been hidden on the cliff all day as well, eliciting greater desperation from those below.

I was sliding back down onto the ledge as the final explosion echoed around the camp, and following that, I saw that only forty men were standing watch now while the others laid in groaning heaps.

A chunk of my ledge had also broken away in the force of the explosions, and rivers of dirt drifted silently down from the edge when I landed.

The pale, warm light of morning sun was touching the sky, and I became sure that my invitation into the camp would come soon.

And, just as I was beginning to worry that I'd been wrong, the General came back out into the clearing.

He stood tall and straight and outwardly unruffled while two of his soldiers stood behind him, gripping their sabres to the throats of the two people who had come to mean everything to me.

'Come out now or your friends will die!'

The last three words of his sentence echoed heavily and boldly around the rocky walls, up to me.

Without any misgivings, I rose from where I had been hiding and held my hands up in surrender.

CHAPTER SEVENTY TWO

Dalin

I became aware of harsh, rumbling voices and the sound of many people moving nearby. My head was throbbing, and I swallowed thickly, my tongue feeling heavy in the dry confines of my mouth.

I groggily opened my eyes to find Noal, already awake and staring glumly at his shackled wrists, and I found my own wrists shackled and chained to a loop that had been hammered into the dirt floor.

'You alright?' I croaked at Noal, trying to lick my lips with a parched tongue that left no moisture.

We were in some sort of tent with all of its canvas windows closed, but the sun's brightness illuminated the space. It emanated through the thin brown material walls, and my stiffened back was warm from the sun radiating where I leaned.

'In one piece,' he whispered glumly, probably avoiding, as I was, thoughts of what Darziates and his men might do if they knew who Noal and I truly were.

There came a shuffling sound and a pitiful moan from a pile of rags at the other side of the large tent, and my heart leapt for a moment until Noal drew my attention again.

'While you were knocked out, I met Agrudek,' Noal told me quietly, trying not to draw attention from anyone outside. 'He's no danger to us.'

I tried to peer at the moaning pile of rags, which was actually a small figure bundled in an oversized robe, and I saw a bloodshot eye peering back at me.

'Hello friend,' I said kindly to the scrunched up person. 'Are you a prisoner too?'

A muffled, tentative voice came from the pile: 'Y–yes.' There was a sad gulp. 'And she... burned off... my hand. The W... Wit... ch,' the small bundle whimpered sickly.

I looked to Noal. 'His accent...?'

Noal nodded. 'He's from Krall. They harm their own too.'

I turned back to the poor, wretched creature. 'We are with you now,' I said, trying to be comforting despite our own misfortune.

'I wish we could say Kiana was here too,' Noal admitted. 'So we could know she was alright.'

'And because she always sees a way out of impossible situations,' I agreed. 'But she wasn't with us when we were caught, so she will have escaped.'

'There'll be no escape,' came an accented grunt, and I couldn't help but jump as the tent entrance was thrust aggressively aside and a colossal guard swept in to drop a lump of bread in the dirt at our feet.

Then the hulking soldier stepped across to tower over Agrudek's wheezing, huddled form, and he pressed a steel-covered war boot into the middle of Agrudek's pile of robes. 'Don't you try anything either, traitor. Or I'll twist your neck.' He sent Agrudek tumbling with a kick that rolled the little man into a pile of bags in the corner before he stalked back out.

'Agrudek? Are you harmed?' I asked the quivering bundle as he laid still in the growing shadows within the tent.

'N... no,' he lifted his head a little and I saw carrot coloured hair that stuck out at all odd ends and in tufts. 'But... I... lost my family.'

I heard faint sobs as the middle of his swaddled shape rose and fell.

'I am so sorry, Agrudek,' Noal said, aghast. Neither of us knew how to comfort him.

'Can you move at all?' I asked Agrudek eventually. 'Try to grab onto one of our bags near you and then get as close as you can to us.'

The small man whimpered, but for the first time I saw him rise on his elbows shakily and drag himself forward with our pack. I noticed with relief that one of our flasks and a cloak had been thrust into that bag.

'There's less chance of the General or anyone bothering to harm him if he's wedged between the two of us,' I explained to Noal. So we both strained to get as close to Agrudek as our chains would allow, and when he was within reach, we pulled the feeble figure close so that he could shelter in the middle of us, covered by the cloak.

Noal grabbed a flask of water and gave the little man a few drops.

'Thank... you,' coughed Agrudek, curling up in our fast darkening tent.

I was about to answer when I was distracted by a sudden increase in the brightness in the tent.

'What in the Gods' names...?' Noal gaped as we heard a whizzing, whistling sound from outside.

It became so shrill that it hurt, until the sound wavered as my ears began to pop and ring.

Agrudek cowered in a ball while Noal and I stared with bulging eyes, our shackled hands clamping on our ears as the tent shook around us; the wind almost seeming to suck the tent from its frame.

Then, the growing light suddenly surged as the piercing whistling was replaced by a booming explosion that forced the tent, and us inside it, into a lean because of the pressure.

I saw the silhouettes of the guards outside as they were thrown back against the tent, and my teeth gritted with the immensity of it until, at last, the waves of pressurised air eased up and passed.

The camp was instantly swept into an uproar and a leader's voice barked orders for a search.

'What the Frarshk just happened?' one of the guards outside our tent grunted.

'Sorcerer's not here. So what in the Other Realm has such power?' asked another husky voice. 'A demon?'

Noal and I just gaped at each other.

'What could wreak such destruction?' Noal whispered, his eyebrows raising.

'Kiana.' I agreed, and a grin spread across my own face. 'She's here.'

The explosions that continued to strike throughout the whole night rocked the camp to its very foundations, and we were rocked as the General entered our tent twice, demanding answers. But we heard the growing panic and silently cheered Kiana on in what could only be her brand of ingenuity.

'The frarshks are getting closer!' our guards kept up a stream of commentary as morning dawned. 'What the Frarshk are we gonna do? Wait until they pick us all off?'

'No. You're going to bring my prisoners out for bait,' a low growl cut across the voices of our guards. We'd come to know that as the General's voice.

Then the flap to the tent door burst open with the two stormy looking guards hurrying to push us out into the daylight. We were quickly surrounded by jeering soldiers as we were led out, many bleeding from torn faces and shredded hands.

The General yelled his threat out through the Forest, promising that he would end our lives, and my guard's blade pressed into my throat, snicking my skin as I swallowed. I could feel his hot breath on my neck and his armour was hard against my back.

But I didn't truly expect that Kiana would take this threat seriously.

I was as surprised as everyone else to see her lone figure standing calmly from a hiding spot near the top of the cliff, with arms outstretched in surrender as the camp beheld her in shock.

'A girl?' the General hissed incredulously. 'Where are the rest of them?' he demanded of us while we waited for Kiana to be led down.

'There aren't any others,' Noal strained to answer truthfully against the knife blade.

'They will be found,' the General guaranteed while the crowd of sneering soldiers parted for Kiana's arrival.

'It's a bad day for you, sweetheart,' grinned one soldier. He had a few bleeding holes in his face, and chunks of what looked like rock embedded into his cheeks and forehead.

'Get too close to the fire?' she asked him, and the grin dropped from his face as the mass surged angrily forward like a swarm of bees.

Then I saw the General clench his massive fist tightly, bringing it up to smash it with a staggering blow into Kiana's cheek. Her head was thrown to the side, but she straightened steadily after a moment.

I looked on in horror, Noal and I frozen in our captor's hands.

'Didn't even feel my eye pop,' she scolded.

There was swift silence from the crowd encircling us, and a sudden gleam of true interest in the eyes of the General.

'I'll do better next time,' he promised her darkly. Then he eyed her captors. 'I'll have this one,' he told them, and shockingly, he lifted a finger to trace her unflinching face. His finger pressed against the bruise already swelling on her cheek and then moved down to cup her chin and lift it.

My heart was beating unbearably fast.

'We'll see if I can't get her to explain all of this.'

A hollow feeling created a cavity in my stomach and I started to strain against the guard holding me.

'Don't touch her!' I growled, managing to struggle free of the guard's grasp for a moment before another stepped forward to add his grip. 'Leave her alone!' I twisted and turned so desperately that another man came out of the crowd and threw a bunched fist into my stomach so that my legs folded. But I fought to get back up.

And then Kiana spoke.

'Dalin, stop.'

Her voice was very close, and I looked up in shock to find she had managed to come to me.

There were grunts of surprise as others noticed one of her guards was keeled over, clutching his throat, while another was wheeling around with his hands over his eyes. Nobody had seen how that had happened.

She allowed two new soldiers to rush forward and seize her arms while I became immediately still; trying to fathom what was really going on, the same as everyone else.

I gaped at her hopelessly, breathing heavily, but I did as she said, no longer struggling.

The General smirked, and they began to turn her away from me, to lead her to his tent.

'Kiana?' I called after her desperately.

But as I stared with horrified distress after her, I saw her head turn, and she looked back to me, over her shoulder.

Then, in a split second, she had winked one brilliant blue eye and turned away.

CHAPTER SEVENTY THREE

Noal

Her screams had stopped. So had the crashing sounds that had come from the General's tent.

Dalin slumped dejectedly beside Agrudek, having given up reassuring us, and himself, that Kiana had given him a sign not to worry. Instead, all we heard now were the filthy speculations of our guards describing what the General must be doing to her.

'Frarshk, I don't think it was information that he wanted! No what he wanted–'

I'd blocked out the rest, feeling sick, and trying not to remember my mother and sister on the day that they had been made to scream as Kiana had.

When the tent flap was finally pushed aside Dalin and I sat up quickly, filled with dread.

Two soldiers dragged Kiana limply between them by her arms, and the tips of her boots scraped along the ground. Her head hung, and her hair was a curtain hiding her face. When they laid Kiana on her back her face was still away from us and she stayed motionless as a pair of shackles were closed around her wrists and linked by a length of chain to the ring in the dirt connecting all of ours.

As soon as the two soldiers were gone, Dalin was sliding his way across to Kiana, lifting her to rest against himself as best he could with restrained wrists.

'Kiana?' he whispered, moving the hair from her face to reveal a mass of blood that had spread down from a slice across her hairline. It had bled so much that hardly any clean skin remained on her face. Blood had leaked down her nose, her eyelids, her cheeks, her neck and had stained her shirt.

The crooked set of her nose suggested that it was broken.

Dalin's eyes were wide. 'Can you speak Kiana?' he asked softly.

We were so unprepared for her frighteningly lifeless form to spring to action then, that Agrudek gasped audibly when Kiana quickly jerked her head up and gestured for us all to be quiet.

It was only at that moment that we noticed the voices of our guards outside of the tent had stopped.

Kiana jabbed at Dalin pointedly and made exaggerated motions for him to keep talking. Dalin caught on. 'She isn't responding,' he delivered the line a little more loudly this time, watching her for approval. 'He really hurt her.'

Kiana gave a satisfied nod when we heard the curse filled conversations begin outside again.

'Frarshk, must've beat her good...'

Kiana propped herself up in Dalin's lap when she was certain our guards were focused on themselves once more.

'I was worried sick about you two!' she whispered, her white smile standing out against the crimson blood soaking her skin.

'What?!' Dalin hissed. 'You...?'

'Shush,' she told him more sombrely, using Dalin's shoulder to pull herself up properly. 'I didn't let him do too much. I was in control.'

With a sickening crunch, Kiana's shackled hands squelched her nose back into line with another spurt of coagulated blood.

'What in the Other Realm is going on?' I asked weakly, while Agrudek simply gaped.

Kiana looked miserable for a moment. 'I'm so sorry I wasn't there to help you,' she said. 'And I'm sorry if I gave you a scare,' she squeezed Dalin's hand and tapped my boot encouragingly with hers. 'But it was the only way I could think of getting myself in.'

We were silent, staring at her, dumbfounded.

'I had to try something, didn't I?' she implored. Then she reached to inspect the back of Dalin's head before he could register her movement. 'You had a good thumping here,' she mused. 'Did either of you have any bleeding from the ears or nose? Have you been dizzy?' she questioned me, releasing Dalin's head as I motioned that we had not.

She slid over to Agrudek next, and he gulped up at her almost demonic, bloodily red face.

'And what's your name, friend?' she asked kindly.

He swallowed nervously. 'Agrudek.'

'What part of Krall is your accent from?' she asked easily, briskly checking him over.

'From... in the main City... near the castle.' He seemed surprised, but didn't resist or cower as she reached for his injured arm.

'That must've been a nice house, in those parts,' she said conversationally.

'Yes... before they... yes.'

'Last time I went to Krall I passed through the east side sectors. It would've been nice if the rainy season hadn't made the roads and houses so muddy.'

'You... you have been to Krall?' Agrudek stammered incredulously. I often forgot myself how well travelled she was beyond the lands I knew.

'Several times,' she told him, tutting as she felt his ribs. 'I know you must ache all over, but we shall try to help you,' she said then. 'When we get free.'

He gazed after her wonderingly as she slid back across to where Dalin and I waited.

'When we get free?' Dalin repeated as she sat comfortably beside him, dabbing at the cut across her own forehead with her shirtsleeve.

'I have chosen to be confident that we can escape with our lives for this Quest,' she affirmed, stretching her legs out luxuriously.

'How did you do it? How did you create the explosions inside the camp?' I asked curiously.

'I did at first lack friends to help me,' she admitted. 'But the incredible Forest provided me with some new friends who were able to breach the perimeter.'

'Friends?' I asked. 'What friends?'

She shrugged. 'You'll understand when you see them, just keep in mind the strange ways of the Forest. It mustn't just effect the creatures of Darziates.'

'But what went wrong? Why did you have to surrender?' Dalin asked, confused. 'Didn't the explosions work well enough to kill at least some soldiers?'

'No, no, no,' she shook her head. 'So far everything's been going just as I'd hoped. I had to put up enough of a fight for them to want to bring me in. And for the General himself to bring me in further.'

I let out a huge breath. 'Well, knocking out a troop of their men and blasting the place was a good start,' I congratulated her.

She crossed her legs and leaned cosily against Dalin's shoulder, somehow getting comfortable on the ground while being held by chafing chains.

'I needed the General to force me to surrender for questioning, as the alternatives were that they would either kill me or at least put me under heavy guard. Instead they saw me as desperate and weak, giving in.'

'Simple,' I puffed.

'So,' Dalin started uneasily. 'What happened when you were with the General?'

Kiana crinkled her face in distaste. 'I've seen his kind before. All he wants is someone small, powerless, and also defiant, who he can have fun breaking. But I broke early,' she said smugly. 'After throwing me around, threatening me and trying to learn of who must have aided my efforts, he was disappointed and disgusted enough by my clearly broken spirit to send me away with little harm done.'

'Little harm done?' Dalin scowled.

'Oh, I did the surface cut to myself to make things authentic,' she reassured him. 'Our weapons were all laid out on a table at one end of his tent. I just had to roll around a lot, subtly block any dangerous blows he delivered, and angle myself around the space until he found himself throwing me into the table.' She became sly as she described his abuse. 'I was theatrical in my screams as I landed on my stomach, facing away from him and taking the opportunity to hide this under my shirt.'

Kiana fleetingly lifted her shirt to reveal her own safely sheathed dagger pushed into her pants so that only the hilt showed.

'A quick nick at my hairline that would bleed like crazy was all I needed as an excuse to faint. That took all the fun out of it for the General, and when I simply refused to be roused he lost interest. He sat on the cot, pulling something out from his cases...'

She paused for effect.

'What was he doing?' Dalin asked obediently.

'From where I was lying, I could see that he was looking into a globe of some sort.' She gave us a meaningful look then. 'And he was talking to it.'

'Talking to a ball?' I asked, my face scrunching in disbelief.

'Yes,' she nodded, her eyebrows raised. 'Please remember that his master is a Sorcerer. And please believe that I saw the ball glowing and heard it start talking back.'

Dalin released an astonished breath as I sat back in bewilderment.

Agrudek was leaning upright and listening with interest. 'Describe... the ball.'

Kiana regarded him for a moment, just as intrigued by his curiosity. 'It was fist sized and red. A deep, rich red. So dark that at first the ball looked black, but then as the General spoke it glowed and became a brilliant blood colour that filled his cupped hands with crimson light. And it wasn't a smooth or perfectly rounded ball, more like a large stone.'

'What did the... General say to the ball... and what did it say back?' Agrudek asked.

She paused, thinking. 'First, the General uttered a strange word. It sounded like 'engrark'. And the light started, before a terrible voice replied–from the ball.' Kiana shivered unconsciously. 'The General confirmed our capture and resistance. And the voice ordered that all three of us, and you Agrudek, had to be taken to Krall immediately.'

'The Sorcerer wants the three of you...' Agrudek sank back, shell-shocked as he sagged against the wall of the tent.

'It definitely seems so,' Kiana grimaced. 'But the General hid the ball in a case beside his bed and ordered me to be removed. So now I am with you again at last,' she eyed us seriously. 'And we do not wish to be taken to pay our respects to Darziates in Krall, so we must begin to plot our way free.'

I felt a grain of hope as resolve crossed Kiana's face and she pulled her dagger out before expertly picking open the locked shackles at her wrists. She had leapt across the tent to grab her medicine bag and had returned to her shackles in moments before rifling through her bag. 'First, I'll show you how to make some real explosives and some real diversions. There'll be no need to hold back on the way out.'

Agrudek watched her, dumbfounded as she set to work, pulling ingredients out of her pack. 'Those are some of the most... reactive plants in the land!' he exclaimed. 'Half of them don't even grow in Krall or Awyalkna! The other half... I didn't realise truly existed!'

'Collecting them was tricky. But they'll serve us well now,' Kiana agreed.

'What a... wonder,' he breathed, mystified.

Dalin and I nodded mutely in agreement.

CHAPTER SEVENTY FOUR

Dalin

Kiana had found Agrudek to be no mere admirer as she hastily prepared what she called 'real' explosives with ingredients from her healer bag. She realised that he was learned in such things himself, and questioned him on his past.

'I was a scientist—an inventor—in one of the poorer City sectors when my two beautiful daughters were born,' he explained timidly when she quizzed him. 'I was unusually good at making gadgets... and putting things together to make them work in different ways. I could do things that other people found impossible. And it drew the notice of ... the King.'

'You would have had no choice but to serve the Sorcerer,' Kiana surmised as she worked.

Agrudek nodded sadly. 'He... was beyond anything I'd ever imagined. The power that I felt, he was much more than just a man... I could hardly stand in the same room as him.' Agrudek's eyes lowered. 'I've never been so afraid of anybody. His own guards and servants trembled when he looked at them, or—or flinched when he moved. I was aware of his every breath! I could barely concentrate over the feeling of dread... but he gave me proper facilities, a good house for my family, and he set me to work.' Agrudek still didn't look up, but he shuddered. 'It wasn't long before the King demanded I make him things for the war. And when they failed... he took my family, and my hand, before I was thrown out. I wandered for so long as a beggar until I was lost in the Forest and found by these soldiers, who do not know what should be done with me.' The little man sagged sadly then.

'I hope to offer you your freedom,' Kiana told him grimly. 'I hope, for you, the worst has passed.'

He smiled faintly in gratitude. 'I don't deserve as much. I would do anything to get my family back. And... the things I made—'

The tent door was suddenly thrust open and a huge Krall soldier burst inside, holding a bowl with what looked like lumps of bread and scraps of meat in it, which he dropped at my feet.

My eyes darted to Kiana, but her dagger was nowhere in sight, and somehow the ingredients she'd just been mixing in a bowl were now hidden with a cloak.

Still, the massive man let out an outraged bark and thundered across to Kiana, grabbing a fistful of her hair before he threw her into the dirt.

'What the Frarshk do you think you're doing with that pack?' he bellowed.

Kiana's bag was incredibly suspicious looking, and with the flap untied I could see the cloths, jars, bottles and assorted herbs packed neatly away in there. The soldier raised his hand to strike her.

Noal gripped my arm to try to restrain me before I even moved to her defence, but we all watched, stricken, as Kiana wailed and threw herself at the soldier's ankles.

'Please!' she cried and sobbed, grasping at his legs. 'Please don't!' she wrapped her arms around his left leg and he stood at his bulky height, frowning down at her in disgust. 'Please! I want to go home! Please!' she wept all over his feet, grovelling and writhing pitifully while he stood at a loss.

He tried to shake her off, but she clung more tightly and howled louder still, seeming every bit a helpless wraith, until he flung her away from himself in aversion.

He shook his head contemptuously and threw the medicine bag to the other side of the tent while Kiana hiccupped and gurgled in a convincing heap on the dirt. He glared under thick eyebrows and stomped back out of the tent to reprimand the two guards outside for having clearly left the packs within reach.

Not until the acidic voices of the two guards resumed did we glance at each other in relief.

Kiana shook off her half open shackles and crossed to grab the healer bag again.

'There's no way we can do this subtly,' she said, pulling her bowl out and continuing as if we had not been interrupted. 'We could never get far with the amount of soldiers, fires and sentries here. It's just impossible. So we're going to have to make a big fuss to get away.'

She poured a splash of red liquid over the orange paste and the whole mixture in the bowl let out a low sizzling sound. Noal and I viewed it with apprehension while Agrudek looked on in appreciation. 'My friends will be ready to help us with the explosives once more,' she added.

'Who are these friends?' I questioned her this time.

She raised an eyebrow. 'Suspend your disbelief, and remember the power of the Forest,' she prepared us again. 'Now, with that in mind – my friends are birds.'

I guffawed, but she held up a finger.

'Accept it,' she told me bluntly. 'You'll see.' She began to scrape the mix, which had thickened into balls that she set aside to solidify and dry.

'Just three explosive balls this time?' Noal asked her as she finished.

'These ones do more than just create damage,' Kiana told him. 'They won't leave much behind at all.'

I eyed the line of explosives with mistrust as she stood up, dusting the seat of her pants.

'Time for stage two.' She turned to me and clicked my shackles open now too. 'I need you to lift me so I can reach the roof.'

'What are you going to do?' I asked warily, rubbing at my chafed wrists.

'I'm going to make a space for one of my winged friends to get in,' she replied.

'And if somebody notices?' Noal fretted.

'It will be the least of their worries,' she informed him darkly, taking my arms and putting my hands around her hips. 'I am ready. I won't need play acting anymore.'

'Alright,' I said, and stooped down lower to wrap my arms around her knees, lifting her easily so that she reached the roof with her outstretched knife and was able to make quick slices in the canvas.

A square of morning sunlight poured in through the hole and she quickly thrust her hand up to wave it about outside. When she brought her hands down I gently let her slide back through my arms until her feet touched the ground and she stood with her face upturned to the hole she'd created.

'So uh, how long do the birds usually take to reply?' Noal coughed awkwardly.

That was when a tiny blur of brown whizzed at top speed through the hole and flapped around Kiana like a whirlwind, letting out soft, excited peeps before spinning to a halt and landing in a flurry on the dirt.

She smiled down at the palm sized puff of feathers that had just burst so happily into our prison, and then Kiana started to converse with it in another language.

It was unlike any language I'd ever heard. Krall and Awyalkna had essentially the same language with only different accents or phrases. I'd heard that Jenrans and the far away desert people of Lixrax spoke completely unique tongues. But the elegant words Kiana quietly spoke sounded almost magical.

The little bird chirped back whenever she paused, even bobbing its small head when her musical voice stopped. I blinked as if waking from a daze when the beautiful words finished and the bird proudly puffed up its feathered breast and flapped its way back through the hole.

'Amazing!' Agrudek breathed as I stared at Kiana in awe.

'You can talk to birds?' Noal spluttered.

'Hurry, please,' Kiana's voice was back to normal, and she ignored our astonishment—instead looking at me pointedly until I scuttled over to lift her again.

'Noal,' she said then. 'Your job is to hand the explosives up. Carefully.'

He approached the three volatile balls with distrust, passing them up gingerly so that one by one she could push them through the hole. And within moments there had been three thumping sounds above where larger birds were landing on the canvas roof to collect each explosive before swooping off.

'You can talk to birds,' Noal breathed again, shaking his head as he marvelled at Kiana's compliant helpers.

'What language was it that you used?' I asked. 'Because those definitely weren't bird sounds.'

'I spoke a different language?' Kiana asked mildly, bringing my shackles back over to me. 'That's interesting.'

She calmly settled the chains to be half closed around my wrists again, and unlocked Noal's as well, not putting hers back on.

'We have only a short time before the first explosion.' Kiana stooped over her medicine bag and pulled out three small tubes with corks tightly stopping them. There was a red liquid like dye inside them that stained the glass.

'When these bottles are opened, if the lids even come off an inch, the red liquid will immediately become a gas with the first touch of oxygen and create a red cloud. The red gas is potent enough to give you cover and the advantage of surprise, but don't breathe it in. It'll strip the lungs of anyone who breathes it, so it can eliminate your enemies and yourself if you're not careful. It dissipates quickly, but only use it if absolutely necessary.' She handed both Noal and myself a finger-sized vial, and we copied when she tucked hers carefully into the top of her own boot.

'I'm going to get rid of our guards now, and with the first explosion I'll collect our weapons. I'll come for you before the second explosion.'

We nodded, and holding her dagger at the ready, she stalked without a sound to the tent door, disappearing through it like a wraith.

Almost immediately the foul discussion outside was cut off as there was a gurgling gasp from first one guard and then the other.

We didn't hear their bodies hit the ground, because the first explosion rocked our tent so hard we were thrown backward into the dirt–the force of the blow so great that we lay in stunned heaps wherever we'd been thrown while the tent sagged and billowed.

I sat up and let my shackles fall free as screams of pain rose outside, and I saw that Noal was already helping the stunned Agrudek to sit up too.

'Report!' the General bellowed over the chaos, his voice sounding hoarse in the dusty, hot air.

I noticed dizzily that our tent roof was smouldering, with patches of the canvas glowing faintly orange.

Some time passed before someone managed to respond to the General. 'Ten dead over here!' a soldier moaned from a distance away.

Kiana reappeared like an apparition at the limp tent entrance.

'Twelve on this side who won't live long,' someone else cried out.

A sour taste crept up from the back of my tongue as I registered twenty-two men had been wiped out in a single blast. I could hear retching outside, but we picked up our packs.

I noted blood on Kiana's dagger as she motioned us silently to come to her.

'Three dead on this side!' sounded another alert, closer to where the General's voice, and his own tent, must have been. 'But they've been marked by a blade!'

Kiana's eyes met mine unflinchingly. And the three of us moved to her side to collect our weapons as she turned to lead us out.

Kiana's sword was already belted at her hip, and her bow and arrows were slung over her shoulder.

'You took...' I heard Agrudek gasp and saw him reach toward where a small, black case was tied at Kiana's belt.

'The General's communication globe,' Kiana affirmed as she peered out to check our way. She held her free hand out as if to shelter us then, and the very earth we stood upon roiled as if enraged as the second and third explosions simultaneously tore their way through the camp opposite to where we were.

Noal and I held Agrudek's frail frame to support him while we were nearly blown backwards ourselves, but Kiana gripped my sleeve, pulling me to move.

My ears were buzzing and my head seemed to throb in time with the ringing, but she drew us out of the now scorched and shredded tent. The ground was still vibrating with shock waves, and my throat burned with the heat that scorched the air.

'Gods,' Noal uttered, as she led us over torn ground, around inert bodies, and through what had become a field of fiery destruction.

CHAPTER SEVENTY FIVE

Dalin

Ash covered survivors stirred in groaning heaps and shouts of confusion echoed all around us. I glimpsed a group of intact soldiers starting to form a panicked gathering, but they hadn't spotted us through the smoke yet, and Kiana moved us onward quickly, heading for the cover of the nearest trees.

It was not enough time before our absence was noticed though, and we were still running across blasted dirt when we heard the General's booming voice.

'FIND THE PRISONERS!'

Moments later the sounds of pounding feet signalled to us that more soldiers were recovering and stumbling after us.

'There! I see th–'

Kiana had turned, drawn her bow and loosed her arrow before the shout had ended, and it was cut short, but too late. The alarm had been raised.

I glanced back to see hulking figures breaking through shrouds of smoke behind us.

'Noal,' Kiana said. 'Run ahead. Help Agrudek.'

I followed Kiana's lead, and turned to face the oncoming soldiers, gripping my sword as Noal half carried Agrudek on towards the trees.

Kiana loosed another arrow at one soldier angling to move around us to attack Noal from the side and then shot her very last arrow at another soldier who rounded a crater ahead of us.

She slung her bow back over her shoulder and drew her sword as perhaps fifty glowering soldiers charged at us from all sides.

'No formation. We have a slight chance,' Kiana grunted, as they sprinted onward individually.

'Their sheer numbers...' I gasped.

Then Kiana sprang to meet a colossal man who engaged with her immediately. She seemed to dash around him, delivering a series of death strokes without breaking fluidity in movement. He fell quickly, and she engaged with her next foe.

I blankly lifted my sword to parry the blows of the soldier who reached me first. I reacted and blocked and lunged with my blade, just as I had always been trained to do. And I was numb as I felt the thick toughness of his stomach quickly give as I lunged forward to spear him with my blade.

He dropped, and I blocked the blades of two other soldiers as they drove down towards my head at the same time.

My life became a blur of curved sabres and I felt a hot bite of a slice opening across the top of my thigh.

Before my foes could take advantage, and quicker than my eye could follow, a straight blade was thrust past me and upward, ringing loudly against the sabres of my opponents.

I glanced back to see Kiana standing behind me, but without pause she'd thrown herself into battle with one of my foes, leaving me to the other.

I heard further fighting a distance away from us and knew Noal hadn't made it to the trees with Agrudek. I let my sword fatally bite into my opponent, only to have to raise it again to deflect the sabre of the next soldier.

Kiana was calmly stabbing at a new outraged enemy, who had clearly been wearing his spiked armour when the blasts went off. She was darting about him like a dancer springing from step to step, but she was leaving her deep marks wherever his armour had an opening.

I lunged automatically at my own current foe, and my blade slid under the soldier's guard. I felt the sluggish resistance that his body at first offered until he crumpled backward, sliding off my sword.

Kiana was gracefully darting about her next opponent, cat-like—leaving neat, precise and life threatening marks on him now too.

Next she made a flashing, neat slice across another man's belly before he'd even had a chance to engage with her, and as he fell to his knees, she spun to decisively slide her blade clean through his throat.

I was amazed to discover my own skill level as I was tested for the first time against true warriors who were not just sparring. Kiana was a blur of action, holding a wave of onrushing attackers at bay, and I found felling each man disturbingly easy. But, while Kiana and I rent the air with continuous strokes through flesh and bone, it was clear that we would be overwhelmed.

I heard Noal shout in frustration, and a glance showed me that he was being surrounded.

Kiana caught my eye.

'Deep breath,' she called, and drew her tube of red liquid from her boot, uncorking it. She threw it into the rushing soldiers and covered her face with the sleeve of her shirt while I hurriedly did the same.

Instantly an explosion of red cloud billowed as if by magic out of the chaos, swallowing the churning group of soldiers while Kiana propelled me away.

We left behind sudden shrieks that quickly turned to coughs, and then to choking rasps as the toxic red mist sounded like it had formed razor blades that, once inhaled, started shredding the lungs of those who had sought to harm us.

Kiana steered me toward Noal and Agrudek, where they were circled by at least fifteen of their own enemies.

Noal still gripped his sword threateningly, and stood over three dead men lying at his feet, but he was outnumbered and they were closing in. Agrudek cowered in terror behind Noal, knowing my brother would not be able to protect him.

An explosion bigger than any that had rattled the Forest took place inside of me, and I found myself sprinting forward and throwing myself at the back of a burly soldier who had just cocked an arrow to eliminate Noal without further fight.

I collided with the man's back so that he was both impaled on my sword and thrown forward to drop his bow harmlessly onto the grass.

Surprised at my sudden appearance, the soldiers nearest me whirled to engage, and I fought with a savagery I'd never known had existed within me—finding it easy to get under their guard or around their attacks, or to throw off those who tackled me. Like two swimmers battling across a raging sea to get to each other, I fought my way towards Noal and he fought fervently to get to me.

The roars and ring of steel against steel were deafening, but all I could seem to hear was the pounding of my heart and the breath coming from my own mouth as I deflected and returned blow after blow.

I never noticed that Kiana wasn't by my side. I only knew that I had to keep fighting, that we had whittled the fifteen of them down to six, and that perhaps we had a chance.

But then I heard the General's voice bellowing from somewhere close by. I turned my head even as I blocked a slice to my chest to see the approaching, mighty General and ten surviving men flanking him. The soldiers who had been stationed at the cliff top.

The disheartened band that had been fighting to surround and subdue Noal and I quickly drew back with new confidence to encircle us from a safe distance, and my body seemed suddenly bare in the space it had been given, without such pressing and scrambling.

Seventeen soldiers now joined together, and I knew using the red bottled poison was not an option this time, as Noal, Agrudek and I would have no way to escape it ourselves.

I moved closer to Noal and Agrudek at last, and we stood together, our bodies heaving as we gasped for air.

'My King will not easily forgive the massacre of over half of this troop,' the General snarled, shoving his way through the ring of soldiers.

He motioned for two men to step forward with him, and both of them were holding knocked bows at the ready. At their gesture, Noal and I had to forfeit our weapons—and releasing the hot hilt of my blade so that the sword fell to the ground, felt like releasing an important part of my own self.

The soldiers came slowly toward us until there was one standing beside me and one beside Noal, arrows poised.

'In fact,' the General continued to growl as he strode forward and lifted his curved sabre to my throat. 'After this, I don't think Warlord Mainyu would mind if all I brought back was your heads. Even if the King demanded he get his hands on you alive.'

I felt the sweat beading on my flesh and tried not to swallow or breathe hard enough to disturb his blade.

'And there's no one here who will stop me,' he said vehemently, stepping closer to scowl in my face.

'You see, I would beg to differ.' Kiana's strong voice echoed around the clearing.

The ring of warriors surrounding us murmured and lifted their weapons nervously, peering about themselves for the invisible speaker.

The General's eyes filled with wild fury as Kiana revealed herself, stepping out into a puddle of sunlight upon the last jutting ledge at the base of the cliff above us.

'You have no power over this,' the General smiled a warped smile up at her, and my throat smarted as the blade wobbled against my skin.

'No. Not from here. Not me,' she called down simply. 'But I think you can be stopped by your master if he is shown what you have allowed to happen. You must heel to your master.'

'How will King Darziates know my plan until it's fulfilled? He is not here to see it,' the General called back confidently, while the warriors about him watched the exchange in growing apprehension.

'I know the word to activate this,' Kiana answered, holding up the dark stone she had told us allowed communication with the Sorcerer of Krall.

'Hurt your valuable prisoners further and I activate the stone. Your King will see your incompetence and your betrayal, and you shall all surely die,' Kiana gazed down at the crowd surrounding us, seeming somehow more in command than the General.

There were outbursts of uncertainty and fear, and the ring of soldiers wavered.

The General frowned at the shifting group in disbelief. 'Hold the lines!' he shouted in fury. But his own men watched him with increasing hesitation and doubt.

The General stepped away from me now, his eyes bulging with wrath.

'Shoot her!' He yelled at the men around him, jabbing a finger toward Kiana.

None of them moved.

'Shoot her!' he bellowed again.

Kiana lifted the rock-like globe defiantly. 'Engrark.'

It was a beautiful word when it slipped past Kiana's lips.

'No!' the General gasped in utter shock, sheathing his sabre and taking a step toward the ledge–but a burst of pure white light surged from where Kiana stood, stopping him in his tracks.

The light filled my vision with such brightness that the Forest, the clearing and everyone around me disappeared. It was like a wave of energy that rushed from Kiana's fist to fill the whole area, and there were gasps and shouts of wonder and amazement.

A blissful, peaceful sensation enveloped me as I breathed the pure light in, and I could tell by the cries of happiness that even the monstrous men of Darziates felt the goodness of the magic from the sea of white light.

Then I staggered, as in a brutal, wrenching moment, the dazzling white emanation was swallowed by a burst of blood red light.

'Engrark,' answered a low, biting voice from somewhere within the stone. The voice, and the feeling that accompanied it, filled me with senseless trepidation, as though shock waves were rippling in my blood.

The voice was that of a Sorcerer, and it made my legs want to run, it made me want to cower and grovel, and made me want to lift my hands to fight it all at the same time.

The men around me cried out in despair and loathing at the stark contrast in what they felt from their King compared to the serenity that had been unleashed from Kiana.

'SHOOT HER!' the General roared again, witless distress across his savagely contorted face. But none of his men would end the life of Kiana now, or evoke the hate of the Sorcerer King.

Kiana let her hand fall, looking at it in shaken surprise. She hurriedly pushed the stone back into its case and the red light vanished.

The General turned in outrage while she did this, knowing his King had seen the destruction that had occurred under his leadership.

'Cowards!' he thundered frantically and snatched the loaded bow from the soldier standing dazed beside me.

Before I could react, I heard the twang of his fingers on the bowstring, and the General had loosed the arrow at Kiana.

Too late, I made a desperate grab for him, and I heard his own warriors shout out in protest and dread.

Kiana glanced up at our sound to register the arrow plunging through the air toward her heart. She swung herself to the side, but the arrow hit her with such force that she was twirled around upon the ledge and nearly toppled from it.

The General let out a triumphant, booming war cry while the strangely converted warriors who had been caught under Kiana's spell gasped and cried out with as much dismay as spilled from the lips of Noal, Agrudek and I.

Then Kiana stopped herself from falling, regained her balance, and without uttering a sound, she straightened.

Everyone below stopped their confused wailing and stared up at her. The General froze mid celebration.

By turning, she had stopped the arrow from piercing her heart. Instead, the arrow had lodged into the skin just below the collarbone on her right side.

An alarming amount of blood was already oozing from the wound, staining the shirt beneath the bodice of her tunic. It dripped thickly like teardrops from the stem of the arrow as it slid along the wood.

Everyone watched wordlessly, as if enchanted. Even the General was still as her eyes held his without blinking.

She lifted her left hand to the deeply embedded arrow, closing her fingers around the feathered end before slowly, harrowingly, drawing the arrow all the way back out of her flesh so that it didn't break.

When it was free the stain on her shirt blossomed more quickly, but as we all gaped, she reached for her bow and knocked the arrow in a flash of fluid movement.

'This is yours,' she told the General.

Without batting an eye, she fired.

The arrow whizzed back through the air, returning along the same path it had taken moments before, until it came to a dreadful stop between the General's eyes.

The impact was audible and the General's body remained tensely upright for a moment. There was a surprised look on his face–disbelief that she'd shot him back, before his vast form crumpled down.

Then sixteen soldiers turned to one another in desperate bewilderment; unnerved. They scrambled together, chaotically yelling over each other and trying to decide what they should do and how they could avoid the King's wrath.

'Kiana!' I yelled up to her.

'Go!' Kiana ordered. 'I'll find you!'

Noal pressed my sword hilt back into my hand as Kiana turned and slid down the other side of the rocks and disappeared from sight.

Noal firmly gripped my arm and Agrudek's, forcing us to follow him in the direction of the trees ahead, not stopping even once we had slipped into their dense shelter.

CHAPTER SEVENTY SIX

He had been on his way to confront the Emperor of Lixrax when he'd felt the calling from one of the many communication globes he'd given to his mortal Generals.

Darziates allowed his scryer to materialise on his open palm, uttering its activation word.

'Engrark'.

The scryer globe burst with a dazzling illumination, casting a crimson light over the walls of his private throne room.

And for the first time in centuries, Darziates, Sorcerer King of Krall, was surprised.

Instead of feeling the General's narrow thoughts, he felt the vast expanses of another mind, and he registered both who and what this being was.

He could see through the scryer, and also feel, the enriched purity flowing from the exquisite woman holding the globe. It filtered through his own globe, filling the stone chamber with a brilliant white radiance along with his own red illumination.

He had not felt anyone so powerful since before he had culled the Larnaeradee, and even then such magic had never existed.

Darziates looked beyond her to see his own mortal soldiers standing enraptured. Somehow this woman, this enigma, and her companions had bested over a hundred of his men.

Kiana. Her name was Kiana.

Yes... though she seemed to be like a mortal at the moment, she had confounded his men. And when he finally forced his will over hers, the contact of such opposing energy against his own sent pulsating, almost nauseating waves of glorious, prickling, spasming torment across his skin and into his core.

It was ironic, and perhaps fateful, that he should suddenly covet one of pure magic such as her, when his life Quest had involved eradicating all others of her kind.

But if she was descended from the Larnaeradee, and if he could corrupt her as she realised her power, she could be the woman he needed for himself and for his cause.

She must have been saved from his slaughtering for a purpose.

To be his.

He saw Agrudek amongst the crowd–which was perhaps grand design again too.

Darziates lost the vision of the scene as, repulsed, Kiana pushed the scryer into its case. 'Engrark,' he repeated, thoughtful, and more energised than before.

He tossed the scryer into the air and it disappeared as if it had never been, with hot desert sunlight replacing the red illumination within the stone room.

Oddly optimistic, Darziates turned his thoughts to Lixrax once more and pooled his power, focusing on penetrating this realm to allow himself access to the next. With a burst he was skimming half through the Other Realm, and half through what would be his own realm–warping across the wastelands toward the Lixrax Takal.

In an instant the scorching desert had passed, and like a phantom he appeared out of thin air, standing calmly in front of the Emperor of Lixrax, Razek.

CHAPTER SEVENTY SEVEN

Razek was sitting in his golden, jewel encrusted throne, and his gleaming temple-like hall was filled with vibrant crowds of dark-haired, bronze skinned citizens who had all just frozen in astonishment.

Wide-eyed servants in loin cloths, rich men and women in gauzy garments littered with gold, and shrouded, dusty peasants all watched the Sorcerer in stupefaction, their almond desert dweller eyes glittering.

People who lounged on silk cushions had paused with food held halfway to their mouths, and even the musicians and the scantily clad dancers who had been whirling and jingling around the enormous crowd had stopped moving. Their bare stomachs were thrust forward, their tanned arms were held paused in the air and their painted eyes were astounded.

'Razek,' Darziates said in the Lixrax tongue as the entire crowd shrank away from him. 'You must speak with me.'

Emperor Razek's dark, creased face turned from Darziates, and then to the crowd.

'You may talk to me, Sorcerer, but you may not harm my children. Let them leave.'

'For now, I have no interest in anyone but yourself,' the Sorcerer replied.

Razek motioned with a hand to clear the room, and the crowd obeyed at once, rising from their feasts, from their instruments, or from their cushioned litters to quietly stream towards the arched doors. Hardly a sound rose from hundreds of tinkling, jewelled belts or moving feet.

When the room was cleared, the great golden doors on both sides of the hall were closed, and Darziates was left with Razek and two advisors. Razek had even motioned for the oiled, muscled guards to leave, knowing that strength would not be enough against a Sorcerer.

Darziates conjured his own steel throne, and with hardly a pause he was seated upon its towering magnificence, directly opposite the Emperor.

Razek sat back in his golden throne, his bearded mouth forming a hard, fearless line.

'What is it you have come for, Crishnarx?' the Emperor glowered, using the

Lixrax word for a servant of the Demon King of the Other Realm.

Darziates considered. 'I assure you I am no servant. The Demon King works for me.'

Razek swallowed, his mouth tightening into an even harder line.

'And I have come for the ferocious battle skills of your armies,' Darziates continued.

Razek clenched the armrests of his throne. Lixrax was smaller in land and population than the other three Kingdoms of men, but its harsh surroundings, isolation and ancient practises of endurance meant that the warriors of Lixrax were highly skilled, and could survive the most brutal of conditions. But citizens of Lixrax were not warlike. They were simply survivors.

'We want no part in your conflict with Awyalkna,' spat Razek. 'And we have no alliances binding us to the likes of you.'

Darziates was impassive. 'You were allied with Krall the moment I decided it.'

Razek fought to maintain calm. 'Lixrax has never made any binding pacts with Krall, not even in the ancient war between Deimos, Awyalkna and the Army for the World. We have no obligations and you have no need to be here, Larza Ez.' Evil One.

Razek's knuckles turned white as his hands tightened over the golden throne arms. 'I know my history.'

Razek and his people had a long memory. Unlike the other mortal races, the people of Lixrax did not believe that the ancient tales of a magical army, or of the existence of magical beings at all, were only myth. The desert dwellers remembered through the ages and still believed the truth.

'Alas for Deimos,' Darziates agreed. 'That he did not conscript the Lixrax fighters. But this is to be more than just a war between Awyalkna and Krall. This is much greater than any of that. Once I have conquered Awyalkna I will conquer Jenra. And then...'

'Lixrax!' Razek's eyes were wide.

'Yes. I will be King of the mortal lands. And then I will cross the seas and claim every other race and land as my own so that I can be ultimate King.'

'So it is greed and ambition that rules you. You're just a tyrant craving more,' Razek glowered contemptuously.

'No,' Darziates told him calmly. 'It seems you don't remember all of your history.' And out of nowhere, the Sorcerer allowed the image of a woman to manifest in the air between them.

Razek and his advisors jumped, thinking that the feared Witch had appeared, but then Razek frowned in realisation.

The woman's image wavered like a dream, but her impression was inked carefully across the pages of many historical scrolls in Lixrax, and Razek knew her. She was the auburn-haired, green eyed Lady of the Forest. The guide of Nature sent to the world at the beginning of time to watch over life.

'Our great Mother...' Razek breathed in wonder.

'This is a memory of her, given to me and stored in my mind for eternity,' Darziates replied, and as Razek watched her, the Lady spoke.

'At the beginning of time, as I journeyed to earth, I carried with me the knowledge and will of the Gods. I held in my hands two prophecies that would reveal themselves to me upon my arrival into the new world. The first prophecy was revealed only moments after my arrival, and the voices of the Gods warned that the world's races would become separate through the ages. The prophecy also told of a deadly threat being born into the world at the end of the ninth age. The voices of the Gods said that the world and her many races must be united once more to survive the threat. If the world does not unite before the beginning of the tenth age, and the threat is able to succeed, the world will be destroyed in a storm of ice and fire. The voices of the Gods ended there, the prophecy laid quiet in my hand, and the second did not reveal itself. Remembering the warnings I have travelled far and wide to spread them, telling all of the prophecy so that in thousands of years the world will be ready, and can be saved...'

The image of the Lady faded to nothingness, and Razek stared at the empty space while his two advisors looked as if they were fighting hysteria.

'How could nobody know of these prophecies? This threat? Why has nothing been done?' Razek demanded, his thick black eyebrows drawing together in alarm.

'The magical and human races chose to do nothing, and drifted apart despite her warnings,' the Sorcerer replied. 'Each civilisation instead became more involved in their own affairs, and before now only Deimos has ever made an effort to conquer and unite each race against the threat.'

Razek gazed at Darziates in disbelief as he perceived the Sorcerer's meaning.

'I have taken up Deimos' cause to unite the world against the unknown threat, and plan to rid the world of its divisions,' Darziates affirmed Razek's suspicions. 'By giving the world one King, one Kingdom for all races, the world may survive.'

The tattooed markings over Razek's crinkled brow stood out as his skin paled. 'You believe that Deimos, who sought to subdue all in a blanket of terror, hunger and injustice... was heroic?' Razek choked.

Darziates inclined his head a fraction. 'The ignorance and selfishness of those who stopped Deimos meant our world continued to spiral towards this unknown destruction. Deimos simply used the help of darker powers and passions to break through his human barriers, changing the very fabric of his being and the essence of life in his blood and bloodline. He did all in his power, no matter the cost, to save the world. I am of his line, and must continue his Quest.'

'How do you know all of this to be true? It was generations ago!' Razek exclaimed while his attendants hovered, pale faced, behind his chair.

Darziates let his cold stare pierce the strong Emperor's deep gaze. 'Because the memory that I showed you is generations old. It has been passed along my bloodline, always shared from father to son so that each son could remember his true identity and purpose.'

Razek felt growing despair as he beheld the impartial face of the being in front of him. Darziates was just a ghoul ruled by the dark, with none of the human flaws or beauties that his flesh suggested he should have.

'You cannot be sure that you act correctly in conquering every race, and Lixrax will take no part in it,' Razek spoke at last. 'There may be a threat. But destruction in the name of survival cannot be the answer.'

Darziates' brow lifted slightly. The two advisors huddled even closer to the throne.

'The words of a mortal such as you, who will be old and returned to dust before I can blink, will do nothing to change what I have decided.'

'Perhaps, like last time, there will be an Army for the World to stand against your cruelty,' Razek answered resolutely. 'The cost of you being our saviour may not be worth the end result, if all that is left is a miserable world and barren lands ruined by your magic.'

Darziates was motionless for a moment.

'Did you know, Razek,' Darziates said at last, speaking dangerously slowly, 'that the ninth age is already waning?' his voice was low. 'I have already dealt with any that could challenge my Quest in these lands. Those who sabotaged Deimos' efforts. And no power has ever been stronger than mine. All who have been tested against it have failed.'

With Kiana at the back of his mind, Darziates created a blur of images and memories for the Emperor again.

The mortified Emperor and his advisors saw a stream of visions of what could only be poisoned Unicorns, rearing frantically as purple feather lines were spreading across their gleaming coats and dark, frothy bile streamed from their snouts. On the ground they writhed and kicked until their chests heaved no more.

'Stop!' Razek cried hopelessly.

But Darziates pushed on ruthlessly. He showed them flashes of hundreds of his mass slaughters of the Unicorns, and then he showed the bodies of multitudes of Larnaeradee, who looked like people, only somehow, more than that.

In flashes, Razek and his advisors saw countless beautiful creatures crushed before their eyes–victims of Sorcery. Creatures of the lands and seas, some big and some impossibly small.

When the dead faces, the screams, the horror of the memories faded, Razek had tears burning upon his fierce, tattooed cheeks. His advisors were crouching on the floor, shuddering.

'Arvix rux Larza!' Razek spat at Darziates.

'Yes.' Darziates replied. 'I am 'King of Evil'. In the name of my Quest.'

'Never will I sacrifice my children for you. These are the children of Lixrax. Men of honour. They will not die for a Demon. A shadow of a human's glory.'

Darziates regarded the Emperor unemotionally.

Without taking his eyes from Razek, he let his reined in power ebb a little.

Razek's eyes widened as the advisor next to him stood to walk across to kneel before Darziates, without Darziates ever moving. Then the advisor took his own sword from its sheath.

'What are you doing?!' Razek cried. 'Stop at once!'

'The magical ones could not defend against me. You most certainly cannot deny me. You don't actually have a choice in anything,' Darziates explained. 'None of you do. Your troops will join mine before the year is out. You will help me to cull enough Awyalknians for them to be controlled too. And then we'll go further.'

The advisor, his eyes wide and mouth gasping, raised his sword and took the hilt in two hands, facing the long dagger toward his own stomach. The advisor's hands were shaking as the blade began to move through the air toward his navel.

'Stop!' Razek was shouting now, but he found himself unable to rise.

'I am being generous.' Darziates continued as the blade got slowly closer. 'Instead of simply overtaking the land and spilling your royal, mortal blood, I offer you this–'

The blade was itching so close that the thin shirt over the advisor's stomach was fraying.

'...I will be King, but will allow you, Razek, to remain as a governor, under my rule. Your people will retain their own minds.'

The blade started to cut into flesh and the advisor screamed.

Razek looked on in horror while the blade slid into the advisor's flesh an inch.

'I will collect the army soon,' Darziates finished calmly, and disappeared as if he had never been there, throne and all.

But as the Sorcerer disappeared, Razek heard a meaty squelching as the advisor's hands were forced to fully plunge his blade into his own belly.

CHAPTER SEVENTY EIGHT

Noal

'Footsteps!' Dalin hissed and pulled us down hastily into a hollow covered by a fallen tree.

We'd been running raggedly for hours, not daring to stop, and now the sun was going down. Setting like a fiery orange jewel in a velvety pink sky.

We tried to rein in our ragged, breathless gasps, and clutched at our sides as we heard the footsteps crashing through the undergrowth only yards away, knowing they were too heavy to be Kiana's steps.

A voice called softly from nearby. 'Nothing?'

I pressed my eyes to a gap between the log and ground.

'Nothing,' replied a second warrior, and they came together within my view.

They were sweating and clutched their spiked helmets under their arms, their curved sabres pointing downward tiredly.

'We have to be back at the meeting place before dark,' one commented, wiping his brow.

'Perhaps one of the other teams found her,' the other said.

I felt Dalin stiffen next to me.

They were after just Kiana?

'We'll search the entire Forest if we have to,' the first soldier told his partner resolutely.

'We do have to,' he agreed. 'We need a powerful prize to ensure the King's forgiveness.'

The first warrior grimaced. 'I have not felt such power before.' He turned on his comrade. 'I feel her white light upon me even now.'

'You have felt the King's power...' began the other soldier uneasily.

'This was different. You know it,' interrupted the first.

The other licked his lips. 'Yes,' he agreed in a wavering voice. 'I know.'

'I would almost say we shouldn't give her to him and keep her safe ourselves. But that would be treason.'

'Aye. That would be treason,' agreed the other, sounding unsure.

There was a noise up ahead and both of them stiffened.

A bird flapped out from the ferns and, as if galvanised by the sound, the two warriors began moving back the way they'd come at once.

After a few moments, Dalin was struggling to sit up.

'What are you doing?' I asked him, although I already knew.

'We need to find Kiana before they do,' he said with an expression of unshakeable determination.

'She told us to keep going. She said she'd find us,' I reminded him uselessly. 'She always does as she says.'

'Perhaps she can't this time!' he whispered agitatedly. 'Perhaps they've got her on the chase or have cornered her. Perhaps she's too hurt to move.'

I gave in to my own dread. 'Why in the Gods' names are they so keen to have her now, anyway?' I groaned.

'They won't hurt her now that they know,' Agrudek reassured us quietly.

'Know what?' Dalin asked.

'That she has magic. Different to the King's.' He glanced at us nervously.

'No human has magic,' I answered with perplexity. 'Only Darziates and Agrona are magical.'

'The white light? The effect she had on Darziates' own poisoned soldiers? The birds?' Agrudek shrugged helplessly. 'There's something different about her.'

Dalin looked bewildered. 'I don't know what they teach you in Krall,' he said slowly. 'But there's nothing wrong with Kiana.' He stood and slid back out of the hollow in the ground we'd hidden in.

I clasped his hand as he bent down to pull me firmly out of the hollow, and we both turned to carefully lift the frail Agrudek out behind us.

'Let's go,' Dalin said grimly then, and we followed him back through the trees, the way we'd come.

We only stopped when it was the dim blue of evening, and we saw the line of soldiers scouring the land ahead of us.

They were keenly following a trail, and what was most likely Kiana's tracks. A few of the warriors held flaming torches above the ground as they moved slowly forward, scouring the Forest floor for the path to their reward. And one of them held Kiana's healer bag.

Dalin pulled us roughly aside, behind a thick patch of massive trees.

'We split up from here,' he whispered, peering around the tree trunk urgently.

'You two search along this side,' he gestured to the left of the searching soldiers. 'I'll take the right.' He drew his sword without a noise. 'We have to find her first.'

'We'll lose each other!' I whispered in protest. I'd rarely been apart from Dalin.

'Every two hours we'll meet up at the stream bank in this part of the Forest,' he told me hurriedly, itching to go. The flame lights of the soldiers were passing by. 'After tonight we'll follow the stream, I'm sure that's what Kiana would be doing. It's our best bet of finding her.'

He was right. It was the same stream we'd been following ever since Kiana had led us into the Forest.

I nodded glumly, beginning to see how he felt now. He needed to find her.
'Be careful.'

'Always brother,' he said before slipping quietly away into the trees.

I looked after him with a lurching feeling in my stomach. Then, with no less urgency, I helped Agrudek as we made our own way to search for Kiana.

CHAPTER SEVENTY NINE

War Lord of Awyalkna, and Angra Mainyu's counterpart, Chayton Conall pushed the canvas door open and stepped into the King's tent with a heavy heart.

He found the King pouring over parchments of reports, looking weary and aged.

Glaidin had been outwardly unshakeable in the months of gathering forces on the border and had maintained determined strength while leading his loyal Awyalknians into Krall. But privately, he was a broken man.

Word of the Dragon attack upon the Palace had only fuelled their forces with further motivation, but the news had drained his King.

Glaidin was already facing a hopeless war, his Queen was far from his protection, and he was haunted by the fact that Dalin and Noal had not been found. Glaidin had felt the weight of their disappearance keenly, feeling sure that his quarrel with Dalin had been the cause of it.

Conall knew that Dalin could be a hot-blooded, often impatient boy, but the Prince was also passionate, good natured and fiercely loyal. The Prince wouldn't have foolishly run away out of spite. Nevertheless, Glaidin could not be consoled on the matter, and as Glaidin had been Conall's closest friend since boyhood, it pained him to now be bringing his friend further upsetting updates.

'Conall,' Glaidin husked tiredly in greeting. 'What news?' He stretched his long legs out and rubbed at an angular, now almost gaunt face.

Conall grimaced. There was no helping it.

'Our spies report that Darziates now has the allegiance of Lixrax,' he reported bluntly.

Glaidin's broad shoulders slumped a fraction. 'The Sorcerer already has nearly double our numbers in troops from his own country. Not to mention his odd creatures.'

Conall toed the dirt unhelpfully. 'And not to mention the fact that he has apparently conjured himself a set of Dragons along with his Witch.'

'But now he also has the fierce blades of Lixrax, as well?' Glaidin grimaced.

'Yes.' Conall nodded. 'He must be quite intimidated by us.'

Glaidin choked, resignedly rubbing his eyes.

The troops had only recently completed their preparations and started a march into Krall. From the moment they had crossed the borders, the whole Awyalknian army had felt a disconcerting shift upon crossing from one land to the next–a draining, unnatural force that could only be the touch of Sorcery.

'It is a hopeless fight against such a being,' Glaidin sighed.

'I know it, you know it. Everyone knew it before we all set out,' Conall shrugged burly shoulders. 'Yet the Awyalknian army does not cower. We go to meet Darziates before he comes for us.'

'The situation is dire,' Glaidin said.

'And it's only getting worse,' Conall nodded.

'So tomorrow...'

'We march ever on. Your people are behind you, my King.'

'I am glad of them. And glad of you,' Glaidin said finally. Ignoring the fact that they desperately needed help. And that Awyalkna had near been emptied, and there seemed no aid to come.

138

CHAPTER EIGHTY

Kiana

The burning had started in the hole where my skin had been punctured. But as blood had oozed down my front in a hot, thickening slick, the blazing fire beneath the surface of my flesh had only intensified.

I blinked sweat from my eyes and clutched my sopping shoulder, feeling the heat radiating in my cheeks and throbbing in my fingers and toes. Gods, it was as if my arteries ran thick with boiling pitch.

Yet somehow shivers were radiating through my core. Somehow my teeth were chattering. And I was dimly aware that on the surface, my clammy skin was cold all over.

There was searing pain as I used my free hand to bat away ferns and branches that scratched at my face, but then the contradictory feeling of a light, trickling tickle as a trail of blood forged a new line down my arm and over my elbow.

I was moving sluggishly, stepping heavily and stooping like a heavy sleep walker drugged with foggy dreams. On I went, one leaning step after another to slowly push through green walls, and to slowly find my boys.

I'd promised them, and I had to hurry, had to drag on, because time was passing. The sun was hazy in my eyes, or my eyes were hazy in the sun, and Dalin would be troubled.

When I glanced down for a moment I saw my white shirt was dripping and stained. I could hear gasping and rasping, but my breaths simply refused to be hushed. And my hands were red gloves, shaking too much now to press the hole in my shoulder closed, shaking too much to even hold them up against the sharp fingers of the ferns.

Red drops on the leaves appeared to lurch and spin before my eyes. Round and round. And I worried dimly that my blood was not thickening, the bleeding was not getting lighter, instead every step meant another warm little spurt from the hole to tickle my ribs and make my hands slippery. I hadn't felt so damaged since Agrona had branded me on the same unlucky spot.

I stopped with a wave of nausea to lean over dizzily. When I moved to force my aching muscles and bones into an upright stance, the sky had become darker. Or my sight had.

Two steps designed to carry me forward took me to the left instead, and then I stumbled because it was so dark in my head.

I made an effort to run blindly, wanting nothing but my boys. But instead I felt myself go down, and the ground dropped away. My eyes rolled upward as I tumbled downward, my limbs dashing uselessly against sharp rocks instead of protecting me so that I felt new hot scratches open all over.

The drop ended with a brutal hardness catching my body, and I felt the splintering of ribs going loose inside me. I retched on the vomit that wanted to explode up upon impact and scrabbled onto hands and knees to open my eyes on a world that was rotating.

The rock below me and the trees all round were alive and twirling as fast as my insides were heaving and my head was pounding—as if my brain was swelling quickly and then shrinking just as fast.

'Dalin...' my voice rolled around the clumsy tongue in my mouth. I heard a wet sob filter out from stinging lips as I wobbled and stood, wondering if I was spinning without meaning to.

Gods, it was hard to walk when carrying my thudding heart became a burden that got bigger in my chest. But the thudding was getting slower, and so was I. My boots were getting too heavy to lift.

The trees blurred and darkened as they passed by, looking like they were marching onward faster than I was. I stopped altogether, and a tree leaned on me to take a break in the fog.

I realised I could hear voices. Faint, faraway, but close voices.

Gods, the pain was a suffocating blanket. It swelled over my whole body.

Then I moved the heaviness of my head to look to my side, where I saw another movement.

His lovely shape was moving fast, leaping over rocks, racing between trees.

'Dalin,' I mumbled. 'Found you.'

It was nearly dark, but I saw his desperate expression.

There was an awful rushing in my ears and black patches blocked bits of the world out in my eyes.

I was so glad when he came to me in an urgent flurry, but when he took my hand to fly away with me, I felt like I was sinking backward, out of balance, like I might just gradually be sucked down into the foliage and stay there, swallowed whole.

Instead of running with him, I sank into his side.

He had my hand, and the blood now fell like sticky raindrops from his fingertips too, but something inside of me was letting go. Untying itself from an anchor so I could sink down to rest.

His eyes were on the hole in my chest. Green eyes. Frantic eyes.

A hole! I thought to myself dizzily. I hate sewing!

My insides had become weights that dragged, heavy with some dreadful, seeping sickness that was spreading through my body from the wound–chasing down my feverish soul with dark, deadly arms outstretched.

Dalin held my hand tighter in a saturated grip. He held me to reality as I noticed torch lights getting closer. I reached towards the lights, the golden globes of flame bobbing prettily in the darkening world, but Dalin pulled me away.

In a sickening lurch, I was up in his arms and looking at the moving stars between the circling treetops.

Body wracking fire raged up and down my side, exploding in my shoulder and chest.

'Dalin.' I gurgled softly to check we were both really there, and I felt warm wetness drizzle down my chin.

Everything was smudging and distorting, as if a painting had been spoilt by raindrops, and only one thing stayed clear and tangible.

The grip that Dalin had on me. Keeping me in this world.

CHAPTER EIGHTY ONE

Noal

'N... Noal...' I heard Agrudek's tired, strained voice as I peered anxiously into the night.

'We'll give Dalin just a little longer,' I cut him off distractedly, knowing that it was getting late. I could see that the moon was high and small as I stood beside the gurgling water of the steadily rushing stream.

'Noal... your boot...' Agrudek quavered, and I realised that his voice held a note of panic.

Then I felt something creep up my ankle, one prickly leg at a time.

I groaned when I looked down to see the dark shape pause in its sneaking to wave its hairy, spiked legs up at me, as if it was pleased to have been found out.

'Granx?' Agrudek whimpered disbelievingly, drawing his legs up onto the rock I'd left him to rest on.

'You're back again?' I asked the beady eyed creature, feeling almost resigned. 'Surely it can't be just to poison me after all of our meetings.'

Its two fangs, glistening with poison, seemed to smile out of the darkness, and I frowned when I saw it waggle its legs towards the trees.

Then Agrudek sucked in a terrified gasp, and I looked up to see six towering, dark shapes watching us from between the trees.

I stiffened as my heart jumped into my mouth and I realised that we were surrounded again.

Though I wanted desperately to reach for my sword and to move to Agrudek, I didn't move. The dark silhouettes that had spread out between the trunks betrayed incredibly tall, imposing figures. Inhuman figures. But not spiked like the beasts.

They were standing silent and still like shadows, but their keen eyes glittered out from the darkness, and the hairs on my arms raised as I noticed that the air seemed filled with something I had felt before, from the Willow. A sizzling energy that made the surface of my skin ripple with shivers.

It was not the kind of feeling that any of Darziates' creatures had given me, and while I was certain these beings were not human, I was also certain they were not of ill design.

'Well met,' I held my hands out non-threateningly. 'I am Noal. This is Agrudek.'

The figures wavered a little, as if addressing them had broken a spell.

One especially tall figure, shrouded like the others in shadow, stepped forward into the moonlight then. I craned my neck upwards to see him, while feeling cascades of that sensation in the air—which could only be described as magical—spread outward from him like a cool mist.

'Well met,' the being replied in a halting voice with a lilting tongue, bowing gently with a graceful sweep of strangely long, lean limbs. 'I am Frey. Granx has summoned us to your aid.'

I was breathless at the sight of his strikingly sharp features, which made him look like something carved by the Gods, like an artwork brought to life. His skin was also unlike that of any other ordinary man I'd seen, being of richest midnight black, flawless and deep. And his hair, rugged and unruly, standing up at all ends, was bone white.

'Arn niela rin lissa?' he asked the Granx then, using a beautiful, foreign tongue.

The Granx plucked a long, spike tipped leg free of my trousers and waved it in a small circle before lowering it, as if in answer to his question. Then it scuttled down my ankle and through the grass, disappearing quickly.

The tall stranger, Frey, raised his smouldering eyes to take in Agrudek, who was gaping wide mouthed, and then back to me. I was waiting with a sense of strange calm. I knew things had changed now, for the better.

'We are Elves of Sylthanryn. We have come with the hopes of offering the Three our help and friendship,' Frey said in a low voice, still pronouncing the Awyalknian words carefully. He was a figure of quiet assurance, but fiery, alert energy burned in his eyes and stance. The power ebbing from him as he focused on me was enough to take my breath away.

'We have known of your Quest and were aware immediately of your entrance into the Great Forest. The power of the One sent shivers through every leaf and blade of grass with her first step under the ancient treetops. However, her power also created a shield over your company that left no trace and kept even animals who may have seen you from being able to recall the details.'

'You are referring to Kiana?' I asked with a slight frown.

'Her power is already great,' Frey inclined his head. 'We could also feel the foulness of Darziates existing within his soldiers as soon as they entered the Forest, and we knew of the capture of yourself and the Raiden because you were not under the One's shield at that time. However, when the One rejoined you we lost our sense of your location once more. Only now have we been able to sense your own presence.'

I was unsure of how to respond, but he spoke once more as if nothing was amiss in his description of our group.

'Where are the One and the Raiden?' Frey asked then, his face serious.

My heart suddenly sank with uncertainty and desperation once more. 'We escaped Darziates' men, but Kiana was separated from us and wounded by an arrow, and Dalin is out searching for her.'

Sounds of concern came like the whispering of a breeze from the trees as the other beings wavered in the shadows.

'The One is injured?' Frey asked sharply, moving forward a step in apprehension.

'Kiana,' I reaffirmed.

Disquiet creased the dark, solemn face of the Elf. 'Let us hope the Raiden and One have found each other.'

At that moment, a growing whirring sound of something speeding through the air reached my ears. Frey was unmoved, but Agrudek and I looked about in consternation to see a fast blur shooting through the Forest towards us.

The blur came to an abrupt stop in the air beside Frey, and I felt surprise pluck at my brow as the blur became clear and took on an, again inhuman, form.

For the second time myth was made reality before my eyes as I beheld a new creature, the size of a small child, flapping little wings to keep herself afloat. Thick wisps of gravity defying, flaming red hair added to her miniature height, as though a bonfire was sparking away on her head.

She began to speak hastily in a different tongue, until Frey gestured to me and she switched to Awyalknian in the slightly higher pitch of voice that children have.

'Well met!' she greeted.

'Noal,' I responded quickly, still trying to recover composure.

'Asha—Nymph. Adorable squad leader,' she explained herself speedily. Then she turned red coloured eyes back to Frey. 'The One's shielding power has weakened, which is worrying, but it has meant we've caught traces of her and the Raiden. The squads are searching, and they're close. We need to move now, though. Because Krall soldiers are also close. The Lady has warned that these soldiers now covet the One in particular.'

Frey nodded. 'Soon your company will be reunited,' he told me, and he held out a midnight hand to Agrudek, who, in awe, reached up to clasp it and allow the lean warrior to effortlessly lift him to his feet.

The other Elves stepped forward then—all of them sharing Frey's exotic skin and bone-white hair, and as I felt the overwhelming effect of their presence adding to that of Frey's and Asha's, I was offered a hand as well.

In wonder, I felt an incredible surge of prickling energy thunder through my fingers as soon as I made contact with the Elf. I felt that I could fly across leagues with a single step, that every cell in my body was being polished and refreshed, that even my hair follicles were more magnificent now.

'Follow me,' Asha instructed, before flying off through the trees at an extreme pace so that I wondered for a moment how we were supposed to catch her.

Then the Elves moved into formation. The Elf who held my hand began to jog, his long legs seeming to make him fly over the ground, and as the burning, prickling feeling travelling from his hand into mine spread upward along my arm, into my shoulder, my chest, my stomach, to explode through my legs–I found I could keep up.

My eyes adjusted to see everything more keenly, and I realised we were moving faster than any human should be able to move.

I passed things too quickly, but I could smell and hear everything with more clarity. Most incredibly, I could feel more clearly. I could feel the overwhelming amount of life and power around me, I could feel Frey's energy and determination, and I could feel Agrudek's fear. I could also feel the severe pain of someone close by as their body was overtaken by something terrible.

The trees rushed by and my feet hardly touched the ground until Asha circled back from what she'd seen ahead and pushed to keep pace with us.

'They're close,' she gasped out. 'Frey, they're being attacked. Only the Raiden's strength is protecting them. But he is outnumbered greatly.'

'How long?' Frey asked, not stopping.

'He will be overtaken in moments. The squad is regrouping now we've found them, but our strength is failing. Our magic is near spent from the days of searching.'

'We'll be there,' Frey grunted grimly, his eyes narrowing.

She nodded, speeding off in the direction she'd come from, and I was amazed as I felt our group somehow pick up pace.

Soon we could hear the shouts ahead and could see torches through the trees. In a rush we broke out into the open and found a scene of chaos–but my enhanced sight absorbed everything instantly.

Dalin was facing sixteen huge soldiers of Krall, still monstrous in their spiked armour and with their gleaming, curved blades. He had a gash across his cheek and a deepened one across his thigh. Sweat saturated his hair and mingled with the blood on his exhausted face. But Dalin was fighting with such courageous force that the men who tried to swarm him were kept at bay.

They fought ferociously to reach Kiana, where she laid motionless upon the grass behind him. Yet he moved faster and with more power and skill in his blows than his opponents. He had always been a match for many of the soldiers we'd grown up with in practice, but this was something more than the mastery he'd shown in drills and matches at the Palace. Something spectacular and unstoppable had been brought out in him in the face of true combat, and the sound of his sword clanging against the sabres and armour of his enemies rang like fast and savage thunder strikes.

Gushing from the trees there now came a flow of flying Nymphs like Asha. They swooped and swiped at the men who had been engaged in battle with Dalin. Their brightly coloured hair, and hands which glowed with balls of coloured light, filled the clearing vibrantly–but the light balls sent their foes hurtling backward as if they'd been struck by lightning, and left the soldiers sprawling on the ground.

Dalin seemed to have taken in the fact that mythical beings had materialised to join with him. He had not wavered, but continued his devoted, unrelenting aggression toward anyone who dared to try to get around him to Kiana.

Dalin roared as a soldier tried to duck past his guard and swung his sword at the hulking soldier with such force that the bulky man only just had time to block the blow. He was sent flying backward by Dalin's shove.

Our Elves left us to hurry to Dalin's side, and Agrudek and I sagged as a deflated feeling of normalcy returned to our limbs.

The Elves drew long, double tipped spears from where they were strapped at their backs, and the blades of each Elf burst to life with green light. But I noticed that the Krall soldiers appeared almost undaunted by the supernatural beings, as they fought single-minded, almost hungry to get to Kiana.

Only when Frey's team joined Dalin to create a semi-circle that blocked Kiana from their view and reach, did they awaken to the hopelessness of their fight.

With Agrudek following, I ran to Kiana's side as the soldiers began to scatter, and I felt as if I lumbered heavily.

'Gods,' Agrudek gasped as we both knelt beside her and I felt a sick ball tighten in my stomach too.

Her breathing was shallow and I could see that her entire side was soaked with blood–the wound still bleeding sluggishly after such a span of time.

The Krall soldiers were dumbfounded and being chased away at last, so Dalin sheathed his sword and whirled to face me, dropping down on the other side of Kiana.

'Who... what are they?' he asked hurriedly, panting.

'Elves. Nymphs. They're friends,' I told him. 'They seem to think we're important and came to aid us.'

'Good.' Dalin gasped, eyeing the unbelievable and enigmatic beings dashing about the clearing. 'We need all the help we can get.' His shoulders were heaving as he fought to get his breath back, but his eyes returned to Kiana.

'She'll get through this,' I told him. 'Kiana's the strong one.'

The Elven warriors were sheathing their double sided weapons, the coloured flames engulfing the blades had disappeared, and the Nymphs sank lower in the air to hover at our height protectively. They didn't extinguish the glowing spheres that they'd before used as weapons, so the small clearing was still filled with light.

Dalin didn't rise from where we knelt by Kiana, but regarded Frey and the beautiful, incredible beings surrounding him. He rubbed his hand against his tunic in an effort to clean it of crimson stains and held it out firmly to Frey.

Frey's intense eyes burned upon Dalin, and he took Dalin's unwavering hand in his own strong grasp. 'Well met Raiden,' he said solemnly, before they released each other's clasp.

'Well met friend,' Dalin replied, controlling the fatigue in his voice. 'I thank you,' he said simply then.

Frey knelt down with us too. 'Will you allow me to see how grave the situation is with your companion?' he asked, and Dalin gave him a weighing look, before moving aside and standing. He sheathed his sword and stood swaying as I rose to stand at his side, worried that he could collapse at any moment.

Frey gently laid his hand upon Kiana's forehead. Then he moved to begin untying the cord of her tunic. I felt Dalin tense next to me, but as I turned to him, I saw one of the tall, dark-skinned warriors reach out a large hand and rest it reassuringly upon his rigid shoulder.

'It will be alright,' the hulking warrior soothed from his great height. 'Frey has healing powers. We will allow no more harm.'

Dalin turned as Frey gently eased the front of Kiana's shirt open enough for the bleeding wound to become visible, and both Dalin and I watched on sickly as we saw Agrona's brand upon her skin.

It was as if red ink had been tattooed into Kiana's shoulder, and the blood that stained all of Kiana's side seemed somehow less alarming than the stark, smooth tear drop shaped branding. The only fault in the shape was where the arrow had pierced the very centre of it.

Frey's face grew increasingly troubled as he held a hand over the wound until finally he rose, his face grim. 'The poison of dark magic in that mark has been reawakened. It has been released from the original brand and is spreading throughout her body. She is feverish and unable to fight it. The poison makes it so that the bleeding won't stop. We need to get her to the magic of the Lady.'

Dalin stumbled slightly for a moment, but I caught at him and saw that the Elf warrior still supported him also.

'We should leave at once,' Frey said, looking at Agrudek, Dalin and myself.

I nodded, and Dalin stepped forward with a strength that almost hid his weariness, and stooped to lift Kiana.

'I'm ready,' he said gruffly.

Frey regarded him sincerely. 'Friend, your courage and strength have been shown tonight as beyond admirable. Will you allow me to carry the One in your stead so that the journey may be faster?'

Dalin looked ready to refuse, having never seen the speed of the Elves as they dashed across the Forest.

'Raiden, we will not separate you from her. We will simply get you all to the care of the Lady as fast as we can, so that she can try to help the One.'

Dalin frowned down at the pale face of Kiana, resting as if in the deepest sleep upon his shoulder.

'Be careful,' he gave in finally.

He stepped warily closer to Frey, and allowed the Elf to cradle Kiana in his own arms, while I went to Dalin's side to support him. I could feel his body shuddering with depletion.

The same warrior who had steadied Dalin before stepped kindly over to him again now. 'Will you allow me to give you help?' he asked, holding out his hand. Dalin nodded his thanks, looking hardly able to stand, and took the huge hand held out to him. Another warrior came to my side, already linked to Agrudek, and offered his hand.

And in moments I was again being carried at a phenomenal speed across the Forest, following the gurgling stream.

CHAPTER EIGHTY TWO

Dalin

Everything ached as I was rushed across the Forest floor. But it was my heart that especially throbbed and drummed like a cramping muscle in my chest.

In the arms of the richly skinned warrior ahead of us, I could see Kiana's boots swinging with his motions.

I was dimly aware that the trees were swelling to impossible sizes as we rushed past. And the gurgling of the stream was getting louder as the size of the channel of water grew into a clear gushing river that churned with enormous sound.

I felt removed when I saw the roaring river split itself in two to create a border, and when we ran over that border, our speed such that our feet barely touched the water. I felt removed even when we suddenly entered a part of the Forest where there were brilliant lights in the massive trees. They were coming from gaps like windows in the twisting trunks of the trees, as if these were living, breathing towers.

We passed onwards in a blur and I hardly registered any wonder as I next found myself looking down into the largest, strangest natural hollow in the ground that I'd ever seen. It was as if a great circle of Forest had once dropped away, and the lower level space had been used to create an impossible City that ended with a monstrous waterfall.

We reached a path winding down along the rocky wall and into the sunken City, and only began to slow as we followed it into the depths of the submerged, magnificent area.

I knew dimly that there were faces and lights and blurred figures and crowds waiting. But I hardly saw them as we came to a stop in their midst. The warrior didn't stop supporting me against his shoulder, and I was grateful because it was getting hard to remain upright.

The whole extraordinary City was alight with golden floating globes that sat like lanterns in the vines all along the cliff walls, in every tree and bush and across every vine bridge hanging gracefully over our heads, but everything still seemed blurry.

Beautiful beings with dark skin and white hair surrounded us, standing in walkways that seemed to be growing out of the trees, and looking out from lit up dwellings that were a part of the cliff faces. Those strange little winged Nymphs hovered like glowing stars amongst leaves and in the air.

There seemed to be thousands of them as we stepped out into the light, and I was swamped by the extent of the magic they exuded.

I squinted at the crowds as they parted to let a small, ordinary looking old woman through. She was faintly recognisable, and though everything else had failed to hold my attention, *she* did. Something about her, underneath the surface, made her seem like a Goddess sent from the heavens down to the lands of men. Swells of power rippled around her—so dense that the air stirred and shifted visibly around her, and her flashing green eyes were mesmerising. For a moment I imagined torrents of auburn hair upon her shoulders, but I blinked hazily and it was silver.

Noal had again come to stand by my side, and I saw my own wonderment reflected in his face. 'She looks familiar,' he breathed.

She stopped before us with her warm, brown face radiating care and a wisdom that was more noticeable to me than anything else in the blurred faces and impossible things pressing in all around. The perceptiveness and strength emanating from this woman was staggering, and it anchored me to reality in a way that I gratefully clung to.

'This was not the welcome we had hoped to give you, honoured guests,' she said in a deep, musical voice that somehow carried all the way up to the top of the round cliff edges.

'We offer you tree towers to rest and recover in,' she told Noal, Agrudek and I warmly. 'And I will tend to the One's healing myself.' She gestured to Kiana with brown, lined hands, and the movement broke my enchanted reverie. I nearly staggered with the memory of my hurts, and Kiana's, but I felt a firm grip of support from the fierce and terrifyingly magnificent being beside me. His hand encompassed my whole upper arm.

'Lady,' I said quickly, assuming this title unconsciously. 'I must go with Kiana.' I took a stumbling step towards the Elf named Frey, and I was surprised at how far away my voice sounded.

The Lady smiled and inclined her head in understanding as Noal and Agrudek stood loyally by me. The warrior whose support I leaned on steered me to follow Kiana as Frey carried her through the parted crowd, and the immense energy that seemed to dwell within him poured over me so that my stupor abated slightly, the blurriness shifting back to the edges of my vision.

We were taken to one giant tree 'tower' among many, and I felt numb when we entered through a gracefully carved doorway at the bottom of the twisting trunk to find a large room that looked like part of a wooden home instead of the inside of a tree. Steps protruded from the wooden walls and wound upward, but the Lady waited for us to stand around her, and before I could blink, I was being sucked dizzyingly upward.

I saw a series of beautifully adorned, round rooms that were within the tree as I hurtled upward, but I vaguely realised that we were whizzing directly through hard objects in these rooms, as if they were nothing, to get to the upmost part of the tree.

Our motion then stopped jarringly quickly when we found ourselves in the highest room where a large, rounded, wooden framed bed nestled against a curved wall.

The softly lit room looked like the safest place in the world in the eyes of weary travellers. There was a large, diamond-shaped window, a vine and branch wrought balcony, and the bed was made up with a plump white cover.

Frey carried Kiana over to lay her on the bed, getting blood on the cover, and I saw how deathly pale her face was.

I fumblingly wormed my way free and crossed the circular room to stand at her side, swaying.

Frey caught me before I toppled over, but I was intent on bending to clutch her icy hand in my own. Buckling knees were an enemy, and I ignored them.

I only looked up at the warm feeling of the Lady's hand upon my shoulder. A shock of rushing energy made my focus shift without my meaning it to.

'Please help her,' I whispered, and the Lady nodded with a kind smile.

'Now that you have seen she is safe, you can be comforted. Frey and I will tend to her, and you can wait in the room below.'

'Thank you,' I told the Lady as the room swam. 'I don't want to be far away from her.'

'Of course,' she agreed as the other warrior collected me good naturedly again and I was led away.

I peered over my shoulder as the warrior helped me down the steps growing out from the walls, and I saw the Lady bending over Kiana.

Then I sent a silent prayer up to the Gods. Over and over again.

Don't let her die.

CHAPTER EIGHTY THREE

Noal

'This gash will need stitches,' a tall, stern looking healer Elf named Ailill remarked. He was inspecting Dalin's thigh from where he had collapsed in a large armchair that looked to be made out of white clouds.

A breathtaking female Elf named Chloris was tending to Agrudek where he slept too.

The third healer, a male named Silvanus, had already approved my health, and I sat out of the way beside Asha and Vidar–the Elf who had supported Dalin on our journey through the Forest. I sipped at a cup of cool water appreciatively.

'Your friends are in the best care,' Asha told me in her high voice, floating down to sit on a polished, intricately carved mahogany desk beside me.

'His stump has been cauterised, and is not infected,' I heard Chloris say quietly as she examined Agrudek.

'Stitches?' I asked, leaning forward nervously to watch Ailill appraising Dalin. 'My friends aren't clothes for mending.'

Asha waved a tiny, dimpled hand. 'The Raiden won't feel a thing. When Ailill is holding sharp things, he's at his nicest.'

'Stitches simply bind a wound so it heals properly,' Ailill explained.

Asha grinned, running a hand through a lock of fiery red hair for a moment, and when she let it go, it floated back up to stand on end with the rest of her hair.

Silvanus crouched beside Chloris and Agrudek. 'Poor little fellow,' the tall being said softly. Next to Silvanus, Agrudek truly did look alarmingly small. 'It's best to let him stay asleep. We can give him something for his pains when he wakes.'

Ailill on the other hand looked far from gentle as he now held a small knife.

I sat further forward in my chair, more nervous than before.

'Relax,' Asha laughed in a bubbling chuckle.

Chloris poured something from a flask into Dalin's mouth and he hardly stirred. Then she briskly began to wipe the sweat and dried blood from the cut on his face, before thoroughly cleaning the deeper gash on his thigh.

Silvanus held Dalin's thigh while Ailill next cut a bigger slice in Dalin's pants leg around the cut there and then threaded a small needle with a thin thread.

I winced as I saw the needle pass into Dalin's flesh and out again, the skin around the gaping cut pulling closed as Ailill calmly drew his stitching tightly together.

Only moments later, a clean white bandage had been neatly wrapped around Dalin's thigh and he and Agrudek were covered with plush blankets, both of them looking drained and pale in their sleep.

'Thank you,' I told the healer Elves meekly as they packed up to leave, but I resolved to stay awake in case I was needed by Dalin or Kiana anyway.

I rubbed at my eyes with my fist, grinding the sleep from them as I was left with just Vidar and Asha for company.

'You could do with a bath,' Asha remarked frankly when they left. 'I can tend to you,' she added wickedly.

I fast felt wide awake again as I stared at the Nymph who was like a flicker of light and life in the room.

'Yes, she is often so suggestive,' Vidar nodded sympathetically from where he sat against the writing desk now too. 'You have to watch out for Nymphs. They're wily ones.'

Asha floated up into a standing position with her hands on her hips, her fiery hair seeming suddenly fierier and sticking out more stiffly than before as her red eyes drew level with his.

'Well with Elves what you have to watch out for is their big fat heads,' she retorted moodily. 'If you're not careful, you fly right into them all the time.'

'Big fat head?' Vidar asked her in an injured tone.

She poked out her tongue, like waving a pink little petal, and floated gracefully back down to sit beside him.

'When Nymphs have such vibrance, and Elves have such big fat heads,' I jested, 'how is it that my kind know nothing of you? Will you explain some things about yourselves to me?'

Vidar patted Asha's cheek lovingly. 'Well, Elves are magical beings,' he started. 'We have longer lives than what you would consider normal.' I gave him a questioning look. 'We are considered to be elders when we reach two hundred years.'

I tried to nod with easy acceptance. The flawless features of the Elves made them appear ageless. But compared to mortals, he was ancient. Only nobility tended to live beyond sixty or seventy years in Awyalkna, and they still at least showed the aging process.

'We thrive from a connection to Nature,' Vidar continued. 'It gives us our life, whereas mortals rely on their own bodies for energy.'

'Right,' I replied weakly. 'So the immortal thing?'

'We could live forever if we chose. But it would be hard for us to keep our grip on reality, and life would be confusing and dangerous; only a half-life as our bodies and minds lose connection – our Nature given souls yearning to return to the earth. Most of us feel tired of this heightened awareness and connectedness at the elder stage, and move onto a new path. Passing from physical life,' Vidar explained. 'And even before old age, if we don't train together or interact with our Nymphs, Elves fast become too introspective. It is like an illness for us.'

'And us Nymphs are the most magnificent, beautiful, intelligent beings you'll ever find,' Asha chirped in flamboyantly. 'For example, have you ever seen hair as good as ours?'

I laughed. 'No, you're right there.'

Vidar grimaced. 'The Nymphs are of course bubbly, free, wild, fast paced, and keep us Elves from sinking too far into our intense seriousness. But,' Vidar said firmly.

'Always a but,' she said crossly, zipping higher above the desk.

'These compact little ones are also tricksters, mischief makers, and in no way to be underestimated,' warned Vidar.

'Can't disagree with that particular kind of but, Vidar,' Asha beamed with a happy smile that engulfed her gorgeous face, and she returned to nestle beside him placidly, hugging his massive arm with both of her teensy ones.

I could hardly imagine such an innocent looking soul as Asha ever being dangerous. 'So how did both of your kinds come together?' I asked curiously.

Vidar sagged a little. 'When Darziates wiped out the Larnaeradee and the Unicorns, the Centaurs, Sprites and other deities, he turned his sights on the Nymphs. They made it to us to seek refuge.'

My stomach did a somersault. I remembered back with a flash to the day that Kiana had told the village children of Wanru the stories of the Fairies and the Unicorns. My mind reeled as I considered that her tales of Farne and Treyun, of Kinrilowyn and Sylranaeryn, as well as the Army for the World against Deimos— could be true.[2] I had seen enough magical beings now that I could believe it.

'Why didn't the Army of the World rise again, if Darziates was doing such things?' I asked, aghast.

'The Larnaeradee and Unicorns were targeted first, and they had always been the ones to keep the uniting language of Aolen alive. When they were no longer there to help each race communicate and rise up, fear and suspicion spread,' Vidar explained.

'Asha's kind, more fearsome than can be imagined by looking at them, were targeted last in these lands.'

Asha snuggled her cheek into Vidar's arm for comfort. 'We used to live in clans and warred for the fun of competition. But we came together at the Sorcerer's threat

---

[2] The 'Tales of the Fairies and Unicorns' are included at the end of this text.

138

and moved into the mountains bordering Jenra and Sylthanryn. He found us with no trouble, and though we threw all we had at him, he was never injured or exhausted. As we tired, he summoned demons of the Other Realm.' She shuddered, the merry spark dying in her eyes. 'A crack tore the atmosphere, and fiends of horror; shapeless monsters of deadly shadow, climbed out. Darziates had created a rift between our two worlds, and dread beyond describing spilled like nightmares into our midst. Abominations upon Nature. None could survive their foul touch; the darkness that made them could suck dry the pure magic that made up a Nymph. So when too few of us remained, we fled.'

Asha wiped a stream of tears that were dripping down her cheeks and chin to fall like raindrops upon the floor. Her emotions were powerful, moving to extremes, and I was amazed at the transformation the cheeky Nymph had undergone.

'Beyond exhaustion, spurred only by our terror, we managed to flee into the Forest's refuge. We could go no further and dared not risk being separated; the only survivors of our entire race. The demons and spirits reached the Forest border, but found that they could not go further into the Lady's domain. They roared and beat against the borders, but Darziates dismissed the Other Realm fiends back to their world. Darziates had no trouble stepping beyond the border, and he was calmly advancing, building up the spell that would obliterate the last of us, when the Elves and the great Lady of the Forest arrived.' Asha drew a deep breath and buried her face completely in Vidar's muscular arm.

Vidar's deep, low voice began then.

'We Elves had long been suffering a sickness of introversion and inactivity–our minds absorbed in Nature. We were becoming increasingly catatonic, trapped in what we called our intense seriousness, but our great awakening was when we felt the Nymphs arrive, and we roused ourselves to speed to their sides.'

He gently enfolded one of Asha's hands in his own, her hand not even half the size of his massive palm.

'The Lady joined her ancient and boundless power with the Elves and the depleted Nymphs, and with such unity we managed to banish Darziates from the Forest. Darziates and his dark creatures could never again enter here, and from that time we sheltered the Nymphs from despair, while they helped us to thrive once more.'

'Darziates had murdered so many of the magical races,' Asha sniffed, 'that soon the mortals who had loved us forgot that we had truly lived. And the magical races dwelling across the seas were all forbidden from coming here to help, as it would only bring them into danger too. The only surviving Unicorns hid in Karanoyar, the single surviving family of the Larnaeradee hid amongst mortals, and the remaining Nymphs remained in the Forest.'

I shook my head, my mind boggled. 'It's a wonder your City has put so much effort into helping us ordinary three then, in the face of all of that. I never realised how huge this all was.'

Asha smiled. 'But you are the Three that we have been waiting for!' she said. 'You do not know of the prophecies. Of your role in them.'

I shrugged my shoulders helplessly. 'I think you've got the wrong people.'

Asha shot back up into the air, ready to persuade me, but Vidar tugged gently at her little foot where it was hanging next to his ear.

'Perhaps leave it for the Lady to explain,' Vidar suggested softly, and she scrunched up her face, but floated back down to his eye level.

I regretted that they'd perhaps rescued us out of mistaken expectation, but Dalin was asleep and safe, and Kiana was in a fight for her life. So I knew I wouldn't have passed up their aid for anything.

CHAPTER EIGHTY FOUR

Dalin

The sound of footsteps had me awake in an instant.

I sprang forward, bracing myself, my heart racing. I'd woken in some unnamed fear, startled forth from a dreamless, deep sleep with my stomach in knots.

I blinked rapidly at the peculiar sunset filled room I was in, with my chest rising and falling fast.

An Elf of splendidly dark skin and enormous build sat at a massive window nearby. He seemed to have been woken by my sudden movement as he gazed at me from beneath protruding, startlingly white eyebrows.

'Dalin?' a firm hand stayed my arm as I moved to stand.

Noal had leaned over from his own chair to calm me, and I saw two other concerned faces peering at me from behind him as well.

An Elf and a Nymph.

I also saw Frey on the stairs–the source of the footsteps.

Everything came rushing back into focus.

'Kiana?' I croaked urgently, my throat dry. 'Is there any news?'

I tried to take a step, but an unexpected bolt of burning pain shot up my thigh, which had been bandaged.

'Sit down and stop putting so much pressure on my new stitches,' the Elf that had awoken at the same time as me instructed, pointing at my leg.

'Stitches?' I vaguely remembered getting sliced. One savage Krall warrior had seen the weakness of a smaller gash there and had widened it for me.

'Yes, stitches,' the stern Elf replied almost primly.

'Ailill mended you like clothing,' the red haired Nymph smirked, floating just over Noal's head, on her back, her arms cushioning her head and her legs crossed in the very picture of comfort. 'But Vidar and I–Asha–we were here to keep you safe,' she told me daintily. She kicked her little legs in the air so that she was propelled lazily away.

'Frey,' I asked him desperately, not relaxing. 'What did you come to say?'

'The Lady has done what she can for Kiana for now,' Frey answered solemnly.

'She is finishing her work, and once you are washed, you may come up.'

I hobbled forward immediately. 'Kiana will live?'

'Kiana will continue the fight for her life,' Frey inclined his head. 'The Lady has given her a chance.'

'I shall go with them to make sure they wash before they visit the One,' Asha suggested nefariously.

But Vidar rose to help me, guiding Noal and I to the washroom instead, where I was under Ailill's strict instructions not to wet my stitches.

The sky was darkening outside and both Noal and I speedily washed, dried and dressed in new, elegant shirts and cream coloured trousers before Noal helped me stumble back up to the other room.

'Despite those being Elfling clothes, you do look regal,' Asha commented with an approving eye, and she somersaulted playfully backward in the air to perch on the ornamental desk across from the window.

'Can I see Kiana?' I husked breathlessly as Frey stood when we made our entrance.

'She clings to life,' Frey warned as I limped towards him. 'And she might not ever regain her full strength or recover full use of her shoulder.'

I jolted toward the steps to Kiana's room.

'Frey, please make sure my stitches aren't torn,' Ailill sighed, and Frey reached out to help me propel up the steps.

'Easy, Raiden,' Frey said quietly, steadying me with one hand, but I hardly noticed. I had struggled up and into the globe lit room in moments.

The Lady was no longer there, but I stopped at the sight of Kiana lying in that large bed.

Careful hands had combed and arranged Kiana's wavy raven hair away from her face. She wore a light cotton shirt, tied loosely so that I could see the layers of white bandages wrapping around her chest and shoulder. Thin white sheets had been draped over her and her arms rested freely upon the bed.

I took a deep breath. I stepped away from Frey and haltingly crossed the distance between us until I stood at her bedside, looking down at the amazing woman who had led two strangers on a foolhardy Quest, through unbelievable, supernatural friends and foes, through injury, and through darkness, to become as dear to me as Noal and my Awyalkna.

I touched her hand lightly, and saw that sweat glistened upon her skin, lying over her like a mist even though she had been dressed in the thinnest possible sleep clothes to ease the fever. Her eyelashes, sweeping downward like fine paint strokes on her cheeks, seemed stark in their darkness against her pallor.

I hadn't heard Frey, but turned when I saw that he had somehow lifted and carried across a heavy white armchair as though it weighed nothing. He lowered it next to the side of the bed, careful to make no noise, and gestured for me to sit.

'My thanks, friend,' I whispered.

'She will sleep for a while now,' he said in a low voice. 'The Lady has given her an elixir to help ease the pain with dreams. You too should try to rest, at least until the elixir fades. Then there will be little rest for you if you stay.'

I nodded and eased myself into the blissfully soft chair, drinking in the sight of Kiana while Frey sat in the window seat that had been carved into the dark wood below the wide-open window.

Gradually the golden, glowing globes floating around the rounded room's walls dimmed of their own accord, and Frey seemed content to lose himself in the stars, his gaze serious and unwavering even as the moon shifted.

Much time had passed in this way before the elixir began to wear off and I began to notice Kiana's glistening brow creasing with a frown of discomfort. Soon she was also restlessly struggling, pushing at the sheets in her sleep.

I sat straighter, rousing from my drifting thoughts.

'We can only keep her comfortable and as stationary as possible,' Frey whispered. 'We have to wait for the fever to break.'

When her hand began scrunching the bed sheets, I gently pried her fingers loose and took them into mine. But as the night passed, she became increasingly unsettled.

She began to toss and turn, and her hand slipped from mine when her body was wracked with a convulsive jolt. She let out a sharp cry and moved under the sheets as if to start defending herself.

Frey came to her bedside quickly. 'The elixir has stopped working. We must hold her still,' he warned.

I immediately took a firm hold of her good arm, stopping her from flailing it about wildly. Frey put a firm hand on her good shoulder and held her other arm carefully against the bed, forcing her to stop agitating the wound.

But she reacted as if we had suddenly sprung an attack upon her, and unconsciously began to thrash aggressively against our hold, crying out in pain and in anger.

Her back arched and her eyes flashed open, glinting gold and blue as she tried to throw our hold off.

Even injured, she was skilled enough to slip out of my hold. With a ferocious half-punch-half-push she sent me reeling backward with her now free hand, and nearly completely bowled Frey off her with a thrashing heave.

'Hold her!' he said urgently now, fighting to keep a grasp on her unexpectedly strong arms while she yelled and lashed out. 'She is injuring her ribs and shoulder further!' he was struggling to keep her lying down without doing her harm himself, and I knew from experience that she would be able to worm out from his hold because of his delicate handling.

Filled with blind delirium, her eyes were gleaming as she made swipes at Frey's face. Yet she didn't truly see either of us.

I swallowed. 'You took away all of the daggers and sharp objects she always has hidden all over the place, didn't you?' I asked Frey.

He gave me the briefest of glances, his usually placid face written with astonishment. 'Yes, of course,' he grunted as her foot connected with his stomach. 'Why?'

'She's having a nightmare,' I told him. 'I've had bad experiences confronting her during her nightmares,' I added.

'Can you make her stop moving? The bleeding will start again if she continues,' he answered with an effort, avoiding her next kick and pinning both her arms while she tried to shake him off.

I winced. 'I can try.'

Even as Frey looked to me for my answer, Kiana aimed an incredible blow at his head, having resorted to using her own brow. She head butted him squarely in the temple, and their skulls connected with a dull, painful thud.

Taken by surprise, Frey was overcome and toppled to land sprawling on the floor. Thankfully, she too had been stunned by the impact and blinked away the dizziness— lying prone long enough for me to pounce. I dived onto the bed beside her before she could resume her attack and tucked her arms in before quickly pulling the sheets taut over her chest and legs again.

Frey got the idea and pulled himself up onto the bed on her other side, his massive, lean frame holding down the other side of the sheets.

She tried to struggle underneath the sheet prison. But with both my weight and Frey's weight pulling the sheets tightly over her from both sides, she was pinned safely between us.

'Hurry...' Frey warned, looking at her shoulder worriedly.

I leaned over Kiana so that she could see my face.

Her feverish eyes glared indignantly back at me, her stare fiery with rage and a burning hate for someone she saw only in her memory.

'Kiana?'

Her tensely straining body froze, her wild eyes fixing on mine properly and her eyebrows coming together in a frown.

'Kiana,' I said softly, 'it's only me, Dalin.'

Frey let out a startled gasp as her body became instantly still and Kiana blinked warily.

'It's alright now,' I shushed her, reaching up a hand to stroke her heated cheek.

'Dalin?' she frowned, saying the word slowly, as if remembering me through a foggy haze. She had been remembering a different time.

'I'm here with you,' I said, settling her hair back away from her face. 'And I need you to rest now.' I could feel the heat from her body through the sheets.

A tear spilled from the deep blue pools of her eyes, and slid warmly down the side of her face, toward her ear. I stopped it with a fingertip.

'The dreams are back,' she whispered. 'It's him, that sabre, and then her, and those cruel hands. And Tommy... my Tommy... with holes all over... but then I'm being chased by the shadows... the shadows breathe... the shadows burn with ice... the Sorcerer is sending them for me... and I can't get away...'

Her breathing was getting faster again, her eyes becoming wide, and I quickly pushed my face back in front of her eyes. 'They're gone now. I'm here. It was just a dream.'

Her eyes burned as they searched my face. 'It was no dream that you found me.'

'I found you and now you're safe. Now you can rest.' I told her warmly.

She didn't seem to be seeing me properly, and never even noticed that Frey was on her other side.

She looked exhausted, and her eyes were becoming less wild, clouded again with pain and sickness.

'Sleep a while,' I coaxed, stroking her forehead.

Her gaze connected tiredly with mine, but it was still strong enough to capture me completely.

'You won't go?' she murmured.

'I'll be right here.'

'...Won't leave me alone?' her voice was almost too faint to hear as her eyelids slowly slid closed.

'No,' I told her. 'I'll be watching over you.'

She nodded faintly, reassured, and her breathing began to settle into the pattern of a sleeper.

Frey let out a sigh of relief and tucked the sheets neatly back into place, settling Kiana more comfortably upon the pillows. Then he eased her arms free of the sheets, looking at the bandages. Faint flecks of blood had seeped through during her struggle.

'We were fortunate,' he said finally.

Kiana let out a small moan and turned fitfully in her new sleep.

'Is there anything you can do?' I asked in concern. 'Can you give her more of that elixir?'

Frey shook his head. 'We have given her the potion three times already. It becomes addictive. We cannot risk giving her any more.'

I looked at her miserably, taking her hand in mine again.

'She is strong, and her body has been cleansed by the Lady's magic. Now it is her turn to fight and to heal.'

She moaned again, her face creased with agony, and I lowered my head into my free hand.

CHAPTER EIGHTY FIVE

Dalin

All through that night I watched over Kiana, firmly holding her against the pillows while she twisted and tossed and turned in her troubled sleep.

She talked in her delirium. Her voice was hoarse and exhausted, and she sometimes spoke in tongues that I couldn't understand.

I heard her talking to Tommy, her mother and her father, and I thought my heart would break. I heard her addressing Noal and I. I heard her trying to get rid of Gangroah's Gloria and I heard her yelling at a distant memory of some beast she had fought.

She constantly shifted in agitation, muttering and raving, sometimes making Frey and I jump as she fought monsters in her dreams.

Time passed slowly, but I didn't notice it.

The Lady came as the days melted by, talking quietly with Frey. Kiana would become still then, as the Lady's strange power spread into the room.

The Elf Chloris would tend to Kiana, and Noal also often came and sat on the end of the bed, bringing water that we tried to help Kiana get down, coaxing her to swallow even though she didn't seem to notice us.

Asha and Vidar, even Ailill and a few others that I came to know would sit with me by Kiana's side.

As time passed, Kiana grew extremely thin and weak. Her bones seemed to protrude at alarming, sharp angles from under her skin. Dark shadows stained under her eyes, and it was clear that her body was exhausted.

The Lady's visits became more frequent, but even with Kiana becoming quieter and frailer as the fever waged war upon her fatigued form, I never thought once that she wouldn't wake again.

I never let my face appear as grim and serious as those other faces. I knew Kiana, and I knew she wouldn't let this sickness and injury get the better of her after surviving so much.

And finally, I was the one watching her pale face when her eyelashes moved for the first time in days. I saw the brilliant blue of her eyes as the eyelashes parted. And I was the first one that those brilliant blue eyes fixed upon.

Looking beyond weary and dazed, but very much alive, she smiled at me.

A fragile, shaky smile that lit me from head to toe.

Noal let out a little cry of amazement as he saw her.

The Lady and Frey immediately turned from where they had been speaking, and Kiana's eyes shifted from my face to fall upon them.

Her features seemed to lighten faintly with joy.

Then, without hesitation, she spoke.

'... Quindinara uona... nell... Sylthanryn dliss lissryn,' she whispered in a lilting tongue.

I didn't understand, but when she spoke those words, shivers and thrills ran up and down my spine.

'Quindinara uona nell dliss lissryn, nell Tru Larnaeradee,' the Lady responded, even as a comforted smile spread across Kiana's lips and as her eyes slowly closed again.

'What did she say?' Noal whispered apprehensively, having obviously felt the same prickling power about Kiana's words that I had.

Asha laughed in glowing pleasure, having come with Vidar to visit. 'She just greeted the beings of the Forest in the ancient tongue. Aolen. There can be no doubt about the prophecy. No mortal could have spoken in that tongue.'

'Kiana has just ended the long silence between races and has shown the lost Larnaeradee to have one surviving member,' the Lady affirmed. 'The Larnaeradee created Aolen as the unifying language of all peoples, and that is why they became the Summoners when the world needed to unite against Deimos. Because it was their magic that helped Aolen to connect everyone. Without them, the language faded.'

'As soon as the One spoke I knew, I felt what she was saying. Never have my spirits soared so high!' Asha sang gaily.

'Are trying to say that Kiana is a Fairy?' Noal asked disbelievingly, trying to keep his voice quiet.

'She is the One of the prophecies, the last of her kind,' Frey nodded. 'The One, or Tru, Larnaeradee. She has yet to find her earth stone, but she already has power.'

I remembered how Kiana's song had created relief in Giltrup. How she'd connected with Ila and Amala, a flock of birds, and a Willow. How she had always lasted longer than anyone else–even against the beasts of Darziates. How she'd created white light from the General's globe and converted those soldiers. How she'd just spoken an ancient language and been understood.

'She truly is the One,' Asha giggled joyously, clapping her hands.

But I didn't care about any of it, and I let the voices of the others fade to the back of my awareness.

Instead, I stared at Kana's sleeping face, beautiful and fearless.

She was still Kiana, even if she might be more than she seemed.

And she was fighting to come back to me.

I watched over her in a committed vigil for the rest of that day, and I was there when her fever finally broke late in that night.

I never left her side.

HISTORICAL TALES

The Tale of the Fairies and the Unicorns

Unicorns were magnificent to behold. Their bodies slender and powerful, built for speed and freedom. Their hooves and horns the colour of stainless gold.

Their horns were the source of their might. Each foal's horn would grow as gradually as a human babe might grow teeth, and with this growth came its magic. Through its horn, a Unicorn could channel Nature's power to create magic.

But for all their power, the Unicorns were a withdrawn race living in an isolated land within a ring of mountains. At that time it was known as Karanoyar, a place later referred to as Jenra.

Karanoyar's perilous border mountains were so high that, even in the warmest weather, their jagged peaks were capped with ice. Protected and secluded, the Unicorns had lived peacefully for many generations, until during one frosty season, a young Fairy was blown off course into their home.

The youthful Larnaeradee, Farne, only just given his earth stone and with only newly formed wings, was found collapsed in the snow by the Unicorn foal Treyun.

Curious and excited, Treyun took Farne back to the herd, and Farne was discussed for a long time by all of the Unicorn elders. At last it was agreed that he did not look or feel dangerous, and so they cared for him as best they could until he woke.

To their surprise, Farne and Treyun soon discovered that they understood each other through shared thoughts. As Farne healed, they became loyal companions, and when it was time for Farne to return home, parting seemed unbearable.

At the same time, upon embracing an outsider amongst their herd, a deep yearning had begun to stir in the heart of each Unicorn. The Unicorns became thoughtful and quiet. The elders again withdrew and discussed many matters. Each Unicorn ached to see the open outside land.

So it was agreed that the herd would visit the outside with Farne, and he was overjoyed that he was to stay with Treyun for a while longer.

THE LAST
LARNAERADEE

A great mountain tunnel was opened by an elder Unicorn, and the whole company was spurred on by their eagerness. They galloped with glee out to the Forest land beyond the mountains, swiftly exploring their surrounds in elation, and moving gaily and freely across the green and sunny plains towards Farne's people.

Amazement followed the company, and while at first the Unicorns were fearful— every human filled village they passed greeted them with only wonder and awe.

The travelling company became happier the further they roamed. The beauty of the land and the kindness of the humans turned the Unicorns from their long desire for solitude.

When they finally reached the valley Farne had grown up in, the Unicorns were so changed from when Farne had first seen them that he was almost shy of them as their elegance and power seemed intensified.

His people crowded the sunny, green valley in spellbound wonder. The Larnaeradee were as in awe of the Unicorns as the Unicorns were of them.

The Unicorns and Larnaeradee grew to love each other like family and became as close in friendship as Farne and Treyun had become.

At last the Unicorns pronounced that they couldn't leave their new family, or the land and the many new peoples and animals they had grown to love.

Over the first few years, the bond between Unicorns and Larnaeradee became incredibly powerful. A bond that had never before existed between any race was developed. Their knowledge was shared, their thoughts were linked and a deep love and understanding for each other grew.

It became that each Fairy linked with one Unicorn, becoming a pair. They melded the magic of the Unicorn horn with the power of the earth stone and eventually achieved such a bond that they became more powerful than any other race.

In their time, they used this great power to the benefits of all peoples, creating a universal language as well as enhancing all life around them. And such abundance has never again been matched in the world.

The Tales of the Army for the World, and Sylranaeryn and her Unicorn.

Evil stirred in the land when, through treachery and darkness, Deimos of Krall discovered the Other Realm and brought a seed of dark magic into the world. He became the King of Krall and turned his people against all other races. Yet he was not satisfied with ruling just his kingdom.

He wanted the world. He wanted every land to be under his command alone, and he wanted every race, mortal and magical, to bow to him alone.

Slowly, through dark and twisted magic, Deimos bred new and terrible beasts, loyal only to himself. Ogres, Griffins, and even shadow creatures known as the Evexus that served as his dreaded personal army, began to plague the lands of mortals. Festering, dark spirits were summoned from the Other Realm, a place of decay and evil ghouls.

So, the tyrant Sorcerer King had built himself a powerful and terrible army of dread to help him win dominion over the entire world.

The Larnaeradee and Unicorns were filled with a deep sorrow. Being linked with the land and each other, they felt the earth's pain from Deimos' corruption as their own, and could not bear it. Together, they began to create their own army to contest Deimos' evil and Sorcery.

An Army for the World.

On golden hooves the Unicorns raced to every part of the Awyalknian and Jenran lands of men. On swift wings the Larnaeradee flew over the seas to the islands of the Giants, the Dragons, Gnomes and Dwarves. Together, the Larnaeradee and Unicorns united the earth's free races.

Under the call of the Larnaeradee, the magical beings crossed the seas to join with mortals and Forest dwellers in the mortal lands. The Army for the World travelled through every village, bringing hope and wonder.

But when they met Deimos' forces in the wastelands of Krall, the battle was too close. With a ferocity that shook the earth, the two forces collided, and the battle was like no other in any Realm.

The fighting raged and the world was dark, shrouded in storm, as if even the earth itself hovered on the outcome of the war. Such power and magic surged back and forth between the forces that even the air seemed to sizzle.

Yet at the peak of battle, when Deimos' armies seemed undefeatable, and the united races were giving up hope, a brave young Larnaeradee named Sylranaeryn flew high above the fighting into the stormy air, and became a clear target. She cast a spell so potent, so powerful, that hundreds of Griffins fell from the sky. The Ogres that had been ploughing easily through the Army for the World's lines also writhed in fear and were defeated, and corrupted men fell screaming to the ground to awaken from Deimos' power as if from a dream.

Her magic was pure enough to weaken their foes, but Sylranaeryn's energy was also spent, and she was no longer able to shield herself in the air.

One Evexus—a creature made from Other Realm spirits, called upon its poisoned magic, and with it, poisoned the tip of a mortal's arrow. With a mighty howl, the beast fired upon the Larnaeradee Sylranaeryn, and she was fatally pierced in the chest.

Kinrilowyn, the Unicorn of Sylranaeryn, reared in fury with a wildness so great that the enemies about him were smote down by the power of his golden horn. He charged through the remaining dark masses, and they scattered in fear before his thundering hooves. He charged to where he could feel the worst of all evil, and he was sure that that place was where the rotten King Deimos stood.

A storm raged in his eyes and his horn glowed with the radiating power of rage. The Evexus who had sheltered the Sorcerer even shrieked and fell back as Kinrilowyn stormed past, unable to sustain their shadow in the presence of his light.

In his grief the Unicorn unleashed all of his magic and he plunged toward Deimos, bearing down with a lowered, fiery horn that pierced the heart of his foe—impaling the evil King.

With Kinrilowyn's entire life force spent in that action, Deimos was ended, and with him, all of the evil he had created died too.

The storm that had splintered the skies lost its ferocity, becoming a downpour of rain that cleansed the earth of blood and scars. The sizzling air became calm, and the clouds evaporated like mist.

With such sacrifices, the land and its peoples were saved, and the earth began to heal. As peace returned, there came a time when the united beings in the Army for the World parted, yearning for long missed homes.

But, before parting, every pure race of the land swore an oath that, should ever evil fester in the world once more, every race would once again unite and triumph. The Larnaeradee and the Unicorns were selected to be the 'Summoners' of each race; if ever the need for the Army for the World arose again.

So, in friendship, the races of the world parted.

The Giants, Gnomes, and Dwarves crossed the oceans to their different island homes. The Dragons returned to their cliffy lofts. The Forest Dwellers disappeared once more, deep into their Great Forest. The men of the mortal races marched with pride back to their villages and were honoured among their kind. And the Larnaeradee and the Unicorns roamed together for many years of peace.

Locations and pronunciation guide:

Sylthanryn: (Sil-than-rin). *The Great Forest. Where the Lady, or the Mother of Nature, and the Elves and Nymphs live.*

Awyalkna: *(A for apple-why-elk-nah)*. A mortal Kingdom under the reign of **King Glaidin** *(G-laid-in)* and **Queen Aglaia** *(Ag-lay-ah)*. The Awyalknian Palace is also known as the 'Awyalknian Jewel,' and is protected by the internal **Gwentorock** *(G-when-toe-rock)* and external **Gwynrock** *(G-win-rock)* walls. The lands beyond the City are green and flourishing, with many self-contained villages.

Bwintam *(B-win-tam)* village was a key provider of Awyalkna's fresh produce, before it was razed by Krall. **Gangroah** *(Gang-row-ah)* and **Giltrup** *(Guilt-rup)* are examples of smaller villages, while **Wanru** *(W-an-roo, an isolated, hilly place)* and **Wrilapek** *(W-rill-ah-peck, a horse rearing place)* are larger and more greatly populated.

Krall: *(Crawl)*. A mortal Kingdom ruled by the immortal Sorcerer **Darziates** *(D-are-zee-eights)*, who is the heir of the first Sorcerer to have lived; **Deimos** *(Day-moss)*. Darziates is assisted by the psychotic Warlord **Angra Mainyu** *(An-gra Main-you)* and the Witch **Agrona** *(Ag-groan-ah)*, and is responsible for the genocide of all of the **Larnaeradee Fairies** *(La-nair-ah-dee)*, the Unicorns and Sprites.

Nature dies around Darziates' unnatural power, so he forces his magic into Krall's earth so that a type of growth and food is produced for his people. However, this has corrupted Krall's seasons, which involve intense heat or extreme cold. Sorcery has reduced the land to barren plains of wastelands and desert.

Jenra: *(Jen-rah)*. A Kingdom circled by and built into the mountains by the sea. The mountain Kingdom is isolated from the rest of the world, and was once known as **Karanoyar** *(Karen-oi-ah)*, the original home of the Unicorns. It has lush valleys, but the peaks of the mountains are infested with Griffin eyries, and **King Durna's** *(Der-nah)* brother—Warlord **Aeron** *(Air-on)* must work tirelessly to contain the infestation.

Lixrax: *(Lix-r-axe)*. A desert nation, with people who have been tempered by the harsh environment. They are skilled survivors, but are a united family because of their surrounds. Their Emperor, **Razek** *(Rah-zeck)* regards all of the tribes and Takal residents of Lixrax as his children.

The Other Realm: a separate plain of malicious spirit beings. When King Deimos wanted to unite the world under one kingship, he used a piece of his soul to bargain with the demons of the Other Realm, who gave him powers to help him in his Quest.

He became so powerful that the Larnaeradee **Sylranaeryn** *(Sil-ran-air-in)* and her Unicorn **Kinrilowyn** *(Kin-ril-owen)* had to deplete their combined magic to defeat him as he faced the Army for the World.

Though he was overthrown by the first Army for the World, he made the first of the experimental Evexus beasts. The **Evexus** (*E-vex-us*) are bestial creatures possessed by the spirits of the Other Realm.

Margate Isle: home of the Giants.

Eirian Isle: home of the **Dargons** (*D-are-gone-s*) and the Dwarves and Gnomes. A cliffy place of soaring heights and deep, tunnelling caves, perfect for creatures of flight as well as rock loving peoples.

Other books by Shelley Cass:

'A Fairy's Tale' trilogy:
Book Two – 'The Raiden'
Book Three – 'The Army for the World'

'The Sleep Sweet Series' of
children's books:
Book One – 'Little Pixie's Christmas'
Book Two – 'The Adventures of
the Bored Baby Ace'
Book Three – 'Mum and Me'
Book Four – 'The Cloud and the Flower'
Book Five – 'Hush'

Stand-alone novels:
'Darkling'
'Awaken Dreamer'

For more information on novels written by Shelley Cass, please visit:
http://shelleycass.com

ACKNOWLEDGMENTS

Thank you so much to the friends who have encouraged me with my writing of this series, a process that has taken over fifteen years.

Thank you to those who put such time into helping me, by reading this novel and offering advice, even when the manuscript was triple the length it is now. Wendy Glover (the most helpful neighbour to have ever lived), June Laurie (the first author I ever befriended, and creator of the 'Blake Collider' series), and my mum, Linda.
Thank you so much mum, dad (Robert), Melissa, Andrew and Leigh, for being the warmth in my world.

Thank you Jack and Elyssia, for making the future world worthwhile.

Thank you to my extended family, for being everything I needed.

Thank you to Jarryd, for being the magic and love of my life.

And thank you to the hesitant little Junior High School version of myself, for picking up that pen to write.

ABOUT THE AUTHOR

Shelley Cass was an awkward, reserved year 8 student–totally in love with the escape and comfort offered by novels she read. She could hear the voices of the authors' characters, she could tune out her stresses and uncertainties as she journeyed with each protagonist through their own troubles. And then one day she could hear the voices of characters who hadn't been written yet, in places that hadn't been created, and she decided to write her own world.

It took a quest of over fourteen years to get that world perfected in three novels– because of course the real world kept getting in the way.

In the real world Shelley Cass became a high school teacher and still faces the epic battle of staying afloat in all the papers she must assess. And in the real world the magic was also sometimes hard to find. Stress and disunity surface like cancer– making the nightly news too hard to watch on most days.

But in the real world there was also inspiration–incredible students, loved ones, golden memories, growing up, warm hugs, big laughs and good people.

So Shelley Cass wrote of the things that threaten the world, and of the things that save it. She wishes for a real world where the air is clean, the trees can grow without concrete borders, the darkness can be cured with the switch of a light, and the people can all have long days and happy lives.

SHAWLINE
PUBLISHING
GROUP

Shawline Publishing Group Pty Ltd

www.shawlinepublishing.com.au

Lightning Source UK Ltd.
Milton Keynes UK
UKHW041215201220
375339UK00002B/13